Disability Studies in India

Disability Studies in India

Global Discourses, Local Realities

Editor
Renu Addlakha

LONDON NEW YORK NEW DELHI

First published 2013 in India
by Routledge
912 Tolstoy House, 15–17 Tolstoy Marg, Connaught Place, New Delhi 110 001

Simultaneously published in the UK
by Routledge
2 Park Square, Milton Park, Abingdon, OX14 4RN

Routledge is an imprint of the Taylor & Francis Group, an informa business

© 2013 Centre for Women's Development Studies (CWDS), New Delhi

Typeset by
Bukprint India
B-180A, Guru Nanak Pura, Laxmi Nagar
Delhi 110 092

All rights reserved. No part of this book may be reproduced or utilised in any form or by any electronic, mechanical or other means, now known or hereafter invented, including photocopying and recording, or in any information storage and retrieval system without permission in writing from the publishers.

British Library Cataloguing-in-Publication Data
A catalogue record of this book is available from the British Library

ISBN 978-0-415-81212-2

CONTENTS

List of Tables	viii
List of Figures	ix
List of Plates	x
List of Abbreviations	xiii
Glossary	xvi
Acknowledgements	xix

Introduction   1
RENU ADDLAKHA

PART I: Disability Movement, Disability Rights and Disability Studies

1. Historicising Disability in India: Questions of Subject and Method   35
SHILPAA ANAND

2. Disability Rights and the Emergence of Disability Studies   61
JAGDISH CHANDER

3. Tracking Disability through the United Nations   78
N. SUNDARESAN

PART II: Family, Care and Work

4. Prenatal Diagnosis: Where do We Draw the Line?   97
ANITA GHAI AND RACHANA JOHRI

5. Burden of Caring: Families of the Disabled in Urban India   122
UPALI CHAKRAVARTI

6. Exploring Constructs of Intellectual Disability and Personhood in Haryana and Delhi   145
NILIKA MEHROTRA AND SHUBHANGI VAIDYA

7. Corporeality, Mobility and Class: An Ethnography of
    Work-related Experiences in Urban India   169
    AMIT UPADHYAY

Part III: Gender and Disability

8. *Bhalo Meye*: Cultural Construction of Gender and
   Disability in Bengal   201
   NANDINI GHOSH

9. Body Politics and Disabled Femininity: Perspectives of
   Adolescent Girls from Delhi   220
   RENU ADDLAKHA

10. Identity Formation and Transnational Discourses:
    Thinking beyond Identity Politics   241
    MICHELE FRIEDNER

11. The Inner World of Adolescent Girls with Hearing
    Impairment: Two Case Studies   263
    SANDHYA LIMAYE

Part IV: Assertion of Difference through Art and Communication

12. Body/Text: Art Project on Deafness and Communication   285
    JOSÉ ABAD LORENTE

13. Blind With Camera: Photographs by the Visually Impaired   303
    PARTHO BHOWMICK

Part V: Contesting Marginality at Micro- and Macro-levels

14. From Mental Illness to Disability: Choices for Women Users/
    Survivors of Psychiatry in Self and Identity Constructions   333
    BHARGAVI V. DAVAR

15. Need for a Framework for Combined Disability and
    Gender Budgeting   363
    ASHA HANS, AMRITA PATEL AND S. B. AGNIHOTRI

16. Sameness and Difference: Twin Track Empowerment
    for Women with Disabilities   390
    AMITA DHANDA

17. Participation, Inclusion and the Law: Moving beyond
    Rhetoric   414
    JEEJA GHOSH

About the Editor   423
Notes on Contributors   424
Index   429

LIST OF TABLES

1.1	Disability Historiography	37
1.2	Sample Survey of Histories of Disablement in India	45
2.1	Disability Models	69
15.1	Allocation Ratio per Person with Disability in Andhra Pradesh, West Bengal, Orissa and Chhattisgarh	375
15.2	Disability Allocation as a Percentage of State Expenditure	375
15.3	Beneficiaries of the NHFDC	381

LIST OF FIGURES

15.1	Total Central Budget Estimate and Expenditure for Welfare of PWDs (in millions)	371
15.2	Central Plan and Non-Plan Budget Estimate for the Welfare of PWDs (in millions)	372
15.3	Central Plan and Non-Plan Expenditure for Welfare of PWDs (in millions)	372
15.4	Disability Budget Analysis of Orissa: Total BE (in millions)	373
15.5	Disability Budget Analysis of West Bengal: Total BE (in millions)	373
15.6	Disability Budget Analysis of Andhra Pradesh: Total BE (in millions)	374
15.7	Disability Budget Analysis of States: Total BE (in millions)	374
15.8	Disability Budget Analysis of Orissa: Non-Plan BE (in millions)	376
15.9	Disability Budget Analysis of Andhra Pradesh: Non-Plan BE (in millions)	376
15.10	Disability Budget Analysis of West Bengal for 2004–5: BE Components (in millions)	377
15.11	Disability Budget Analysis of Chhattisgarh (Non-Plan and Plan) for 2005–6	377
15.12	Disability Budget Analysis of West Bengal: Components	378
15.13	Disability Budget Analysis: Central Plan Allocation (in millions)	378
15.14	Disability Budget Analysis of Orissa: Total AE (in millions)	379
15.15	Disability Pension in States (in millions)	381

LIST OF PLATES

12.1	*Disability Rights* (2008). Interpreted by Bahar Alan, Rishikesh Anand, Karan Kumar and Pravesh Behl.	285
12.2	*Life Bricolage* (2006). Performance and photography by José Abad Lorente.	287
12.3	*Making the Way* (2008). Interpreted by Navneet Kaur, Bahar Alan, Rishikesh Anand and Pravesh.	293
12.4	*Cyber Connections* (2008): 'Computers and the internet mean communication.' Interpreted by Bahar Alan.	294
12.5	*Expressions of Learning* (2008): 'I want to read and write. These make me feel good.' Interpreted by Karan Kumar.	294
12.6	*SMS Boon* (2008): 'Mobile phones help us to communicate. SMS brings us together.' Interpreted by Mohod Haroon, Pravesh Behl and Hira Singh.	295
12.7	*Definition, Discrimination, Debilitation* (2008): 'We don't like to beg, cry or get beaten because of our disability.' Interpreted by Mohod Haroon, Pravesh Behl and Hira Singh.	295
12.8	*Signs for Living* (2008): 'I feel independent with sign language. It helps me to work and succeed in life.' Interpreted by Rishikesh Anand, Navneet Kaur, Bahar Alan and Sudesh Kumar.	295
12.9	*Variegations* (2008): 'Justice for the disabled. Red, black, yellow, and white people. Learning equals prosperity. Our flag is orange, white, and green.' Interpreted by Bahar Alan, Rishikesh Anand, Karan Kumar and Pravesh Behl.	295
12.10	*Body Calligraphy: Lotus I* (2008). Interpreted by Rishikesh Anand, Bahar Alan and Sudesh Kumar.	296

12.11	*Body Calligraphy: Lotus II* (2008). Interpreted by Bahar Alan, Navneet Kaur, Rishikesh Anand and Sudesh Kumar.	296
12.12	*Body Calligraphy: Cobra* (2008). Interpreted by Navneet Kaur, Rishikesh Anand, Sudesh Kumar and Bahar Alan.	297
12.13	*Body Calligraphy: I Love You x 8* (2008). Interpreted by Bahar Alan, Rishikesh Anand, Karan Kumar and Pravesh Behl.	297
12.14	*Salute Colors* (2008). Interpreted by Bahar Alan, Rishikesh Anand, Karan Kumar and Pravesh Behl.	298
12.15	*Goodbye* (2008): Fragment from the poem 'Goodbye' by Federico García Lorca. Interpreted by Guruvendra Jhar, Mohod Haroon, Akshay Bhatnagar and Hira Singh.	299
12.16	*It's True* (2008): Fragment from the poem 'It's True' by Federico García Lorca. Interpreted by Guruvendra Jhar, Kalaparthi Sudhir, Kara Kumar, Akshay Bhatnagar and Hira Singh.	300
13.1	A visually challenged person experiences a 'touch & feel' raised photograph at an exhibition by Blind With Camera. Photograph by Harsh Vyas (2011).	311
13.2	*Memory of Touch* by Bhavesh Patel (2009).	312
13.3	*Chair and Door* by Rahul Shirshat (2006).	313
13.4	*Light and Shade* by Satvir Jogi (2009).	314
13.5	*Closed Door by Closed Eyes* by Mahesh Umrrania (2006).	314
13.6	*Sound is My Eye* by Rahul Shirshat (2006).	315
13.7	*Clapping Hands* by Sujit Chaursia (2006).	315
13.8	*Cycling by The Sea* by Ravi Thakur (2010).	315
13.9	*Maths Teacher* by Nikhil Mundhe (2006).	316
13.10	*Subway* by Rahul Shirshat (2006).	317
13.11	*Pigeon Series* by Bhavesh Patel (2009).	318
13.12	*Building* by Ravi Thakur (2009).	318
13.13	*Big Life* by Kanchan Pamnani (2006).	319

13.14 *Designer Shadow* by Mahesh Umrrania (2006).   320
13.15 *Self Portrait* by Mahesh Umrrania (2006).   321
13.16 *Visual Handshake* by Dharmarajan Iyer (2006).   322
13.17 *Mumbai* by Raju Singh (2006).   323
13.18 *Pillars* by Raju Singh (2006).   324
13.19 *Getting Close* by Raju Singh (2006).   325
13.20 *Pointing Fingers* by Vaibhav Girkar (2009).   326
13.21 *The Face* by Vaibhav Girkar (2009).   327
13.22 *This is My Sight* by Nikhil Mundhe (2006).   327
13.23 *Puddle* by Satvir Jogi (2009).   328

LIST OF ABBREVIATIONS

AADI	Action for Ability Development and Inclusion
AE	actual expenditure
AFA	Action for Autism
AIFD	All India Federation of the Deaf
ALIMCO	Artificial Limbs Manufacturing Corporation of India
ASL	American Sign Language
BE	budget estimate
BTE	behind-the-ear
CAT	(UN) Convention against Torture
CBR	community-based rehabilitation
CEDAW	Convention on the Elimination of All Forms of Discrimination against Women
CEHAT	Centre for Enquiry into Health and Allied Themes
CII	Confederation of Indian Industry
CMD	common mental disorder
CP	cerebral palsy
CRC	Convention on the Rights of the Child
CSP	centrally-sponsored plan
CWDS	Centre for Women's Development Studies
DDRC	District Disability Rehabilitation Centre
DDRS	Deendayal Disabled Rehabilitation Scheme
DEDAW	Declaration on the Elimination of Discrimination against Women
DEOC	Diversity and Equal Opportunity Centre
DFDW	Delhi Foundation of Deaf Women
DPI	Disabled Peoples' International
DPN	Deaf President Now
DRDP	Declaration on the Rights of Disabled Persons

DSaRI	Disability Studies and Research Institute (Australia)
DSM	*Diagnostic and Statistical Manual of Mental Disorders*
ESCAP	(UN) Economic and Social Commission for Asia and the Pacific
FDA	Food and Drug Administration (U.S.)
FXS	Fragile X syndrome
ICCPR	International Covenant on Civil and Political Rights
ICESCR	International Covenant on Economic, Social and Cultural Rights
ICF	International Classification of Functioning, Disability and Health
ICIDH	International Classification of Impairments, Disabilities and Handicaps
ICRC	International Convention on the Rights of the Child
ICRD	International Convention on the Elimination of All Forms of Racial Discrimination
IDC	International Disability Caucus
IDCSK	International Disability Convention Solidarity in Korea
IFSHA	Interventions for Support, Healing and Awareness
ILO	International Labour Organisation
ISIC	Indian Spinal Injuries Centre
ISL	Indian Sign Language
ITI	Industrial Training Institute
IYDP	International Year of Disabled Persons
LON	League of Nations
MASUM	Mahila Sarvangeen Utkarsh Mandal
MCA	Master of Computer Applications
MDG	Millennium Development Goal
MI Principles	Principles for the Protection of Persons with Mental Illness and the Improvement of Mental Health Care
MNC	multinational corporation
MR	mental retardation
NAD	National Association of the Deaf
NCF	National Curriculum Framework
NCW	National Commission for Women
NFB	National Federation of the Blind

NGO	non-governmental organisation
NHFDC	National Handicapped Finance and Development Corporation
NIMHANS	National Institute of Mental Health and Neuro Sciences
NMHP	National Mental Health Programme
NPRPD	National Programme for Rehabilitation of Persons with Disabilities
NSSO	National Sample Survey Organisation
OBC	other backward class or caste
PIL	public interest litigation
PNDT Act	Pre-Natal Diagnostic Techniques (Regulation and Prevention of Misuse) Act
PPD	postpartum depression
PWDs	persons with disabilities
RCI	Rehabilitation Council of India
RE	revised estimate
SGSY	Swarnajayanti Gram Swarozgar Yojana
TSP	Tribal Sub-Plan
UDHR	Universal Declaration of Human Rights
UISL	Urban Indian Sign Language
UNCRPD	United Nations Convention on the Rights of Persons with Disabilities
UNDP	United Nations Development Programme
UNESCO	United Nations Educational, Scientific and Cultural Organisation
UNGA	United Nations General Assembly
UNICEF	United Nations Children's Emergency Fund
UNIFEM	United Nations Development Fund for Women
UPIAS	Union of the Physically Impaired Against Segregation
VDPA	Vienna Declaration and Programme of Action
WFD	World Federation of the Deaf
WHO	World Health Organisation
WPA	World Programme of Action
WSDC	Women's Studies and Development Centre
WWDs	women with disabilities

GLOSSARY

aadhaar	support
aashrit	dependency
amman	mother
bahir	outside
baje meye	bad girl
banjh	barren
baper bari	father's home
bechchaari	pity (also, poor thing)
bhalo meye	good woman; also, good girl
bhola/bawla	simple, innocuous or innocent
Caraka Samhita	one of the oldest and most authoritative texts on Ayurveda, composed around 400–200 BCE
chuha	rat or mouse
dalit	designation for groups traditionally regarded as untouchable in the caste heirarchy of Hindu society
dharma	Sanskrit term meaning law, order or duty
diksha	vow
dukh	misfortune
ganda kaam	filthy work
ghar	home (inside) (cf. *sansar*)
gharer kaaj	housework (cf. *sansarer kaaj*)
gram panchayat	people's court referring to one of the tiers of *panchayati raj* or system of local self-government at village level in India

karma	Sanskrit term meaning deed or action, which is the central concept in ancient Indian philosophy accounting for the cycle of life and death, and of creation and destruction
khap	caste *panchayat*
Mahisya	a peasant OBC caste
Mariamma	Mother Mari, who is considered to be an incarnation of *durga* or *kali*, Hindu goddesses
mudra	(symbolic) hand gesture
paagal	mad
panchayat	see *gram panchayat*
panchayati raj	system of local self-government in India, Pakistan and Nepal
para	neighbourhood, cluster of houses
salwar kameez	Indian women's attire comprising a long tunic-like top and loose trousers
sansar	entire family and household (cf. *ghar*)
sansarer kaaj	household work (cf. *gharer kaaj*)
sasur bari	father-in-law's home
seva	service; to serve
shok sabha	mourning meeting
Sitala	the cool one; also, Hindu goddess responsible for smallpox and other diseases, who is appeased to ward off afflictions
Surdasi	blindness (deriving from the blind Indian poet, Surdas, who lived during the 15th century)
viklangta/apangta	disability, particularly locomotor impairment

ACKNOWLEDGEMENTS

Disability is one of the key components of the research agenda of the Centre for Women's Development Studies (New Delhi). I would like to acknowledge the unstinting support of the faculty and staff of CWDS, particularly Dr Mary E. John, Dr Malavika Karlekar and Ms Leela Kasturi, in bringing this work to fruition.

This volume is the product of the collaboration of twenty contributors, whose patience and enthusiasm never flagged from conceptualisation of ideas through multiple revisions to the final product. It has been both my honour and pleasure to work with such a lively group of authors.

I would like to acknowledge with gratitude the incisive and helpful comments of the anonymous Routledge reviewer, which helped me in tying up some loose ends of the book, particularly the sequencing of the different chapters.

Last but not least, I would like to express my gratitude to the Routledge India team whose warmth and meticulous management made the publication process an effortless experience.

Renu Addlakha
New Delhi
1 October 2012

Introduction

RENU ADDLAKHA

Since the 1970s, the international disability rights movement, the United Nations and national governments have attempted to ameliorate the status of the disabled population through a range of policy and legislative measures, primarily in the areas of health, education, employment, accessible environments and social security. For instance, India enacted the Persons with Disabilities (Equal Opportunities, Protection of Rights and Full Participation) Act in 1995.[1] More recently, India is a signatory to the landmark United Nations Convention on the Rights of Persons with Disabilities (UNCRPD) that was passed by the General Assembly in 2006. While the discourse in the disability sector in India has largely shifted from charity and welfare to human rights, disability studies, as an interdisciplinary academic terrain that focuses on the contributions, experiences, history and culture of persons with disabilities, has not yet taken root. Although a number of Indian scholars, activists and policymakers are engaged in path-breaking work on disability,[2] it remains marginal within the wider research and advocacy communities.

The present volume is the outcome of a two-day conference on gender, disability and society organised by the Centre for Women's Development Studies (CWDS), New Delhi, and the Women's Studies and Development Centre (WSDC), University of Delhi, on 21 and 22 August 2008. Going beyond the original exclusive focus on gender, it collates some of the most recent work on disability studies from across the country. The essays in this volume seek to engage with the concept of disability from a variety of disciplinary positions, sociocultural contexts and subjective experiences within the overarching framework of the Indian reality. The collection is a compilation of existing and ongoing research with a particular focus on the intersections of disability with other socio-demographic variables such as gender, class, caste, ethnicity, age, urban–rural residence, etc., in the diverse areas of law, policy, medicine, family and culture. Eight of the 17 articles have appeared in a special issue of the *Indian Journal of Gender Studies*, guest-edited by Renu Addlakha (2008a). The remaining nine essays are being published for the first time.

The contributors come from different disciplines and practice contexts, from universities, the government, the NGO sector and civil society. They are researchers, teachers, activists, policymakers and artists. Some of them are themselves persons with disabilities lending an unmatched authenticity to their work.

Disability Studies vis-à-vis the Study of Disability

Self-advocacy by members of the disability community in Europe, the United States and Canada, over the past three decades, has not only led to enabling legislation and public policy measures to ameliorate the life conditions of persons with disabilities, but it has also resulted in unravelling the epistemological underpinnings and ontological status of taken-for-granted conceptual categories. Notions of normality and abnormality, ability and able-bodiedness, difference and deficit, health and illness, strength and weakness, dependence, independence and inter-dependence, etc., have been analysed threadbare. In the process, a new perspective on disability as primarily a sociopolitical phenomenon rather than a given biological reality has emerged. Disability studies is the academic discipline that embodies this perspective. Simi Linton (1998) offers perhaps one of the most comprehensive definitions of this emerging discipline that articulates both its theoretical and activist dimensions. According to her:

> Disability studies takes for its subject matter not simply the variations that exist in human behavior, appearance, functioning, sensory acuity, and cognitive processing but, more crucially, the meaning we make of those variations. The field explores the critical divisions our society makes in creating the normal versus the pathological, the insider versus

the outsider, or the competent citizen versus the ward of the state. It is an interdisciplinary field based on a sociopolitical analysis of disability and informed both by the knowledge base and the methodologies used in the traditional liberal arts, and by conceptualizations and approaches developed in areas of the new scholarship. Disability studies has emerged as a logical base for examination of the construction and function of "disability". These scholarly explorations and the initiatives undertaken by the disability rights movement have resulted in new paradigms used to understand disability as a social, political, and cultural phenomenon (ibid.: 2).

Unpacking this definition highlights some of the main features of disability studies. First, it challenges the definition of disability as a purely medical category that is the domain of specialised applied fields such as special education, rehabilitation and health. Furthermore, viewing disability largely through a non-biological lens reframes it as primarily a social, cultural, economic and political category, opening it up as an interdisciplinary or transdisciplinary domain of study. Third, it weaves in the activist agenda of the disability rights movement, which has preceded its entry into the academy.

Making a strong pitch for the incorporation of disability studies in the academy, Linton goes on to state:

> Hidden and disregarded for too long, we are demanding not only rights and equal opportunity but are demanding that the academy take on the nettlesome question of why we've been sequestered in the first place. For, in disregarding disability as subject matter, disabled people as subjects, and disabled people's subjectivity, academics have been complicit in that confinement. Yet each of these elements, worked through the curriculum, can serve not only to liberate people but to liberate thought. Disability studies introduces contradiction into the polarized categories of weak and strong, normal and abnormal, revered and reviled, dependent and independent, expendable and essential. It reveals these as false dichotomies, and reveals the epistemological underpinnings of the privileged position in each pair. Other fields have described the consequences of the splits between public and private, personal and political, mind and body, or biological and social. Disability studies demonstrates how such compartmentalization often serves some groups better than others but ultimately serves no one well (ibid.: 185–86).

Following the minority group argument, Linton draws attention to the connection between the segregation of persons with disabilities in the population and the marginalisation of disability in the context of knowledge production. In that sense, disability studies is the logical outcome of a trajectory pioneered by the interdisciplinary domains of ethnic and race studies, women's studies and queer studies, which also entered the academy after hectic activist politics and social mobilisation.

It is not as if disability studies is the first systematic approach to the study of disability.[3] Indeed, as already mentioned, disability has been a major concern of medicine, social work and education, giving rise to the subspecialities of rehabilitation and special education. The fields of health, illness and ageing have been particularly important sites for the study of disability. Even within the social sciences, disability has been a prominent topic in the study of the sick role (Parsons 1951), illness behaviour (Mechanic and Volkart 1962) and deviance (Goffman 1968). Indeed, disability studies scholars like Tanya Titchkosky (2000) critique the medical view of disability as pathology and the traditional sociological approach to disability as deviance. Although medicine and sociology have different conceptual frameworks, they share the same perspective, namely, that disability is a problem in need of remedy.

Repositioning disability in an alternative perspective, Titchkosky grounds her work in the new disability studies genre that questions the medical model that has historically dominated the mainstream study of disability. Disability studies contests disability as an undesired, and undesirable, asocial, apolitical individual bodily condition. It reconfigures it as a category of analysis that presents different accounts of the self and the world on the lines of class, gender, race and sexuality.

A key concept that has played a critical role in the emergence of disability studies as an academic speciality is the social model developed in Britain during the 1970s and 1980s by a group of largely disabled social scientists (Barnes 1991, 1998; Barnes and Mercer 1996; Barnes, Oliver and Barton 2002; Campbell and Oliver 1996; Finkelstein 1980; Oliver 1990, 1996). It was in a seminal document of the Union of the Physically Impaired Against Segregation (UPIAS) that this term first appeared in 1976. As against the medical model, the social model of disability asserts that material barriers, social prejudice and exclusion define who is disabled and who is not in a particular society. While some people have physical, intellectual, or psychological differences from a statistical norm, these impairments do not have to lead to disability unless society fails to accommodate and include them in the way it would those who are 'normal'. Many would regard the social model as a paradigmatic shift in the study of disability. While the social model does not reject medical knowledge and technology in dealing with the problem of bodily impairment, it shifts the spotlight of research and advocacy to analysing how society disables its impaired members. Consequently, the focus of inquiry and intervention is on how physical, social, economic, political, communication and attitudinal barriers create disabling environments that lead to the oppression of disabled persons.

The social model was developed by a group of British social scientists with a strong socialist agenda, which is reflected in its Marxian and materialist perspective. They linked the systematic oppression of disabled people to the rise of industrial capitalism, which created a market where those who could not sell their labour power were devalued and stigmatised. Modern medicine played an important role in providing the ideological justification for their marginalisation. In the United States, minority group politics deriving from the prevailing black civil rights and women's movements influenced the development of disability activism and disability studies with the resulting emphasis on tackling social subordination, exclusion and developing strategies for empowerment (Charlton 1998; Driedger 1989). The minority group perspective and the social model of disability paradigm provide a backdrop to the configuration of disability studies as an intellectual enterprise that examines the world from the distinctive vantage point of disability as a social, political and cultural category.

Postmodernist and poststructuralist disability researchers, largely influenced by the work of Michel Foucault and Jacques Derrida, like Marian Corker, Tom Shakespeare and Sally French (Corker and French 1999; Corker and Shakespeare 2002) provide another perspective on disability that shifts the primary focus of analysis from sociostructural determinants to linguistic, discursive and cultural practices. Rather than configuring it as a fixed essential category with a definite genesis in capitalist social formations, the latter perspective looks at disability through the categories of power/knowledge, social construction and individual agency. While disability and impairment continue to be foundational concepts in disability studies, postmodernism recognises the variability of categories and goes beyond the simple impairment–disability dualism by interrogating the social embeddedness of embodiment itself (Hughes and Paterson 1997; Thomas 2001). Postmodernist perspectives in disability studies acknowledge the plurality in meaning construction and recognise that disability would have very different meanings, both historically and cross-culturally.

So, what are the defining characteristics of disability studies as it struggles for academic legitimacy? In terms of disciplinary location, it is an interdisciplinary and transdisciplinary domain spanning the humanities, social sciences and cultural studies. As already discussed, the overarching theoretical insights in the discipline are provided by the materialist/Marxist and postmodernist/-structuralist perspectives. Coming to more specific concerns, disability studies examines reality from the standpoint of disability, i.e., from the perspectives of persons with disabilities in society. Since disability has hitherto almost exclusively been conceptualised and studied by non-disabled persons, one of the goals of the discipline is to provide centre stage to the voices of disabled persons, namely, their thoughts, feelings and experiences as members of an oppressed minority group and an oppressive culture.

Disability studies does not regard disability as a problem but as a location or position for gaining valid knowledge and understanding. In this connection, it is very critical of the expertise or 'professional disability knowledge' (Titchkosky 2000: 214) generated by the helping professions and mainstream sociology, psychology, education, etc., which construct disability as a problem in need of management, if not resolution. Disability studies eschews the application of such terms as deviance, overcoming, coping and cure, adjustment and acceptance, which reduce persons with disabilities to bearers of signs and symptoms of pathology.

Disability is a relational concept, since even mainstream notions underwriting the medical model place it in relation to a taken-for-granted notion of normalcy. Disability studies questions not only the hegemony of the norm but configures it more as an ideological construct than as an actual condition of embodiment. So, while it accords primacy to the standpoint of disability, it is equally mindful of the standpoint of normalcy, as both are complementary. Indeed, disability is over time a common fate of all bodies, and not just impaired bodies. In the ultimate analysis, is not each one of us only temporarily able-bodied? The ideal of normalcy is an attempt to conceal the associations with fear, vulnerability and death that the disabled body evokes in the 'non-disabled mind' (Davis 1995; Zola 1982).

In keeping with its critical epistemology and radical politics, disability studies has also reconfigured research paradigms. Michael Oliver (1997) proposed the notion of emancipatory disability research, which transforms the material and social relations of research production. Essentially, this is a form of participatory action research that questions the possibility of objectivity and value neutrality in which research has traditionally been determined by non-disabled professionals and academics. Persons with disabilities have been 'cases', and the results of the research have been used largely to serve the interests of policymakers. Indeed, the rationale for emancipatory research is to displace control from non-disabled persons to persons with disabilities. This research stance not only has an empowering potential, but it also questions the systems of expertise deployed to define and manage disability by medicine and the helping professions (Finkelstein 1998). By having persons with disabilities and disability organisations involved in the entire research process (including agenda-setting and finances), attempts are made to ensure that it has positive and practical outcomes for them.[4] By being upfront about its political commitment and goal of empowerment of its constituency, emancipatory disability research attempts to ensure both academic authenticity and social accountability of knowledge production and its application.

Phrases like 'new disability studies' and 'critical disability studies' highlight the counter-normative and counter-hegemonic spirit of engaging with disability as a historical, social, cultural and epistemic reality that goes beyond medical management and rehabilitation, social mainstreaming, and cultural acceptance of individuals with disabilities. Disability studies, at core, involves an engagement with the experiential reality of disability, historicisation and politicisation of the category, intersectional analysis, epistemological recognition and social transformation — all this and more.[5]

Disability Studies in India

It is ironic that while India probably has the largest number of persons with disabilities in the world after China, if total population size is taken as a reliable indicator, accurate clinical, empirical and demographic data on disability is not available. According to conservative estimates derived from the Census of India 2001, 1.8 to 2.1 per cent of the population suffers from some form of disability, which in absolute numbers comes to approximately 18.49 to 21.92 million persons.[6] It needs to be remembered that estimates of the total number of persons with disabilities in a country vary depending on the definition of disability adopted, degree of impairment recognised as disabling and survey methodology, including use of scientific instruments for identification and measurement of disabling conditions. Thus, the 2001 Census only took account of five loosely defined disabling conditions, namely, problems of seeing, hearing, speech, movement and mental conditions — i.e., mental retardation and mental illness. Using a wider definition of disability, which includes conditions like diabetes and cardiovascular disease, the World Health Organisation (WHO) estimates that 6–10 per cent of the population suffers from identifiable physical or mental disability. That comes to over 90 million persons in India. Phenomena such as war, ethnic conflict, HIV/AIDS, natural disasters, industrial injuries and road accidents are increasing the number of persons with disabilities. Ironically, enhanced life expectancy has also increased manifold the incidence of old age-related, chronic disease-induced disabilities worldwide.

So, while on the one hand the social model of disability has tangentially entered the public domain in India largely through the work of disability rights activists, the concern with issues of prevalence, incidence, management and prevention of disabilities is still a stark reality in the government and NGO sectors, highlighting the strange and uneasy coexistence of the medical and social models. This situation is further complicated by India's official commitment to the UNCRPD that seeks to operationalise many of the basic tenets of the social model. The absence of a valid empirical database on disability[7] is a serious limitation highlighting the fact that the meaning of disability and its social ramifications largely remain invisible in both public understanding and policy formulations.

A social context in which the charity and human rights discourses on disability uneasily sit side by side points to the urgent need to inaugurate a serious discussion on disability from a disability studies perspective, which is the explicit purpose of this book. In the United Kingdom and the United States, disability activism has produced an interdisciplinary domain of disability studies within the academy. Many disability rights activists and policymakers in India are attempting to take a Western agenda on disability to a reality which has different epistemological and ontological moorings. Hence the need for a perspective that not only critically assesses the relevance of concepts and theories on disability developed in the West, but also engages in uncovering meaningful discourses and developing strategies that address the local realities of disability in the Indian context.

An analysis of available literature on disability in India shows the existence of a large number of empirical studies on impairment and handicap generated by professionals in the fields of special education, rehabilitation, clinical psychology and other paramedical specialities. It is only in the past decade that the issue of disability has been explored from a social model perspective. A number of books focusing on mental — or what is now referred to as psychosocial — disability pioneered an exploration of the issue from a critical institutional standpoint. The works by Bhargavi Davar (1999, 2001), Amita Dhanda (2000) and Renu Addlakha (2008b) engage with this theme from the perspectives of the women's movement, the law and the psychiatric profession, respectively.

More phenomenological accounts started emerging from 2000 onwards. Insa Klasing's study (2007), examining the social exclusion of disabled persons in rural India, falls in the category of area-specific empirical studies. More specifically addressing the issue of women with disabilities are Anita Ghai's account (2003) of the emergence of disability feminism within Western feminism vis-à-vis the marginalisation of the issue within the Indian women's movement; and Asha Hans and Annie Patri's edited collection (2003) of an international seminar on women with disabilities. Then, Rukmini Sekhar's (2005) and, more recently, Malini Chib's (2011) works make a beginning in the area of autobiography and disability.

The collection of papers in the present volume opens yet another window on disability in India. First, unlike the works by Ghai, Hans and Patri, all the essays are India-centric. Second, unlike the works by Addlakha, Davar and Dhanda, this volume engages simultaneously with physical, sensory, communication, psychosocial and intellectual disabilities. Third, it moves beyond both the medical and social models of disability to situate the debate within the context of disability and impairment as universal experiences of the human condition. The essays address different aspects of disability, raise complex questions and make a case for culture, class/caste, area and gender-sensitive interdisciplinary and multidisciplinary research. They lay the foundation for beginning a serious engagement with disability studies in the academy and providing insights for formulating culturally sensitive and socially and economically viable public policies on disability in this country.

This volume is divided into five sections: the articles in Part I historicise the category of disability and document the important role of the disability rights movement and the United Nations in giving it social and political legitimacy. Part II presents micro-level accounts of the experiences of disability in everyday life, both from the perspective of persons with disabilities and their caregivers. Part III carries forward the phenomenological approach with a particular focus on disability as a gendered reality. Part IV discusses aesthetics and disability in the context of photographic projects with persons with hearing and visual disabilities, highlighting the creativity of persons mistakenly considered incapable of such endeavours. The last section discusses some concrete micro- and macro-level strategies to mainstream the issue of disability and persons with disabilities in Indian society.

Historicising Disability and Disability Studies

Scholarship on the history of disability in disability studies attempts to create a pan-human historiography, but as Shilpaa Anand points out in Chapter 1, being a field of inquiry that has originated in the West, it tacitly draws on historical material that is peculiar to the West's experiences of the world. Consequently, historicising disablement in non-Western cultural contexts using the Western paradigm for mapping out African, South Asian, Japanese and Middle Eastern histories of disability is problematic. Such a perspective, for example, excludes historical experiences, such as colonialism, that the West's collective experience cannot conceptualise. Anand proposes a solution through a re-evaluation of the historical method(s) adopted. She excavates the concepts of monstrosity and feeble-mindedness from colonial records at the interface of the encounter between biomedicine and local epistemic categories in India. One of the historical stages that Anand identifies in her delineation of the history of disability in the disability studies literature is the human rights paradigm that recognises disability as both a valid individual identity and political category. It is within this framework that both the social model of disability and the United Nations disability-related interventions took shape. The two remaining chapters in Part I examine these developments presenting a contemporary historiography of disability that complements Anand's critical historical analysis.

Identity politics is epistemology inextricably tied to praxis. It not only involves a common group experience of injustice and a collective effort (in the form of a social movement) to overcome the common oppression, but also involves cultivating a sense of pride and reclaiming a positive identity. The second half of the 20th century has seen the emergence of large-scale political movements — black civil rights in the US, second wave feminism, gay and lesbian liberation and, more recently, the disability rights movement. Drawing upon American, British and Indian literature, Jagdish Chander (in Chapter 2) presents a historical analysis of key concepts in disability studies such as 'impairment' and 'disability', the 'medical/individual' and 'social/minority' group models. Chander points out how, prior to the 1970s, the disability rights movement was, by and large, what is described as an 'impairment specific' movement, i.e., the blind canvassed for the rights of the blind and the deaf activists worked only for the deaf. Most often, such impairment-specific activism was undertaken by non-disabled persons. Subsequently, disability rights organisations led by disabled people themselves took centre stage, and disability became a unifying category in a movement that realised the value of self-advocacy and coalition-building. An important consciousness-raising strategy was to show how disability is not an individual tragedy that requires medical management, but a social problem that demands collective action. Being a disability scholar specialising in research on the blind, Chander highlights throughout the paper the historically overlooked contribution of the blind activists in India in developing a rights-based advocacy perspective, much before the rise of a cross-disability rights activism in the country during the 1990s.

Complementing Chander's analysis of the critical engagement between the disability rights movement and disability studies is N. Sundaresan's examination of how disability has been configured in the mandate of the United Nations, mainly through an analysis of its disability-specific instruments (Chapter 3). Ever since its inception after the Second World War, the United Nations has played an important role in affirming disability as an important human rights issue through a range of disability-specific recommendations, resolutions, declarations, guidelines, treatises, programmes of action and conventions, which in turn have influenced national-level laws, policies and programmes of its member states. For instance, a radical redrafting of the national Mental Health Act, 1987, and the Persons with Disabilities (Equal Opportunities, Protection of Rights and Full Participation) Act, 1995, are currently underway in India in an attempt to make disability legislation compliant with the UNCRPD.

Disability at Home, at Work and in the Community

Prejudice against and exclusion of disability and persons with disabilities are entrenched in society. They are not just confined to academic, legal, political and medical discourses but pervade experiences of life in general. They are embedded in the family, in social relationships and at the workplace. The four essays in Part II excavate the experiential reality of disability from the perspectives of different stakeholders in these different domains. The analysis of the experiences of living with a disability, caring for someone with a disability or working as a professional in the disability sector shows how disability intersects with other categories like gender and class, and in the process, contests the homogeneity of the concept highlighting its diverse dimensions and manifestations.

Drawing upon an analogy between sex determination and disability selection in the Indian context, Anita Ghai and Rachana Johri examine issues of freedom of choice, gender and disability-based oppression, and notions of motherhood and childhood in Chapter 4. In light of the declining sex ratio in the country, antenatal sex determination has been made illegal. However, the more liberal abortion regime has also led to the possibly unwitting legitimisation of the abortion of children with disabilities. The authors question the ideology that regards abortion as the only option, when prenatal testing reveals a birth abnormality, an option sanctioned by both the Medical Termination of Pregnancy Act, 1971, and the Pre-Natal Diagnostic Techniques (Regulation and Prevention of Misuse) Act, 1994. Furthermore, the abortion of disabled foetuses is also endorsed by many feminists on grounds of the right of women to autonomous decision-making in the domain of reproductive health.

Viewing disability as largely a social construct and drawing upon interviews with mothers of children with disabilities and non-disabled children, as also the testimonies of young women with disabilities in Delhi, Ghai and Johri contest societal attitudes that view the lives of people with disabilities as tragic, worthless and a burden. They feel that the pro-choice stance, promoting antenatal testing for elimination of defective foetuses, feeds into prevailing notions of bodily perfection. Furthermore, there is a singular focus on the costs of disability in terms of time, money and suffering for both persons with disabilities and their parents.

Indeed, one of the reasons for avoiding continuation of a pregnancy that may result in the birth of a child with disabilities is the not entirely incorrect expectation of the extra material resources and personal care that such a child would require. Issues central to care work and caregiving are raised from different perspectives in the two articles by Upali Chakravarti (Chapter 5), and Nilika Mehrotra and Shubhangi Vaidya (Chapter 6), respectively. Chakravarti examines parenting through the lens of ongoing caregiving in a social context where the entire responsibility is put squarely on the family[8] and, more particularly, the mother. The non-availability of state-sponsored support and limited family resources for the care of members with disabilities also highlight another important issue, namely, it is not just individual medical care that persons with disabilities require, but families also require a range of support services to be able to successfully care for a member with a disability. Families not only require material resources, but also continual psychological support, as highlighted by Chakravarti's interviews with parents of adults with cerebral palsy (CP).[9] Many issues germane to their day-to-day lives, such as feelings of anger and helplessness, apprehensions about the child's future, especially after the death of the primary caregiver, and religious faith are discussed. Unfortunately, these concerns are invisibilised by society, and the resulting personal and social suffering ignored.

It is in this light that the need for a comprehensive package of outside family support services covering long-term physical, financial and psychological requirements is reiterated. Chakravarti's informants spoke with appreciation of the help extended by NGOs like the Delhi-based Action for Ability Development and Inclusion (AADI). An interesting point raised by the author is that, historically, NGOs working in the disability sector in India have been started for child-related services. They do not have services to cater to the needs of adults with disabilities.

Mehrotra and Vaidya provide another perspective on care, family and the NGO interface through the lens of intellectual disability[10] and autism,[11] with specific reference the notion of masculinity and the manner in which disabled males are feminised and infantilised. Femininity and masculinity are not only ascribed biological characteristics but are enacted in a cultural milieu. Acquiring a masculine identity and proving their manhood are considered beyond the competence of males with intellectual disability who are, thus, notionally clubbed with the community of women and children in places like rural Haryana. They are described as naïve or innocent, ridiculed, and assigned household chores. They continue to be looked after by their female family members.

Using ethnographic data collected from two pioneering disability NGOs in Rohtak (Haryana) and Delhi, an attempt is made by the authors to understand how individuals with these disabilities and their families seek social spaces for themselves and negotiate the social compulsions for 'normalcy' and competent adulthood. Conversations with NGO functionaries and families of some of the male attendees revealed that coming to the centres gives the latter 'something to do' — they are provided with a routine; they spend the day in surroundings that are congenial, respectful of their differences, and are amidst peers.

Unlike the practices of labelling, segregation and institutionalisation observed in the West, the sociocultural milieux in non-Western societies, including India, have historically tended to absorb persons with disabilities within the circle of family and social networks, creating spaces for them to function according to their capacities. The fact that Mehrotra and Vaidya's informants appeared more socially integrated in the rural areas of Haryana than in the urban landscape of Delhi highlights the role of traditional community-based care strategies. But with urbanisation, nuclearisation of the family, women's outside employment and rapid social change, traditional support structures are breaking down and NGOs have stepped in to fill the vacuum in a context where a neo-liberal state is withdrawing from the social sector. It is interesting to note that while in the West, the last two decades have seen a shift from institutionalisation to family and community-based support for persons with intellectual disability, in urban India the reverse seems to be taking place.

When it comes to adults with disabilities, work becomes a central concern since, like gender, it is a critical category of identity construction. In the last article (Chapter 7) in this section, Amit Upadhyay examines the prospects of employment of disabled persons in urban India. The productive capacities of persons with disabilities have always been suspect: they carry the taint of partial personhood casting them with a die of weakness, incapacity, incompetence, passivity, dependence and socioeconomic futility. While data on work participation rates clearly shows the almost total absence of persons with disabilities in the labour force, this is, as Upadhyay's essay shows, more likely to be the outcome of social prejudice and discrimination rather than individual incapacity.

Delineating perceived barriers to employment, in both finding and holding down a job, of a subset of persons with locomotor impairment in Bangalore, Upadhyay points to such architectonic obstacles as public transport and staircases, and attitudinal barriers like employers' negative perceptions. Interestingly, socioeconomic status and family income were stronger determinants of employment success and quality of work experience than the disability per se. Middle class respondents repeatedly managed to circumvent physical barriers, such as transport, in comparison to their more impoverished counterparts. Of course, overcoming social prejudice and exclusion was a more arduous task, which even a higher socioeconomic status could not easily overcome.

Femininity and Disability

We have already seen how gender ideologies frame caregiving within the family and emasculate men with disabilities. Even though the principle of 'the personal is political' shows up very starkly in the way in which women with disabilities are portrayed in society, they have been missing from the mainstream agenda of feminism. Women's studies all over the world, including India, has tended to reflect a non-disabled or able-bodied perspective, and it is this perception that has generated a critique from within feminism itself by women with disabilities. This critique has been done through the concepts of gender roles, body image, sexuality and care. Feminist disability scholars (Begum 1992; Fine and Asch 1988; Ghai 2003; Meekosha 2002; Morris 1993; Thomas 2001) have highlighted how women with disabilities are often considered asexual and incapable of taking on sexual, reproductive and maternal roles. However, the expulsion from traditional gender roles has not protected them from the threat of male violence. On the one hand, there is pervasive desexualisation and rolelessness of women with disabilities, and on the other, there is the evidence of higher rates of sexual exploitation and abuse in comparison to non-disabled women.

Heterosexuality, work and motherhood are 'normally' associated with women in general, but are not used to describe women with disabilities who are uniformly considered to be passive, dependent and deprived. Feminists have critiqued the traditional roles of daughters, wives and mothers as oppressive, but these may be the very roles that women with disabilities aspire to, precisely because they are denied to them. Consequently, the feminist struggle against the oppression of the institutions of marriage, family and childcare will be different for women with disabilities.

It is precisely these issues that Nandini Ghosh raises in her essay (Chapter 8) on constructions of femininity and disability in Bengali culture. Her feminist ethnography is based on a cohort of women with different kinds of disabilities from both urban and rural backgrounds, who are largely from the lower middle classes. Using a life cycle approach, the paper reveals their experiences during childhood, adolescence and adulthood in their natal and affinal families. It specifically explores the subjectivity of the disabled female body in structuring notions of femininity, desirability and sexuality. Bengali gender/ability regimes draw heavily on the concept of the *bhalo meye* (good woman), an ideological construct of femininity manifested through representations, images, norms, practices, activities and ideas regarding acceptable female bodies, appearance and behaviour, qualities and characteristics. For a woman with disabilities, the ideology of the *bhalo meye* deems her as falling short of the ideal in almost all spheres, while at the same time creating pressure on her to actualise the concept in her own life.

How do individual disabled women and their families negotiate the gender order in such a context? Strategies, like over-protectiveness of the daughter — reinforcing her 'special' status —

and encouraging her to study with the aim of being financially independent, reflect a tacit acceptance of the idea that women with disabilities do not have the same life options as non-disabled women in the form of marriage and motherhood. Underlying such ableist assumptions is a denial of their sexuality, excluding them, by inference, from the domains of desirability, pleasure, procreation and responsible adulthood. Ghosh's informants were not radical feminists. Given the material reality of the impairment, most of them learnt to struggle against, accept and manage their bodies according to gendered constructions decreed by the culture. But it must be remembered that oppression is always accompanied by resistance, and individual agency penetrates cracks within hegemonic systems; for instance, most of Ghosh's interviewees engaged in housework and some of them were also gainfully employed outside the home.

How individuals conceptualise and contest social representations, particularly the negative social messages they receive about sexuality, is the theme of Renu Addlakha's essay (Chapter 9). The essay explores the opinions of a sample of young women with different disabilities in Delhi, who formulate and articulate a sense of self that straddles the slippery terrain between normative and disabled femininity.

The analysis of the voices of young people with disabilities shows that the embodied female self of the disabled subject is primarily constructed through a formal allegiance to the sexual and aesthetic norms and values of the non-disabled patrifocal world. Agency emerges in the choice of areas of relative focus and appropriation, which are critically dependent on the specific experiences of impairment. For instance, visual disability may predispose affected individuals to develop a non-visual aesthetics of the body, while mobility impairment may push the affected person to construct a politics and aesthetics of the body that shifts the focus away from the dynamics of physical grace and movement. Indeed, notions of beauty and attractiveness that accentuate mental abilities and moral rectitude may be strategically highlighted in place of physical characteristics in the presentation of the self.

The remaining two essays in Part III present two contrasting views on deafness, namely, as a cultural identity and as hearing impairment, respectively. Working on the boundary between deafness and Deafness in Chapter 10, Michele Friedner develops an exegesis of Deaf identity that is both gendered and culturally embedded. Deaf, written with a capital 'D', is distinct from deaf, written with a lower case 'd'. A 'Deaf' individual is a member of the Deaf culture, the Deaf community, communicates using sign language, sees the world through Deaf eyes and possesses Deaf pride. In contrast, someone who is 'deaf' has a medical condition or impairment, does not identify with Deaf culture and, most likely, does not use sign language. Deafness is an identity, a culture and a community — and not a disability — for those who identify with it.

Friedner's interviews with members of the Delhi Foundation of Deaf Women help her examine how discursive flows contribute to the constitution of Deaf identity in a context, wherein ideas and resources flow from the global North to the global South.[12] How do deaf women belonging to a lower socioeconomic urban context negotiate with such concepts as Deaf culture and Deaf identity? Friedner comes to the conclusion that culture plays a critical role in their construction of selfhood. The universality and cultural neutrality underlying Deaf studies[13] are challenged by her informants' privileging of their kinship identities and the domestic sphere over all other identities (including Deafness). Most theory coming out of Deaf studies has ignored, until relatively recently, the category of gender. This chapter seeks to explore how culture and gender modify the experiences and articulations of Deaf identity in a non-Western setting.

While Friedner looks at Deaf identity in the context of global flows and transnational discourses, Sandhya Limaye presents two detailed case studies of hearing-impaired adolescent girls in Mumbai. The essay (Chapter 11) is framed in the context of the developmental tasks of adolescence.[14] Adolescence is one of the critical developmental stages of the life cycle involving a distinct set of developmental tasks, which include awareness and acceptance of the changing body, development of peer relationships, internalisation of gender role expectations and development of a distinct personal identity, in addition to exercising autonomy, training for and acquiring work for economic independence, and entering marriage and family life. While adolescents with hearing impairment face the same developmental challenges that confront all hearing adolescents, their passage through this stage is more difficult since the basic deprivation due to deafness is more than sensory, as basic communication skills are seriously affected. Since most deaf children are born to hearing parents, absence of communication and/or actual miscommunication in the family may have adverse consequences for socialisation. Limaye's two young female interviewees, Radha and Hasina, challenge the discrimination and marginalisation meted out to them by their families, teachers and the wider society. They attempt to exercise autonomy by choosing life partners, planning careers, and forging social lives that contest the notion of deaf persons as secluded and dependent. The girls emerge as assertive, individualistic and high-spirited persons who contest popular negative stereotypes of persons with disabilities. This is the life context in which oralism[15] is the almost exclusive mode of communication. One wonders how their lives would have panned out had they been part of a milieu in which Deaf culture was the norm.

Disability Aesthetics and Creative Diversity

The intersection between aesthetics and disability is an emerging area that seeks to capture the multiple representations of disability and the production of art by persons with disabilities. Disability art culture is the term used for this genre of academic inquiry and aesthetic appreciation. Representations of the disabled body in the visual arts like painting, sculpture and photography often equate disability with evil, pain, suffering and mortality. This objectification of the disabled body by non-disabled artists is often in sharp contrast to the production of art by artists with disabilities. Underlying the latter is a different and a unique aesthetics that is prefigured on the experience of disability. The two papers in this section explore the disability–art configuration through photography by the Deaf and the blind respectively.

In Chapter 12, José Abad Lorente, an artist and curator who can only use one of his hands, describes a collaborative and interdisciplinary art project undertaken with the Deaf community in New Delhi in 2008. 'Life Bricolage' explores disability and representation through contemporary visual art practices. In the context of the ongoing battle for Indian Sign Language (ISL) to be recognised as a natural language of the Deaf, the project aimed to prompt discussion by representing the language corpora of the Deaf minority. Using participatory techniques, it attempted to map the qualities or abilities that Deaf people have developed as a result of using their whole body as a natural medium of communication in response to the need to both communicate among themselves and to respond to the challenges of a hearing world that stigmatises them.

Abad prefaces his photographic project with a discussion on sign language and the dominant oralist tradition in deaf education in India, highlighting the fact that deafness continues to still be configured as an audiological disability. But like Michele Friedner, he writes from the perspective of Deafness, with a capital 'D', which is a paradigm shift in the Indian context. The photo sessions he organised explored ways of using the body as a site for text and representation. The photographs project a positive message about the Deaf community and their language.

Partho Bhowmick examines the creativity–disability dyad in the context of yet another innovative project. He presents his work with a group of blind photographers in Mumbai. 'Blind with Camera' (Chapter 13) challenges the taken-for-granted equation between reality, knowledge and the gaze. Photography by the visually challenged is neither a paradox nor a contradiction in terms because it offers alternative ways of visualising the world, apprehending and constructing reality and valorising identity. Photography by the blind has developed in the past quarter century and is an integral part of the new field of disability art culture. Blind With Camera is the first step towards systematically promoting disability art culture in India.

Writing from the perspective of a sighted person, Bhowmick offers interpretations of a collection of photographs taken by a group of visually impaired persons. The basic premise of the essay is that sight and blindness are complimentary and inextricably intertwined concepts; and that in blindness, pure art exists. As a corollary to this, seeing is conceptualised as not a taken-for-granted activity derived from sight, but a learning process. Consequently, just as the sighted learn to see, so can, and do, the blind. The unique perceptions of the world and complex processes of representation by the blind are captured in photographs under labels such as 'Memory has eyes', 'The hand has eyes' and 'The eye has new eyes'. Indeed, art by persons with disabilities offers novel perspectives on the world and the self.

Destigmatisation, Recognition and Empowerment

The four essays in the concluding section (Part V) offer concrete proposals to ameliorate the life conditions of persons with disabilities through micro- and macro-level approaches. Suggestions are made to replicate strategies of the women's movement for empowerment in the disability sector. Phenomenological exploration of the lived reality of exclusion, gender budgeting and engendering legal instruments and policy documents are put forward as concrete possibilities to this end.

In her passionate self-reflective account of her engagement with the Indian women's movement over the past two decades, Bhargavi V. Davar (in Chapter 14) delineates the tensions between a feminist politics of empowerment that seeks social transformation in gender relations and the personal experiences of distress of individual women in search of healing. Davar's article follows other feminist disability scholars in their critique of the allegiance of the mainstream women's movement to a homogenous notion of womanhood that does not adequately valorise how disability, for example, creates fundamental differences among women. Davar traces the critical engagement of the Indian women's movement with psychiatry, mental health and disability. She discerns three phases in this engagement: the first was a phase of radical intellectual disbelief about the very existence of mental illness as a valid knowledge category. In the second phase, the experiential reality of women, who had to manage their own emotional states, found expression in a variety of discourses about women and mental health. The marginalisation of women by mainstream medicine was addressed, and the right to care was redefined as the creation of gender-sensitive sciences. In the third present phase, Davar reflects on the paths taken in the creation of such gender-sensitive mental health practices. According to her, a mental illness language has been exhausted of any positive content.

Using the emerging concept of 'psychosocial disability', Davar feels that the disability paradigm offers both theoretical justification and strategic opportunities for understanding and legitmating women's experiences of mental distress and illness.

She bemoans the Indian women's movement's prioritisation of socioeconomic and political issues at the expense of psychological distress and suffering of individual women. This has resulted in a strange and uneasy alliance between the feminist movement, the psychiatric profession, state policies and laws, and the pharmaceutical industries. It is in such a context that a sociopolitical discourse provided by disability studies that valorises individual experience can be helpful in thinking about the personal and the private that the politicised and medicalised rational discourses, cited earlier, have obstructed.

From the political to the personal, and back to the political! In Chapter 15, Asha Hans, Amrita Patel and S. B. Agnihotri show that allocating resources is not enough when the social, political and cultural realities block access of persons with disabilities, particularly women with disabilities, to such resources. Using the paradigm of gender budgeting to analyse allocations and expenditure in the disability sector in four of the poorest states in India, they highlight the yawning gap between policy rhetoric of rights and empowerment and inadequate resource allocations to match it. One of the most startling findings of their research is the steadily diminishing utilisation of resources in the disability sector. Bad governance, structural adjustment programmes, and lack of awareness about such programmes by persons with disabilities and their families are major reasons for this underutilisation. The authors strongly recommend the need for a concerted national campaign of awareness-building on the entitlements available to persons with disabilities in the country. By highlighting the total absence of gender sensitivity in budgetary allocations in the disability sector, they alert us to the multiple layers of exclusion within the category of disability in its intersections with other sociodemographic variables, such as gender, caste, class and region.

The discussion on the UNCRPD initiated by N. Sundaresan (Chapter 3) and Bhargavi V. Davar (Chapter 14) allows us to move to examine the critical interface between disability, law and gender.

Historically, law has been one of the most powerful institutions that has systematically contributed to the dehumanisation and disempowerment of persons with disabilities. Imputation of legal incompetence has been used to deprive disabled persons, particularly persons with intellectual and psychosocial impairments, basic human rights to livelihood, property, marriage, parenthood and political participation. Functioning under an illusory garb of gender neutrality, law has ensured an even worse deal for women with disabilities. For instance, in her analysis of legal judgements involving a diagnosis of mental illness, Amita Dhanda (2000) has shown the overwhelming use of a psychiatric diagnosis in divorce cases wherein the petitioner is a man. Ironically, or expectedly, a weapon can also become a saviour. For instance, the plethora of disability legislation during the 1990s, such as the Americans with Disabilities Act, 1990, the Disability Discrimination Act, 1995, in the United Kingdom, and the Persons with Disabilities Act, 1995, in India, testifies to the role of law being envisaged as a powerful tool of social change and justice. From country-specific disability laws, it was only one step to formulating an international law in the form of the UNCRPD.

Amita Dhanda (in Chapter 16) analyses the in-depth country-level discussions that went into arriving at a mutually-acceptable approach for engendering the UNCRPD. It is an intriguing case study of the development of international legal instruments from the perspective of an insider, as Dhanda was one of the participants in the negotiations on the Convention. The 'twin track' approach that it embodies attempts to both mainstream and provide special measures for ameliorating the lives of women with disabilities in the laws, policies and programmes of member states. Article 6 of the UNCRPD on women with disabilities is critically evaluated by the author; she notes that its diluted wording considerably diminishes its capacity to induce radical change. Even gender mainstreaming appears to have been selectively done in the Convention — for instance, rejection of the gender dimension in the articles on education (Article 24) and work (Article 27) is a serious lacuna, but its incorporation in the health article (Article 25) is clearly a gain.

A general pattern of law becoming a springboard for social change, be it in the realm of reducing caste inequities, empowering women or mainstreaming disability, is discernible in India. Enabling legislative enactments and the subsequent case law intersect with public policy initiatives. For instance, 3 per cent reservation in government employment, mandated by the Persons with Disabilities Act, 1995, has resulted in legal redressal in some cases where this provision was violated. However, as Jeeja Ghosh clearly points out in the concluding essay, law on its own cannot guarantee substantial change without social participation of the marginalised constituency, which she defines as 'access to leisure activities, participation in social functions, interaction with family, friends and outsiders, and opportunities to socialise with the peer group to develop intimate relationships' (Chapter 17). This formulation makes the important observation that inclusion cannot be actualised without factoring in the critical issue of sexuality, which is a real challenge in a social context that systematically desexualises disability, particularly the sexuality of women with disabilities. Discussing different provisions of the UNCRPD, Ghosh reiterates the need to move beyond education and employment guarantees to ensure rights to recreation, leisure and family life of persons with disabilities in India. Highlighting the intersections between economic exclusion, sexuality, leisure and accessibility, Ghosh foregrounds with particular emphasis the plight of women with disabilities.

Conclusion: Subversion, Interdisciplinarity and Intersectionality

So what is the emerging paradigm of disability studies in India? Given the nascent stage of development, it is difficult to articulate its definite features; but certain observations of the process underway may be highlighted on the basis of the contributions contained in this volume. First, even though the social model of disability is seeping into disability activism and the state's thinking on disability, the disability studies perspective has a long way to go before it becomes the dominant way of looking at disability, because of the hitherto relatively unchallenged status of the medical model. The academy can make a contribution to institutionalising it, but there are as yet hardly any programmes or courses on disability studies (as distinct from studies on disability in the paramedical, social work, clinical and legal fields) in Indian universities. On the other hand, a range of policy-level endeavours underway, such as amendments to existing disability laws to make them compliant with the UNCRPD, which India has signed and ratified, may eventually result in creating the much needed momentum to mainstream the disability studies perspective not only in the university but also in the public domain. As an academic specialisation, disability studies would incorporate the rich insights of already institutionalised interdisciplinary fields such as women's studies, and *dalit* and tribal studies, sharing common experiences of social exclusion and mobilisation. An added and distinctive dimension in the case of disability is its dependent, yet deeply contested, relationship with medicine and the health industries, which foreground critical issues of care, treatment and management. This volume presents an outline of the key issues that would be germane to any disability studies endeavour that is in the process of taking shape in the Indian context.

A Note on Terminology

As language is a key tool of oppression, naming is critical when a socially disadvantaged section of the population seeks recognition and rights. Analysis of key linguistic terms and the replacement of pejorative with more value-neutral and positive terms are essential preliminary steps in any movement towards collective self-affirmation and empowerment. The disability rights movement has promoted a move away from a language of handicap towards a more empowering language that emphasises self-determination and personhood. In the American context, this people-first language approach (Vaughan 1993) has given rise to the use of the term 'person with disabilities'. On the other hand, the impact of the social model, which emphasises structural and attitudinal barriers as a source of oppression lying outside the individual, has resulted in 'disabled person' becoming more commonplace in Britain. In the Indian context, where political correctness is a prickly issue, the tendency is to use a mix of terms like 'differently-abled', 'challenged', 'person with a disability' and 'child with special needs' in policy documents, media reports and even by disability activists.

No attempt has been made in this volume to standardise terminology about disability across the different papers. Choice of language is not just about political correctness but more about reality construction. Hence, when such terms as 'madness', 'impaired person', 'handicapped person', regarded as inappropriate if not downright stigmatising, have been used by authors, they have not been edited because they carry a semantics that might otherwise have been erased had they been replaced by other more politically correct substitutes.

Although the contributors in this collection have, by and large, taken a disability studies perspective, some have used terms such as hearing impaired, visually impaired, etc., which to a purist might be objectionable. Instead of reading such expressions as disabling, I leave it to the reader to interpret their usage in the light of the authored text. For my own part, I prefer the American usage of 'person(s) with disabilities' simply because it moves beyond the singular negative master status attribution of disability to a configuration of physical/mental, social, cultural, political and economic factors that obstruct the person, but do not constitute the person per se. On the other hand, I have also used terms like 'blind' and 'deaf', which are self-consciously used by members of these communities as well as by activists involved in the disability rights movement in this country.

Notes

1. Presently, there is a revision of disability legislation in India in order to make the legal regime compliant with the UNCRPD that India has signed and ratified.
2. A distinction has to be made between disability as a medical issue largely focusing on provision of clinical and rehabilitation services and disability studies, a scholarly approach to examining various dimensions of disability as a form of difference along the lines of race, class, caste and gender. Refer to the section 'Disability Studies vis-à-vis the Study of Disability'.
3. In his historical excavation of the concept of normalcy in Europe, Lennard J. Davis (1995) informs us that disability first became an analytic category with the Enlightenment when the disabled were bureaucratically tracked, counted and managed.
4. Attempts are being made to mainstream disability in society through creation of Disabled Persons' Organisations (DPOs), which are the new buzzword in the disability sector. As the name suggests, the majority of persons running these organisations are persons with disabilities.

5. A third perspective that developed within disability studies in the context of the welfare state, specifically in the Nordic countries of Denmark, Sweden and Norway, is normalization. This standpoint emphasises community participation of disabled persons attempting to make their lives as close as possible to the ordinary conditions of life in society. Since this perspective has not really played a major role in the development of disability thought and services in India, it has not been elaborated upon in this work.
6. The figures are outdated, but the results of the latest Indian Census, conducted in February 2011, were not available in the public domain when this book was sent for printing.
7. It needs to be noted that getting reliable prevalence data is in itself a herculean task. Commenting on the limitations of a study undertaken to map social exclusion in Rajasthan and Andhra Pradesh, Insa Klasing notes: 'Despite the enormous motivation and sensitivity of the researchers [most of whom were themselves disabled], the intensive nature of the survey and multiple sources and methods of identification used, the survey team could barely identify half of the disabled people believed to exist in each village' (2007: 56). Barely 2 per cent of the total persons with disabilities could be identified in any given area in a situation where modest estimates point to 5 per cent of the population being disabled. Klasing continues, 'Even as the survey teams were leaving the villages after finishing their investigation, more disabled people were discovered. So deep is the social invisibility of disabled villagers that even these high participatory and intensive surveys could not identify all disabled people' (ibid.).
8. Although disability pensions and other minimal welfare measures are provided to persons with disabilities by the state in an ad hoc way, there is no assistance to families caring for an adult with disabilities.
9. Cerebral palsy (CP) is an umbrella term for a group of congenital disorders affecting body movement, balance, and posture. CP is caused by abnormal development or damage in one or more parts of the brain that control muscle tone and motor activity (movement). The resulting impairments first appear early in life, usually in infancy or early childhood. Physiotherapy and medication may ameliorate the condition but there is as yet no cure. Taking the case of CP is particularly relevant in connection with care because individuals often require lifelong assistance in the management of even the most basic activities of daily life like eating, using the toilet, bathing, dressing, etc.
10. Earlier known as mental retardation (MR) and also referred to as cognitive disability, intellectual disability is characterised both by a significantly below-average score on a test of intelligence and by limitations in the ability to function in areas of daily life, such as communication, self-care, and getting along in social situations and school activities.
11. Autism is a neurological developmental disorder. The prominent characteristics of the disorder include the absence of a theory of mind, failure in interrelatedness, failure to establish an experiencing self and executive function deficit, that is, inability to plan, monitor and direct

activities and achieve goals (Jordan 1997). In India, the World Health Organisation estimates that 1.7 million individuals may be afflicted with this disorder. Only a miniscule number of the affected are correctly diagnosed. Many persons with autism are either regarded as mentally retarded or mentally ill. Over 85 per cent of persons diagnosed are males. For a variety of unknown reasons, both autism and intellectual disabilities predominate in males.
12. Many disability activists feel that the minority view predominates in the international disability movement, that is, the perceptions and experiences of disability prevailing in the Western world (Priestley 2001). As Shanaaz Majiet points out, 'If one looks at the [disability] agenda, we can ask who sets the agenda globally for human rights. My impression and humble opinion is that this agenda is very much set by the North and that we need to take issue with that' (cited in Priestley 2001: 3). While the focus in the South is more on nutrition, education, employment and other issues of survival, in the North, independent living services, assistive technologies, leisure and recreation are regarded as of prime importance, because issues of basic survival have been taken care of. Disability studies appears to privilege the minority worldview, since the theoretical perspectives and empirical data have so far largely come from accounts in Western Europe and North America, which comprise a minority of the total world population of persons with disabilities.
13. Deaf studies is a relatively new interdisciplinary academic domain devoted to the study of Deafness as a sociocultural, historical and linguistic phenomenon. By conceptualising Deafness as a culture and Deaf persons as a distinct linguistic minority group, it challenges the medical definition of deafness as hearing impairment. There are both similarities and differences between disability studies and Deaf studies.
14. According to the psychoanalyst Erik Erikson (1982), psychosocial development is achieved by the passage of an individual through eight developmental stages from infancy to late adulthood. At each stage, new challenges have to be mastered before the individual can pass onto the next stage.
15. Oralism is the system of teaching deaf people to communicate by the use of speech and lip-reading, rather than sign language.

References

Addlakha, Renu. 2008a. 'Disability, Gender and Society' (Special Issue), *Indian Journal of Gender Studies*, 15 (2): 191–207.
———. 2008b. *Deconstructing Mental Illness: An Ethnography of Psychiatry, Women and the Family*. New Delhi: Zubaan.
Barnes, Colin. 1991. *Disabled People in Britain and Discrimination: A Case for Anti-Discrimination Legislation*. London: C. Hurst & Co.

―――.1998. 'The Social Model of Disability: A Sociological Phenomenon Ignored by Sociologists?', in Tom Shakespeare (ed.), *The Disability Reader: Social Science Perspectives*, pp. 65–78. London: Cassell.
Barnes, Colin and Geoff Mercer (eds). 1996. *Exploring the Divide: Illness and Disability*. Leeds: Disability Press.
Barnes, Colin, Mike Oliver and Len Barton (eds). 2002. *Disability Studies Today*. Cambridge: Polity Press.
Begum, Nasa. 1992. 'Disabled Women and the Feminist Agenda', *Feminist Review*, 40 (1): 71–84.
Campbell, Jane and Mike Oliver (eds). 1996. *Disability Politics: Understanding Our Past: Changing Our Future*. London: Routledge.
Charlton, James I. 1998. *Nothing About Us Without Us: Disability Oppression and Empowerment*. Berkeley, CA: University of California Press.
Chib, Malini. 2011. *One Little Finger*. New Delhi: SAGE Publications.
Corker, Mairian and Sally French. 1999. *Disability Discourse*. Buckingham: Open University Press.
Corker, Mairian and Tom Shakespeare (eds.) 2002. *Disability/Postmodernity: Embodying Disability Theory*. London: Continuum.
Davar, Bhargavi V. 1999. *Mental Health of Indian Women: A Feminist Agenda*. New Delhi: SAGE Publications.
――― (ed.). 2001. *Mental Health from a Gender Perspective*. New Delhi: SAGE Publications.
Davis, Lennard J. 1995. *Enforcing Normalcy: Disability, Deafness and the Body*. London: Verso.
Dhanda, Amita. 2000. *Legal Order and Mental Disorder*. New Delhi: SAGE Publications.
Driedger, Diane. 1989. *The Last Civil Rights Movement*. London: C. Hurst & Co.
Erikson, Erik Homburger. 1982. *The Life Cycle Completed: A Review*. New York: Norton.
Fine, Michelle and Adrienne Asch. 1988. 'Introduction: Beyond Pedestals', in Michelle Fine and Adrienne Asch (eds), *Women with Disabilities: Essays in Psychology, Culture and Politics*, pp. 1–37. Philadelphia, PA: Temple University Press.
Finkelstein, Victor. 1980. *Attitudes and Disabled People: Issues for Discussion*. New York: World Rehabilitation Fund.
―――1998. 'Emancipating Disability Studies', in Tom Shakespeare (ed.), *The Disability Reader: Social Science Perspectives*, pp. 28–49. London: Cassell.
Ghai, Anita. 2003. *(Dis)Embodied Form: Issues of Disabled Women*. Delhi: Shakti Books; New Delhi: Har-Anand Publications.
Goffman, Erving. 1968. *Stigma: Notes on the Management of Spoilt Identity*. Harmondsworth, Middlesex: Penguin Books.
Hans, Asha and Annie Patri (eds). 2003. *Women, Disability and Identity*. New Delhi: SAGE Publications.
Hughes, Bill and Kevin Paterson. 1997. 'The Social Model of Disability and the Disappearing Body: Towards a Sociology of Impairment', *Disability and Society*, 12 (3): 325–40.

Jordan, Rita R. 1997. *Education of Children and Young People with Autism.* Paris: UNESCO.
Klasing, Insa. 2007. *Disability and Social Exclusion in Rural India.* Jaipur: Rawat Publications.
Linton, Simi. 1998. *Claiming Disability: Knowledge and Identity.* New York: New York University Press.
Mechanic, David and Edmund H. Volkart. 1962. 'Stress, Illness Behavior and the Sick Role', *American Sociological Review,* 26: 51–58.
Meekosha, Helen. 2002. 'Virtual Activists? Women and the Making of Identities of Disability', *Hypatia,* 17 (3): 67–88.
Morris, Jenny. 1993. 'Feminism and Disability', *Feminist Review,* 43 (1): 57–70.
Oliver, Michael. 1990. *The Politics of Disablement: Critical Texts in Social Work and the Welfare State.* London: Macmillan Press.
———. 1996. *Understanding Disability: From Theory to Practice.* New York: St. Martin's Press.
———. 1997. 'Emancipatory Research: Realistic Goal or Impossible Dream?', in Colin Barnes and Geoffrey Mercer (eds), *Doing Disability Research,* pp. 15–31. Leeds: The Disability Press.
Parsons, Talcott. 1951. *The Social System.* New York: Free Press.
Priestley, Mark. 2001. 'Introduction: The Global Context of Disability', in Mark Priestley (ed.), *Disability and the Life Course: Global Perspectives,* pp. 3–14. Cambridge: Cambridge University Press.
Sekhar, Rukmini. 2005. *Naseema: The Incredible Story,* trans. Aasha Deodhar. New Delhi: Viveka Foundation.
Thomas, Carol. 2001. 'Feminism and Disability: The Theoretical and Political Significance of the Personal and the Experiential', in Len Barton (ed.), *Disability, Politics and the Struggle for Change,* pp. 48–58. London: David Fulton.
Titchkosky, Tanya. 2000. 'Disability Studies: The Old and the New', *The Canadian Journal of Sociology,* 25 (2): 197–224.
Union of the Physically Impaired Against Segregation (UPIAS). 1976. *Fundamental Principles of Disability.* London: UPIAS.
United Nations. 'Convention on the Rights of Persons with Disabilities', http://www.un.org/disabilities/convention/conventionfull.shtml (accessed 9 March 2011).
Vaughan. C. 1993. People-First Language: An Unholy Crusade, *Braille Monitor,* 36 (8): 868–70.
Zola, Irving Kenneth. 1982. *Missing Pieces: A Chronicle of Living with a Disability.* Philadelphia: Temple University Press.

PART I

Disability Movement, Disability Rights and Disability Studies

1

Historicising Disability in India: Questions of Subject and Method

SHILPAA ANAND

> It would certainly be a mistake to try to discover what could have been said of madness at a particular time by interrogating the being of madness itself, its secret content, its silent, self-enclosed truth; mental illness was constituted by all that was said in all the statements that named it, divided it up, described it, explained it, traced its developments, indicated its various correlations, judged it, and possibly gave it speech by articulating, in its name, discourses that were to be taken as its own.
>
> Michel Foucault (1989a: 35)

The Problem

Disability studies as a field of inquiry has developed certain methods of organising and narrating histories of disability. It engages with certain events, themes and subjects as seminal to offering an explanation for the present treatment of disability as a human condition, a social category and a concept. These events and themes are drawn primarily from Western histories, as the field of study itself was by and large constituted in the USA and UK during the latter half of the 20th century. As a consequence of the locale of its disciplinary evolution, disability history appears to have tacitly assumed a universal project of unearthing the factors responsible for the present marginalisation of disabled people in different parts of the world, disregarding its own genealogy. As a result, the discourse of disability studies presents us with a template of subjects, themes and methodological frameworks with which to study the history of disability as a category of human condition. How, then, does a scholar invested in studying the historical trajectory of disability in a non-Western context undertake his or her enterprise? One finds that many scholars are compelled to go about their research using the Western scholarship as their template; the disability history of parts of Africa and Asia, then, reads like the histories of disability of Europe and America. This essay offers a critique of such dominant trends in history-writing that have become a blueprint for subsequent histories, while proposing a methodological intervention to better understand how corporeal differences are conceptualised in the Indian (South Asian) cultural context.

The essay is divided into three sections: the first is an overview of existing currents in the historical discourse of disability within the field of disability studies, the second section outlines the historical sources identified by existing scholarship on disability in India, and the third submits a proposal for future avenues of study.

Disability History: An Overview of Subjects and Themes

Disability historians have examined religious events and practices, past episodes of plagues and other epidemics, traditions of institutionalisation — asylums, poor houses and lazar houses — medical diagnoses and treatment of blindness, deafness, feeblemindedness, etc., as well as the role of industrialisation in Western society in producing notions of ability, able-bodiedness, normalcy and the productive body (Foucault 1973; Rose 2003; Stiker 2002; Yong 2007). It is possible to plot the features of disability history in three parts — events and moments in the past, classification of these moments into themes and categories, and finally the explanatory capacity of each event and theme. Facilitating the task of surveying the trends of doing disability history, Table 1.1 sketches major approaches employed within disability studies discourse to establish histories of disability.

Table 1.1: Disability Historiography

Events/Subjects (A)	Themes/Concepts/Ideas (B)	Project/Intent (C)
Monsters, miracles, religious institutions — Christianity, Judaism	Religious/moral model of charity; Christian influence on constructing abnormality; what the Bible says about disability — attitudes towards disability, charitable or welfare models; theology; Medieval studies (bodily aberrations and early Christian interpretations of aberrance as sub-natural or sub-normal) and Judaism[1]	To describe and explain social attitudes to disablement and disabled persons in present times. To understand theological contexts and the emergence of concepts of charity, institutionalisation, segregation and social stigma.
Greco-Roman culture — evolution of Western society	Infanticide; endorsement of physical beauty[2]	To find explanations for contemporary trends in discrimination against physical difference. To understand contemporary veneration of beauty and perfection.
Medical science; scientific advances; social reactions to some adverse uses of medical research	Charles Darwin's theory of evolution as 'ableist', survival of the fittest thesis; theories of normalcy; development of medical intervention — diagnosis, classification, treatment, cure; the medical model of disability	To explain the overdependence of human thought and action on notions of normalcy and the subsequent emergence of the disabled body as abnormal.[3] Reject the medical model as a discriminatory model of disability and emphasise its dehumanising tendency.
Wars — veterans of war;[4] political paradigms	Heroism ensuing from disability; eugenics and the holocaust[5] — exclusion based on bodily markers of difference; impairments resulting from courageous acts — positive connotations of disability	To understand the origins of perceptions of disabled persons as respectable, as achievers and heroes. Political discrimination of disabled bodies and the hegemony of 'ableist' societies.
Industrialisation	Disability oppression as a result of industrialising society; Marginalisation of disabled persons as a side effect of capitalist societies (Barnes 1997; Finkelstein 2004; Oliver 1996). Emphasis on economic capabilities predicated on the ability to work, and allied notions of work ethics.	To put in perspective current trends in social treatment of disabled persons. Establish the emergence of disability as a category of historical changes of Western society.

(cont.)

(cont.)

Human rights, governance of disability as a human category, minority category; disability rights movements[6]	Rights framework of disability, the social model of disability, individual's rights, disability as an individual's identity and political identity; Civil rights movement's motivation	To change negative attitudes towards, and perspectives of, disability. Recognition of disability as a minority political category and the disability rights movement as akin to civil rights movements and class struggles. Politicisation of the category, disabled persons, and implementing the role of disability as an identity politics issue.
Freaks and freak shows[7]	Normative notions of wholeness, perfection and normalcy that society adheres to, which shape the zeitgeist; Social relations and attitudes based on physical difference.	To establish social history and social behaviour which show the early forms of some present-day treatment of disabled persons; Reflection of social reform

Note: This table has been developed using an assorted selection of literature on disability studies that circulates within the discipline, primarily in universities in the US and UK.

The first column (A) of the table provides a broad historical–cultural context. The second column (B) presents the explanations of these contexts and the third column (C) underlines the choice of the corresponding elements in the first column as constitutive of the history of disability. Indeed, it is being argued that shifts in (C) are constituted by epistemic shifts relevant to the West. There is an interdependence between events (A), discursive themes that frame the events (B), and the motivations (C) behind knowledge production in the development of disability history. It needs to be noted that the nature of this interdependence is characteristic of the West alone.

Studies of the history of disability are heavily dependent on identifying instances of social unrest and strife, such as the institutional criminalisation of madness, the Holocaust, industrialisation, etc., to show that contemporary responses are coded in these historical experiences. Furthermore, the practices and routines of modern medicine place the burden of difference on the individual, thus making the person with disability the object of scrutiny — diagnoses succeed in pathologising physical and developmental differences as deviance. Many histories also find that confinement practices that emerge at different moments in the history of the West are responsible for discriminating against and subsequently 'othering' people lodged in the lazar houses, the lunatic asylums and the poor houses (Foucault 1973; Stiker 2002). Industrial, economic, scientific, religious and social discourses put in place notions of normalcy that actively constituted and produced exclusionary norms of wellness and able-bodiedness.

Indeed, items in (B) (Table 1.1) are instrumental to establishing crucial links between the three columns. There appears to be some consensus on the themes, ideas and concepts that populate (B), in that there is little confusion as to the meanings of 'social', 'medical' or 'religious' — for instance, the scholarship reflects little or no conceptual difficulty in classifying events and moments in history as 'social', 'medical' or 'religious'.

Using these themes, disability studies scholars have been able to classify the Western historical experience of disablement as belonging to, and at times, transitioning to and from the charity model/moral model, the medical model and the social model. Such a classification, however, seems largely dependent on the thematic allotment (B) of different events and instances. If we look more closely at how disability as a concept as well as a category has been historicised, we find an array of answers consistent within the frames of the table above. It appears that much of the exercise to historicise disability resembles 'the evolution of a species' and charts 'the destiny of a people' (Foucault 1977: 146). Foucault would have argued that it is these processes that float and sustain the chimera of an 'unbroken continuity' in the life of a concept, meaning that such retrospective categorisation imposes a historical sequence and conceptual resemblance on a series of events (ibid.). Nevertheless, the table does present a variety of theories and perspectives that organise events and themes into explanatory sequences.

The idea of disability in Marxist understanding, for instance, depends on one's functionalism in society, and the emphasis is on a person's utility to his community and environment (Barnes 1997). Talcott Parsons' work (1951) on the concept of the 'sick role'[8] has been identified as an important source for sociological consolidation of the medical model of disability. Some historians have elaborated on the conception of disability having roots in notions of abnormality, subnormality and, more essentially, the fear of the unknown. The study of institutions of confinement became popular with Foucault's groundbreaking work *Madness and Civilization* (1965). Isolation as the logic of institutional segregation has been studied variously as a historical form of oppression shown to disabled persons such as lepers, lunatics and poor people (Buckingham 2002). Many of these studies reckon that when they discuss terms and notions such as disability, disablement and social stigma, they signify the now normalised sense in which these words discursively operate.

A relatively recent channel of work is the theological history of disability and disablement. Studies, in disability and theology consistently offer contextualised debates, which animate the examination of relationships between present-day universalised social notions of disablement and theological discussions about very specific concepts like charity that emerged at a particular time in relation to the church. The pioneering work in this domain is Henri-Jacques Stiker's widely acclaimed *A History of Disability* (2002). The author is cautious enough to state from the outset that he is dealing with 'Western history', a tag that often slips under the radar of his readers. Stiker's history begins with representations of disability in texts like the Old Testament and maps out prominent notions such as prohibitions prescribed by the Bible, teratology[9] of antiquity and segregation during the times of plague and leprosy. From such analysis, he arrives at certain conceptual typologies like:

profanity = defect = impurity = blemish = deformity = subnormal

The development of ideas in the Judaic traditions offers Stiker a canvas where these words and concepts were interchangeably or causally associated. Blindness, lameness, certain illnesses and other deformities were all considered to be impurities of the flesh. This necessarily theological context lent specific definitions to 'impurity' and 'flesh' that bolstered deformities and illnesses as deviations from accepted notions of purity and wholeness as morally hinged norms. So also the prescription, which Stiker refers to as an ethical component of social responsibility required 'to situate the disabled within society' (ibid.: 30). The act of restraining violence against deformed individuals was codified in terms of moral behaviour. With the New Testament, there is a sense of religion as an evolving entity. Stiker claims that according to the new text, only 'the evil of mind', 'the wicked', were outcast. Intentionality is appended in delineating a person's subjectivity. Correspondingly, he argues, there is an imposition of appropriate attitude towards outcast persons, namely that of charity, where charity is defined and understood as 'disinterested love of one's fellow human beings' (Stiker 2005: 236).

Examining other studies elucidating different conceptions of 'charity' in Western society, we are led to find that its theological emergence is embedded in debates about faith, hope and love. St Augustine, we are told by Tim Stainton (2008: 494), clarified the volitional connection between charity and attainment of salvation for the almsgiver in Christian society. The recipient of alms may profit from the alms but 'social reform' is not the ultimate aim of almsgiving. Both Stiker and Stainton offer us something to think about regarding the changing perspectives on almsgiving and charity in Western society. Present-day objections to charitable treatment in the West ensue from historical connotations of charity, having religious intention and containing an inherent sense of indifference to the object of charity. We see in Stainton's work that the interpretation of charity as oriented towards social reform may have been a popular misconception, emerging at a time of religious significance and carrying forward to later secular times. He makes this point with specific reference to the institutions of charity that developed from and around the church, for instance, the almshouse. With regard to intellectual disability, Stainton has argued that paradigms erected by the early church have fathered many of the modern conceptions of and attitudes towards people with intellectual disability (ibid.). For instance, he considers Augustine of Hippo (354–430 CE), among other key interlocutors involved in the development of church doctrine, as having articulated certain associations between reason, human value and citizenship, which shaped societal responses to intellectual disability in terms of charity and confinement. However, these notions cannot be conveniently categorised as discriminatory or favourable. Augustine's contributions, Stainton reveals, dwelt on the inclusiveness of monstrous beings who, within his logic, qualified as lacking reason within God's divine plan.

Along similar lines, Amos Yong (2007) has argued that an important aspect of disability history of the West is the emergence of institutions of care in the light of theological concepts of care, charity, shelter, etc. Yong suggests that 'biblical and theological emphasis on healing' is responsible for contemporary medical traditions in general and mental health in particular (ibid.: 43). Indeed, our present-day 'medical understandings' of Down's syndrome and other intellectual disabilities 'are fundamentally based on theological presuppositions' (ibid.). Yong, like other scholars, extends Foucault's thesis of power exuded via asylums, to present the institutional history of developmentally disabled persons as oppressive. He refers to the continual scrutiny that disabled persons came under by being 'at the mercy' of a variety of experts — physicians, psychologists and scientists to name a few (ibid.: 54). Sterilisation was adopted as a method to prevent future births of feeble-minded children by those who were institutionalised. Asylums were short-staffed and the immense pressure on the staff forced them to privilege maintenance over rehabilitation. When atrocities committed within the asylum on patients and inmates became public knowledge, it led to a demand for deinstitutionalisation.

The idea that medicalisation of a biological or intellectual condition necessarily implies discriminatory attitudes towards persons with that condition has its roots in the history of the West.[10] I would like to formulate the problem of medicalisation of conditions in non-Western contexts like India in the following manner. As part of scholarly writing, we often adopt concepts that materialised in one culture's historical context to investigate other cultural contexts. In the second culture, there is no experiential history of these concepts; they have emerged because of colonial rule and the imposition of a new way of observing and knowing the world. For instance, scholars of the medical history of India have demonstrated that the concept of 'disease' was not familiar to the Indian context till the entry of modern medicine via foreign rule and encounters with European culture and education. Thus, if we discuss the history of smallpox in India as the history of a disease, we are likely to discount the experience of it within the semantics that it inhabited outside of or prior to modern medicine's disease theory.[11] Similarly, if disability history — as it exists at the moment in content and form as a discourse drawn from the West's historical experience — establishes itself as a blueprint for the exercise of historicising disability in all cultural contexts, then it is likely that what we will have is the same tale told with different cultural inflections. As a result, culturally different historical experiences are likely to be compromised. My aim is to precisely avoid such a pitfall as I try to excavate and understand the indigenous experiences of bodily difference rather than disability in the Indian context.

Disability History in India: Same History, Different Inflection?

Disability history in India has received some attention among both Western and Indian scholars. This section develops a list of subjects and instances selected from existing scholarship on the history of disability in India and compares it with the list populated in the previous section about disability history in the West. The intention of this comparative exercise is to examine the nature of these subjects and sources, and examine their use within the discourse on disability in India.

As far back as 1963, Usha Bhatt discussed some facets of historical attitude towards disabled people in India. According to her, there are four stages in the development of social attitude towards persons with disability: exposure and destruction, care and protection, training and education, as well as social absorption. Referring to Darwin's theory of natural selection, Bhatt restates the assumption that during a 'pre-historic' time, many tribes killed off people who were deemed physically unfit to survive in the world (ibid.: 84). She also mentions a more altruistic trend common to the Todas, an Indian tribe and natives of the Andaman Islands, who were respectful towards adults and children with disabilities and did not sacrifice them. Among the Todas, it was a sin to harm those considered to be 'deformed' or the 'weaklings' of society (ibid.: 85). Under 'care and protection', Bhatt reflects on the ideals of Christianity in the West and Buddhism in the East that put an end to harsh practices of killing disabled people, but by and large maintained traditions of social ostracism towards blind and lame people (ibid.: 87).

Bhatt further offers that a largely charitable and benevolent attitude was promoted by epics such as the *Mahabharata* and the laws prescribed by Manu. While the story of the *Mahabharata* portrays people with different kinds of disabilities in a sympathetic manner, Manu's laws provide context-specific laws to the householder, the king, etc. Through these instances, Bhatt concludes: 'although the handicapped were treated with pity and compassion in ancient India, their rights to social equality were never recognized' (ibid.: 95). Applying the theory of *karma*, disability was considered the result of 'wrong actions' in one's past life or the present one. According to Caraka, a medical scholar in ancient India known for the *Caraka Samhita*,[12] diseases in the present life were the result of undesirable actions in the past life. However, care for disabled people was provided for by the administration:

> In ancient India, when the State and the joint family, and to a certain extent, the caste, took care of the individuals who needed shelter and protection against the rigours of life, the physically handicapped did not present a problem. In the compact rural community, the headman was entrusted with the task of looking after the welfare of its distressed and disabled members (ibid.: 96).

Buddhism intervenes later and promotes a more tolerant attitude towards disabled people by emphasising the virtues of 'mercy, charity, truth, purity, kindness, goodness and above all, non-violence' (ibid.). The reign of Chandragupta Maurya, according to Bhatt, saw the initiation of what we would now regard as vocational rehabilitation of those who were considered physically, socially and economically handicapped within the kingdom. The benevolence of the king, Ashoka, extended philanthropic work on a mass scale in keeping with the precepts of Buddhism.

Usha Bhatt's history of disability in India traces many of the seminal instances that later scholarship on the subject reiterates, however differently. Anita Ghai (2003) has argued that in the epics *Mahabharata* and *Ramayana*, many characters with disabilities are presented in a negative light. She specifically points to Dhritarashtra, the blind king in the *Mahabharata*, being deprived of the throne, and the portrayal of Shakuni (*Mahabharata*), who has an orthopaedic disability, and Manthara (*Ramayana*), a dwarf woman, as characters with evil intent. Narasimhan and Mukherjee (1986), Miles (2001) and Dalal (2006) allude to one or more of these historical moments to qualify social reactions to disabled people in the past reflecting discriminatory as well as inclusive approaches. Drawing up a table similar to the one of disability historiography in the West (Table 1.1) would show that while historians find equivalent moments in Indian history to corroborate the items in the first column (A) and can also argue in terms of the items in (C), they appear to struggle while attempting to fit their evidence into the items in (B). Consider that Bhatt is able to supply moments in Indian history that compare with instances in Western history, e.g., religious attention to disabled people and institutional care. However, claiming that these instances are evidence of charitable treatment of disabled persons is inconclusive. The categorisation of these instances into thematic categories, such as religious, social, institutional and charitable, is dubious. For one, within their historico-cultural contexts, they were not representative of these themes; two, the sources that provide these instances are not exact equivalents of their Western counterparts like recorded histories and doctrinal texts.

Table 1.2 is a replica of Table 1.1 attempting to historicise disability in India. It is not as exhaustive a representation as the latter, but serves as a sample of the prominent subjects, themes and intentions that constitute the project of historicising disability in India. It aims at providing a comparison between two sets of efforts rather than function as an overview.

Table 1.2: Sample Survey of Histories of Disablement in India

Events/Subjects (A)	Themes/Concepts/Ideas (B)	Project/Intent (C)
Hindu/Buddhist/ Islamic traditions — miracles, blessings, curses	Charitable treatment of deformed persons as part of religious practice.	To describe and explain social attitudes to disablement and disabled persons in present times.

(cont.)

(cont.)

	Deformity as result of past actions — *karma* (Miles 2001) (**blessing** or **curse**?) **Reverence** of persons with deformities/**Pity** shown to persons with deformities.	To understand theological contexts and the emergence of concepts of charity, institutionalisation/ segregation and social stigma.
Ancient and medieval culture and traditions	Social ostracism in the face of religious exclusion of disabled persons. Medical texts such as *Caraka Samhita* — disease as result of wrong actions in the past (Bhatt 1963). *Caraka Samhita* as instance of medical knowledge; evidence of moral model of Hindu practices; prescription of social behaviour? Manu's laws: **Legal precepts**? **Religious prescriptions**? King Ashoka's methods of vocational rehabilitation: Instance of royal administrative governance method? Instance of religious (Buddhist) influence on governance. Aurangzeb's need to hide his weak knee.	To explain current reactions to disability in India as a curse or as a shameful feature and study the history of this negative perception to one's disability being the result of individual fault.
Colonial intervention in the form of schools, hospitals and institutions	Beginning of formal care and rehabilitation of disabled people. Disruption of the old order of familial care; implementation of segregation of sick and ill persons; methods of modern medicine isolate the person with disease/ disability from community-based care (Arnold 1993; Bhatt 1963; Miles 1995).	India treated its disabled people as faulty and punished or cursed. Colonial modernity reinstated maligned people to charity, care and rehabilitation. Present attitudes as a result of traditional fatalistic attitude and superstitious mindset of Indians. India had a glorious past when disabled people were treated with respect; this was disrupted by British rule.

Note: This table contains an overview of the trends prevalent in contemporary scholarship on the subject of history of disability in India. Table collated by author from relevant texts.

Histories of disability and disablement in India appear to resemble similar history projects in the West, but present certain problems in terms of themes, ideas and concepts because of the intrinsic aspects of the culture in question. The emphasised portions (in bold type) of the text in (B) represent the difficulty faced by scholars in classifying certain incidents and subjects as belonging to particular themes. A problem that, at first, might appear innocuous is of greater magnitude because of the bearing it has on establishing a viable history of disablement in India. Some of these conundrums offer significant insights.

There appears to be a temptation to use texts such as the *Mahabharata* and Manu's laws as equivalent to the Bible and other Semitic theological texts within Western history. However, there are several problems with doing so because epics such as the *Mahabharata* are not governed by doctrinal authority as the Bible is; there are no semantic constraints placed on the interpretation or narrativising of the *Mahabharata*.[13] While Manu's laws can be considered prescriptive, they only offer prescriptions that are sensitive to context and cannot be applied in a generic manner.[14] The *Mahabharata* is rendered severally in folklore, stories and texts. While renditions of the story can be interpreted as containing records of social responses to characters that are blind, hunchbacked and disfigured, they only serve as context-specific responses that vary from narrative to narrative with regard to each kind of disability or deformity. This aspect disqualifies the epic from functioning as a suitable example of a religious text that prescribes certain actions to its readers and listeners. It is, at best, a story that expresses a set of propositions that depict actions, and cannot be regarded as explanatory. It is not intrinsically directive in that its intention is not to teach; it is another matter that some of these texts are deemed as part of Hindu scriptures.[15] Stories in the Asian context provide information about actions that can be performed in certain situations, but cannot be construed in the same way as theories are in the Western context. Theories are inherently explanatory and offer causal logic, while stories do not purport to connect their several features. When the *Mahabharata* is used to serve a function within disability history discourse, by virtue of its discursive location in that situation and its identification as an explanatory text, it results in a conceptual misrecognition. To illustrate, I'd like to refer to Anita Ghai's assertion that characters in ancient discourses such as Surdas, a blind poet-singer, and Ashtavakra, known for his eight deformities, are representative of those who fought disability oppression. The line of inquiry pursued by the present essay would challenge such assertions by asking if these categories of disability oppression and anti-oppression strategies are conceptually available within the spatio-temporal and epistemic contexts of Surdas, Ashtavakra and the *Mahabharata*.

M. Miles, a British scholar with years of research on culturally different experiences and histories of disability, has a deep investment in disability histories of South Asia. While he also uses the *Mahabharata*, Manu's laws and the example of the Surdasis[16] to serve as illustrations of recorded responses to disability in the past, he is aware that absence of terms for disabilities and aspects of disability in the Indian context may be indicative of absence of these concepts. However, he interprets this absence as proof of discrimination. Though Miles argues in one of his essays that disability is possibly conceptualised differently in Indian history, he seeks to find these varying concepts in 'religious, legal, medical, folkloric' material, suggesting tacitly that these categories and themes are universal to all cultures (Miles 2001: 143). His presupposition of themes of knowledge leads him to misrecognise historical events under definitive categories, whereas Table 1.2 clearly shows that there is no consensus among the historians as to these themes and categories.

Miles also believes that the cultural differences in conceptualising disability can be revealed only when Asian scholars work on research and interpretation of Asian records and archives. In reality, as we can see from our table, the problem is not with the cultural identity or roots of the individual historian or scholar but with the epistemic training and pedagogic approach they bring to their material. How would Miles otherwise explain the presence of an Usha Bhatt, who qualifies as an Indian scholar interested in disability research, but whose work tacitly utilises Western themes, subjects and methods?

A Proposal

The challenge posed to Miles and other historians of disability can be addressed by approaching a body of work that is yet to be engaged with from a disability studies perspective, namely, the history of colonial medicine in India. Medical history of India during the colonial period offers a favourable standpoint as it presents a context of the encounter between two cultural ways of knowing, or ordering knowledge. The question I engage in this essay concerns whether the ways of knowing alterity or bodily difference, as intrinsic to Western concepts transferred to India, indeed corroborated or were commensurate with Indian ways of knowing alterity of body and mind. This study's focus on the history of concepts and the corresponding transformations in discourse demand that our mode of inquiry follow a genealogical route. I have predominantly adopted a mode of 'discourse'[17] analysis keeping in mind Foucault's notion of a genealogical study.

Genealogy is a way of finding out why we think what we think, or how we have come to think of an object in a certain way. Genealogy traces the descent of an idea, while history ascertains an origin. History varies from genealogy in that it believes in the idea of developing a trajectory to its conclusion; it is synchronic in its approach and is invariably wedded to the idea of an eternal truth. Unlike history, genealogy cannot take the constancy of any concept or idea for granted; it depends on fractures in themes and follows a diachronic route. The aim of genealogy is to trace the discontinuities that a concept is bound to traverse along: 'It was a matter not of digging down to a buried stratum of continuity, but of identifying the transformation which made this hurried transition possible' (Foucault 1977: 75).

In the case of a concept like 'monstrosity' for instance, we have a situation where the idea is inserted into a context that did not have a tradition of indexing corporeal difference as monstrous. Here, I mean not just the use of the term or its synonym, but the very grid of ideas that hold monstrosity or monstrousness in place — for instance, morality, normalcy and bodily perfection. To illustrate such conceptual disjunctions over space and time, I have chosen certain concepts and theories that are extensively used in understanding disability history of the West and investigated the careers of these concepts in India.

Colonisation impacts culture and, thereby, the way people think about and organise the world into an order, or learn about the world that is ordered as such, a process that Balagangadhara

(1988) characterises as 'colonial consciousness'. The study of a concept or assemblage of concepts that is inherent to one culture undergoes some change when it is transposed into another cultural context. Concepts don't exist in a vacuum. What then is the environment that makes it possible for disability to exist as an idea — philosophical, intellectual, semantic, epistemic and cultural? Let us take two cases to begin to formulate an answer to this question: monstrosity and feeble-mindedness.

There have been attempts within medicine and psychiatry to study Indian forms of bodily and mental deviance in the hope of exploring culture-specific conditions. My interest is in the emergence of monstrosity and feeble-mindedness within the medical discourse about India in the late 18th and 19th centuries. At this juncture, it would be important to keep in mind that both these concepts have long careers within the West before they come to assume diagnostic status within the discipline of medicine. How do categories that are generated within one epistemic-cultural context travel and maintain their corresponding concepts in another context? In due course, this investigation will question the easy compartments — medical, religious, social — that South Asian disability history has been organised into in recent scholarship.

Studying the history of monstrosity is relevant to the present project because the history of monstrous bodies is considered significant within Western studies of disability genealogy (Fiedler 1978; Shildrick 2002, 2005; Thomson 1997). It would be useful to examine the impact and mobilisation of the concept in the Indian context at the time it began to flourish in the early and middle colonial period. Second, the presence of Shah Daula's *chuha*s is interpreted severally as one of the earliest instances of religious–institutional care of young feeble-minded adults in South Asian history.[18] It would be worthwhile to investigate the conceptual frames and discursive canvases that confer it such a status.

Monstrosity and Feeble-mindedness in India

Evidence of monstrosity and monstrous bodies in the history of the West is linked to explaining how we treat disabled people in the present moment. Examining historical sources for India shows that this may not hold true for the Indian context. In the West, the idea of monstrousness is largely constituted by the fact of social reception and social attitudes to the monstrous body. The attitude is based, in one historical moment, on theological conceptions of monstrousness, where within Christian tradition, a body that was classified as inhuman also implied aberrations in the moral cosmos. One notion is that a monstrous body was the symbol of intercourse between human and animal forms, thereby violating moral sexual practices. Monstrousness in this case was an evaluative notion, given the dominance of Christian values. From another perspective, as the concept, monstrous, furthered by Darwinian notions, gathered a scientific explanation, its constitutive terms of reference changed but it still carried the meaning of deviating from a norm — this time, scientific norms of what a human body should be. However, these conceptual transitions only marginally changed the societal attitude to monstrous bodies. That social attitude was one of repulsion, a phenomenon that disability historians in the present cash in on to explain contemporary discriminatory attitudes towards disabled people.

Monstrousness as a concept is not intrinsic to Indian historical experience or to Indian ways of categorising corporeal difference, until this can be proved through extensive research. Indeed, when we look for evidence of it in archival material, we find that it arrives in India as a medical category. Scholarly journals at the time record instances of monstrous bodies. Although they dwell on the rational–scientific aspect of monstrousness, their descriptions don't dispossess the term of its theological and social meanings. But there is no corresponding evidence in India to corroborate those two sets of meanings. I draw on two sources, one from a letter that was published in the journal, *Philosophical Transactions of the Royal Society* in London (Home 1790), and another from a report in the *Indian Medical Gazette* (Browning 1886) to illustrate the point. Everard Home, an esquire in India, once wrote to an esquire in England about a double-headed child found near Burdwan in Bengal. The child, he explained, was carried around to collect alms. When he died due to extraneous circumstances, the child was buried under customarily appropriate norms. In this account, Home intervenes to interpret the carrying of the child for money as evidence of a social consensus on the child's monstrousness; that is, it was perceived as repulsive based on a set of norms.[19] We have little account of the social circumstances in which the child's life was lived out. In the second instance, recorded by Browning, a boy in Hyderabad in 1886 was born with an extra set of limbs. We are also informed that regardless of the extra limbs, he ran around and played freely. These two instances, if found in Europe, would have been conceived differently. It is possible that the boy with extra limbs would have been used in freak shows where his monstrousness would have been the object of ridicule and mirth. Disability historians in Western scholarship detail the presence of such monstrous bodies and their uses in their historical contexts to draw our attention to the fact that when disabled people are ridiculed or discriminated against in the present moment, this follows a long tradition.

Let us consider that if social attitude towards a person with monstrous features determines his or her monstrosity, then what we have in the case of the boy in Hyderabad is not monstrousness in the Western sense. There may have been other concepts and categories that define and value his corporeal difference, but they are context-specific and unknown quantities. The documentary evidence available disallows us from configuring other notions of corporeal difference, because the terms it uses and the way it uses those terms lead us to conclusions of a certain type.

To illustrate further, let us take the second case of Shah Daula's 'rats', an instance commonly identified within the literature (Overbeck-Wright 1921) as an Indian form of feeble-mindedness. Colonial reports tell us of the presence of rat-like creatures at the shrine of Shah Daula in the Punjab region in the 19th century. The accounts, depending on the time period and disciplinary affiliation of the author, allow for the following disclosures:

  a. The collection of rat-like human beings at the shrine was due to the benevolence of the Muslim saint Shah Daula who was kind to animals.
  b. Microcephalic[20] boys collected at the shrine and begged for a living because their human abilities were limited. Note that this explanation classifies the erstwhile rat-like creatures under a medical diagnostic category, microcephaly.

c. *Chuha*s, who gathered at the shrine of Shah Daula, are evidence of an Indian or South Asian brand of feeble-mindedness. We note here that a medical category is now more specifically a psychiatric classification.

Moving away from colonial accounts to the 1980s, we see scholars in psychiatry and psychology using the colonial evidence as proof of Indian forms of mental illnesses. More recently, Miles (2001) develops the idea that Shah Daula's shrine is probably evidence of one of the earliest care and rehabilitation centres for mentally retarded children in parts of South Asia. Shah Daula's shrine, in this case, was akin to a church-like institution that welcomed persons with limited physical and mental capacity as a charitable gesture.

The colonial authors as well as our contemporary Miles also tell us that they draw their evidence from hearsay that circulated locally about the shrine and the saint. Common knowledge that circulated locally consisted of different theories and stories:

a. Women came to the shrine to be cured of their infertility and were expected to donate their first-born to the shrine as a gesture of thanksgiving.
b. Women who came to the shrine to be cured of infertility, consummated with one of the *chuha*s at the shrine; and, therefore, the child that was born to her, was also a *chuha* who was returned to the shrine.
c. Shah Daula was a saint who was kind to all animals, and he cared for human beings that were animal-like.

While the scholars attend to the hearsay, they build their theories based on their specific temporal and disciplinary affiliations. Their theories are, then, religious, folkloric, medical and psychiatric interpretations of stories they heard and observations they made. Their accounts never supply us with enough evidence to believe that the *chuha*s were indeed there because of their medical or psychiatric conditions. To construct a history based on such flimsy evidence is not insightful. What is more intriguing is that this history is then disseminated as empirical evidence for the existence of Indian forms of feeble-mindedness and as proof of religious rehabilitative services for individuals with intellectual disability. Whereas, if we were to study Indian cultural ways of classifying and acting towards corporeal difference or intellectual difference, if that scale indeed was significant, we would have had to examine the language and rhetoric of the hearsay that was in circulation.

Conclusion

This essay suggests that disability can best be understood as one theory of corporeal difference. It follows then that what we will find, when we thoroughly investigate the history of concepts of bodily and mental difference in the Indian context, is not another theory of disability but possibly another cluster of ways of thinking and knowing such differences. Contemporary trends in historicising disability cross-culturally reflect a paucity of historical method. Scholarly naïveté is apparent in uncritically adopting Western histories of disablement as the blueprint for histories of disability in different cultures. The monstrosity and Shah Daula cases show that corporeal difference is undoubtedly acknowledged in the South Asian context, but the process and discourse of its identification resists a large number of the grid of ideas that govern the conception of disability in the Western tradition. In each case of monstrosity, the recognition of corporeal difference is under diverse conceptual circumstances and the value attached to these markers of difference in each context is distinct. In that sense, the Indian context of conceptualising corporeal difference seems to parallel notions of disability in Greek antiquity, where every conception of disability was context-sensitive (Rose 2003).

This paper has also suggested that methods of history will have to be recalibrated if the task at hand consists of constituting the history of corporeal difference in the Indian/South Asian context. Such an exercise, from its very inception, must be conscious of the impact that colonisation has had on the history of thought and not merely on the events of colonial rule. Studying the colonial encounter as an inauguration of different systems of thought in a cultural context, where others were in place, allows us to understand why Usha Bhatt or Ajit Dalal would view and research their own context with lenses borrowed from Western traditions of thought and epistemology. The intention of this essay must not be misconstrued as romanticising one culture's attitude to disability in the past nor should it be conceived as providing a new blueprint for the disability histories of South Asian, African or Japanese societies. It merely offers a critical analysis of existing methods and suggests possible avenues to study culturally distinct modes of conceptualising corporeal difference.

Notes

1. On the embodiment of the monster, Margrit Shildrick (2002) examines the various representations of monstrousness in the light of medieval discourse on the subject — the monstrous body, she finds, is reflective of internal aberrance in the sense of corporeal alterity as well as a fulfilment of a disruptive force that acts as an external threat to the existing cosmic order.
2. Lennard Davis' work (1997) on representations of beauty and perfection in Greek antiquity engages with reading notions of disability represented in cultural artefacts of another era and place. He discusses the values that body parts assume and how their absence or incapacity implies a kind of devaluing of the whole body. Martha L. Rose's work (2003) follows the more Foucauldian mould which distinguishes Greek antiquity as not only historically distant but also culturally distinct from the contemporary landscape of the West.
3. In a seminal essay on the history of the concept of normalcy, Davis (1997) links the emergence of the word 'normal' and its semantic cluster of 'normalcy', 'normality', 'average', etc., in the 19th century in most European languages with the inauguration of statistical studies.
4. In his landmark essay, David Gerber (2003) discusses war veterans and the consequent constitution of disablement as a trophy of war.
5. Zygmunt Bauman's writing (1989) on the holocaust and the political selecting out of 'lives not worth living' is one of the early instances of this theory. Later exponents of the subject include Poore (2007), Shildrick (2002, 2005) and Thomson (1997).
6. Prominent exponents of this area of historical research are Longmore and Umansky (2001), Fleischer and Zames (2001), Baynton (2001), Shapiro (1994), Finkelstein (2007), Shakespeare (1998) and Oliver (1996).
7. Rosemarie Garland Thomson's (1997) and Leslie Fiedler's (1978) expositions on freak shows are suitable examples of this genre of historicising disability.
8. Parsons' notion of the 'sick role' was considered an innovative intervention in the 1950s because for the first time 'being sick' was identified as a socially endorsed temporary state (Sherry 2005: 908). However, it was later discarded by disability studies scholars because it

relied heavily on ideas of health and illness and did not necessarily supply disability a positive value.

9. Derived from the Greek words meaning the study of *monster* or *marvel*, as early as the 17th century, teratology referred to a discourse on prodigies and marvels of anything so extraordinary as to seem abnormal at that time. In the 19th century, it came to be equated with biological deformities, mostly in the field of botany. Currently, its most instrumental meaning is that of the medical study of teratogenesis or individuals with significant malformations.

10. One of the reasons for this argument is that it was medical agencies that animated eugenic activities in Europe's past, be it the case of Darwin's thesis of natural selection or the holocaust in Germany (Shildrick 2002: 763).

11. Both historians and anthropologists in the last two decades have pointed to the fact that smallpox in India was revered as *amman* (mother), *Sitala* (the cool one) or *Mariamma* (Mother Mari, who is considered to be an incarnation of *durga* or *kali*, Hindu goddesses), as the case may be, and several aspects of this way of thinking prove that it did not resemble a disease in the local imagination. How accurate will our characterisation of smallpox as a disabling disease be, given these circumstances? If the aim of our study is to unravel the history of bodily difference in India, then this way of going about it falls short because implicit in our characterisation of smallpox in India is a historical experience of smallpox in the West, where it was configured as a disease producing disabling conditions such as disfigurement and blindness. David Arnold's study (1993) of smallpox in colonial India from a historical perspective and Frédérique Apffel-Marglin's treatment of the subject (1990) from an anthropological viewpoint offer important insights for discussions of disabling diseases in the South Asian context.

12. *Caraka Samhita* (400–200 BCE) is considered to be the most ancient and, perhaps, also the most authoritative text on Ayurveda, a form of treatment practised in parts of South Asia.

13. A detailed discussion on this subject is inappropriate given the focus of this essay, but S. N. Balagangadhara's book, *The Heathen in his Blindness* provides the necessary attention to delineating the differences across cultures regarding relations between doctrinal texts, religion and their interpretations (1994: 195).

14. A. K. Ramanujan (1989) recommends that while Indian system/s of thought offer context-sensitive formulations, solutions and prescriptions, Western systems of thought tend to universalise and generalise precepts.

15. Balagangadhara (1988) distinguishes culturally different ways of organising content and methods of learning. While the West's learning is based on theoretical structures, the Indian context appears to employ the mode of action knowledge where the form of learning is through stories. When stories are interpreted as if they were theories, what occurs is a category mistake and conceptual confusion. Elsewhere, Balagangadhara

(1994) elaborates on historical processes, colonial intervention and the impact of the two on popularising texts such as the *Mahabharata* and Bhagavad Gita as scriptures.

16. 'Surdasi', a title lent to blind singers, takes its name from a medieval Bhakti poet, Surdas, who was blind. Scholars like Narasimhan and Mukherjee (1986) have traced the contemporary presence of blind beggars on the streets of India as an act that invokes the Surdasi tradition of singing for alms. Ingstad and Whyte (1995) employ this reference to illustrate their claim that many cultures consider blindness a 'valuable qualification' for begging (ibid.: 15). Surdas is also iconic in India for the equation between visual impairment and musical talent.

17. My understanding of discourse in this dissertation is linked to Foucault's ideas of discourse in *The Archaeology of Knowledge* (1989a) and *The Order of Things* (1989b). Foucault proposes a framework of archaeology as a way of studying the groundwork of bodies of knowledge. The archive implied here is the depth knowledge which is buried in that knowledge, something that its users cannot be conscious of. Discourse, then, is the superficial manifestation of that depth knowledge — everything on the surface, all that is said or stated. As Ian Hacking sums up, 'Systems of thought have a surface that is discourse' (2004: 91).

18. Shah Daula's *chuha*s, or 'Shah Daula's rats', is the phrase used to refer to several youth who were found near the shrine of Shah Daula (in Gujrat city, Punjab, Pakistan). They were so named because of the size and shape of their heads, which were small like those of rats or mice. This phrase is used in a variety of documents found in archives such as the *Indian Medical Gazette*, and in colonial reports.

19. The fact that the parents carried their child around to elicit attention and alms is not directly revealing of the notion of monstrosity. To understand this better, it would be useful to turn to Raymond Geuss's elaboration on notions of public and private in ancient Greece, and the idea of disattendability. Disattendability is a tacit principle that governs public behaviour in large parts of Europe and the Western world about how one should comport oneself in public places (Geuss 2001). In other words, not staring and not providing reason to stare would both constitute norms of social behaviour and explicate the notion of disattendability. For the object that violates disattendability to be rendered 'monstrous', certain Christian theological prerequisites need to be fulfilled. So, in the absence of a moral/social environment that fulfils these requisites, can the presence of a child with a double head still be considered monstrous?

20. Microcephaly is a medically diagnosed condition in which the circumference of the head is small and the diminutive size is attributed to incomplete development of the brain. Within psychiatric classification, microcephaly is associated with developmental disabilities like autism and Rett's syndrome.

References

Arnold, David. 1993. *Colonizing the Body: State Medicine and Epidemic Disease in Nineteenth-Century India*. Berkeley: University of California Press.

Balagangadhara, S. N. 1988. 'Comparative Anthropology and Moral Domains: An Essay on Selfless Morality and the Moral Self', *Cultural Dynamics*, 1 (1): 98–128.

———. 1994. *'The Heathen in His Blindness...': Asia, the West and the Dynamic of Religion*. Leiden; New York: E. J. Brill.

Barnes, Colin. 1997. 'A Legacy of Oppression: A History of Disability in Western Culture', in Len Barton and Mike Oliver (eds), *Disability Studies: Past, Present and Future*, pp. 3–24. Leeds: The Disability Press.

Barnes, Colin, Geof Mercer and Tom Shakespeare. 1999. *Exploring Disability: A Sociological Introduction*. Cambridge; Malden, MA: Polity Press.

Bauman, Zygmunt. 1989. *Modernity and the Holocaust*. Ithaca, NY: Cornell University Press.

Baynton, Douglas C. 2001. 'Disability and the Justification of Inequality in American History', in Paul K. Longmore and Lauri Umansky (eds), *The New Disability History: American Perspectives*, pp. 33–57. New York: New York University Press.

Bhatt, Usha. 1963. *The Physically Handicapped in India: A Growing National Problem*. Mumbai: Popular Book Depot.

Browning. 1886. 'Mr. Browning's Notes of a Case of Monstrosity', *Indian Medical Gazette*, 21: 219–21.

Buckingham, Jane. 2002. *Leprosy in Colonial South India: Medicine and Confinement*. New York: Palgrave.

Dalal, Ajit K. 2006. 'Social Interventions to Moderate Discriminatory Attitudes: The Case of the Physically Challenged in India', *Psychology, Health and Medicine*, 11 (3): 374–82.

Davis, Lennard J. 1997. 'Constructing Normalcy: The Bell Curve, the Novel and the Invention of the Disabled Body in the Nineteenth Century', in Lennard J. Davis (ed.), *The Disability Studies Reader* pp. 9–28. New York: Routledge.

Fiedler, Leslie A. 1978. *Freaks: Myths and Images of the Secret Self*. New York: Simon and Schuster.

Finkelstein, Vic. 2004. 'Modernising Services?', in John Swain, Sally French, Colin Barnes and Carol Thomas (eds), *Disabling Barriers — Enabling Environments*, pp. 206–11. London: SAGE Publications.

———. 2007. 'The "Social Model of Disability" and the Disability Movement', The Disability Archive UK, Centre for Disability Studies, University of Leeds, http://www.leeds.ac.uk/disability-studies/archiveuk/finkelstein/The%20Social%20Model%20of%20Disability%20the%20Disability%20Movement.pdf (accesses 19 May 2012).

Fleischer, Doris Zames and Frieda Zames. 2001. *The Disability Rights Movement: From Charity to Confrontation*. Philadelphia: Temple University Press.

Foucault, Michel. 1973 (1965). *Madness and Civilization: A History of Insanity in the Age of Reason*. New York: Vintage Books.

———. 1977. 'Nietzsche, Genealogy, History', in Donald F. Bouchard (ed.), *Language, Counter-Memory, Practice*, pp. 139–64. Ithaca, NY: Cornell University Press.

———. 1989a. *The Archaeology of Knowledge*. London and New York: Routledge.

———. 1989b. *The Order of Things: An Archaeology of the Human Sciences*. London: Routledge.

Gerber, David. 2003. 'Disabled Veterans, the State, and the Experience of Disability in Western Societies, 1914–1950', *Journal of Social History*, 36 (4): 899–916.

Geuss, Raymond. 2001. *Public Goods, Private Goods*. Princeton, NJ: Princeton University Press.

Ghai, Anita. 2003. *(Dis)Embodied Form: Issues of Disabled Women*. New Delhi: Shakti Books.

Hacking, Ian. 2004. *Historical Ontology*. Cambridge, MA: Harvard University Press.

Home, Everard. 1790. 'An Account of a Child with a Double Head'. In a letter from Everard Home, Esq. F. R. S. to John Hunter, Esq. F. R. S., *Philosophical Transactions of the Royal Society of London*, 80: 296–305.

Ingstad, Benedicte and Susan Reynolds Whyte. 1995. *Disability and Culture*. Berkeley, CA: University of California Press.

Longmore, Paul K. and Lauri Umansky (eds). 2001. *The New Disability History: American Perspectives*. New York: New York University Press.

Marglin, Frédérique Apffel. 1990. 'Smallpox in Two Systems of Knowledge', in Frédérique Apffel Marglin and Stephen A. Marglin (eds), *Dominating Knowledge: Development, Culture, and Resistance*, pp. 102–44. Oxford: Clarendon Press.

Miles, M. 1995. 'Disability in an Eastern Religious Context: Historical Perspectives', *Disability and Society*, 10 (1): 49–69.

———. 2001. 'Studying Responses to Disability in South Asian Histories: Approaches personal, prakrital and pragmatical', *Disability and Society*, 16 (1): 143–60.

Narasimhan, M. C. and A. K. Mukherjee. 1986. *Disability, a Continuing Challenge*. New Delhi: Wiley Eastern Ltd.

Oliver, Michael. 1996. *Understanding Disability: From Theory to Practice*. New York: St. Martin's Press.

Overbeck-Wright, Alexander William. 1921. *Lunacy in India*. London: Baillière, Tindall and Cox.

Parsons, Talcott. 1951. *The Social System*. Glencoe, IL: Free Press.

Poore, Carol. 2007. *Disability in Twentieth-Century German Culture*. Ann Arbor, MI: University of Michigan Press.

Ramanujan, A. K. 1989. 'Is There an Indian Way of Thinking? An Informal Essay', *Contributions to Indian Sociology*, 23 (1): 41–58.

Rose, Martha L. 2003. *The Staff of Oedipus: Transforming Disability in Ancient Greece*. Ann Arbor, MI: The University of Michigan Press.

Shakespeare, Tom (ed.). 1998. *The Disability Reader: Social Science Perspectives*. London and New York: Cassell.

Shapiro, Joseph P. 1994. *No Pity: People with Disabilities Forging a New Civil Rights Movement*. New York: Three Rivers Press.

Sherry, Mark. 2005. 'Identity', in Gary L. Albrecht, Jerome Bickenbach, David T. Mitchell, Walton O. Schalick III and Sharon L. Snyder (eds), *Encyclopedia of Disability*. Thousand Oaks, CA: SAGE Publications.

Shildrick, Margrit. 2002. *Embodying the Monster: Encounters with the Vulnerable Self*. London: SAGE Publications.

———. 2005. 'The Disabled Body, Genealogy and Undecidability', *Cultural Studies*, 19 (6): 755–70.

Stainton, Tim. 2008. 'Reason, Grace and Charity: Augustine and the Impact of Church Doctrine on the Construction of Intellectual Disability', *Disability and Society*, 23 (5): 485–96.

Stiker, Henri-Jacques. 2002. *A History of Disability*, trans. William Sayers. Ann Arbor, MI: The University of Michigan Press.

———. 2005. 'Charity', in Gary L. Albrecht, Jerome Bickenbach, David T. Mitchell, Walton O. Schalick III and Sharon L. Snyder (eds), *Encyclopedia of Disability*. Thousand Oaks, CA: SAGE Publications.

Swain, John, Sally French, Colin Barnes and Carol Thomas (eds). 2004. *Disabling Barriers — Enabling Environments*. London: SAGE Publications.

Thomson, Rosemarie Garland. 1997. *Extraordinary Bodies: Figuring Physical Disability in American Culture and Literature*. New York: Columbia University Press.

Yong, Amos. 2007. *Theology and Down Syndrome: Reimagining Disability in Late Modernity*. Waco, TX: Baylor University Press.

2

Disability Rights and the Emergence of Disability Studies

JAGDISH CHANDER

> Disability only becomes a tragedy for me when society fails to provide the things we need to lead our lives — job opportunities or barrier-free buildings, for example. It is not a tragedy to me that I'm living in a wheelchair.
> Judy Heumann (Cited in Shapiro 1993: 20)

The 20th century has been marked by a host of social movements all over the world, including the socialist revolution in Russia and the anti-colonial struggles in Asia and Africa. In the United States, the second half of the 20th century witnessed a spurt of social movements starting with the black civil rights movement followed by the feminist and the gay rights movements (Scotch 2001; Shapiro 1993). One of the most recent such movement in this series is the disability rights movement which began in the 1970s (Barnartt and Scotch 2001; Fleischer and Zames 2001; Scotch 2001; Shapiro 1993).

Just as the civil rights movement of the African-Americans, or the feminist and the gay rights movements created the ground for the emergence of studies in their respective spheres, the disability rights movement challenged traditional understanding of disability and offered a new perspective, contributing significantly to the emergence of the discipline. It is, therefore, rightly argued that the philosophical foundations of disability studies are rooted in the activism and experiences of the disabled people (Priestley 2003). Consequently, there is no doubt that disability studies as a discipline springs from the disabled people's international movement (ibid.). It has been developing as an inter-disciplinary field of inquiry since the 1980s in the United States, and subsequently in Britain, Canada and Australia among other countries. It is also in the process of establishing a presence in India since the early part of the first decade of the 21st century.

Traditional Meaning of Impairment

Impairments are a universal reality found all over the world in all times, but the significance and meaning attached to them have varied from time to time and from one society to another. In most cases, the meaning attached to physical, sensory and cognitive impairments has been highly negative (Ingstad and Whyte 1995; Bhatt 1963: 84–90), though in certain cases the impaired persons have been fully integrated in their respective communities (Groce 1985). Manu, the founder of the Hindu law, preached the exclusion of the disabled from the holy and the auspicious events and places (Bhatt 1963: 94–95).

In traditional societies, there was a religious meaning attached to the occurrence of disability in several cases. In the Indian society, for instance, occurrence of any kind of impairment was considered to be punishment for one's sins in the past life under the *karma* theory, a belief which still persists in popular culture. As Bhatt observes:

> The theory of *Karma* was instrumental in depriving the disabled of their inherent right to lead an independent life. It was believed that the disabled were reaping what they had sowed (sic) in lives bygone and any attempt to ameliorate their lot would, therefore, interfere with this divine justice (ibid.: 96).

During the medieval ages, too, disability continued to be attributed to supernatural factors, and the disabled were considered to be responsible for their plight in the Indian society (ibid.).

With the dawn of the modern era, many superstitious beliefs were replaced by rational and secular ideas deriving from new medical findings. As a result, all types of impairments began to acquire a medical meaning. Around the end of the 19th century in America, there was the beginning of what was called 'hospital schools' (Byrom 2001: 141–51). Under what came to be known as the 'medical rehabilitation approach' (ibid.), efforts were made to 'cure' impairments. In case medical science could not offer a cure, then rehabilitation or necessary measures were to be extended to the educational and occupational areas of life of the impaired person in an attempt to 'normalise' him/her. As elaborated further in this chapter, the medical approach towards disability led to the creation of what is today described by disability studies scholars as the 'medical model' of disability.

The disability rights movement and the narration of the experiences of the disabled people challenged the traditional meaning assigned to impairment based on the medical approach. This is in contrast to the new meaning assigned to 'disability' under the disability studies perspective, which interprets it in social and contextual terms. A number of publications have appeared, particularly in the last two decades, which incorporate the voices and the perspective of disabled people. Some of these leading publications include: Barnartt and Scotch (2001); Campbell and Oliver (1996); Charlton (1998); Davis (2002); Ferguson (2001); Fleischer and Zames (2001); Ghai (2003); Groce (1985); Hans and Patri (2003); Ingstad and Whyte (1995); Jernigan (1999); Linton (1998); Longmore and Umansky (2001b); Matson (1990); Oliver (1990, 1996); Russell (1998); Scotch (2001); Shapiro (1993); Taylor, Blatt and Braddock (1999); tenBroek and Matson (1959); Thomson (1997); and others. These publications deal with disability-related issues, particularly the struggle of disabled people for their rights, by incorporating their voices and perspectives.

Due to a host of factors, the disability rights perspective initially began in the United States during the 1970s. It is important to discuss the origins of this perspective.

Disability Rights Movement and the Origins of Disability Studies in the United States

As Scotch rightly notes:

> Demands for greater participation by disabled people occurred in the wake of the wide spread and highly visible social conflicts of the 1960s. These conflicts included the struggle for civil rights by black people, the anti-war and student movements, and a revitalized feminist movement. A number of disabled people had been active participants in these movements, and they came to see their disability in the same political sense as blacks viewed their race or women their gender. Along with this new consciousness came an appreciation of how the change strategies of other movements could be adopted. While models of change-oriented advocacy did not guarantee success, they did suggest a method for stirring up latent support among a constituency and among the general public, and for channelling that support in attempts to influence governmental and institutional decision-makers (2001: 35–36).

Thus, while certain groups among the disabled had been waging a struggle for their rights from a much earlier period in the United States, the 'disability rights movement', as it came to be known, originated and gained momentum in the 1970s (Scotch 2001, Shapiro 1993). Prior to this, certain impairment-specific groups like the deaf (Baynton 1996) and the blind (Matson 1990; Jernigan 1999) were very active in demanding equal rights since early 20th century. But they always maintained themselves as a separate category, and did not identify with the larger section of the disabled population in sharing the stigma. This disability-specific activism notwithstanding, the disability movement prior to 1970 remained, by and large, what is described as an 'impairment-specific' movement (Barnartt and Scotch 2001; Scotch 2001; Shapiro 1993).

During the 1970s, the disability rights movement was primarily led by disabled people themselves, who waged a struggle for their rights based on the philosophy of self-advocacy through organisations in different parts of the country. These included groups like Center for Independent Living, founded by Ed Roberts in Berkeley, California, and Disabled In Action, founded by Judy Heumann in New York in 1971 (Scotch 2001; Shapiro 1993). The movement started gaining momentum when these groups were joined by other smaller groups from different parts of the country. Unlike the earlier movements led by the blind and the deaf people, this movement was known as the movement of the disabled people rather than the movement of the blind or the deaf. With increasing consciousness about their identities and realisation of the importance of alliance-building, the leaders of this newborn movement of the disabled people identified themselves as those who were deemed and rendered by society as 'disabled'. Their slogans reflected this newfound consciousness: for instance, the well-known 'You have given us your dimes, give us our rights now!' (Scotch 2001: 36). Today, one of the most popular slogans of the disability rights movement at the international level is 'Nothing about us without us' (Charlton 1998).

Disabled people came to take an increasing pride in their identities and began to demand their rights like other socially and politically marginalised minorities in the United States (Shapiro 1993). The population of the disabled people in the United States at the time of passing of the Americans with Disabilities Act (ADA) in 1990 was considered to be something between 35 and 43 million (ibid.: 6). Going by this statistic, they formed the largest minority in the country and, thus, demanded their rights as a socially and politically marginalised minority group. Citing Mary Johnson, the editor of *The Disability Rag*, the irreverent magazine of the disability rights movement in the United States, Shapiro (ibid.: 20) draws an analogy with the gay rights movement and emphasises that the disabled people came to realise that there is nothing to be ashamed of in having a disability. The understanding of the disabled people of themselves as a 'socio-political minority group' gave rise to the theorisation of the 'minority model' of disability, which replaced the traditional 'medical model' (Longmore and Umansky 2001b; Linton 1998; Russell 1998; Scotch 2001; Shapiro 1993; Thomson 1997). Thus, a politics of recognition embedded in a notion of civil rights came to characterise the disability discourse in the United States.

This understanding based on the 'socio-political minority group' model also resulted in the emergence of the discipline of disability studies. The first wave of disability studies began in the United States during the 1980s when disability came to be studied with a new perspective as a part of policy studies, political science and sociology (Longmore and Umansky 2001a: 12–13). Though it was studied primarily within these disciplines, its impact began to be seen in various other subjects as well. Subsequently, the second wave of disability studies began in the 1990s when disability came to be studied within the humanities. Michael Bérubé, a parent of a disabled child and a scholar of cultural studies, urged his colleagues in humanities, in an article written in *The Chronicle of Higher Education* in 1994, to study the cultural representation of disability (ibid.: 13). In her seminal textbook on disability studies published in the late 1990s, Simi Linton (1998) strongly argued the case for working on housing the discipline of disability studies in humanities. Syracuse University, New York, and the University of Illinois, Chicago, have been among the pioneering universities in the United States which introduced disability studies at the doctoral level. The fact that the doctoral programme at Syracuse University has been housed in the Department of Cultural Foundations of Education under the School of Education, and the department from which this programme is run at the University of Illinois is called Department of Disability and Human Development, reflects the perception that disability studies is being accepted as a part of the humanities.[1]

Disability Studies: Definition and Meaning

This section deals with the definition and meaning of 'disability studies' in the context of the theorisation of the disability studies perspective by the American and the British scholars, particularly the 'social model' as formulated by Oliver (1990, 1996). But before engaging in a detailed discussion of the disability studies perspective, it is useful to mention Erving Goffman's theory (1963) of 'stigma', which has been used by several scholars to build the disability studies perspective (Thomson 1997).

In his classic work, *Stigma: Notes on the Management of Spoiled Identity*, Goffman (1963) identified three characteristics which lead to stigmatisation and separate the stigmatised individuals from the other assumedly 'normal' individuals. These are the presence of: first, individual characteristics such as physical disability, deformity and anomaly; second, behavioural characteristics such as addiction, dishonesty, unpredictability, lack of education or manners and certain sexual habits; and last, social characteristics such as race, religion, ethnicity and gender (ibid.: 4). Consequently, according to Goffman, the ideal typical normal individual constructed by the modern western society free from these stigmatising characteristics would be someone who is 'a young, married, white, urban, northern, heterosexual, Protestant, father, of college education, fully employed, of good complexion, weight and height, and a recent record in sports' (ibid.: 128).

The ideal type delineated by Goffman is the updated version of the 'self-possessed individual of the 19th century America' (Thomson 1997: 29–32), which creates an illusory majority of the ideal types and an equally illusory and overwhelming minority of the non-conforming, a process described as 'normate subject position' by Thomson (ibid.: 7–10). This has led to the construction of what she described as 'normate bodies' (ibid.). Thus, persons embodying 'differences' not falling within 'normate subject positions', such as homosexuals, women, non-white, unemployed, unmarried and short people were excluded from the definition of 'ideal-type'. Similarly, disabled people were also considered to be a deviance from the norm. This definition of the ideal type constructed by the modern Western society came to be vehemently challenged in the 20th century by the feminist movement, the movement of the African-Americans and the gay rights movement (ibid.: 29–32). More recently, the disability rights movement has also followed the same trajectory of challenge and assertion of difference as a legitimate subject position in a pluralistic society.

As implied in the discussion, disability has traditionally been understood as an individual problem arising from sensory, physical and cognitive impairments. In other words, before the emergence of the disability studies perspective, it was primarily regarded as a medical problem or deficit affecting an individual based on what is described as the medical model by some American scholars (Linton 1998; Thomson 1997) or what is also considered to be an 'individual model' by some British scholars (Oliver 1990, 1996; Priestley 2003). This traditional approach towards disability in the Western societies presents disability as a 'deficit', a 'deviance from the norm', an 'individual burden' and a matter of 'personal tragedy' (Byrom 2001; Linton 1998; Oliver 1990, 1996; Priestley 2003; Thomson 1997). It is considered to be a physical, sensory or cognitive impairment and the focus is either to prevent its occurrence or to find a cure for it. In case the impairment cannot be cured, then the individual has to come to terms with it. The appropriate social response according to this traditional approach towards disability is, therefore, to then help the impaired person to rehabilitate himself/herself (Byrom 2001). Hence, disability under the medical model is considered to be a 'loss' to be compensated rather than a 'difference' to be accommodated.

The disability studies perspective has challenged this traditional notion based on the medical approach, and has instead proposed the theory that disability is a social problem rather than an individual one, and is a product of social construction rather than a medical condition. As argued by several American scholars, this approach has theoretically replaced the 'medical model' of disability with the 'minority model' (Davis 2002; Linton 1998; Russell 1998; Scotch 2001; Shapiro 1993; Thomson 1997). Some British authors also describe it as the replacement of the 'individual model' with the 'social model' (Oliver 1990, 1996; Priestley 2003).

Although there seems to be a difference of terminology, the perspectives of both the American and the British scholars of disability studies are not substantially different. For instance, Oliver (1996) refuses to consider the traditional model as medical model and would rather call it an individual model. He, however, accepts that medicalisation is a very important aspect of the individual model (Oliver 1990, 1996; Priestley 2003). By and large, both American and the British scholars agree on the major differences between the individual-based traditional approach to disability and its new progressive understanding in terms of social interpretation which emphasises physical, social and attitudinal barriers. The distinctions between the traditional individual model and the social model of disability described by Oliver (1996: 34) are clearly articulated in Table 2.1.

Table 2.1: Disability Models

Individual Model	Social Model
Personal tragedy theory	Social oppression theory
Personal problem	Social problem
Individual treatment	Social action
Medicalisation	Self-help
Professional dominance	Individual and collective responsibility
Expertise	Experience
Adjustment	Affirmation
Individual identity	Collective identity
Prejudice	Discrimination
Attitudes	Behaviour
Care	Rights
Control	Choice
Policy	Politics
Individual adaptation	Social change

Source: Prepared by the author.

Theorisation of the 'socio-political minority group model' by Scotch (2001) in the first edition of his book was primarily based on the analyses of the disability rights movement in the United States. This analysis was further endorsed by other scholars of disability studies (Linton 1998; Shapiro 1993; Thomson 1997). Similarly, Oliver developed the 'social model' of disability originally in 1983 (Priestley 2003) on the basis of a definition evolved by a British organisation of disabled people called the Union of the Physically Impaired Against Segregation (UPIAS) in the 1970s. As cited in Priestley (2003), the UPIAS argued: 'Disability is something imposed on top of our impairments by the way we are unnecessarily isolated and excluded from full participation in society. Disabled people are therefore an oppressed group in society' (ibid.: 13).

As explained by Priestly, a close analysis of this definition highlights the following:

a. Disability is something which is imposed on top of the impairments;
b. disability leads to exclusion from social participation;
c. the most important point is that this exclusion from social participation is neither necessary nor inevitable. By

implication, it is possible to have a society which is a fully participative society that includes all its members;
d. the disabled people form an oppressed group (ibid.: 14–15).

Disability Studies in India, 1980–2005: A Review of Literature

Initially, the rights-based approach came to influence the activists of the advocacy movement of the blind in India in the 1970s with the founding of the National Federation of the Blind Graduates in 1970, which was renamed as National Federation of the Blind (NFB) in 1972 (Chander 2008a: 1). The NFB waged a struggle for the rights of the blind during that decade through a moderate form of advocacy. This struggle was joined by some Delhi-based organisations of the blind, like the National Blind Youth Association, and acquired a radical form by the early 1980s (ibid.: 2). Subsequently, activists from other categories of disability also came to follow the rights-based approach beginning early 1990s (Bhambhani 2004; Chander 2008b). This approach is now firmly embedded in the discourse of the current generation of disability rights activists from cross-sections of disability in the country (ibid.). and likely to grow stronger over time as it crystallises at the international level. It is this approach which triggered the development of disability studies in the United States and United Kingdom and is beginning to influence disability scholars in India. With the exception of some recent publications (Ghai 2003; Hans and Patri 2003) which could be put in the category of works written with a disability studies perspective, most of the literature available on disability in India falls within the medical model. In order to substantiate this argument, a review of some important works on disability in India is presented in this section.

A significant publication which presents an in-depth analysis of social attitudes towards disability is a book by Usha Bhatt (1963). This book is a refined version of her Ph.D. dissertation submitted at the Department of Sociology at Bombay University. It remains a highly cited reference on disability in India. Bhatt examines the changing social attitudes toward disability in different historical periods through an analysis of the religious scriptures and main currents in Western philosophy. She elaborates the *karma* model (actions of past lives exerting an influence on the present life) and explains the reasons for the lack of development of rehabilitation services for the disabled in India.

Bhatt argues that while the break-up of the institution of the extended family and two World Wars have had a tremendous impact on social attitudes toward disability in the West, India remained relatively unaffected by such events: the disabled segment of the society did not get the due attention of policymakers and planners. As a result, social attitudes toward disability continue to be highly influenced by the moral and charitable approaches arising out of the traditional Hindu notions of *karma* and *dharma* (religious duty). Although a pioneering work at the time when there was hardly any focus on disability as a subject of academic pursuit, it must be admitted that Bhatt's largely sociological understanding is based more on a moral rendition than a disability studies perspective.

Around the same time when the civil rights and women's movements were taking shape in the United States in the 1960s and 1970s, India witnessed the emergence of strong communist movements adhering to Marxist and Leninist philosophy (Vanaik 1990: 182) and a socialist movement based on the ideology of Gandhi led by Jai Prakash Narayan and Ram Manohar Lohia (Limaye 1984; Mohan 1984). While the radical communist movements did not acquire a broad-based legitimacy, the socialist movements were more influential. As elaborated in certain other writings of mine (Chander 2008a, 2008b), there was a sustained and radical movement carried out by the NFB and certain other advocacy organisations of the blind since the early 1980s, which paved the path for implementation of the disability law in India. During the early and mid-1980s, this movement was focused on the implementation of the Office Memorandum of 1977. This Office Memorandum was the first government measure to ensure the reservation for three categories of the disabled — 1 per cent each for the blind, deaf and the physically impaired in certain selected categories of jobs under the Central Government Services and public undertakings (Mani 1988: 60–62; Pandey and Advani 1995: 100–102). The blind activists achieved several successes in terms of employment of the blind through this movement by the later part of the 1980s, most important being the recruitment of 239 qualified blind persons in 1987 in Delhi.[2] Thereafter, this movement focused on the demand for enactment of a comprehensive disability rights law resulting in the passing of the Persons with Disabilities (Equal Opportunities, Protection of Rights and Full Participation) Act (Government of India, 1996).[3]

In such an atmosphere of vibrant social and political movements emerging in different parts of the country, and a sustained and radical movement of the blind for their rights since the early 1980s, it is surprising that neither of the two important publications on disability of the time (Chaturvedi 1981 and Mani 1988) mentioned the advocacy movement of the blind, its accomplishments and its approach. A similar line was adopted by Kitchlu (1991) in relation to welfare services for the blind in India in the second half of the 20th century. While Mani and Chaturvedi dealt with disability issues from a policy angle in a broad way, Kitchlu claimed to analyse the educational and employment measures adopted for the blind by the welfare State of India. The clear message sent to readers through these three books was that the disabled people had received all the benefits accorded to them as a part of the welfare philosophy of the Indian State and not as a result of the struggle carried out by them for their rights (Chander 2008a). The authors completely ignored the advocacy carried out by organisations like the NFB. It is disturbing to note the apathy displayed by middle class intellectuals towards the advocacy movement led by blind activists for their rights in the 1970s and 1980s, at a time when India was so influenced by Gandhian thought, which strongly emphasises advocacy for the rights of the oppressed (Limaye 1984; Mohan 1984).

It is only during the 1990s that Indian books on disability accorded some recognition to the importance of the disability studies approach, acknowledging the advocacy potential of the disabled activists. The passing of the Americans with Disabilities Act (ADA) in 1990 and the movement preceding it in the United States laid the foundation for a broader disability rights movement in India in the early 1990s (Bhambhani 2004). The passing of the Persons with Disabilities (Equal Opportunities, Protection of

Rights and Full Participation) Act in 1995 (Government of India 1996) and the growing literature on disability studies in the West gradually started to influence intellectual work on disability in India, though initially in a very minor way. Three publications in the 1990s deserve special mention: an earlier book by Ali Baquer (1994), another co-authored by R. S. Pandey and Lal Advani (1995), both published in the year preceding the passing of the PWD Act, and finally, a co-authored book by Ali Baquer and Anjali Sharma (1997), published in the immediate post-PWD Act period. While the co-authored book by Pandey and Advani, as well as that by Baquer and Sharma, discussed the issues relating to disability law, they were still quite in line with the traditional medical model of disability as they basically presented status reports on disability-related issues in India. However, interestingly, it was Baquer's earlier analysis (1994) which was more embedded in a disability studies perspective. The underlying emphasis by Baquer was on the argument that the government should take serious account of the demands of the disabled for comprehensive disability rights legislation — and that the more the government delayed the passing of such legislation, the stronger would be the movement for and wider the scope of legislation demanded by the disabled activists.

Lately, more works are reflecting a clear disability studies approach. For instance, Asha Hans and Annie Patri (2003), and Anita Ghai (2003) have incorporated the disability studies perspective in their analysis. However, these are the only two identifiable publications by Indian scholars that can be put in the category of disability studies in the early part of the decade of 2010. Interestingly, both of the works are grounded in a strong feminist perspective. Hans and Patri's edited volume (2003) is significant as it adopts a disability studies perspective in the discourse on identity of disabled women by including contributors who either happen to be disabled themselves, or are the siblings or parents of the disabled, or are women scholars working on theorising the academic discourse on disabled women's identity. This book will, therefore, always be regarded as one of the pioneering works initiating a new intellectual tradition that examines disabled women's identity in the South Asian context. Drawing upon the marginalisation of women with disabilities in Western feminist discourse, Ghai (2003) develops her argument regarding a similar process of marginalisation of women with disabilities by feminist theorists in India, and discusses the multiple forms of oppression disabled women face in Indian society. Ghai's work should inspire young scholars interested in the discipline.

Conclusion

As a field of academic inquiry, disability studies is an emerging discipline in its nascent stage. It is based on a perspective that differs radically from the traditional models of disability such as the medical or the individual model. According to this perspective, disability is no longer considered to be an individual problem leading to personal tragedy, but something rooted in the social values and the physical environment that are not accommodating of any kind of difference based on physical, sensory or cognitive impairments. Disability, therefore, is a difference to be accommodated rather than a loss to be compensated. A new vocabulary has been designed to explain disabling processes starting from individual prejudice to institutionalised discrimination. Various terms have been coined to describe discrimination on the bases of impairments such as 'handicapism' (Bogdan and Biklen 1977), 'ableism', (Linton 1998), or 'disablism' (Oliver 1996). Whatever may be the term used to describe this discrimination, the essence of the new perspective in disability studies is that the disability lies in social structures and processes rather than in individual physical, sensory or cognitive impairments.

Notes

1. For details on The Center on Human Policy, Law, and Disability Studies, Syracuse University, see http://disabilitystudies.syr.edu/default.aspx (accessed 9 September 2010), and for Department of Disability and Human Development, University of Illinois, Chicago, see http://www.ahs.uic.edu/dhd/academics/phd.php (accessed 9 September 2010).

2. S. K. Rungta, personal interview, 18 March 2005.
3. For details of the Act, see http://socialjustice.nic.in/pwdact1995.php.

References

Baquer, Ali. 1994. *Disabled, Disability, and Disablism*. New Delhi: Voluntary Health Association of India.
Baquer, Ali and Anjali Sharma. 1997. *Disability: Challenges vs. Responses*. New Delhi: Concerned Action Now.
Barnartt, Sharon and Richard Scotch. 2001. *Disability Protests: Contentious Politics 1970–1999*. Washington, DC: Gallaudet University Press.
Baynton, Douglas C. 1996. *Forbidden Signs: American Culture and the Campaign against Sign Language*. Chicago: University of Chicago Press.
Bhambhani, Meenu. 2004. 'From Charity to Self-advocacy: The Emergence of Disability Rights Movement in India'. Unpublished MA dissertation, University of Illinois, Chicago.
Bhatt, Usha. 1963. *The Physically Handicapped in India: A Growing National Problem*. Bombay: Shivlaxmi Bhuvan Publication.
Bogdan, Robert and Douglas Biklen. 1977. 'Handicapism', *Social Policy*, 7 (5): 14–19.
Byrom, Brad. 2001. 'A Pupil and a Patient: Hospital-Schools in Progressive America', in Paul K. Longmore and Lauri Umansky (eds), *The New Disability History: American Perspectives*, pp. 133–56. New York: New York University Press.
Campbell, Jane and Mike Oliver. 1996. *Disability Politics: Understanding our Past, Changing our Future*. London and New York: Routledge.
Chander, Jagdish. 2008a. 'History and Disability in India', *The Disability History Association Newsletter*, Spring, 4 (1), http://dha.osu.edu/news/spring08/chandler.html (accessed 8 September 2010).
———. 2008b. 'The Role of Residential Schools in Shaping the Nature of the Advocacy Movement of the Blind in India', in Susan Lynn Gabel and Scot Danforth (eds), *Disability and the Politics of Education: An International Reader*, pp. 201–24. New York: Peter Lang Publishing.
Charlton, James I. 1998. *Nothing About Us Without Us: Disability Oppression and Empowerment*. Berkeley: University of California Press.
Chaturvedi, Triloki Nath (ed.). 1981. *Administration for the Disabled: Policy and Organizational Issues*. New Delhi: Indian Institute of Public Administration.
Davis, Lennard J. 2002. *Bending over Backwards: Disability, Dismodernism and Other Difficult Positions*. New York and London: New York University Press.
Ferguson, Ronald J. 2001. *We Know Who We Are: A History of the Blind in Challenging Educational and Socially Constructed Policies (A Study in Policy Archaeology)*. California: Caddo Gap Press.

Fleischer, Doris Zames and Frieda Zames. 2001. *The Disability Rights Movement: From Charity to Confrontation*. Philadelphia: Temple University Press.
Ghai, Anita. 2003. *(Dis)Embodied Form: Issues of Disabled Women*. New Delhi: Shakti Books.
Goffman, Erving. 1963. *Stigma: Notes on the Management of Spoiled Identity*. New York: Simon & Schuster, Inc.
Groce, Nora Ellen. 1985. *Everyone Here Spoke Sign Language: Hereditary Deafness on Martha's Vineyard*. Cambridge: Harvard University Press.
Hans, Asha and Annie Patri (eds). 2003. *Women, Disability and Identity*. New Delhi: SAGE Publications.
Ingstad, Benedicte and Susan Reynolds Whyte (eds). 1995. *Disability and Culture*. Berkeley: University of California Press.
Jernigan, Kenneth. 1999. *Kenneth Jernigan: The Master, the Mission, the Movement*. Baltimore, MD: National Federation of the Blind.
Kitchlu, T. N. (ed.). 1991. *A Century of Blind Welfare in India*. Delhi: Penman Publishers.
Limaye, Madhu. 1984. 'Socialist Movement in the Early Years of Independence', in G. K. C. Reddy (ed.), *Fifty Years of Socialist Movement in India: Retrospect and Prospects*, pp. 38–53. New Delhi: Samata Era Publication.
Linton, Simi. 1998. *Claiming Disability: Knowledge and Identity*. New York: New York University Press.
Longmore, Paul K. and Lauri Umansky. 2001a. 'Disability History: From the Margins to the Mainstream', in Paul K. Longmore and Lauri Umansky (eds), *The New Disability History: American Perspectives*, pp. 1–32. New York: New York University Press.
——— (eds). 2001b. *The New Disability History: American Perspectives* (History of Disability Series). New York: New York University Press.
Mani, D. Rama. 1988. *The Physically Handicapped in India: Policy and Programme*. New Delhi: Ashish Publishing House.
Matson, Floyd W. 1990. *Walking Alone and Marching Together: A History of the Organized Blind Movement in the United States, 1940–1990*. Baltimore, MD: National Federation of the Blind.
Mohan, Surendra. 1984. 'The Turbulent Years: 1952–55', in G. K. C. Reddy (ed.), *Fifty Years of Socialist Movement in India: Retrospect and Prospects*, pp. 54–60. New Delhi: Samata Era Publication.
Oliver, Michael. 1990. *The Politics of Disablement*. London: Macmillan Press.
———. 1996. *Understanding Disability: From Theory to Practice*. New York: Palgrave.
Pandey, R. S. and Lal Advani. 1995. *Perspectives in Disability and Rehabilitation*. New Delhi: Vikas Publishing House.
Priestley, Mark. 2003. *Disability: A Life Course Approach*. Cambridge: Polity Press.
Rudolph, Lloyd I. and Susanne Hoeber Rudolph. 1987. *In Pursuit of Lakshmi: The Political Economy of the Indian State*. Chicago: University of Chicago Press.

Russell, Marta. 1998. *Beyond Ramps: Disability at the End of the Social Contract.* Monroe, ME: Common Courage Press.

Scotch, Richard K. 2001. *From Good Will to Civil Rights: Transforming Federal Disability Policy,* 2nd edn. Philadelphia: Temple University Press.

Shapiro, Joseph P. 1993. *No Pity: People with Disabilities Forging a New Civil Rights Movement.* New York: Times Books (Random House).

Taylor, Steven J., Steven D. Blatt and David L. Braddock (eds). 1999. *In Search of the Promised Land: The Collected Papers of Burton Blatt.* Washington, DC: American Association on Mental Retardation.

tenBroek, Jacobus and Floyd W. Matson. 1959. *Hope Deferred: Public Welfare and the Blind.* Berkeley: University of California Press.

Thomson, Rosemarie Garland. 1997. *Extraordinary Bodies: Figuring Physical Disability in American Culture and Literature.* New York: Columbia University Press.

Vanaik, Achin. 1990. *The Painful Transition: Bourgeois Democracy in India.* New York: Verso.

3

Tracking Disability through the United Nations

N. SUNDARESAN

According to the Preamble of the Convention on the Rights of Persons with Disabilities (UNCRPD), persons with disabilities continue to face barriers in their participation as equal members of society and violations of their human rights in all parts of the world.[1] Multiple physical, social and attitudinal barriers prevent their integration and full participation in the community. As a result, millions of people throughout the world are segregated and deprived of virtually all their rights and end up leading a miserable life (Campbell and Oliver 1996).

Proponents of the social model of disability have developed a twofold materialist definition of disability that connects the biological and social barriers experienced by disabled individuals through the concepts of impairment and disability. While impairment means lacking part or all of a limb, or having a defective limb or mechanism in the body, disability is the socially imposed state of exclusions or constraints which physically impaired individuals may be forced to endure (Oliver 1990, cited in Gleeson 1999: 25).

The manifold problems faced by disabled people are basically a consequence of the violation of their human rights; namely, the absence of the conditions for the development of the innate characteristics that nature has bestowed upon them as human beings. It is this ongoing struggle for the protection and promotion of human rights of persons with disabilities that colours the endeavours of national governments and the United Nations (UN).

All human rights instruments are embedded in notions of universality, equality and non-discrimination. However, not all instruments carry equal legal status within the UN framework; for instance, conventions and treaties like the UNCRPD are legally binding on States Parties that have ratified them, while declarations, resolutions, programmes and guidelines of the United Nations General Assembly (UNGA) like the Declaration on the Rights of Disabled Persons (DRDP) are not. They are in the nature of soft laws that express generally accepted principles and represent a moral and political commitment by states to guide national-level legislation and policies. At times, these standards may even be incorporated as part of the national framework of laws, though in principle they remain non-justiciable.

In addition to a General Comment[2] on persons with disabilities in the International Covenant on Economic, Social and Cultural Rights (ICESCR), several disability-specific non-binding international instruments have been adopted at the international level, which include:

a. Declaration of the Rights of Mentally Retarded Persons (1971)[3]
b. Declaration on the Rights of Disabled Persons (1975)[4]
c. World Programme of Action concerning Disabled Persons (1982)[5]
d. Tallinn Guidelines for Action on Human Resources Development in the Field of Disability (1989)[6]
e. Principles for the Protection of Persons with Mental Illness and the Improvement of Mental Health Care (1991)[7]
f. Standard Rules on the Equalization of Opportunities for Persons with Disabilities (1993b)[8]
g. ILO Recommendation concerning Vocational Rehabilitation of the Disabled (1955)[9]
h. ILO Recommendation concerning Vocational Rehabilitation and Employment (Disabled Persons) (1990)[10]
i. Sundberg Declaration on Actions and Strategies for Education, Prevention and Integration, adopted by the

UNESCO World (1989) Conference on Actions and Strategies for Education, Prevention and Integration, Malaga (Spain), 1981[11]

j. Salamanca Statement and Framework for Action on Special Needs Education, adopted by the UNESCO World Conference on Special Needs Education: Access and Quality, Salamanca (Spain) (1994a)[12]

The UN and its specialised agencies, such as the International Labour Organisation (ILO), the World Health Organisation (WHO), the United Nations Children's Emergency Fund (UNICEF), and the United Nations Educational, Scientific and Cultural Organisation (UNESCO) among others, have a long history of engagement with the issue of disability. In fact, some of the earliest universal disability policy statements were put forward by its predecessor, the League of Nations, which adopted a Crippled Children's Bill of Rights in 1931. In 1955, the ILO issued its Recommendation 99, an instrument which served as the basis for national legislation and practice concerning vocational rehabilitation, training and placement of disabled persons. In its attempt at standardised classifications, the WHO developed the International Classification of Impairments, Disabilities and Handicaps (ICIDH)[13] and the International Classification of Functioning, Disability and Health (ICF).[14] Disability became a more central concern from the 1980s onwards, with the Declaration of 1981 as International Year of Disabled Persons and the period 1983–1992 being designated as United Nations Decade of Disabled Persons. This was followed by regional initiatives such as the Asia-Pacific Decade of Disabled Persons (1993–2002) supported by the United Nations Economic and Social Commission for Asia and the Pacific (ESCAP). All these developments coincided with the rise of the disability rights movement in the West, which engaged in self-advocacy at both local and global levels. The culmination of these efforts is the UNCRPD in the formulation of which national disability organisations from all member states of the UN have played a pivotal role.

The subsequent sections of this paper will examine the major provisions of the UN legal framework on disability with a view to highlight its seminal contribution to protection of the human rights of what is often termed as the largest and most invisible minority group.

The Beginnings

The Charter of the United Nations is the first international document which explicitly and unconditionally advocated for the human rights and fundamental freedoms for all persons. It stated that all men are created equal and they are endowed by their Creator with certain inalienable rights, and among these are the rights to life, liberty and the pursuit of happiness. Subsequent covenants, such as the International Covenant on Civil and Political Rights (ICCPR) (1966), International Covenant on Economic, Social and Cultural Rights (ICESCR) (1966), International Convention on the Elimination of All Forms of Racial Discrimination (ICRD) (1969), International Convention on the Elimination of All Forms of Discrimination against Women (CEDAW) (1979), UN Convention against Torture (CAT) (1984), and the International Convention on the Rights of the Child (ICRC) (1989), took forward the same principles. Every human being, by virtue of being human, is entitled to liberty, equality, non-discrimination, and the right to a decent and secure life without distinction of race, class/caste, gender, age, and disability. Human rights are the tools for the realisation of social justice for all.

Given the universality, indivisibility, interdependence and interrelatedness of all human rights and fundamental freedoms, and the need for persons with disabilities to be guaranteed their full enjoyment without discrimination, the UN passed the Declaration on the Rights of Mentally Retarded Persons in 1971. It sought to affirm the essential humanity and right to the enjoyment of all rights and fundamental freedoms by the most marginalised among the disabled. The Declaration begins with the categorical assertion that:

> The mentally retarded person has, to the maximum degree of feasibility, the same rights as other human beings.[15]

In addition to the rights to medical treatment and rehabilitation, education, training and appropriate occupation, the Declaration clearly pitches for deinstitutionalisation by highlighting the mentally retarded person's right to residence with his/her family — natal, foster or adoptive, as the case may be — in the community. Interestingly, the Declaration uses the (now) stigmatising term 'retardation' and does not make a distinction between mental illness and mental retardation (MR). However, it does entitle the affected person to due process of law and legal representation keeping in view his/her degree of mental responsibility.

The Declaration on the Rights of Disabled Persons (1975) defined a disabled person as any person who is unable to ensure by himself or herself, wholly or partly, the necessities of a normal individual and/ or social life as a result of a deficiency, either congenital or acquired, in his/her physical or mental capabilities. While disability was narrowly defined in terms of the medical model, i.e., as deviations from normative standards of physical and mental functioning of the individual human body, the Declaration acknowledged the intersections of disability with other socioeconomic variables such as gender, ethnicity, nationality or class. It goes on to affirm the fundamental rights of all disabled persons to the same rights and freedoms available to other citizens, including '. . . the right to enjoy a decent life, as normal and full as possible' (Clause 3). An important connection between this Declaration and its predecessor is the rider placed on mentally retarded persons in the area of political and civil rights, where their freedom may be curtailed, after due process and periodic review, to ensure that there is no abuse or exploitation of such persons (Clause 4).

Around the same time as the passage of the above Declarations, the WHO, with a view to distinguishing between the biological and social dimensions of disablement, proposed a threefold classification, namely, impairment, disability and handicap through its International Classification of Impairments, Disabilities and Handicaps (ICIDH). While impairment is a more or less permanent biological condition subject to correction by the level of medical knowledge and intervention, disability is inextricably linked with activities that an individual has to (walk) or wants to (dance) undertake. It is a situation-dependent phenomenon. Handicap, on the other hand, emphasises the inequality with non-disabled persons and the disadvantages thereof.

Intensification of Efforts

The first major global programme for the welfare of persons with disabilities was the declaration of 1981 as International Year of

Disabled Persons by the General Assembly in 1976. It called for a plan of action at the national, regional and international levels, with an emphasis on equalisation of opportunities, rehabilitation and prevention of disabilities. The motto was 'full participation and equality'. Other objectives included: increasing public awareness; understanding and acceptance of disabled persons; and encouraging them to form organisations for advocacy.

The International Year of Disabled Persons was celebrated with numerous programmes, research projects, policy innovations and recommendations. Many conferences and symposiums were held during the Year, including the First Founding Congress of Disabled Peoples International, in Singapore (30 November–6 December 1981). The Trust Fund for the International Year, established in 1977, collected over $510,000 in contributions from member States. In 1982, the General Assembly took a major step towards ensuring effective follow-up to the International Year by adopting, on 3 December 1982, the World Programme of Action concerning Disabled Persons (WPA) by resolution 37/52.

The WPA is a global strategy to enhance disability prevention, rehabilitation and equalisation of opportunities, which pertains to full participation of persons with disabilities in social life and national development. The WPA also emphasises the need to approach disability from an interdisciplinary and multi-sectoral perspective. Its three chapters provide an analysis of principles, concepts and definitions relating to disabilities; an overview of the world situation regarding persons with disabilities; and set out recommendations for action at the national, regional and international levels. Moving beyond health, education, employment, communication in appropriate formats and other access concerns, the WPA also pitched for enhancing the recreational, cultural and creative fulfilment of disabled persons. Special emphasis was put on the important role of families, the mass media and disabled persons organisations in all aspects of programme conceptualisation and implementation. Inter-regional co-operation was also emphasised.

The WPA sought to define disability as the relationship between persons with disabilities and their environment. The imperative to remove societal barriers, which impede the full participation of persons with disabilities was recognised. An important principle underlying this theme is that issues concerning persons with disabilities should not be treated in isolation but within the context of normal community services. This laid the foundation for the community-based rehabilitation (CBR) model and the promotion of integrated education of children with disabilities. It also assigned a critical role to civil society organisations, especially organisations of disabled persons, in planning, implementing, monitoring, evaluation and research in the disability sector in collaboration with national governments. An important modality to maintain momentum of activities throughout the decade was the creation of a Voluntary Fund for the United Nations Decade of Disabled Persons (1983–1992) with a priority to invest resources in programmers and projects for the least developed countries. This was an important modality in an era when bilateral funding was the dominant paradigm of international aid.

The linkages between disability, citizenship and overall development were highlighted. For instance, in 1989 the Tallinn Guidelines for Action on Human Resources Development in the field of disability clearly stated: Effective implementation of the World Programme of Action will make an important contribution to the process of development of societies through the mobilisation of more human resources. The intersections of disability with other variables such as class and gender was also acknowledged. For instance, the WPA called for mainstreaming disability in national women's empowerment programmes.

The Tallinn Guidelines emphasised the potential of persons with disabilities for self-reliance. Instead of just formal skills education, it pitched for social and special skills training to enable independent living, particularly for women and girls in rural areas (Guideline 28). The 'equal pay for equal work' principle and concrete affirmative action to recruit disabled persons in the labour force were also set forth as important goals in this document. For the actualisation of overall development of disabled persons, there was a need to invest national resources for the development of adequate and appropriate infrastructure and manpower in the areas of health, education, employment and social services both by the public and private sectors.

Dovetailing with CEDAW, Article 37 of the Tallinn Guidelines underscored the need for affirmative action for the employment of disabled women. Mainstreaming disability became a major agenda with subgroups of disabled persons such as children, girls and women, disabled migrants and refugees and the elderly being identified as special groups for targeted programmes.[16]

A multi-pronged perspective on disability is embedded in the UN approach. While on the one hand it is acknowledged as a sociomedical condition requiring both medical and social interventions at individual and collective levels, on the other, there is also a recognition of the hierarchy of disabilities in which persons with multiple disabilities, mental retardation and mental illness occupy the bottom of the pyramid.

The next major development in the disability sector in the UN system was the adoption by the UNGA of the 'Principles for the Protection of Persons with Mental Illness and the Improvement of Mental Health Care', known as MI Principles, in 1991. The MI Principles established standards and procedural guarantees, providing protection against the most serious human rights abuses that might occur in institutional settings, such as misuse or inappropriate use of physical restraint or involuntary seclusion, sterilisation, psycho-surgery, and other intrusive and irreversible treatment for mental disability.[17] While innovative at the time, today the value of the MI Principles is disputed.

At the end of the UN Decade of Disabled Persons, the General Assembly adopted the 'Standard Rules on the Equalization of Opportunities for Persons with Disabilities' in 1993. In essence, they reiterate the WPA mandate. 'The Standard Rules consists of 22 rules summarizing the message of the World Programme of Action'. They 'incorporate the human rights perspective which had developed during the Decade'. The 22 rules cover all aspects of life of disabled persons in 'four chapters — preconditions for equal participation, target areas for equal participation, implementation measures, and the monitoring mechanism'.[18] In addition, they provide for the appointment of a Special Rapporteur to monitor the implementation of the Rules. The Standard Rules became the principal United Nations instrument for guiding State action on human rights and disability, and constituted an important reference in identifying State obligation under existing human rights instruments. Many countries have based their legislation on the Standard Rules. Like other UN disability-specific instruments, they are not legally binding and do not protect the rights of persons with disabilities as comprehensively as does the new convention.

Disability in General UN Programmes

In addition to the disability specific declarations, recommendations and conventions, separate mention of disability has been incorporated in all major UN documents since the 1990s. For instance, in 1993, the Vienna Declaration and Programme of Action (VDPA) emphasised that special attention should be paid to ensure 'non-discrimination and the equal enjoyment of all human rights and fundamental freedoms by disabled persons, including their active participation in all aspects of society'. It reaffirmed that 'all human rights and fundamental freedoms are universal and, thus, unreservedly include persons with disabilities . . . Any direct discrimination or other negative discriminatory treatment of a disabled person is therefore a violation of his or her rights'.[19] Similarly, in 1994, the UN International Conference on Population and Development (Cairo Programme of Action) stressed 'equal opportunities for persons with disabilities and the valuing of their capabilities in the process of economic and social development' as also the dignity and promotion of self-reliance of persons with disabilities.[20] The Copenhagen Declaration in 1995 committed itself to ensure 'that disadvantaged and vulnerable persons and groups are included in social development, and that society acknowledges and responds to the consequences of disability by securing the legal rights of the individual and by making the physical and social environment accessible'.[21]

Although separate reference to the plight of girls and women with disabilities and the need for special measures to alleviate their lives were explicitly stated in all disability relevant documents, it was only in the Beijing Platform for Action in 1995 that their reproductive health concerns were addressed. It advocated the design and implementation of gender-sensitive health programmes that 'address the needs of women throughout their lives' and take into account the special needs of women with disabilities, as well as to 'ensure that girls and women of all ages with any form of disability receive supportive services'.[22]

The provision of full accessibility was a central goal of the Habitat Agenda. It underscores that

> Persons with disabilities have not always had the opportunity to participate fully and equally in human settlements development and management . . . owing to social, economic, attitudinal and physical barriers, and discrimination. Such barriers should be removed and the needs . . . of persons with disabilities should be fully integrated into shelter and sustainable human settlement plans and policies to create access for all.[23]

Specialised UN Agencies and Disability

Among the various organisations of the UN, organisations directly concerned with disability are ILO, WHO, UNESCO and UNICEF. The contribution of WHO to the classification of impairments and disabilities has already been cited. In addition, it plays a major role in prevention, detection and management of disabilities through its numerous health programmes.

The four main activities of ILO, viz., (*i*) standard setting, (*ii*) technical co-operation, (*iii*) education and training, and (*iv*) research and information, have impacted the working and living conditions of workers, particularly in developing countries, paving the way for various national and state rules and legislations particularly in the matter of rehabilitation, compensation, minimum wage fixation and regulation of working hours. ILO was the first UN agency to develop detailed policies for not only the employment of persons with disabilities, but more importantly, for protection of workers injured at the workplace, giving rise to the whole area of occupational health. ILO also put forward the idea of governments giving incentives to enterprises for employing disabled persons, which has become a cornerstone of affirmative action programmes in many countries.

According to the ILO, provision for vocational rehabilitation of the disabled should be included as an essential component of health, social welfare and manpower schemes in all national development plans. In effect, the economic value of a country may be assessed by the number of disabled persons in its workforce. In 2001, the ILO formulated a code of practice for managing disabilities in the workplace. The code is meant to guide employers in all sectors and sizes of enterprise to adopt a positive strategy in managing disability-related issues.

In its focus on child survival and wellbeing, the UN International Children's Emergency Fund (UNICEF) places special emphasis on mainstreaming disability in its agenda, be it in health, education, child protection, HIV or advocacy.

United Nations Convention on the Rights of Persons with Disabilities (UNCRPD)

The UNCRPD is the response of the international community to the long history of discrimination, exclusion and dehumanisation of persons with disabilities who constitute over 10 per cent of the world's population. The Convention comprises 50 articles and its Optional Protocol has 18 articles. This historic comprehensive, rights-based, integral convention is groundbreaking in many ways, being the first and fastest negotiated human rights treaty ever in the 21st century. It is the result of three years of negotiation involving civil society, governments, national human rights institutions and international organisations, and most importantly, persons with disabilities and their organisations from across the globe. Since then, a record number of countries have signed to demonstrate their commitment after it was opened for signature in March 2007.

UNCRPD (2006) is the culmination of 25 years since the 1981 International Year of Disabled Persons (IYDP) that brought global attention to the issues affecting persons with disabilities. During the period, many societies have moved away from considering the persons with disabilities as objects of charity and pity by acknowledging that society itself is disabling. The Convention embodies this attitudinal change and is a major step towards altering the perception of disability. During the first major international review of the implementation of the World Programme of Action concerning disabled persons, held in Stockholm in 1987, participants recommended drafting a convention on the human rights of persons with disabilities. Despite various initiatives including proposals made by the governments of Italy and Sweden, and the Commission for Social Development's Special Rapporteur on Disability, and strong lobbying from civil society, the proposition did not win enough support to lead to the negotiation of a new treaty.

In a way, UNCRPD summates the goals and recommendations of earlier disability-specific instruments, especially the World Programme of Action and the Standard Rules on the Equalization of Opportunities in a comprehensive, legally binding, disability-specific instrument that is internationally accepted. It sets out in detail the rights of disabled people, covering civil and political rights, accessibility, participation and inclusion, education, health, employment and social protection. The treaty recognises that equality for persons with disability cannot occur without changes in attitudes.

UNCRPD recognises that disability is an evolving concept resulting from the interaction between persons with impairments and attitudinal and environmental barriers that hinder their full and effective participation in society on an equal basis with others (Preamble (e)). The Convention does not consider it appropriate to give a specific definition of disability, owing to the fact that definitions of disability vary in different countries and regions, depending upon many factors — political, social, cultural and legal. It only states that persons with disabilities include those who have long-term physical, mental, intellectual or sensory impairments, which in interaction with various barriers may hinder their full and effective participation in society on an equal basis with others (Article 1).

UNCRPD covers many areas such as access to justice, participation in political and public life, education, employment, freedom from torture, exploitation and violence, as well as freedom of movement. Under the Optional Protocol, individuals who allege violations of their rights and who have exhausted national remedies can seek redressal from an independent international body. There are two exclusive Articles (6 and 7) on women with disabilities and children with disabilities, respectively owing to the peculiarity of multiple discrimination that women with disability and children with disability are confronted with.

Millennium Development Goals (MDGs) and Disability

The United Nations began the new millennium by launching the historic Millennium Development Goals in 2000 to address major world problems through a concerted international agenda. MDGs are eight international developments goals that all 193 United Nations member states and at least 23 international organisations have agreed to achieve by the year 2015. They include eradicating extreme poverty, drastically reducing child mortality and improving maternal health, providing universal primary education, fighting disease epidemics such as AIDS and malaria, promoting women's empowerment ensuring environmental sustainability and developing a global partnership for development. MDGs are specifically designed to address the needs of the world's poorest citizens and the world's most marginalised populations through sustained international collaboration.

While MDG No. 3 specifically targets gender equality and women's empowerment, there is no mention of persons with disabilities. MDGs cannot be achieved, however, if the concerns of more than 10 per cent of the world population associated with 20 per cent of global poverty are not taken into consideration as a separate constituency.[24]

The international community needs urgently to act to mainstream disability in the MDG processes. This requires policymakers and technical experts, specifically tasked with the programming, monitoring and evaluation of current MDG programmes, to begin to consider disability so that the next phase of the implementation of the MDGs will include disability as an important component of its core mission.

It is obvious that all MDGs are relevant to and affect the lives of persons with disabilities. It is equally important to note that being one of the most vulnerable among the vulnerable, special efforts will have to be made to ensure that the concerns of persons with disabilities are integrated in planning, implementation, monitoring and evaluation of MDGs at global, regional, national and local levels for short-, medium- and long-term results. Existing data gaps on disability within the context of the MDG evaluation and monitoring is a major challenge. Available data, however, could be used to support the inclusion of disability in current MDG evaluation and monitoring processes, while ongoing and new MDG evaluation and monitoring efforts should add a disability component as part of their overall data collection endeavours. Where data is not available, options of where and how disability could be addressed should be provided. Indeed, the absence of data is an indication, among other things, of the lack of attention that disability may receive in the context of a particular issue.

Conclusion

Since its inception, the United Nations has played a seminal role in making disability a human rights and developmental issue. Through a range of general and disability-specific declarations, resolutions, treaties and conventions, it has been able to push national laws and policies to ameliorate the living conditions of perhaps the most marginalised social group. The UNCRPD, which was negotiated with direct involvement of persons with disabilities over a three-year period, is a shining example of this. Nonetheless, there is scope for more concerted engagement. For instance, disability is not mentioned in any of the eight Millennium Development Goals, the 18 targets set out to achieve these goals, or the 48 indicators for monitoring their progress. How can sustainable development and total wellbeing be achieved without the incorporation of the largest minority group in the world?

Notes

1. See http://www.un.org/disabilities/convention/conventionfull.shtml (accessed 4 July 2012).
2. See http://www.unhchr.ch/tbs/doc.nsf/0/4b0c449a9ab4ff72c12563e d0054f17d (accessed 4 July 2012).
3. See http://www2.ohchr.org/english/law/pdf/res2856.pdf (accessed 4 July 2012).
4. See http://www2.ohchr.org/english/law/res3447.htm (accessed 4 July 2012).

5. See http://www.un.org/disabilities/default.asp?id=23 (accessed 4 July 2012).
6. See http://www.un.org/documents/ga/res/44/a44r070.htm (accessed 4 July 2012).
7. See http://www.un.org/documents/ga/res/46/a46r119.htm (accessed 4 July 2012).
8. See http://www.un.org/documents/ga/res/48/a48r096.htm (accessed 4 July 2012).
9. See http://www.ilo.org/dyn/normlex/en/f?p=NORMLEXPUB:12100:3524675008826556::NO:12100:P12100_ILO_CODE:R099:NOon (accessed 4 July 2012).
10. See http://www.ilo.org/public/english/standards/relm/ilc/ilc86/r-iii1b.htm (accessed 4 July 2012).
11. See http://www.unesco.org/education/nfsunesco/pdf/SUNDBE_E.PDF (accessed 4 July 2012).
12. See http://www.unesco.org/education/pdf/SALAMA_E.PDF (accessed 4 July 2012).
13. See http://www.leeds.ac.uk/disability-studies/archiveuk/Barnes/rehab2.pdf (accessed 4 July 2012).
14. See http://www.who.int/classifications/icf/en/ (accessed 4 July 2012).
15. See http://www2.ohchr.org/english/law/pdf/res2856.pdf (accessed 4 July 2012).
16. See http://www.un.org/womenwatch/daw/cedaw/; and http://www.un.org/documents/ga/res/44/a44r070.htm (accessed 4 July 2012).
17. See http://www.un.org/documents/ga/res/46/a46r119.htm (accessed 4 July 2012).
18. See http://www.un.org/esa/socdev/enable/dissre00.htm (accessed 4 July 2012).
19. 'Vienna Declaration and Programme of Action (Part 1, Paragraph 22 and Part II, Paragraphs 63–64)', adopted by the World Conference on Human Rights, 25 June 1993, http://www.unhchr.ch/huridocda/huridoca.nsf/(symbol)/a.conf.157.23.en (accessed 9 September 2010).
20. ICPD, Cairo Programme of Action, 5–13 September 1994 in Cairo, Egypt, (Paragraphs 6.29 and 6.32), http://www.iisd.ca/cairo/program/p06000.html (accessed 9 September 2010).
21. Paragraph 26(i) and Commitments 2(d), 6(8) of the Copenhagen Declaration on Social Development, http://www.un.org/documents/ga/conf166/aconf166-9.htm.
22. Platform for Action, Chapter I—Mission Statement, 'Actions to be Taken'; Paragraphs 106(c) and 106(o), http://www.un.org/womenwatch/daw/beijing/platform/health.htm (United Nations 1995).
23. Paragraphs 16, 40(1) and 43(V). See http://www.unescap.org/huset/publications/localizing.pdf (accessed 4 July 2012).

24. See http://web.worldbank.org/WBSITE/EXTERNAL/TOPICS/EXTSOC IALPROTECTION/EXTDISABILITY/0,,contentMDK:21162907~menu PK:3265756~pagePK:210058~piPK:210062~theSitePK:282699,00. html (accessed 16 July 2012).

References

Campbell, Jane and Michael Oliver. 1996. *Disability Politics: Understanding Our Past, Changing Our Future*. London and New York: Routledge.
Gleeson, Brendan. 1999. *Geographies of Disability*. London and New York: Routledge.
Oliver, Michael. 1990. *The Politics of Disablement*. London: Macmillan.
United Nations. 1979. Convention on the Elimination of All Forms of Discrimination against Women (CEDAW), UNGA Resolution No. 34/180, 18 December 1979, http://www.un.org/womenwatch/daw/cedaw/ (accessed 7 September 2010).
———. 1980. The Convention on the Rights of the Child (CRC), UNGA Resolution No. 44/45, 20 November 1989, http://www.unicef.org/crc/ (accessed 7 September 2010).
———. 1981. International Year of Disabled Persons, UNGA Resolution No. 36/77, 8 December 1981, http://www.un.org/documents/ga/res/36/a36r077.htm (accessed 9 September 2010).
———. 1995. 'Beijing Platform of Action of the International Conference on Women, 1995', http://www.un.org/womenwatch/daw/beijing/platform/ (accessed 9 September 2010).
———. 2006. United Nations Convention on the Rights of Persons with Disabilities (UNCRPD), adopted by the UNGA vide Resolution No. A/RES/61/106, 13 December 2006, http://www.un.org/disabilities/default.asp?id=311 (accessed 7 September 2010).

PART II
Family, Care and Work

4

Prenatal Diagnosis: Where do We Draw the Line?

ANITA GHAI AND RACHANA JOHRI*

When prenatal diagnosis first became a part of the Indian reality, feminists were quick to point out that the techniques, aimed to detect foetal abnormalities, were also capable of providing information about the sex of the unborn child. It seemed evident to them that given the extremely patriarchal nature of much of Indian society and the marked preference for male children, such techniques were more likely to be used for sex-selective abortions. The history of the debates between the state and activists is well known (Patel 2007; Rao 2004). Responding to the massive protest generated by the spread of sex-selective abortions, the central government passed the Pre-Natal Diagnostic Techniques (Regulation and Prevention of Misuse) Act or PNDT Act in 1994. Despite the legal regulation, the 2001 Census showed an alarming decline in the juvenile sex ratio in the under-5 category.[1] In 2003, a public interest litigation (PIL)[2] prompted the central government to place the onus of action against providers of sex-selective abortions on the state governments. In recent years there has been a noticeable increase in media attention, although criminal action[3] against medical practitioners is only now becoming a reality.

In this essay, however, we are interested in exploring a less visible aspect of the PNDT Act. A careful reading of the Act shows that while selection on the grounds of sex is unambiguously banned, there is a positive sanctioning of selection on the basis of disability. Consequently, this results in the legitimisation of one kind of selection, that is, on the basis of disability, while prohibiting it on grounds of sex. The debate on whether selection on the grounds of disability should be legal evokes mixed reactions. The existing arguments suggest that antenatal screening is not understood in any uniform way, either within feminism or in the disability movement, particularly in India.

While many scholars writing on the interface between feminism and disability activism see the right to abortion as creating a gulf between the two perspectives (Hubbard 1997; Shakespeare 1998; Sharp and Earle 2002), others (McLaughlin 2003; Menon 2004; Parens and Asch 2000) think that there is a possibility of reconciliation between the two apparently divergent perspectives. The former believe that for feminists the critical factor in all abortion debates is women's uncontested right to choose. Proponents of this perspective do acknowledge the fact that choice is not always unconditionally autonomous and free. However, many activists in the disability movement object to this unqualified right to abortion, as it has serious implications for the discrimination experienced by disabled persons. This anomaly has been noticed by feminists like Sunita Bandewar, who says:

> A new problem comes up when considering the right to abortions of a foetus with a disability. One might argue that the same reasoning can be applied: since women face the most profound impact of such children upon their birth, they should be the sole decision makers to either continue or terminate pregnancy (2005: 20).

This position potentially strengthens the normative conceptualisation of disability which is value-laden. It sets a precedent for elimination of so-called unfit people. Nivedita Menon echoes Keith Sharp and Sarah Earle (2002), and Bandewar, when she warns that:

> Once we accept that there can be a hierarchy of human beings based on physical characteristics, and that it is legitimate to withhold the right to be born to those at lower levels of this hierarchy, then this reasoning can be extended to other categories, whether female, inferior races or any other (Menon 2004: 96).

One line of reasoning taken by pro-life supporters like Marsha Saxton (1998) and Mary Jane Owen[4] is that the right to abortion is at the root of all discrimination against disabled persons. However, while we are of the opinion that women must retain an unfettered right to abortion, it is also apparent to us that the construction of abortion as individual choice needs considerable rethinking, since women face familial, social and cultural constraints in the exercise of free choice in their everyday lives. Data from across the world, and particularly from India, shows that even when the legal system allows it, many abortions are illegal, thus increasing the morbidity for women. In a review of several researches, Visaria, Ramachandran, Ganatra and Kalyanwala (2004) found that husbands and mothers-in-law play a predominant role in decision-making around abortion. Two other interesting features emerged from this review. First, women reported that while abortion is an immoral act per se, it could be condoned if it was performed for the sake of family honour. Second, women who opt for abortion after giving birth to several daughters receive more support than those who opt for it for other reasons. Many women also reported being forced violently to undergo abortions. Furthermore, in the case of sex-determination and subsequent female foeticide, families make the decision after a cost-benefit analysis factoring in the relative long-term gains of saving on dowry.

Feminists are, therefore, in the difficult position of supporting abortion, even while they recognise the limited agency that women possess in the exercise of free choice. The underlying logic is that abortion rights are necessary in an imperfect system, even where a woman has limited capacity to control her reproductive life. The question, both practical and ethical, is that if women have the right to choose, how can a distinction between abortion and selection be maintained? We believe that it is the category of the unborn child or the foetus which is the critical variable in this debate. Before prenatal diagnosis came into routine use, debates around abortion focused almost exclusively on the mother's ability to bear and rear a child. Such decisions were largely guided by the legitimacy of motherhood for the woman: they did not involve the 'qualities' of the foetus. With the advent of prenatal diagnosis in clinical practice, the conception of the foetus has changed from a generic entity to one with specified properties. The first of these properties, namely, the sex of the child, has already shown itself to be problematic. The case of sex selection points to a critical need to differentiate between abortion and selection. The latter needs to be located within discussions of hegemonies of gender, normalcy and normativity, be it male sex or absence of disability. This paper seeks to draw upon both the feminist and disability rights discourses to interrogate the unqualified right to abort foetuses with disability, as articulated in the PNDT Act.

Context of Sex Selection

The Indian context provides us with a setting to reflect on the ethics of selection. Since sex selection is pervasive in India, feminists have had no choice but to grapple with the dialectic of structure and agency within which the issue is framed. The majority of feminists argue that since women possess limited agency, legal systems have to be strengthened to protect them. At the same time, as highlighted by Menon (2004), individual women who have 'opted' for sex selection should not be punished. Instead, the onus of responsibility lies with the medical practitioner who provides the information about the sex of the unborn child, and the sociocultural context that valorises sons over daughters.

The intricacy of the issue is evident in the perspective of feminist Manjula Padmanabhan (1993), who asks whether there can be:

> . . . anything more grotesque than to be forced to carry an unwanted living presence within the sanctum of one's own body? . . . In a twisted sort of way, women who abort their female foetuses are voting against their own misogynist culture and in that sense, are subverting it . . . Given the world we have now, it is far better to enable women to take this life-denying decision of their own accord, under medically and legally safe conditions than to saddle them with babies whom they will revile and devalue as they were reviled and devalued (cited in Menon 2004: 94).

It is important to understand the mindset of the woman who aborts her unborn daughter as a partial protest against her own oppression, because women do participate consciously in sex selection. In the absence of an alternative viewpoint, a woman, who is rejected for bringing yet another daughter into the world, is likely to hate her and see in her the reasons for her own oppression.

When sex selection has evoked so much debate, the issue of selection on grounds of disability is clearly even more contentious. Again, central to this discussion is the difficulty in conceptualising women's agency. Both the mother of an unwanted daughter and that of a disabled child face tremendous difficulties. To choose to give birth to a child with disability is to challenge dominant social constructions of both motherhood and childhood. If it is possible to argue that the desire to abort a female foetus arises from the conditions of patriarchy, is a similar logic not applicable to disability selection? We try to delineate this nuanced picture by drawing upon research on gender, motherhood and disability carried out by the two authors in the course of several research projects. We come to this debate from different vantage points — Anita Ghai is a disability researcher and activist, and Rachana Johri is a researcher on motherhood.

The essay draws upon data from three qualitative research studies, primarily involving in-depth interviews with mothers. The first set of voices is from an ongoing study by Rachana Johri (2001) in which mothers of young children are asked about the specific circumstances under which they would opt for abortion. One of the issues discussed in detail is what the informants would do in the face of a potentially disabled foetus. All the participants in this study are college-educated and belong to the urban middle class. At the time of writing, interviews had been conducted with 20 mothers, each with one or two children. The selection of the participants was based on the age of their children. Thus, mothers with children below six years of age were chosen as they are in the peak of their reproductive lives. A second data source is another research, conducted in 2007, in which 30 mothers of children with developmental disabilities are interviewed. Again, the women belong to the middle class and are residents of Delhi. The third study that has been cited is a research conducted by Sanjana Singh (2005) as part of her Bachelor's degree under the supervision of Anita Ghai. The participants were 14 visually impaired girls between the ages of 16 and 18 years studying in a residential school for the blind in Delhi. Among other issues on which detailed qualitative interviews were conducted, the students were also asked to respond to a dilemma about prenatal testing for the determination of potential disabilities.

We argue that, as in many other issues, there is no homogenous or essential woman's voice concerning the legitimisation of the abortion of a disabled foetus. Nonetheless, despite an absence of homogeneity, the dominant voice does favour abortion of the disabled foetus. Exploring the underlying reasons for justifying or rejecting such action helps to better comprehend the contexts in which such choices are made, and to arrive at an alternative rendering of the question of abortion of disabled foetuses. In the remaining part of the paper, our attempt is precisely to foreground the voices of a sample of women on disability selection and abortion. But before proceeding any further, it will be worthwhile to develop a better understanding of the dynamics of disability construction.

Medicalisation of Disability

As Anita Ghai (2003) has argued elsewhere, part of the difficulty in understanding disability lies in that it is unequivocally embedded within the medical model. The location of the problem as residing within the individual's body perpetuates the image of the disabled person as sick, flawed, afflicted and suffering. Consequently, the medical model sees the availability of reproductive technologies, such as prenatal diagnosis, as a blessing that may pre-empt and, consequently, prevent congenital disability. This perspective is well represented in the advice columns of magazines like *Parenting India*.

Responding to a query about the safety of ultrasound examination during pregnancy, the gynaecologist in the advice column begins by highlighting the benefits of ultrasound to detect the age of the foetus, its position and other features. Then, she proceeds to emphasise the need for a second ultrasound during the 13th week of pregnancy to:

> [l]ook for certain congenital abnormalities like Down's syndrome or anencephaly.[5] In these cases *'timely intervention'* can prevent a lot of mental trauma to parents as these pregnancies can be easily terminated at that stage. A third ultrasound is done at 22 weeks as most organs have developed at that stage and parents can be given proper counselling (*Parenting India* 2007: 97; emphasis added).

The discursive construction of the perfect pregnancy and, hence, the perfect child is apparent in this brief extract from an advice column of a popular magazine. Indeed, most medical professionals would not find this scenario exceptional. It is worth noting that the advice does not contain any information on the nature of disability, its severity and the possibility of raising a disabled child. If professionals, such as obstetricians and counsellors, are ethically committed to assisting prospective parents make informed choices, they should be providing detailed and reliable information about what life is like with a disabling condition, so that their clients can imagine the ways in which such a life can be both rewarding and difficult for themselves and their potentially disabled child. However, not only do medical professionals tend to medicalise non-medical conditions like normal pregnancy and menstruation, they adopt a directive approach when they should be helping clients engage in a process of autonomous decision-making. Thus, procedures like prenatal diagnoses are not only projected as usual, but also as highly necessary and desirable.

Josephine Green (1994) studied consultant obstetricians and found that they favour selective abortion when they come across any foetal abnormality. Although Green's research comes from a different cultural context, the power of medical discourse seems to be quite universal. This is evident in the narratives of young mothers in our research, who were overwhelmingly in favour of aborting a disabled foetus. They were greatly influenced by medical practitioners who strongly urge pregnant women to have tests. The fact that doctors and genetic counsellors speak from the position of experts makes their suggestions all the more critical.

As Puneeta, a homemaker with a 10-month-old daughter, puts it, 'My doctor told me this when she sent me for the first ultrasound: "We want to check if there is any abnormality. After the third month if there is any abnormality, then abort the child".'

Thus, the medical discourse appears to 'empower' couples by offering tests for a growing range of conditions. Medical professionals claim to provide non-directive counselling,[6] enabling parents to make their own choices. Yet, the ethical issues and the theoretical and practical possibilities of non-directive counselling have remained largely uninterrogated. Recent research voices serious concerns about the extent to which a genetic counsellor simply reproduces the biases of the larger society. As Annette Patterson and Martha Satz point out:

> Serving both as purveyors of genetic information and as guides in decision-making, genetic counsellors often preside over prenatal sessions where parents are considering whether to continue or terminate a pregnancy. This evaluation process has profound implications for society in shaping attitudes about what constitutes a 'life . . . worth living' and, potentially, the provisions society will make for those with disabilities (2002: 119).

Examples abound of mothers who were told at the time of the birth of their disabled children that they would not survive for more than a few years, or would show extremely poor intellectual development. Many such children have survived for years and often reached levels of capability exceeding medical expectations. A particularly poignant account is presented in the autobiographical film '39 Pounds of Love'. Ami Ankilewitz[7] was diagnosed with an extremely rare and often fatal form of spinal muscular atrophy that severely limits his physical growth and movement. He is 34 years old, having outlived the doctor's prediction of his life expectancy by 28 years. The film follows Ami's journey in search of the doctor who predicted his early demise.

One of the mothers from the study on the choice of abortion being done by Johri narrated the case of a friend who was advised to undergo abortion, but whose baby was ultimately born without any disability. It is clear that although medical knowledge is uncertain and disability is often used as a catch-all phrase for all kinds of avoidable conditions, experts push decisions towards abortion. With the detailed mapping of the human genome underway, medical technology will enable the detection of individual predispositions to a number of diseases, such as diabetes, depression, Alzheimer's disease, heart disease, arthritis and breast cancer in the not so distant future. Will the fantasy of a perfectly able-bodied society entail the elimination of all foetuses predisposed to developing a spectrum of possible conditions?

Cost of Disability

Yet another reason, and possibly a very effective one, reminds parents that the rearing of a disabled child would invariably entail extra time, money and suffering[8] for the child as well as the family. Multiple costs are involved in bringing up a child with disability, which may include emotional pain and suffering, loss of the child, loss of opportunities, loss of freedom, isolation, loneliness, fear, guilt, stigmatisation, and financial hardship. In fact, people who argue in favour of disability selection often accuse activists of being insensitive to the 'costs' to women that such a choice entails. As Rayna Rapp reminds us:

> Women judge the acceptability of specific fetuses for entry into their communities because there are so few limits on women's responsibility for the quality of life that the child would have. In other words, our gendered responsibilities for producing acceptable children as well as our embodied responsibilities for the pregnancies that produce them overdetermine our need to think deeply about the consequences of knowing about and possibly eliminating disabled fetuses prenatally (2000: 308).

Since patriarchy determines the social location of care, caretaking usually gets added to the unpaid labour of women in the home. As a result, it is both the disability as well as perpetual motherhood that shape genetic decision-making. The fear of extensive caretaking and responsibility are evident in the voices of the young mothers in our research. Sudha, a homemaker with a 4-year-old son, for example, was sure that she would definitely have had an abortion if she discovered that her unborn child might be disabled. She says, 'There is no doubt about it. I am very clear about it.' Her clarity stems from the fact that her mother's friend had a son who was intellectually challenged. She says:

> I've seen the mother suffering and the child suffering. Maybe it is not the case now because people are more open-minded. But even then, people don't look at physically or mentally handicapped children as equal to theirs.

Mothers fear the greater responsibility that comes with a disabled child, a responsibility that they often have to bear the brunt of. As one of the young mothers comments:

Have tests to find out if there are any abnormalities? I suppose so. Sounds selfish, but probably I think I would abort the child. I guess you feel the amount of responsibility. You're not strong enough to bring up a special child.

In a similar vein, another mother says, 'To bring up that child is the responsibility of a lifetime. No one else will take care [of the disabled child] especially after you die.' In her case, the doctors had indicated a problem with the heart. She continues:

> I had to go to Escorts.[9] Then, I had thought that if there was a problem, I'd get an abortion done. The thought of the baby being born and getting tubes and all put all over was very uncomfortable. Any deformity would make a difference. If you don't know, then you cannot help it; but once you find out, then don't take up the responsibility. If she is born, then you have to take care of it, but otherwise it is better to prevent [the pregnancy].

From the point of view of mothers, the responsibility is particularly frightening, since it is routine to blame them for anything that is regarded amiss with the child, be it female sex or disability. Many women who participated in Johri's doctoral study (1999) described how they were blamed and ostracised by their conjugal families and the larger community for their failure to give birth to a son. Archana, a mother of three daughters, who was the Principal of a school, narrated the painful days following the birth of her first daughter. When her mother-in-law finally came to visit her in the hospital, Archana said:

> She behaved as if I had committed a crime. On the nurses asking for a gift (*inaam*), she commented, 'You are asking for a gift. We are bereft (*Hum to kahin ke na rahe*). She may as well have not survived.'

Archana was devastated and said, 'I felt very bad. Today, if I had a son, everyone would have gathered around me — celebrations would have taken place. And they have not even brought me food.'

Archana's trauma was heightened because her husband did not support her at all in the face of the hostility and ostracism inflicted upon her by his family and community. After the birth of their third daughter, her mother-in-law stopped eating for three days. Such is the lamentation following the birth of daughters that her community conducted a '*shok sabha*' (mourning meeting) for her, the poor woman who has three daughters, none of whom have died. The psychological cost of bearing the less than perfectly desired child are indeed considerable for the mother.

Apart from the psychological costs experienced directly by the mother, the disabled child is viewed as an economic liability and, therefore, a burden on both family and society. Such a child is perceived to contribute little and require disproportionate investment from society. The parallel with the girl child is evident. In a globalising context where the profit paradigm predominates, the justification for preventing the birth of disabled children is that society has to bear the cost of disability. While the billions spent on wars (that are the major source of disablement) are not lamented, the money spent on disabled people is constructed as high cost. Economic factors are at the root of the persistent devaluation of disabled lives. This rationale is, however, flawed. Prenatal diagnosis creates an illusion that disability will be wiped out if research in genetics is successful. However, under no circumstances is a total erasure of disability possible. We know that barely 2 per cent of all births are affected by disability in the womb.[10] Disability may occur during pregnancy, delivery or at any other time during the lifespan. Many impairments have no clear aetiology, and since prenatal testing can carry some risk for the foetus, it is likely that only women with high risk pregnancies will undergo testing. Though many disabilities such as sickle-cell anaemia, Down's syndrome, adult-onset Huntington's chorea, cystic fibrosis and haemophilia are considered grounds for abortion, in reality, many persons with these disabilities do become independent and lead productive lives if given the opportunities to do so. This is not to say that there would be no disabled persons who will require care, but such an expectation is legitimate within a just society.

Enrichment of Parental Autonomy

Another rationale offered in support of prenatal screening is the enrichment of parental autonomy. Peter Singer, a well-known contemporary bioethics scholar, uses this argument to justify genetic/prenatal testing and subsequent termination of a disabled foetus. According to him:

> [O]n the one hand we are naturally sympathetic to the claims of a disability rights movement that models itself on movements defending the rights of women and ethnic minorities, and, on the other hand, we all accept that to have a disability is to be worse off than to be without the disability. . . . There are many things that people who are paralysed below the waist could not do in any society, no matter how constructed. They cannot visit untracked wilderness, go ice skating, or play football. And many other things that they can do, they can do only with difficulty, and with more time than it would take those who have the use of their legs. . . . The decision to abort a fetus that has, say, Down syndrome, is not a decision that is 'antichildren', still less 'anti-life'. It is a decision that says: 'Since I will only have two children, I want them to have the best possible prospects for a full and rich life. And if, at the outset, those prospects are seriously clouded, I would rather start again (2000: 246).

In this discourse, the choice to determine the nature of the foetus is constructed as a parental right. But a reading of the narratives from our research indicates that parental rights and autonomy are differently constructed, depending upon a mother's social location and experiences. Although some mothers of non-disabled children did argue in favour of this right, other mothers of disabled children held a different view. These children were, however, born before the technology was routinely available for clinical use. For instance, Shanti, a 60-year-old disability advocate and mother of a 28-year-old disabled son, admits that she would have had the abortion had the choice been made available to her. She says, 'I was too perfectionist — too intellectual.' However, when asked whether she would give similar advice to young mothers, she responds in the negative. She feels living with a Down's syndrome child has given her an opportunity for deep learning. She would not like to exchange this experience for anything. Many parents like Shanti will attest to the potential for self-transformation that comes about as a result of bringing up a child who has Down's syndrome.

Prenatal screening and other future selective technologies make us lose sight of the possibility of transforming the hostility and prejudices that we carry for anyone who is different. The changing understanding of disability within the social model[11] challenges us to question the assumption that disability is to be avoided at all costs. As Meeta, a mother of two sons, who works in an NGO for disabled children, puts it:

> There is no problem in accepting the baby. Suppose the disability happened after birth, the baby loses an eye, and then you will accept it. You won't throw it away. There is a girl here at our NGO; she is handicapped but she has gone to England. Since I work here, I have seen how a mentally retarded child can take out a comb from the drawer. I have told my husband that in case I cannot have another child, I would like to adopt a disabled girl. That feeling of pity (*bechchaari*) has gone. A six-year-old has gone abroad; can we think of doing it?

Parental choice can only be meaningful within a society that provides knowledge about disabled lives. There is considerable difference between living with the disabled and their stereotypical portrayal in the popular imagination. The gap between stereotype and lived reality is evident in the narratives of visually impaired girls in a research study by Singh and Ghai referred to earlier. While visual disabilities are often not genetic, the issue concerns the difference between the construction of disability and the experience of living it. Therefore, we thought that it would be insightful to look at the views of those who are stigmatised to ascertain how they view the issue of disability and parental autonomy. Radhika is a 17-year-old visually impaired girl, originally from a remote village in the neighbouring state of Uttar Pradesh and presently studying in a residential school for the blind in Delhi. Responding to a hypothetical query regarding what she would say to a mother who might give birth to a disabled child, she says, 'There are good and bad traits in everyone. I would tell her not to abort the child, but help the child to develop an identity, to teach him/her how to live in this world.'

Similarly Puja, her schoolmate, adds, 'I'll also tell her that you should be teaching your child to live, to face this world . . . And we should be doing something throughout our life, so that they (society) can remember us.'

In focus group discussions, the right of the disabled to life was affirmed by visually challenged adolescent girls. Like non-disabled girls growing up in patriarchal society, some disabled children may internalise the dominant voice of the culture and argue for the abortion of disabled foetuses. Many others, as the narratives show, disagree.

From another perspective, it is in the context of potential motherhood that the issue of disability takes on added meaning in the lives of disabled women. This issue is poignantly addressed by Deborah Kent (2000) when she writes about the gulf between herself and her beloved husband, between herself and her parents, regarding her blindness, a gap she was herself unconscious of until she and her husband decided to have children. She writes, 'What I understood was that Dick, like my parents, was the product of a society that views blindness and all disability as fundamentally undesirable' (ibid.: 58). Thus, Kent does not look at life with disability as one of unmitigated suffering.

If, nevertheless, some mothers of disabled children believe that they would advise a prospective mother to abort the foetus, what might be the underlying process? Diya, a 72-year-old, middle class woman, is actively involved in advocating the rights of intellectually challenged adults. She herself has a 24-year-old son with Down's syndrome. Though committed to caring for her son, she points to the discrepancy between her own feelings and the dominant construction of disability. This is reminiscent of the arguments put forward by mothers who have daughters. Diya is of the view that if a young mother discovers any genetic defect such as intellectual impairment, she should abort the child. She feels that although there has been greater awareness about disability over the past two decades, the negative mindset of people has not really changed. She recalls with horror the agony and turmoil that she experienced while getting her daughter married because the whole family was stigmatised. She was equally perturbed by the frustration of her son who was not allowed to be present at many social events — her relatives would often explicitly tell her to leave her son at home.

Similarly, another mother, who has a 37-year-old son with Down's syndrome, was distressed when he expressed a desire for marriage — she has no solutions to offer him. Then, Kamal, mother of a grown son with developmental disability, said that although she herself did not do so, she would advise a mother expecting a potentially disabled child to get the foetus aborted. She feels that even though society might have changed, disability is still perceived negatively.

All the interviews indicate that disabled children are perceived as socially unwanted children. Although the narratives included here refer to mothers with intellectually challenged children, we feel that the findings apply in the case of other disabilities as well. While it is possible to deconstruct the voices of mothers with or without disabled children, the contrasting narratives of visually impaired girls bring out the real paradox in the notion of choice and disability selection. Indeed, the disabled often do not experience their life as one of unmitigated suffering.

Many feminists have repeatedly cautioned against the notion of universal womanhood. We are of the view that the specificity of their social locations will generate a difference in the voices of mothers and daughters on disability. Nonetheless, what is not in dispute is that women have an inalienable right to free choice in the area of reproduction. Health professionals and the wider society do not sanction the birth of a disabled child. Therefore, if women make choices that go against societal norm, they are likely to be blamed. Even in the case of polio, it is often presumed that the mother must have been at fault for not having had the child immunised. Instead of getting support, counselling, understanding and information, people are pressurised into conforming to societal norms and expectations. It is important to note that a focus on individual reproductive choice overlooks the underlying assumption of prenatal diagnosis, namely, that only certain kinds of people should be born in this world. The very existence of prenatal tests assumes that parents will want to select against atypical results. Consequently, is there really a notion of free choice in the true sense of the word in decisions related to elimination of disabled foetuses? As a parent, Michael Bérubé (1996), the father of a boy with Down's syndrome, feels:

> Obviously I can't and don't advocate abortion of fetuses with Down syndrome; indeed, the only argument I have is that such decisions should not be automatic. A fetal diagnosis of Down syndrome should not be understood, either by medical personnel or by parents, as a

finding to which abortion is the most logical response . . . Nonetheless, although this is my belief, it is only my belief. I would not want to see it become something more than belief — something more like a coercive social expectation (ibid.: 79).

Individual Choice: Myth or Reality

It is evident that an emphasis on individual rights does injustice to the complexity of a woman's as well as a disabled person's experiences. Let us consider the scenario that disabled people confront in a society where being normal is the ruling ideology. Considering that disability is defined in medical terms and normality is defined by powerful social normative standards, choice can be anything but free. Furthermore, there are people with a range of different disabilities, different life experiences, different material needs and different ideological perspectives. Although technological developments enhance the sense of choice, in reality they tend to push decisions in a predictably socially desirable direction. In contemporary India, the technology of prenatal determination of foetal characteristics has disadvantaged both girls and the disabled. With the advent of these technologies, more and more pregnant women are encouraged by doctors to go in for prenatal screening. In such a context, the pressure on women to exterminate that which seems to depart from the norm is immense. But, as Veena Das (1986) has argued, this decision is in itself by no means based on autonomous choice implied in discussions on the morality of abortion. Furthermore, as she points out, it is not inscribed in the nature of things that a physically or mentally retarded individual should have a poor quality of life. It is the great value accorded to autonomy and competition that appear to make this a self-evident fact.

Indeed, new technological innovations have already made it possible to select an embryo at the outset rather than abort an unwanted foetus afterwards. The abortion debate may, thus, become irrelevant in the not so inconceivable future. The critical question, then, is the issue of choice. As a recent report on assisted reproductive technologies by SAMA Resource Group for Women and Health states:

It is difficult to distinguish between latent choice and social choice shaped by family, market, and other agents. Unless we draw this line, there is no limit to theoretical choice and everything, including sex selection, can be justified in the language of choice. What society does is to promote one variety of choice while silencing the range of options. The society closes the option that women can be happy without children [or, in our words, without daughters, or disabled children] (2006: 101).

While individual choice must be promoted, what needs to be addressed is that this choice takes place in a particular social space in which disability has a negative connotation. Consequently, it is difficult to say how much real choice is involved. If you choose to bear and rear a disabled child, it appears to be illogical and ridiculous. As Adrienne Asch has written:

Suppose Down syndrome, cystic fibrosis or spina bifida were depicted not as an incalculable, irreparable tragedy but as a fact of being human? Would we abort because of those conditions or seek to limit their adverse impact on life? (1988: 87)

To communicate that 'You must have a test' or 'You must have a termination', without analysing the implications, needs to be problematised. We need to provide mothers and fathers with multiple accounts of how they might lead a life with a disabled child. As Jason Kingsley, a 17-year-old boy with Down's syndrome, puts it:

I have a disability called Down syndrome. My bad obstetrician said that I will never learn and send me to an institution and never see me again. No way Jose! Mom and Dad brought me home and taught me things. He never imagined that I could write a book. I will send him a copy of the book so he will know. I will tell him that I play violin, that I make relationships with other people, I make oil paintings, I play the piano (Kingsley and Levitz 1994: 27–28).

What needs to be clarified is that these choices are made in a context where disability is accepted as an oppositional category to normality. Disabled lives are not considered worthwhile. Whether the argument stresses suffering or economic cost, disability is conceived of only as a medical category. Such a framing misses the socially constructed nature of disability. The fact that some part of the body or mind is limited in functioning is not the problem; but the barriers in society are the real problem — for instance, stairs without elevators or ramps, information not available in Braille or digital format, and most importantly, people's negative attitudes. These represent a complex form of institutional discrimination, which is as deep-seated in our society as gender bias, caste structures and heterosexism/homophobia. Thus, the 'cure' to the problem of disability does not lie in medical technology but in the restructuring of society. Marsha Saxton eloquently sums up the sense of outrage experienced by disability activists when she says:

> The message at the heart of widespread selective abortion on the basis of prenatal diagnosis is the greatest insult: some of us are 'too flawed' in our very DNA to exist; we are unworthy of being born . . . fighting for this issue, our right and worthiness to be born, is the fundamental challenge to disability oppression; it underpins our most basic claim to justice and equality — we are indeed worthy of being born, worth the help and expense, and we know it! (1998: 391)

For a feminist audience, it might be worthwhile to understand the role played by capitalist economies in casting disability as a deficit, something extensively discussed in the social model of disability. As Michael Oliver has written:

> Whatever the fate of disabled people before the advent of capitalist society . . . with its coming they suffered economic and social exclusion. As a consequence of this exclusion, disability was produced in a particular form; as an individual problem requiring medical treatment. Old age [and, I would suggest, madness and distress] suffered a similar fate (1996: 127).

It is not uncommon to find people, impaired due to work-related injury, forced to lead a marginal life thereafter because of the disabled-unfriendly environment. Thus, disabled people are disempowered because bodies, which do not fit in or require additional resources to become a part of the production process, are rejected in a system which emphasises profit. Factors such as the reluctance to provide disabled-friendly environments, and the non-availability of materials in alternative formats for visually and hearing-impaired people, are all geared towards keeping the employment rates for the disabled abysmally low. This image of not being able to contribute to production constructs the disabled as dependent, which is ultimately the root cause of their exclusion.

For a mother, the realisation that her disabled child may never be able to attain fulfilment of all his/her needs is very painful. As the narratives above show, many mothers will choose not to go ahead with the pregnancy in such circumstances. A woman's choice to abort a disabled foetus is constructed within dominant notions both of motherhood and disability. To feel fulfilled as a mother, it is assumed that a woman must produce a healthy, non-disabled baby. Any deviation will produce not only dissatisfaction but also increase her burden and result in mother-blaming. Consequently, it is not difficult to empathise with a woman who selectively aborts a disabled foetus. The difficulty, both logical and ethical, arises when a similar argument is used for the abortion of female foetuses. Mothers report that a woman without sons is *banjh* (barren) and that life without a son is a life spent in darkness. They fear their husbands will leave them, and indeed many do (Johri 1999). If mothers' desires are not sufficient grounds for aborting female foetuses, the same rationale applies to the case of disability. Clearly, the notion of individual choice is problematic.

The new reproductive technologies have eugenic potential as they reinforce the notion that there is an ideal of physical and mental perfection that humanity must aspire to. Such a position considers most differences as deficits. It is, however, a slippery slope to other forms of selection, and thus eventually to a world of a new designer baby eugenics. If new technologies make it possible to fulfil desires and satisfy preferences, is that reason enough to use them? More precisely: If we can, does that mean we should? If one is going to be consistent about choice, then why stop at impairment? But then, can women never be conscious agents? To cite Jennings, the notion of free choice only provides an 'illusion of freedom' (Jennings 2000: 130). Then, how are we to make sense of the situation? Equating choices that women are compelled to make, that is, aborting a female or disabled foetus, is not the same as saying that they are participating in discrimination. Instead, it points to the ways in which women are themselves constrained by the burden of knowledge. Our fantasy might be that women should avoid selection. However, it is unjust to expect that they would not abort when the problem is not a matter of autonomous choice, but the context in which such choice is made. What is perhaps required is an analysis of prenatal screening in the light of the social values and structural inequalities that influence the decision to abort. Therefore, if prenatal screening is to be made available, it must be accompanied by efforts to re-educate the public, including prospective parents, about disabled people's lives. It has to be coupled with efforts to improve financial and other support systems for them and their families. If the danger of increased prejudice is real for sex, then it is even more real for disability. Our contention is that there is a critical need to interrogate the silence around the routinisation and rapid growth of prenatal testing. To our mind, a public debate is extremely important to understand whether elimination of disability is a legitimate goal. Marcy Darnovsky (2004) reminds us:

> This constellation of technological, economic, cultural, and ideological developments has revived the issue of sex selection, relatively dormant for more than a decade. The concerns that have always accompanied sex selection debates are being reassessed and updated. These include the prospect that selection could reinforce misogyny, sexism, and gender stereotypes; undermine the well-being of children by treating them as commodities and subjecting them to excessive parental expectations or disappointment; skew sex ratios in local populations; further the commercialization of reproduction; and open the door to a high-tech consumer eugenics.

The belief that marginalised communities need to be empowered is equally true for both women and the disabled. As Roger S. Gottlieb (2002), a philosopher with strong Marxist leanings, suggests:

> Whether or not someone is disabled is partly a function of what resources are available at a given time, what conveniences are 'standard' in a society, and how we are expected to behave . . . The nature of paraplegia will change when wheel chair ramps are as standard as elevators . . . Similarly, the question arises: what changes are to be made — the institutional equivalents of wheelchair ramps — in equalising the participation of caretakers of the disabled to make our society more just? (ibid.: 231–32).

Conclusion

This essay has argued that both in sex selection and disability selection, discursive constructions of socially acceptable and desirable traits completely eclipse the wide range of subjectivities that are involved in such decisions. What appears to be free choice is largely determined by the dominant social ideologies and institutions. Supporters of the right to determine characteristics of the unborn need to remember that in an era marked by unprecedented technological interventions on the body, the tendency to construct desirable babies is likely to work to reinforce already existing hierarchies. It is opening a Pandora's Box as selection of one trait implies the legitimisation of other traits as well. Therefore, the ethics of what appear as free choices need to be interrogated. The disability community in India is so involved with issues of basic survival that there is yet no space for discussion of the implications of new reproductive technologies. We need to make efforts to incorporate the perspectives of disabled individuals in genetic counsellors' education and practice, thereby reforming society's view of the disabled. This will help in lessening possible negative effects of genetic counselling on the self-image and material conditions of disabled individuals.

As part of a campaign aimed at the Human Fertilisation and Embryology Authority,[12] the UK-based bioethics group Human Genetics Alert writes:

> If we allow sex selection it will be impossible to oppose 'choice' of any other characteristics, such as appearance, height, intelligence, etc. The door to 'designer babies' will not have been opened a crack — it will have been thrown wide open' (2002: 2).

Do we want that to happen?

Notes

* This essay first appeared in the *Indian Journal of Gender Studies*, 15 (2): 291–316, 2008, New Delhi: SAGE Publications. Editorial changes have

been made to the original published chapter with permission from the Centre for Women's Development Studies, New Delhi.
1. See http://www.india-seminar.com/2003/532.htm (accessed 29 August 2007).
2. The PIL was initiated in February 2003 by three petitioners: Dr Sabu George, the Centre for Enquiry into Health and Allied Themes (CEHAT), Mumbai, and the Mahila Sarvangeen Utkarsh Mandal (MASUM), Pune, in the Supreme Court. It called for the implementation of existing legislation banning prenatal sex-selection as well as taking cognisance of newer reproductive technologies for sex determination of the foetus.
3. According to Sandhya Srinivasan (http://www.infochangeindia.org/analysis121.jsp, accessed 29 August 2007), there are some 350 cases filed under the PNDT Act. Of these, 226 are for running a diagnostic clinic without registration, while 26 are for not maintaining accounts. Just 37 are for communicating the sex of the foetus, and 27 are for advertising sex selection. The first conviction involving a prison term was ordered on 28 March 2006, when a doctor and his assistant were sentenced to two years in prison and levied a fine of ₹5,000 in Palwal, Haryana. More recently, a sex-selective abortion racket was unearthed in Pataudi, a town 40 km from New Delhi. The police say that A. K. Singh, the quack arrested for the murder of several unborn children and for conducting illegal diagnostic tests, has confessed to aborting over 260 female foetuses in the past decade.
4. Mary Jane Owen is Founder and national Director of Disabled Catholics in Action. She was formerly Executive Director of National Catholic Office for Persons with Disabilities.
5. Anencephaly is a fatal birth defect that happens when the neural tube does not fully close at the top. As a result, part of the skull and brain are missing. Babies with anencephaly die before or shortly after birth.
6. Non-directive counselling is a psychotherapeutic or counselling technique in which the therapist takes on an unobtrusive role in order to encourage free expression and problem resolution by the client or patient.
7. Ami, who weighs only 39 pounds, works in Israel as a 3-Dimensional animator, and creates his art despite the fact that his bodily motion is limited to a single finger on his left hand. Through his efforts, he continues to redefine notions of a 'normal' life.
8. It is interesting that while suffering associated with disability is assigned a negative value, suffering that is inflicted voluntarily on the self in order to achieve physical perfection is valorised. As Wolfgang Welsch puts it, 'The current aestheticization seems to attain its consummation in individuals. We are experiencing everywhere a styling of body, soul and mind — and whatever else these fine new people might want to have (or acquire for themselves). In beauty salons and fitness centres, they pursue

the aesthetic perfection of their bodies . . . Future generations should then have it easier straight away: genetic technology will already have come to their aid, this new branch of aestheticization which holds out the prospect of a world full of perfectly styled mannequins' (1996: 6).
9. The reference is to the Fortis Escorts Heart Institute, a private speciality hospital in New Delhi. It was earlier known as Escorts Heart Institute and Research Centre.
10. See http://www.ias.ac.in/currsci/nov25/articles9.htm (accessed 20 August 2007).
11. As against the medical model of disability which conceptualises bodily difference in terms of impairment requiring medical intervention, the social model puts the onus of disability not on the individual but on the society in which s/he lives. Architectural, educational and employment barriers created by society disable the individual, not his body.
12. 'The Case against Sex Selection, Human Genetics Alert Campaign Briefing', December 2002. A copy of the report was obtained from Human Genetics Alert, Unit 112 Aberdeen House, 22–24 Highbury Grove, London N5 2EA, t +44 (0)20 7704 6100.

References

Asch, Adrienne. 1988. 'Reproductive Technology and Disability', in Sherrill Cohen and Nadine Taub (eds), *Reproductive Laws for the 1990s*, pp. 69–127. Clifton, N.J.: Humana Press.
Bandewar, Sunita. 2005. 'Exploring the Ethics of Induced Abortion', *Indian Journal of Medical Ethics*, 2 (1): 18–21.
Bérubé, Michael. 1996. *Life As We Know It: A Father, a Family, and an Exceptional Child*. New York: Random House.
Blumberg, Lisa. 1998. 'Reproductive Technology and the Threat to Diversity', *The Ragged Edge*, July–August, http://www.ragged-edge-mag.com/0798/a798ft1.htm (accessed 24 October 2007).
Darnovsky, Marcy. 2004. 'Revisiting Sex Selection'. *Gene Watch*, http://pol285.blog.gustavus.edu/files/2009/08/Darnovsky_Revisiting_Sex_Selection.pdf (accessed 21 May 2012).
Das, Veena. 1986. 'Deciding on Moral Issues: The Case of Abortion', in Diana L. Eck and Devaki Jain (eds), *Speaking of Faith: Cross-Cultural Perspectives on Women, Religion and Social Change*, pp. 211–20. New Delhi: Kali for Women.
Ghai, Anita. 2003. *(Dis)Embodied Form: Issues of Disabled Women*. New Delhi: Shakti Books, Har-Anand Publications.

Gottlieb, Roger S. 2002. 'The Tasks of Embodied Love: Moral Problems in Caring for Children with Disabilities', *Hypatia*, 17 (3): 225–36.

Green, Josephine M. 1994. 'Serum Screening for Down's Syndrome: Experiences of Obstetricians in England and Wales', *British Medical Journal*, 309: 769–72.

Hubbard, Ruth. 1997. 'Abortion and Disability: Who Should and Who Should Not Inhabit the World?', in Lennard J. Davis (ed.), *The Disability Studies Reader*, pp. 187–202. London: Routledge and Kegan Paul.

Human Genetics Alert. 2002. 'The Case against Sex Selection', December, http://www.hgalert.org/sexselection.PDF (accessed 27 January 2012).

Jennings, Bruce. 2000. 'Technology and the Genetic Imaginary: Prenatal Testing and the Construction of Disability', in Erik Parens and Adrienne Asch (eds), *Prenatal Testing and Disability Rights*, pp. 124–46. Washington, DC: Georgetown University Press.

Johri, Rachana. 1999. 'Cultural Conceptions of Maternal Attachment: The Case of the Girl Child'. Unpublished Ph.D. dissertation, Department of Psychology, University of Delhi.

———. 2001. 'The "Freedom" of Choices: A Discursive Analysis of Mothers' Narratives', *Psychological Studies*, 46 (3): 192–201.

Kent, Deborah. 2000. 'Somewhere a Mocking Bird', in Erik Parens and Adrienne Asch (eds), *Prenatal Testing and Disability Rights*, pp. 57–63. Washington, DC: Georgetown University Press.

Kingsley, Jason and Mitchell Levitz. 1994. *Count Us In: Growing Up With Down Syndrome*. New York: Harcourt Brace & Co.

McLaughlin, J. 2003. 'Screening Networks: Shared Agendas in Feminist and Disability Movement Challenges to Antenatal Screening and Abortion', *Disability and Society*, 18 (3): 297–310.

Menon, Nivedita. 2004. *Recovering Subversion: Feminist Politics Beyond the Law*. Delhi: Permanent Black.

Oliver, Michael. 1996. *Understanding Disability: From Theory to Practice*. London: Macmillan.

Padmanabhan, Manjula. 1993. 'Outlawing Sex Determination: No Solution', *The Pioneer*, 22 September.

Parens, Erik and Adrienne Asch. 2000. 'The Disability Rights Critique of Prenatal Genetic Testing: Reflections and Recommendations', in Erik Parens and Adrienne Asch (eds), *Prenatal Testing and Disability Rights*, pp. 3–43. Washington, DC: Georgetown University Press.

Parenting India. 2007. 'Ask Dr. Telang', March.

Patel, Tulsi (ed.). 2007. *Sex-selective Abortion in India: Gender, Society and New Reproductive Technologies*. New Delhi: SAGE Publications.

Patterson, Annette and Martha Satz. 2002. 'Genetic Counselling and the Disabled: Feminism Examines the Stance of Those Who Stand at the Gate', *Hypatia*, 17 (3): 118–42.

Rao, Mohan (ed.). 2004. *The Unheard Scream: Reproductive Health and Women's Lives in India*. New Delhi: Zubaan; Panos Institute.
Rapp, Rayna. 2000. *Testing Women, Testing the Fetus: The Social Impact of Amniocentesis in America*. New York; London: Routledge.
SAMA. 2006. 'ARTs and Women: Assistance in Reproduction or Subjugation?'. New Delhi: SAMA-Resource Group for Women and Health.
Saxton, Marsha. 1998. 'Disability Rights and Selective Abortion', in Ricky Solinger (ed.), *Abortion Wars: A Half Century of Struggle, 1950–2000*, pp. 374–93. Berkeley, CA: University of California Press.
Shakespeare, Tom. 1998. 'Choices and Rights: Eugenics, Genetics and Disability Equality', *Disability and Society*, 13 (5): 665–81.
Sharp, Keith and Sarah Earle. 2002. 'Feminism, Abortion and Disability: Irreconcilable Differences?', *Disability and Society*, 17 (2): 137–45.
Singer, Peter. 2000. 'Severe Impairment and the Beginning of Life', *American Philosophical Association Newsletter on Philosophy and Medicine*, 99 (2): 246–48.
Singh, Sanjana. 2005. 'Capturing the Inner Realities of Visually Impaired Girls: An Exploratory Study'. Unpublished thesis submitted as partial requirement of Bachelors in Psychology degree, Department of Psychology, Jesus and Mary College, University of Delhi.
Visaria, Leela, Vimala Ramachandran, Bela Ganatra and Shveta Kalyanwala. 2004. 'Abortion in India: Emerging Issues from Qualitative Studies', *Economic and Political Weekly*, 39 (46–47): 5044–52.
Welsch, Wolfgang. 1996. 'Aestheticization Processes: Phenomena, Distinctions and Prospects', *Theory, Culture and Society*, 13 (1): 1–24.

5

Burden of Caring: Families of the Disabled in Urban India

UPALI CHAKRAVARTI*

Care is defined with reference to activities and relationships in connection with categories of vulnerable groups such as the very young, the ill and the elderly (Daly and Rake 2003). Care is both a social exigency and a form of interpersonal relations. These authors also point out that although social policy is very important in determining the form and consequences of care, the political economy of care extends beyond public provisions. Even in societies in which the state provides many services, most care is provided informally in families and communities, and has invisible costs attached to it (ibid.).

It has been estimated that about 10 per cent of children have developmental disorders requiring long-term access to the healthcare system and extensive care into adulthood (Raina et al. 2004). The cerebral palsies are an example of such a condition which can serve as a prototype of childhood disability. Cerebral palsy (CP) presents itself in early childhood as a set of functional limitations stemming from disorders of the developing central nervous system. The current estimated incidence of CP is 2.0–2.5 per 1,000 live births. Although impaired motor function is the hallmark (manifesting as complex limitations in self-care activities such as feeding, dressing, bathing and mobility), many children also experience sensory and intellectual impairments. These limitations require long-term care far exceeding the usual needs of children and the expectations of their families. This can become burdensome, adversely impacting both the physical and psychological health of caregivers.

A number of factors in the recent past have contributed to assigning a bigger caregiving role to families. For instance, decline in family size and medical advancements (leading to increased survival rates of children with disabilities) have been accompanied by shifts in healthcare provision from institutional to ambulatory and community-based settings. This combination of factors leaves smaller family units shouldering the responsibility for care, highlighting the need for providing outside support to caregivers. Studies in the West have shown that those undergoing the unexpected 'career of caregiver' for a child with a disability (Boaz and Muller 1992; Hoyert and Seltzer 1992; Keith 1995; Pruchno, Patrick and Burant 1997) experience a stressful life situation that can have negative consequences if the healthcare and social service systems cannot assist such families. Becoming an informal caregiver is not typically chosen or planned; people do not envision being in a caregiver role when they project themselves into the future. Thus, the preparation for this role will often occur after it has already been acquired. In addition, an informal caregiver lacks rights, privileges and prerogatives that come with a formal career status. This is not a career recognised by society as a worthwhile pursuit. The role also differs from occupational careers in that movement along its pathway is driven not by personal ambition, but rather by the progression of the disorder and the functional dependencies it creates. Finally, a caregiving career cannot be entered into and left at will, especially by women who shoulder the major burden of caregiving responsibilities in the home. Indeed, the essay highlights how deeply gendered care for the disabled is within the household.

This chapter examines experiences of caregiving in families of young people with cerebral palsy through interviews with parents conducted during 2001–2 in Delhi. Informants were accessed through NGOs in the disability sector in Delhi, such as Action for Ability Development and Inclusion (AADI),[1] formerly the Spastics Society of Northern India. Semi-structured interviews were done around 10 open-ended themes, such as case history, initial reaction at onset of CP, treatment and other services accessed, family support and coping strategies, social interactions, economic adjustments, thoughts on the future of the disabled child, role of the government in the field of disability, and any other issue the interviewees desired to discuss. CP was chosen due to a number of reasons: it is the third highest cause of locomotor disability in India (NSSO 2002). CP imposes a range of limitations on the individual requiring long-term care far exceeding the usual needs of children as they develop, or the expectations of their families as they parent. The amount of physical care required is much greater than in other disabilities, with the level of care being directly proportionate to the severity of the condition. Children, whose parents were interviewed, were in the 14–25-years age group; and the families belonged to different socioeconomic groups.

Even though the narratives are derived from a small sample of the urban middle and lower middle classes, a range of issues emerge that are relevant to all households having a disabled member, especially in the lower income groups. This snapshot view of family caregiving and disability leads one to speculate on the scenario in different parts of India, among diverse population groups, such as agricultural workers, daily wage earners, manual labourers, domestic workers and migrant population, who would not have access to the most basic facilities for diagnosis and treatment.

Narrativising Caregiving

Narrative 1: 'Time seems endless'

Ramesh[2] is the mother of two boys having cerebral palsy and mental retardation. Sumit is 21-years-old and also suffers from speech and hearing impairment. He is bedridden. Dheeraj is 15-years-old, and in addition to speech impairment, he also gets convulsions. He needs constant monitoring as he is hyperactive and unsteady on his feet. The family lives in a small room that serves as a tailoring shop and living quarters. Ramesh's husband has poor vision; he attends mostly to outside work like purchasing threads and beads in connection with the family's tailoring work. Looking after the two boys, doing housework and attending to customers ensure that Ramesh's day is packed from 5 a.m. to midnight. The couple manages to earn ₹2,000 to ₹3,000 per month, of which ₹600 is spent on medication for the children. Sumit and Dheeraj had been taken to AADI and prescribed physical therapy, but due to paucity of finances, absence of familial and social support, and a general feeling of hopelessness, the couple has not been regular with the physical regime.

Reflecting on her life, Ramesh regrets the loss of her earlier physical vigour and optimism. She says, 'One is growing older, and I am no longer physically fit to deal with the situation. I am also anxious about the future.'

In the recent past, her anxiety reached such a peak that she had to consult a doctor, who told her she had to go out of the house for at least half an hour during the day in order to retain her 'mental balance'. Ramesh fought the guilt of leaving her children unattended as she visited a neighbour or went shopping in compliance with the doctor's advice. After one month, the feelings of being boxed into an existence with no life outside of her two disabled children and a financially troublesome existence diminished. Nonetheless, she still feels resentful of her situation — if only she were more qualified to get a proper job; if she had only known the consequences of getting married within the same family; and if only she could shift out of this cramped space and go back to her village.

Ramesh is tired of caring for two invalid children, crippled by financial worries and consumed by anxiety about her own and her children's future. Provision of medical and palliative services by the government would have made a crucial difference in the initial years; and such services could still make a difference. But she has no expectations from the government or from any organisation.

Narrative 2: 'No miracle can happen'

Surinder is a 21-year-old man with profound cerebral palsy. He lives with his parents and a younger brother. He is homebound and totally dependent on help from others for his daily needs and mobility. Surinder's mother had contracted malaria in the eighth or ninth month of her pregnancy for which she was taken to a nearby government health centre in a village in Haryana. The family attributes Surinder's affliction to the treatment given by the doctor there. Describing their reaction upon learning that their child was disabled, Surinder's father says, 'Initially, we were not depressed, for we didn't realise it would be a lifelong thing.'

When they took him for immunisation, the doctors in a children's hospital informed them that something was seriously wrong with Surinder, and that a lot of exercises had to be done with him. Surinder's father said he tried not to waste time being emotionally overwhelmed by the situation, and instead focused on helping his son do the exercises, which was the only treatment that would enable him to become minimally physically self-reliant. A physiotherapist was hired for this purpose. However, despite the regular regime of exercises, there was no significant improvement in his condition. Surinder's mother had emotional outbursts and spells of crying. As she was employed, both her natal and marital families provided support in caring for Surinder.

The parents acknowledge the help provided to them by AADI in the initial years. They were counselled not to expect a miracle through which their child would become 'normal'. This counselling made them stop looking for a cure, which does not mean that they stopped hoping for one. They have struggled over the years to get Surinder to walk, talk, eat, dress, and use the toilet on his own. However, now, at the age of 21 years, he can only speak a few words. The regular exercise routine notwithstanding, he cannot walk on his own and needs to be carried. His father can no longer carry him because Surinder is too heavy. Even though he has been toilet-trained, he still needs someone to feed and dress him. Surinder is also on medication for convulsions.

Until a few years ago, Surinder went to the AADI School. However, since he was incapable of benefitting from the vocational training offered, the school asked his parents to remove him in order to make place for another child who could be trained. Now, Surinder is left without a daily routine and, more importantly, has no interaction with the outside world. This is a great blow to him, because he really enjoyed going to school. His parents have now enrolled him in a nearby crèche, where he goes for a few hours during the day — it is the only source of contact with the outside world, which he eagerly looks forward to.

After years of shifting from one rented accommodation to another, the family has purchased a house of their own. Explaining the reasons behind this decision, Surinder's father says:

> We had difficulties in finding accommodation with such a child. Initially, the house would be rented on sympathetic grounds, but then we would face humiliating remarks. We have tolerated so many things ... At least, here, we don't have to bear with that torture.

During the past five years, Surinder's parents have undergone spells of ill-health themselves. His father developed severe back pain, rendering him incapable of lifting his son onto his wheelchair. Next, his mother was diagnosed with breast cancer. It was a trying period for the family when his mother had to go for chemotherapy and his father was bedridden for a month. Luckily, there was the support of the extended family to help them tide over this crisis.

When asked how they handle feelings of helplessness and depression, Surinder's mother says:

> I can't explain it to you, but at such times God gives us some inner strength. So, with God's grace, and with the help of some of our relatives and some people in my office, we have overcome difficult times.

Similarly, her husband says, 'We are God-fearing people. As difficulties come, solutions or ways to handle them also emerge.'

This is not to say that they are not anxious about the future. Surinder's mother, in particular, experiences a lot of anxiety regarding the fate of their son after their death. His parents express the hope that his younger brother, who is very fond of Surinder, would look after him. But they wonder how he would manage his own life if he has to also look after his disabled brother. Furthermore, they are of the opinion that no one can look after a disabled child as well as his parents can.

Surinder's condition has restricted the family's spatial mobility and social life. Physical barriers, the need to take Surinder in a wheelchair and the absence of disabled-friendly toilets, as also the negative reactions of people to their son, have led the family to lead a more sequestered life.

Narrative 3: 'She, too, has the right to live'

Living in a big house in one of the lanes of a wholesale market in Delhi is Anjana. She is 25-years-old, and has four siblings. Madhu, her mother, is a widow who lives in her marital house. Anjana has severe CP — she is dependent on help from others for her daily needs. Her speech is also severely affected. She uses a wheelchair that is wheeled by an attendant. Till a couple of years ago, she was a student at the AADI School. However, given her highly dependent status and inability to acquire any vocational skills, the school asked her mother to withdraw her admission. Like Surinder, she now goes to a crèche for disabled children run by the Railway Hospital. This is a way of ensuring she is in a safe environment while her mother goes out to work.

For Madhu, life has not been easy bringing up four children, especially after the death of her husband. Whenever the family faced a lot of financial hardship, Madhu's parents have helped her in bringing up the children.

Anjana is Madhu's second daughter. As the first child was a girl, Madhu's mother-in-law wanted to make sure that the second child was a son. She brought Madhu some medicines, claiming they would ensure the birth of a son. Initially, Madhu resisted taking them but, eventually, gave in due to family pressure. Even though she had a normal hospital delivery, Anjana got fever for 10 days soon after birth. After treatment by a local doctor, she was taken to the Kalawati Saran Children's Hospital.[3] Pneumonia was diagnosed and hospitalisation advised. Having heard horror stories about hospitals, combined with superstitious beliefs about children dying there, the family decided to take her to another doctor near their home. When they went to purchase the medicines prescribed by the neighbourhood doctor, the chemist had remarked, 'Such a heavy dose for a small baby is not right.' The parents, however, gave her the medicine, and within two days she was much better.

When the family noticed that Anjana could not hold her head up even by the fourth month, they took her to yet another local doctor, who told the parents that had they delayed any longer in getting her medical attention, the chances of her survival would have been bleak. He was the first person to explain Anjana's condition to them. He said, 'Whatever she does will be delayed, and progress is going to be very slow.'

Time went by, but Anjana could neither sit nor walk on her own. Her parents again took her to the Kalawati Saran Children's Hospital, where a special chair was made for her. Madhu was taught some exercises to do with her daughter. After seeing an advertisement, Madhu took her daughter to AADI when she was 2 years old. Once Madhu was told about the nature of Anjana's disability, and her interaction with the AADI staff and parents grew, she found the strength to cope and never visited any other doctor.

She shares her anxiety about Anjana's future with her sister, but never in front of Anjana. Sometimes, she is filled with pity for her daughter and pain at the thought of the bleak future that may await her. However, there have been events which have helped her develop a new perspective on the situation. For instance, one day soon after her husband's death, as Anjana sat in her wheelchair near the front door, a neighbour passed by and said, 'It is not the father who should have gone; it would have been better if something had happened to this girl instead.'

This upset Madhu terribly. Commenting on this event, she says, 'My daughter has also come into the world like everyone else; doesn't she, too, have the right to live?'

Madhu realises that Anjana's situation is relatively much better than that of many disabled persons. She hopes that her other children will look after their sister after her death. Madhu is a member of an association of parents, which plans to set up independent accommodation for disabled persons.[4] However, she still hopes that her children will take the major responsibility, because she feels it is eventually only the family that can provide the protection and love needed by a disabled person.

According to Madhu, Anjana is a very sensitive and perceptive young woman. She is not demanding or fussy and tries to manage things for herself as far as possible. When she was young, she used to wave her hands and bang them against the wall, but now she is calmer. Her family has not pampered her — she has been treated at par with her siblings, and scolded and praised on the basis of her behaviour. The family has also never tried to conceal Anjana's condition — they always take her with them wherever they go; she is an integral part of the family and they are proud to have her.

Madhu laments that even 50 years after independence, the government has not done anything for the disabled; and she does not expect any substantial improvement in the future. However, she feels that NGOs have a crucial role to play in disseminating information and providing services. Her critique of the NGOs in the disability sector is that their focus is on childhood services — which are essential — but they need to also develop programmes for disabled adults and their families.

Although Madhu has come to accept Anjana as she is, she is plagued by anxiety about her future. Past incidents of sexual harassment and abuse exacerbate her worries. There was a male helper at AADI, who would touch Anjana inappropriately. She told her siblings about it, but they thought she was just trying to seek attention and did not believe her. When she told her mother about it, Madhu informed the teachers. Subsequently, the helper was dismissed. Similarly, in another incident, a boy in the neighbourhood had misbehaved with Anjana. Whenever this boy visited their home, Anjana would start yelling and asking him to leave. When Madhu tried to reassure her about his good intentions, she protested violently. Later, she told her mother how he had on one occasion touched her in a bad way, when she was sitting outside in the lane. It is such instances of possible abuse in the future which worry Madhu.

Anjana's case highlights the lack of knowledge about disabilities like CP among laypersons as well as among the different care providers accessed by families a few decades ago. Madhu feels that there is now wider awareness about disability and general childcare. Nowadays, disability campaigns emphasise that it is not something to be hidden, ashamed of, or be ostracised for by society. Families are also now aware that they are not alone. For instance, initially, Madhu just could not sit through the parents' workshops at AADI. The moment the parents started talking about their problems, she would have tears in her eyes and would want to walk out. She felt so helpless and incapable of coping with Anjana's condition. 'But see the situation today,' she remarks. 'Now I go about helping and explaining to other parents, boosting their confidence to handle the situation.'

Narrative 4: 'Dedicating oneself to service (*seva*)'

Manav is a single child in a nuclear family. He was born through normal delivery in a hospital in Panipat, in the state of Haryana. When he was about a year old, the family went on a pilgrimage to the city of Haridwar, in Uttar Pradesh. Upon their return to Panipat, Manav had high fever and was unconscious for two days. They took him to a private clinic and then to Delhi after a fortnight. Although the fever subsided, Manav seemed to have forgotten how to sit, stand and walk. The doctors told the family that it might be a case of encephalitis. They were not given any other information, and so they returned to Panipat. However, the parents grew alarmed when Manav did not start walking even by the age of four. They took him to the Kalawati Saran Children's Hospital in New Delhi. It was there that they were informed that there was no medical treatment or cure for Manav's condition, and that he should be admitted to a special school. So, the family shifted permanently to Delhi.

Now, at the age of 21 years, Manav is a tall, lanky young man with a rigid gait, stiff arms and fingers. He has an enlarged tongue due to which his mouth does not close properly, and he drools. Although he is unable to learn any vocational skills at the AADI School, he still attends classes there because his mother wants to ensure a daily routine for him. Otherwise, left at home, he develops behaviour problems.

Describing their initial reaction, his mother says, 'We have left our life's boat in God's hands, and wherever He wishes to take us with Manav, we are willing to go.'

She says she has 'sacrificed' her ambitions to look after him. She had wanted to be a teacher, but she gave that up in order to do *seva* for (serve) her child. In the initial years, she felt very frustrated, not only because of the high level of care required, but also due to anxiety about the future. But over time, religion has helped her come to terms with the situation. As she puts it, 'Now we are in God's hands; so there is nothing to be upset about.'

She adds that even if she has to look after '10 such children', she is willing to do so, as she has developed much patience over time.

Her husband also went through great trauma in coping with their situation in the initial years. Manav's mother narrates an incident to illustrate this. When one of his friends took Manav's father to a female seer and she asked him what he wanted, he said, 'I have not come to ask for anything, I have only come to ask for strength to deal with my *dukh* [misfortune].'

This response surprised the priestess, as she was used to addressing people's material wishes and/or discoursing on the futility of material possessions for salvation. The couple has become very spiritual-minded over time, and they have taken a *diksha* (vow) to serve their child and any such child who comes their way.

Although the extended family did not display any negative feelings towards Manav, the couple was pressurised to have another child. They, however, decided against it and have no regrets. They only want to look after Manav. His mother reasons that if they had a second child who was not disabled, not only would their attention have been divided, but they might have given preferential treatment to the latter, and had greater expectations from him/her. Furthermore, she says that if there are no expectations, there is no cause to be unhappy. She explains, 'From him [Manav], we have no expectations and he is everything for us; and we are not dissatisfied with life.'

Manav's parents are not disturbed by the pity shown by others. As his mother explains, 'Once the parents have accepted their situation, there is nothing that can hurt them or weaken their determination to look after their child. When parents themselves are disappointed with what they have, it is then that what others say hurts them.'

Manav's parents are of the opinion that the disabled are not a priority of the government. Manav's mother wants the government to ensure that doctors do not neglect episodes of minor illnesses such as colds and sore throats, because they might be manifestations of more serious diseases which could cause lifelong disability. Timely diagnosis and medication can make a world of difference. Before Manav became disabled, they viewed disability as the result of accidents, if not congenital in rare cases. They feel no anger towards the doctors for Manav's condition any more. His mother sums it up tersely, 'What has to happen has happened.'

Even though the parents are resigned to their fate, the anxiety uppermost in their minds is who will look after Manav after their death. They hope and pray that some relative will take on that responsibility. When the anxiety becomes overpowering, it leads the mother to wish that the three of them should die together. She feels that since looking after such a person is considered *ganda kaam* (filthy work) by society, the parents are the best caregivers.

Narrative 5: 'There was no choice but to lock her up'

Umul, a 21-year-old woman with cerebral palsy, lives and studies in Chennai. Her parents and younger brother live in Bangalore. When Umul was very young, her mother (who had a job) would take her to the hospital for exercises every day. But once she had exhausted all her leave, the exercises had to be discontinued. Since both parents were employed, her mother had no option but to lock Umul in the house during the day. The enforced immobility resulted in her legs getting locked.[5]

When the parents later took Umul to a *unani*[6] hospital, the doctor recommended that the mother should leave her job, and stay at home to do the exercises, if she wanted her daughter's condition to improve. It was not possible to follow this advice because the family was in debt. The stress due to the family's dire financial situation resulted in Umul's father suffering a heart attack and losing his job. Since then, he has not been able to do any strenuous work. Fortunately, Umul's mother continued to hold her job as a schoolteacher even though the wages were very low. In search of better employment opportunities, her father shifted to Bangalore from Chennai. Despite a tight financial situation, they managed to procure medicines for their daughter. Umul's mother would commute regularly between Chennai and Bangalore by train, carrying her 8-year-old daughter in her arms because they could not afford a wheelchair. In Chennai, she learnt about the Spastics Society of India, Tamil Nadu, and admitted Umul there. However, since the expenditure in running two households was so high, her mother resigned from her job within two years, without completing the term of service that would have rendered her eligible for a pension, and moved permanently to Bangalore. Umul started attending the vocational training programme at the Spastics Society of Karnataka, in Bangalore, where she learned stitching and embroidery. But Umul was not satisfied — she had other aspirations. When in Chennai to attend a wedding, she tried to contact the Spastics Society of India, Tamil Nadu. It was after much difficulty in obtaining a contact number that she finally managed to meet the Director. She expressed her intense desire to make something of her life and become independent. The Director asked her parents to allow Umul to undergo an independent living programme for three months. Finding that Umul had an aptitude for academics, she was admitted to the open school. Her parents said to the functionaries of the society, 'She is your child — do as you like and make her someone worthy. We don't have the resources to do it.'

Since then, Umul has been living in the Spastics Society premises in Chennai and pursuing her studies through the open school. She wants to become a lawyer and fight for the rights of the disabled.

Caring and Caregiving

When parents learn that their child has a disability or chronic illness, they begin a journey that is filled with strong emotions, difficult choices, interactions with many professionals, and an ongoing need for information and services. The narratives show that the burden of caring falls on the family, and within the family, more specifically on the mother. This continuous responsibility, in the absence of any formal support networks, has many negative consequences for caregivers, including the suppression of feelings such as not wanting to do it anymore. For instance, even though Ramesh's husband is supportive, he doesn't actually do the exercises with his two disabled sons because, seeing no apparent improvement in their condition, he feels that there is 'no point'. Although Ramesh also has similar feelings, she still goes ahead with the regime reasoning that 'it is our duty'. As a woman and a mother, the option of not doing so does not arise. Similarly Manav's mother gave up her aspirations to work, since she thought it would result in her disabled child being neglected. She has internalised her commitment to do *seva* for (serve) her son, to the extent that she is willing to look after '10 such children'.

Whenever support from the extended family is available, it is a tremendous help, especially during difficult times. Interestingly, it is usually the maternal grandmother or aunt who gets involved in caregiving. It is women who substitute for each other's labour out of affection and a sense of responsibility. In Madhu's case, however, there has been no support from either the natal or marital families. Families of interviewees fortunate enough to get ongoing support from AADI highlight the urgent need for outside support services. The model of family support or family-like caring is an aspect of societies and states that have few institutional facilities. As Gillian Dalley writes: '... in societies, which do not have formal segregated care systems, the principal structure of kinship has to provide the basis for caring' (1998: 92).

In India, institutional care is almost totally absent. So when the responsibility for providing care falls on 'society', the form of care adopted is either modelled closely on the family, or falls upon individual families directly.

In the absence of support services, the hardship families have to undergo is enormous. They are often not in a position to access outside help due to several reasons. First, they face financial constraints. Second, even though it is specialised work, it is difficult to find persons willing to take on care work, because it is not only underpaid but also considered menial and degrading. Manav's mother puts it aptly when she describes it as '*ganda kaam*'. Even in families where finances are not a constraint, as in Surinder's case, the service is unreliable, and the turnover of helpers is very high.

In the absence of support, the mother has to make a difficult choice between working and caring. For instance, Umul's mother had to take up work in order to ensure the basic survival of the family, and she could only do this by locking Umul inside the house. This had the adverse effect of Umul's legs getting locked,[7] neutralising the mother's efforts of doing daily exercises with her before leaving for work. This Hobson's choice situation was not helped by the doctor's callous query, 'Do you want your daughter or your job?' The mother was forced to handle her feelings of guilt and the financial imperative to work on her own. In the absence of familial support, Manav's mother gave up her dream of becoming a teacher, because she felt that her child's needs were more important than her own desire for independence and creativity.

Ramesh's situation is even more poignant because she has to look after not one, but two disabled children. The parents have to balance the double burden of caregiving with earning a living. Their only support, Ramesh's mother, can help now and then, but only for limited periods, because she is aged and requires support herself. She took Ramesh's youngest non-disabled child to the village when he was small, and still visits whenever possible to help her daughter look after the other children. The limited availability of family support to the primary caregivers is heavily tilted in the direction of the women's natal family, something that cuts across classes. Even in Anjana's case, it was the maternal grandmother who provided financial support in the initial years after her daughter became a widow. While concern for the daughter is an important factor, a more important reason for the involvement of the natal kin may be her ongoing stigmatisation in her marital home for bearing a disabled child.

According to Ms Naidu (Chakravarti 2002),[8] the disabled child's mother has stronger alliances with her natal family, with her mother or sister offering substantial assistance in caregiving. The husband's family rarely provides any support, because they think 'the problem has come from the mother's side'. Consequently, organisations in the disability sector, like AADI, give a lot of information to the mother who undergoes a transformation in personality and behaviour. For example, she learns to go to the institution by bus and to handle people. Through such learning experiences, her world expands. However, one does not find the same thing happening with the fathers. Given the nature of male socialisation, they are left with no outlet to vent their anger and grief. Therefore, as the woman becomes more capable of managing her disabled child, she becomes more independent, challenging normative constructions of wifehood and motherhood. Such mothers develop good problem-solving skills and, thus, demystify disability (ibid.). What needs to be facilitated is the incorporation of the husband into caregiving in a cultural context in which the husband–wife roles are rigidly structured. So, while the mother is becoming more 'empowered', the question is: will she succeed in educating the husband? Ms Naidu feels that over time, both parents need to restructure the way they look at disability and caregiving.

Another interesting observation emerging from the narratives is that despite the small number of organisations for the disabled in existence two to three decades ago, the services offered, especially emotional support, are perceived to have been tremendous by disabled persons and their families who had the opportunity to access them. Even though the number of such organisations has grown over the years, their services have not diversified. The new organisations also continue to provide the same basic services as AADI and other organisations when they started their programmes several decades ago. Even though these organisations now have disabled adults and acknowledge their changing needs, they have not been able to develop support services to address the educational, vocational, psychological and social needs of this group and their families. This is evident from the refrain of parents that children with special needs require opportunities for social interaction and activities to keep them occupied. The parents are caught in a dilemma: they realise that at some point their wards have to make way for other disabled children to avail of the services of the organisations in a situation of resource constraint, but they also want the organisations to recognise that it is not possible for them to address all the needs of their adult offspring on their own. They are exhausted by the ongoing physical care and apprehensions for the child's future. Since organisations like AADI have played a critical role in supporting them in the initial difficult years of bringing up the child, they are not only dependent on the organisations for concrete medical and social assistance, but also have high expectations from them. Consequently, there is a sense of betrayal manifested in the lament that 'the organisation is not doing much for the children now'. Indeed, the question arises whether institutions can cater to the multiple felt needs of disabled persons and their families. Given the meagre facilities in the disability sector, there is a long way to go as far as meeting all the felt needs of this marginalised group is concerned.

Long-term institutional care, especially for severely disabled persons, has not been seriously considered in the Indian context. Consequently, support services provided by institutions mainly focus on prevention and early detection of disability and training of professionals. The Western model of the 'modern' institution, which can take over the caring functions performed by the family, has not been considered. However, the case of Erwadi[9] and the rural study of 41 villages in Andhra Pradesh (Mander 2002) highlight the need for institutional support for long-term care, especially of severely disabled persons. Mander shows how, in rural Andhra Pradesh, the disabled are left without food and care for long periods as families go out to labour. Erwadi brings out the indigenous variant of the institutional solution to care linking it to faith and traditional healing, a system existing outside of the state structure. This leads us to think about locating such issues as the rights of the disabled, care and caregiving in a broader political economy and cultural context. Neither from the narratives of disabled persons and their families nor from the secondary writing on disability in India do we get a picture of either the state or alternative traditional structures providing any feasible, humane and acceptable way of caregiving.

The gendered nature of caregiving is also implicit in the narratives. Although from the parents' responses it appears that both the mother and father are equally involved, in most cases, the mother is a housewife or has sacrificed her professional ambition to devote herself full-time to caregiving. In other instances, financial considerations compel the mother to engage in both earning a livelihood and looking after her disabled child. The mother, in the majority of cases, is the principal caregiver. Feminists have advocated for a change in social attitudes, drawing attention to the need to recognise that caring is not the duty or the prerogative of women alone.[10]

The narratives also underscore the limited family resources and the non-existence of wider support systems for the care of disabled persons. One important issue they highlight is that it is not just medical treatment and physical care that persons with disabilities need, but what is equally imperative is a range of support services to be provided to their families to help them cope. The family burden is not just financial in nature — as in the case of Surinder, money was not a constraining factor, yet reliable help was scarce.

Community, Family and Gender

The organisation of caring in a given society is closely linked to the ways in which it organises the general system of social relations.

According to Gillian Dalley (1998), under normal circumstances, the responsibility for caring functions in relation to child rearing and servicing of adult family members falls upon women. They are also expected in 'extra-normal' circumstances to care for the chronically dependent, namely, the disabled and elderly. In traditional societies with limited division of labour, dependency is managed collectively in a social context in which the public–private dichotomy is blurred. What has been termed as the social construction of dependency is of a different order in capitalist societies. In the latter case, those who cannot engage in productive work due to physical or mental impairment, or those who have passed the age limit imposed by society to mark the end of working life, automatically become dependent either on the State or on the family. Dalley argues that their dependency is not intrinsic to their physical or chronological condition; instead they have been 'socially constructed' as dependent, because they are arbitrarily ruled out from being party to the contract which non-dependent individuals are able, or obliged, to enter into with society. Systems of support and care may vary according to the degree to which the confinement of the disabled is compounded by the social constraints of marginalisation and stigmatisation, or mitigated by the social supports of integration. In societies that do not have formal segregated care systems, the principal structure of kinship provides the basis for caring. In situations where such a society takes on the responsibility for providing formal care, the form of care adopted has tended to be modelled closely on the family.

Analysing the meaning of caring from the perspective of affect, Dalley states that a distinction can be made between 'caring for' and 'caring about' (ibid.: 8). The first is to do with the tasks of tending to another person; the second is to do with the feelings for another person (Parker and Graham, cited in Dalley 1998: 8). Caring for and caring about are deemed to form a unitary, integral part of a woman's nature. In the 'extra-normal' situation of a child being chronically dependent beyond the definition of dependency dictated by its age — through sickness and handicap — the mother automatically extends, and is expected to extend her 'caring for' function. Just as the affective links which form at birth are tied into the mechanical links of servicing and maintenance in the case of healthy children, the same affective links in the case of disabled and chronically dependent family members get tied to the servicing and maintenance functions. In the public sphere, too, the same forces are at work — women go into the caring occupations because their 'natures', and their intertwined capacities for caring for and caring about, are thought to suit them well for those types of jobs.

The mixing of the caring dimensions (for and about) has implications for both parties in the caring relationship. Love, in this context, often becomes fractured or distorted by feelings of obligation, burden and frustration. But the prevailing ethos of family-based care suggests that normal tasks are being performed, that roles enacted are straightforward, expected and unproblematic. Evidence suggests that the boundaries of obligation and willingness are indeed carefully delimited, and the willingness to care is highly relational and context-specific. As long as a disabled daughter or son is a child, caring falls within the normal parameters (even though it may be arduous) and, therefore, is acceptable. Once the child becomes an adult, tensions in the caring relationship may develop — love, obligation, guilt, dislike may all be intermingled.

The ambivalence frequently felt by those involved in caring is further complicated by public discourses, which insist that there can be no separation between caring for and caring about. Official and lay perspectives on community care all assert the conjunction of the two, but in reality this conjunction is enacted in gendered ways with particular consequences for women. The gender dimension of caring, in which the man is assumed to be the provider and the woman the carer, is considered a natural given, but is actually a social fact. Studies have shown that for most women, especially working-class women, the gendered model of caring, drawing upon women's assumed natural propensity to care results in the triple burden — child rearing, housework and wage labour. Land and Rose have discussed womanhood in the context of altruism (ibid.: 17). They define the personal servicing that women do — caring for and caring about — as *compulsory altruism*, which encapsulates both the self-sacrifice and selflessness involved, and the prescriptive expectations of society that women shall perform that role. They show how social policies have been built on the same assumptions — to such an extent that the altruism, which women come to see as a natural part of their character, becomes compulsory. These policies could not be implemented if women declined to be altruistic.

Both Eva Feder Kittay (2001) and Fiona Williams (2004) see the work of caring for dependants at home as a crucial issue affecting the social inequality of women. Holding that women are often subtly coerced by social norms into shouldering the burden of caring for a dependant, Williams argues that any solution to the problem would have to involve two fundamental shifts (ibid.). One is the reallocation of domestic responsibilities between men and women in the home. The second is a greater role of the State. The State may lighten the burden of people who care for dependants through a wide range of policies.

Conclusion

Disability is socially constructed, but it is largely perceived as an individual problem even by policymakers, medical professionals and disability rights activists. This is largely due to the fact that stigma and charity still continue to structure the way disability is viewed. But as the narratives in this essay show, stigma is only one element of the larger political economic context that contributes to the social construction of the experience of disability.

Although people have to deal with disability at an individual level, the suffering is not simply an individual experience; it is inter-subjective largely enacted in the space of families as Arthur Kleinman et al. (1995) has pointed out. The lack of medical knowledge, difficulties in accessing health services, acquiring aids and appliances, and developing skills for training (that would enhance self-help skills) combine to diminish the quality of life of disabled persons and their families. In the absence of opportunities for developing the social, psychological, educational and employment potential of disabled persons, the need for care in the widest sense of the term creates enormous suffering for those affected by disability.

Even in the case of those disabled persons for whom economic factors are not a major constraint, the political economy determines the way disability is perceived. For example, when a person, especially a man, becomes disabled in old age, he is not undervalued because he is judged by the fact that at one time he was a productive individual. The capacity to be productive, or its absence, is a structural factor that configures the understanding of disability. The fact that a man disabled in later years is not marginalised, as a disabled child is from the beginning of life, tells us something about the need to rethink the relationship between the individual and the social, and between disability and society.

To sum up, unlike the women's movement which has managed to highlight the need for an expanded understanding of work to include housework and care work, the disability movement is still struggling to get recognition for disabled persons as citizens, for caring needs of families and for formulation of social policies that respond to their distinctive experiences. Disability continues to be seen as a burden that must be borne by the family with fortitude and patience. It is constructed as a situation where 'suffering' is inevitable. As Anita Ghai, a prominent feminist disability scholar and activist in Delhi noted, families are told by counsellors that the way to deal with adversity is to 'tough it out', that is, if you can avoid showing the pain, then you have been stoic and dealt with the problem 'competently' (cited in Chakravarti 2002). The relationship between the State, society and family in the context of disability is also yet to be adequately conceptualised. The political economy affects us all, whether we recognise it or not. And until then:

> Across our countryside, shrouded from our collective view and conscience, people with disability and their care-givers somehow are living out their lives, surviving, but only just, most often at the precipice of dark despair. It is probably only when they organise into a social and political collective voice . . . that an uncaring state and society will finally be forced to act (Mander 2002).

Notes

* This essay first appeared in the *Indian Journal of Gender Studies*, 15 (2): 341–63, 2008, New Delhi: SAGE Publications. Editorial changes have

been made to the original published chapter with permission from the Centre for Women's Development Studies, New Delhi.
1. AADI was formed in 1978 and is located in New Delhi. The word 'aadi' means 'beginning' in Sanskrit.
2. Pseudonyms have been used to protect the identity of informants.
3. A government hospital located in Central Delhi.
4. AADI has facilitated the formation of a parents' support group. One of its activities is building a respite-cum-residential complex where disabled adults can live as a community, especially after their parents' death.
5. In any coordinated movement, some muscles relax while others contract. Spasticity occurs when this coordination is impaired and too many muscles contract at the same time. It can cause a leg to 'lock' and refuse to bend.
6. The Unani system of medicine, which owes its origin to Greece, was introduced in India by the Arabs. An outstanding physician and scholar of Unani medicine, Hakim Ajmal Khan (1868–1927) championed the cause of the Unani system in India.
7. Refer to $n5$.
8. Ms. Naidu was one of the author's informants. She is an activist in the disability sector, and has worked with the Spastics Society of Tamil Nadu in their community rehabilitation programme.
9. The reference is to the burning to death of 28 inmates in a private mental asylum in Tamil Nadu in 2001.The inmates of the Erwadi Dargah had been chained to their beds and, hence, could not escape the flames that engulfed their thatched huts. Their cries for help were ignored by the asylum owners, who mistook them for the usual outbursts of the mentally ill. The Supreme Court took suo motu cognisance of this horrific incident and called for a nationwide review of treatment facilities for the mentally ill, both in the public and private sectors.
10. An interesting observation on the gendered nature of caring was provided by the father of a young adult with Down's syndrome. Presenting the flip side of the father's peripheral role in caring, he felt that through the 'process of daily routine, caregiving, mothers were able to give vent to their emotional distress and emerged more resilient in crisis situations'. By contrast, fathers, bound by stereotypes of masculinity that excluded them from participating in routine care, ended up suffering from depression, because they had no cathartic release for their pent-up emotions following care work.

References

Boaz, Rachel F. and Charlotte F. Muller. 1992. 'Paid Work and Unpaid Help by Caregivers of the Disabled and Frail Elders', *Medical Care*, 30 (2): 149–58.

Chakravarti, Upali. 2002. 'Is Suffering Inevitable? State, Society and Disability'. Unpublished M.Phil. thesis, Centre for Community Health and Social Medicine, Jawaharlal Nehru University, New Delhi.

Daly, Mary and Katherine Rake. 2003. *Gender and the Welfare State: Care, Work and Welfare in Europe and the USA*. Cambridge: Polity Press.

Dalley, Gillian. 1998. *Ideologies of Caring: Rethinking Community and Collectivism*. London: Macmillan.

Hoyert, Donna L. and Marsha Mallick Seltzer. 1992. 'Factors Related to the Well-Being and Life Activities of Family Caregivers', *Family Relations*, 41 (1): 74–81.

Keith, Carolyn. 1995. 'Family Caregiving Systems: Models, Resources and Values', *Journal of Marriage and the Family*, 57 (1): 179–89.

Kittay, Eva Feder. 2001. 'From Welfare to a Public Ethic of Care', in Nancy J. Hirschmann and Ulrike Liebert (eds), *Women and Welfare: Theory and Practice in the United States and Europe*, pp. 38–64. New Brunswick: Rutgers University Press.

Kleinman, Arthur, Wen-Zhi Wang, Shi-Chou Li, Xue-Ming Cheng, Xiu-Ying Dai, Kun-Tun Li and Joan Kleinman. 1995. 'The Social Course of Epilepsy: Chronic Illness as Social Experience in Interior China', *Social Science and Medicine*, 40 (10): 1319–30.

Mander, Harsh. 2002. 'At the Precipice of Despair'. *Frontline*, 19 (15), July–August, http://www.frontlineonnet.com/fline/fl1915/19151100.htm (accessed 30 October 2007).

National Sample Survey Organisation (NSSO). 2002. 'Disabled Persons in India'. Report No. 485. New Delhi: Government of India.

Pruchno, Rachel, Julie Hicks Patrick, Christopher J. Burant. 1997. 'African American and White Mothers of Adults with Chronic Disabilities: Caregiving Burden and Satisfaction', *Family Relations*, 46 (4): 335–46.

Raina, Parminder, Maureen O'Donnell, Heidi Schwellnus, Peter Rosenbaum, Gillian King, Jamie Brehaut, Dianne Russell, Marilyn Swinton, Susanne King, Micheline Wong, Stephen D. Walter and Ellen Wood. 2004. 'Caregiving Process and Caregiver Burden: Conceptual Models to Guide Research and Practice', *BioMed Central*, 4: 1, 14 January, http://www.pubmedcentral.nih.gov/articlerender.fcgi?artid=331415 (accessed 30 October 2007).

Williams, Fiona. 2004. *Rethinking Families*. London: Calouste Gulbenkian Foundation.

6

Exploring Constructs of Intellectual Disability and Personhood in Haryana and Delhi

NILIKA MEHROTRA AND SHUBHANGI VAIDYA*

Disability, Personhood and Gender

Disability is a universal human experience that has been defined in a number of ways. The World Health Organisation subsumes the diffuse, unspecified concept of disability under three broad categories, namely, impairment, disability and handicap (WHO 1980). Impairment refers to damage or loss of physiological, psychological or anatomical structure or function, for example, loss of hearing or vision, deformity of limbs, etc. Disability is specified as the functional limitations in performing daily activities that are age- and gender-appropriate. Thus, we may speak of communication, locomotor and cognitive disabilities. Handicaps connote the social disadvantages faced by individuals with impairments and disabilities, the loss or limitation of opportunities to take part in the life of the community. Thus, impairment, disability and handicap constitute a tridimensional set that marks the individual experiences of persons with significant physical and/or psychological limitations.

Moving beyond the physical malfunctions, deficiencies and disease paradigms promoted by the WHO, social scientists have highlighted socio-historical and cultural dimensions of disability. For instance, Benedicte Ingstad (1995) has focused on alterations in kinship expectations and domestic duties, Henri-Jacques Stiker (2000) has brought attention to circumscribed economic and productive roles, and Erving Goffman (1963) has examined social and community responses and obligations. This wide range of meanings underscores the multiple implications and understandings of the lived experience of disability, covering actual bodily experiences, cultural constructions and social expectations. Goffman's sociological analysis of stigma is frequently cited as foundational in theorising disability (ibid.). According to him, the experience of disability is marked by an ongoing struggle to keep at bay the personal discreditations and devaluations that constantly assail the self of the person with impairment. If the individual is unable to manage stigma successfully, s/he internalises a stigmatised identity and is relegated to the margins of humanity. Significant for our purpose in this essay is Goffman's distinction between 'discredited' persons who have a visible stigma (such as physical impairment or deformity) and 'discreditable' persons with a non-visible impairment (for example, the intellectually disabled). Goffman argues that the major social dilemma in the case of 'discredited' persons is managing the tensions of social encounters, whereas for the 'discreditable', it is a question of managing information about oneself in such encounters to avoid possible discreditation or exposure (Gill 2001).

Drawing upon his personal experience of a spinal tumour and subsequent neurological loss, Robert Murphy (1987) uses the anthropological concept of liminality[1] to describe the disability experience as one that is 'betwixt and between'. For Murphy, the experience of disabled people is marked by a pervasive exclusion from ordinary life and the denial of full humanity. The social and cultural perception of the disabled individual as 'damaged goods', permanently weak, childlike, suffering and needy — no matter how autonomous they might actually be — has implications for their 'personhood', freezing them, in a sense, on the liminal threshold where their social and human status remains ambiguous.

Robert Edgerton (1967) presents one of the first anthropological accounts of deinstitutionalised, mildly intellectually disabled persons living in the community. He attempted to show the combined impact of institutionalisation, stigma and attribution of labels like 'incompetent' on their lives, and concluded that they relied heavily on the support of non-retarded benefactors (ibid.: 193) to cope with life outside the institution. They accumulated personal belongings to convey the appearance of normality, invented biographies that hid their past institutionalisation, and resisted the label of 'retarded', claiming that there was nothing wrong with them. However, despite such denial, they had to deal with the stigma of being labelled incompetent, resulting in feelings of humiliation, worthlessness and the perception of being considered not quite human (Klotz 2003).

The notion of personhood is particularly problematic in the case of intellectual disabilities, and reveals great cross-cultural variability (Ingstad and Whyte 1995). Jani Klotz (2003) notes that in Western cultures, personhood is defined in individualistic terms, which emphasise independence, autonomy, self-reliance, initiative and success. These are usually associated with the attributes of productivity, intelligence and literacy. However, cultures that emphasise sociality tend to value attributes like interdependence, relatedness and affiliation (Devlieger 1998; Jenkins 1998; Nuttall 1998; Whyte 1998). The latter configure the intellectually disabled person in more relational terms focusing on a range of attributes other than just intelligence.

The feminist turn in the social sciences has led to a reconceptualisation of gender as social doing constituted through interaction, a social web through which we continually produce each other as male or female (West and Zimmerman 2000). Most societies hold consensual ideas about what it means to be masculine or feminine, and individual conduct is evaluated in terms of gender-specific norms. David Gilmore (2001) asserts that while femininity is more often construed as a biological given, which is culturally augmented, the social construction of masculinity encapsulates more than biological 'maleness' — it has to be proved, often through traumatic testing (for instance, initiatory rites). Earning a masculine identity and proving their manhood are considered beyond the competence of intellectually disabled males, who are thus notionally clubbed with the community of women and children. Intellectually disabled women face a double discrimination — the stigma of the intellectual impairment combines with rigid stereotypes of femininity to exacerbate their life situation. Their prospects of marriage and motherhood markedly diminish, as they are perceived to be in need of care themselves than in a position to satisfactorily perform maternal and nurturing roles. There are also misgivings about their ability to become homemakers. In addition, there are unsubstantiated fears that children of intellectually disabled women would also necessarily be disabled (Mehrotra 2004b; Thomas and Thomas 2002).

Disabled men experience masculinity as an oppressive social construct as they fail to measure up to socially accepted definitions (Fine and Asch 1988). Since they have limited access to cultural resources to negotiate the gender order, they do not enjoy the power and privileges accorded to non-disabled men (Shakespeare 1999). Disabled men can subvert their devalued disabled status, either by redefining hegemonic constructions of masculinity through alternate principles and practices, or by denying the importance of conventional notions of masculinity in their lives altogether.

Perspectives on Intellectual Disabilities

According to Trevor Parmenter (2001), the idea that a defect of the human mind can reduce its possessor to a sub-human level is found in the natural philosophy and social and ethical writings of both Plato and Aristotle. During the Middle Ages in Europe, people with intellectual disabilities were also considered less than human, even regarded to be possessed by the devil (Judge 1987). In other contexts, however, such people were protected by the Church as 'holy innocents' or 'sacred fools', their intellectual deficits interpreted as signs of spiritual grace and simple states of nature that were closer to God than normal people corrupted by culture (Jenkins 1998).

Michel Foucault (1967) views society's sequestering or confinement of 'abnormal' persons as a form of social control. The criminal, unemployed and insane were incarcerated during the Enlightenment in Europe, as they were seen as a threat to public order. Thus, it is only by controlling the abnormal that the normal can exist. From another perspective, symbolic interactionist approaches in sociology (Goffman 1961; Scheff 1966), which explain human behaviour in terms of shared expectations, meanings and beliefs, regard deviance as labelling of persons who breach social norms and expectations. These labels are internalised and become self-fulfilling prophecies in that the social reaction to deviant individuals results in persons so labelled to actually contravene those very same norms and expectations. Both these approaches aptly demonstrate what James Trent (1994) calls 'inventing the feeble mind'.

In addition to a range of academic perspectives, medical and technological advances and social movements have influenced changing notions of intellectual disabilities and their management. The eugenics movement[2] has, for instance, played a major role in the institutionalisation of the intellectually disabled, what Parmenter (2001) calls the reification of intelligence.[3] Although the eugenics perspective has been discredited over the years, genetic research has unravelled the role of heredity in intellectual disability, for instance, the discovery of the Fragile X syndrome.[4]

The 'normalization principle', articulated by the Swedish scholar Bengt Nirje (1992), aims at the provision to the disabled of conditions of everyday living as close as possible to the regular lifeways of the community. In North America, Wolf Wolfensberger's formulation of normalization (1972) emphasised the need for intellectually disabled persons to adapt to the cultural norms of their community by minimising their differences so that they could pass undetected in society. The normalization principle and its offshoots set into motion a paradigm shift from institutionalisation to community-based rehabilitation programmes (CBR),[5] special education and intervention. However, cultural constructs about the 'otherness' of intellectually disabled persons underlie special education programmes. Derrick Armstrong (2003), Mal Leicester (1999), Gary Thomas and Andrew Loxley (2001), and Sally Tomlinson (1982) highlight the iniquitous power relationship between professionals on the one hand, and impaired individuals and their families on the other, wherein the 'voices' of the disabled are simply not heard, and categories are created by state and society in order to manage 'difference'.

In conjunction with the discourses of normalization, the human rights approach stressed the importance of the inalienable right of the mentally deficient individual to the same dignity as fellow human beings (Oliver 1990). This has found expression in several proclamations of the United Nations and pro-disability legislation in many countries, including India.[6]

Conceptions of Intellectual Disability in Non-Western Societies

Unlike the practices of labelling, segregation and institutionalisation observed in the West, the sociocultural milieux in non-Western societies, including India, tended to absorb the intellectually disabled within the circle of family and social networks, creating spaces for them to function according to their capacities. In her ethnographic study in rural Uganda, Susan Reynolds Whyte (1998) demonstrates how the notion of 'competence' is linked with the way the individual conducts him/herself in the social sphere, in the context of family and neighbourhood relations. Mark Nuttall (1998) highlights how the Inuit of Greenland regard the ability to hunt and fish in a subsistence economy as competence, rather than the ability to read or write. Tsung-Yi Lin and Mei-Chen Lin (1980) highlight long-standing Chinese traditions of interfamilial coping with stress, including the stress of mental illness and disability.

Underscoring the role of family and kinship in the disability experience, Veena Das and Renu Addlakha (2001) argue that parental anxieties in north Indian families about the welfare of a disabled child, especially a daughter, intertwine with fears of interrupted and tainted lives voiced by members of the extended kin group. The authors locate disability not merely 'in' individual bodies but rather as 'off' the body of the individual, extending into the network of social and kin relationships (ibid.: 512). The notion of 'connected body-selves' (ibid.: 520) links the physicality of the body with the identity and meaning of personhood; and then specifies that the experience and meaning of personhood are fused with a network of other body-selves. Exercise of individual agency is linked to how the disabled persons are positioned or excluded within the domestic configuration. This approach also allows us to see how individuals move within and beyond the domestic sphere, and mobilise resources that enable them to combat social pressures and exercise some control over the course of their lives.

The Hindu perspective on disability, as articulated in the scriptures, can be explained through the *karma* theory, wherein illnesses and disabilities in this life are a consequence of past misdeeds. They are regarded as the outcome of cosmic factors and, in the absence of cure, are to be accepted in a spirit of resignation (Dalal, Pande, Dhawan, Dwijendra and Berry 2000; Dube 1990). Such beliefs work against efforts to ameliorate the life conditions of those so afflicted. In general, Indians pay less attention to mental than to physical illness. In the context of rural Haryana, Nilika Mehrotra (2004a) points out how the intellectually disabled are described as naïve or innocent by the use of such adjectives as *bhola* or *bawla* (simple or innocuous). They are often ridiculed and are assigned household chores. Their reduced mental capacities are viewed as disabilities, only if coupled with some kind of visible physical impairment. One outcome of this is that being mentally defective is not stigmatising in itself — only the severely intellectually disabled carry stigma. Similarly, in his study of community attitudes towards disability in south India, which corroborates the sociocultural variability of constructs like intellectual disability, Raymond Paul Lang (2000) found that the principal aspirations of disabled people were twofold — employment and marriage. By making an economic contribution to the household, their self-esteem and dignity in the eyes of the local community were enhanced. He strongly advocates CBR initiatives, addressing the whole range of medical, social, economic and cultural needs of disabled individuals.

Urbanisation, the dwindling of traditional support networks like the extended kin group and neighbourhood, and the stress on formal educational attainments as the critical factors in charting out careers have resulted in the categorisation as incompetent of those individuals whose mental limitations would, otherwise, have been managed within the ambit of the family and social networks. The labelling of the intellectually disabled as incompetent is an outcome of changing notions of what constitutes competence in a rapidly changing world (Jenkins 1998). The growing influence of Western biomedicine in the developing world, particularly in its urban conclaves, is leading to the salience of categories like learning disorders and intellectual disabilities. At the same time, local models of causality, traditional treatments and remedies and distinctive patterns of help-seeking behaviour continue to exist side by side in such contexts (Kleinman 1980).

This brief overview of the cross-cultural and historical conceptions of intellectual disability shows the highly contextual and culture-specific connotations of the term. However, we also need to understand how intellectually disabled persons actually experience and perceive the world. Jani Klotz (2003) points out that while people with milder intellectual disabilities may be capable or desirous of conforming to the social and cultural norms and expectations of their communities, those with severe intellectual disabilities are rarely able or willing to participate in normal social activities like work and recreation. Indeed, many of them are neither aware of nor appear to care about their own differences from others. For instance, persons with autism have been described as lacking a theory of mind (Baron-Cohen 1997) or the ability to apprehend and orient their behaviour in relation to the mental states of others.

We now present case material culled from our ethnographic studies of intellectually disabled persons and their families in Haryana and Delhi.[7] We demonstrate how intellectual disabilities are increasingly being seen as medical and psychological conditions that need external intervention, and draw attention to the complex interplay between adult identity, masculinity and intellectual disability in the lives of the disabled, their families, and the organisations set up to support them.

The case of Haryana

Disability in the state of Haryana is commonly defined in terms of *aashrit* or dependency (Mehrotra 2004a: 38) of an individual on others in the community. It is understood primarily as a physical defect, specifically a limb deformity. Such a formulation is in consonance with the importance of manual labour in the agrarian economy of the area. Disability is, thus, addressed as *viklangta* or *apangta*, mainly referring to locomotor disorders, which are visible and circumscribe the capacity to undertake physical labour.

Intellectually challenged persons are not recognised as 'disabled' in this sense, as their deficiencies are not visible and do not significantly affect their participation in agriculture. When addressed or spoken of, they are referred to as *bawla* or *bhola*. Intellectually challenged men are usually assigned women's work (*auraton ke kaam*) like fetching water, weeding or grazing cattle. If their mental slowness is coupled with a visible physical impairment, then they are considered 'disabled' like those with deformed limbs (ibid.: 38). On the other hand, 'feeble-mindedness' as deviance is associated with hot temper, erratic behaviour and impotence, and people manifesting such characteristics are described as *paagal* or mad (Mehrotra 2006: 408).

Household resources are usually channelled towards the support of disabled persons. A disabled woman is usually married to a disabled man, a widower, into a household whose economic condition is lower than that of her natal home, or to a man who cannot find a spouse due to any reason — illiteracy, low income or caste endogamy. There are also reports of heavy dowries paid by parents of disabled girls. Their traditional gender roles as producers and reproducers are strictly enforced as in the case of non-disabled women (ibid.). After marriage, disabled women perform the usual household chores — fetching water from the well, cutting fodder, cooking, cleaning, etc. Domestic violence is a routine occurrence, and disability gives another excuse for wife-beating, since the negotiating power of women with disabilities is even less than that of their non-disabled counterparts.

The denial of masculine status to the intellectually disabled male must be located in a social and cultural context, wherein employment and marriage are seen as crucial markers of masculinity. For disabled men, both goals are elusive. Engaging with the complexities of masculinity in present-day Haryana, Prem Chowdhry (2005) contends that the increasing number of unemployed, unmarried and elderly men in the state constitute a problematic category for both society and the state. In conjunction with new technologies, globalisation and consumerism, regressive trends are being strengthened. The tight employment situation and adverse sex ratio have converted these categories of men into loose cannon. Their frustrations and untapped energies are being used for furthering the nefarious ends of illegal and unconstitutional bodies like caste *panchayats*.[8] Unemployment is one of the major challenges to masculinity, and unemployed men are considered a burden on society. To win the approval of family and community, they resort to supporting elders upholding regressive traditions and iniquitous caste–cultural norms, so that they may at least acquire the positive identity of good or obedient sons, albeit unemployed. Their support to caste *panchayats* in matters dealing with breach of marriage norms, such as elopements, runaway marriages and liaisons between *dalits* and non-*dalits*, is particularly conspicuous. These *panchayats*, with unemployed youth as their musclemen, have inflicted illegal penalties, including death, forced divorce and public humiliation on those who have dared to infringe age-old marital and kinship codes (ibid.).

We may speculate that disabled men, particularly intellectually disabled men, are not even regarded as 'men' in the first place on account of their being subsumed in the 'women and children' category. They are pitied as they are seen to be incapable of enacting any masculine role, even though they are not explicitly excluded from community and family life in the rural areas. The demands of manhood put enormous pressures on young men in general to conform. The cultural construction of masculinity places a heavy premium on work (manual and white-collar) and marriage. Men who are poor, sick or disabled find themselves at an enormous disadvantage. Not only are they the butt of social ridicule, but in the prevailing situation of a skewed sex ratio,[9] they are put in the category of the 'non-marriageable' in society.

State and NGO intervention: Arpan Institute, Rohtak

In Haryana, awareness of intellectual disability, as a medico-psychological condition requiring rehabilitation, has been promoted in no small measure by NGOs in conjunction with the Department of Social Justice and Empowerment, Government of Haryana. In accordance with the Persons with Disabilities (Equal Opportunities, Protection of Rights and Full Participation) Act, 1995, a Commissioner of Disabilities has been appointed, and a

State Coordination Committee and State Executive Committee have been constituted. Meetings of both committees are regularly conducted, and representatives from NGOs have been inducted as non-official members. Some of the state-level provisions for the intellectually challenged are special schools and disability pensions to persons above the age of 18 years with more than 70 per cent disability at the rate of ₹600 per month. The state government provides grants-in-aid to voluntary organisations working with the disabled for salaries of staff and provisions for the maintenance of inmates. A state-level 'Home for Mentally Retarded', constructed at a cost of ₹2.18 million at Rohtak, is now operational.[10] There are other schemes and provisions in place for other categories of disabled individuals (physically, visually and hearing impaired). These programmes are largely routed through the Indian Red Cross Society, which runs one of the largest networks catering to the differential needs of the disabled in Haryana.

One of the pioneering residential institutions focusing on the special needs of the intellectually disabled is the Arpan Institute For Mentally Handicapped Children at Rohtak. It was established in 1983 on a small plot of land sanctioned by the state government. It has been functioning under the aegis of the Indian Red Cross Society and currently runs a school. While the Arpan Institute caters to children below 18 years of age, the adjacent Sraban School, established in 2004, provides services for those above 18 years of age. Arpan is the first multi-speciality institution for the mentally handicapped in Haryana. It conducts special education programmes for mentally challenged children and has on its rolls a team of professionals, including special educators, psychologists, speech therapists, and occupational therapists. The level of intellectual disability is assessed through a combination of measures, including evaluation of the present functioning level of the child, IQ scores and other medical and psychological testing protocols.

One of the significant initiatives undertaken by the Arpan Institute was to encourage the active involvement of parents in the child's training programmes. The Principal insisted on a fortnightly meeting between parents and teachers of day scholars and a monthly meeting in the case of hostellers. In fact, a parents' association was formed in 1993, which gained momentum from 1996. Interestingly, the school was initially advised by some local people to avoid involving parents as that would result in the child's difficulties becoming public knowledge. It was felt that this would not only lead to additional problems for the school, but would also result in the stigmatisation of families of children attending the school in the larger social networks of kinship and community.

Of the 150 children enrolled in Arpan at the time of fieldwork, 120 are boys. In an interview, the Principal of the school admitted that parents are usually not open to sending daughters to the school. Girls with disabilities are rarely sent to acquire any education and training on account of the multiple discrimination faced by them, that is, depreciated for being female in a highly patriarchal society, and further devalued on account of being disabled. Many girls with disabilities are subject to absolute neglect by their families in the hope that they will die; those who do survive are accommodated within the ambit of family and kin, and are expected to perform chores within the household. The family emerges as the social unit that both protects and controls them. As already mentioned, a disabled woman in Haryana, especially in the reproductive age group and living in a rural area, is expected to work like any 'normal' woman. She is not perceived as having any special requirements like special schooling (Mehrotra 2006).

Male children with disabilities tend to be the main beneficiaries of state and NGO initiatives, but, as has already been indicated, this does not make their participation in society unproblematic. Parents have to be persuaded that it is not enough to provide the child two square meals a day and, thereafter, let him remain idle. The notion of a mental disability is a difficult concept for most families to grasp. They tend to believe that 'the child will learn' (*bachcha seekh jaaega*), and the problem will resolve itself with age. The Arpan Institute functionaries spend a great deal of time enlightening parents about the nature of intellectual disability and its implications for the child and his family. In one of the cases described, it took the mother of the boy almost two years to understand the problem. Early diagnosis and intervention are at the core of the CBR initiatives launched by Arpan. Many of the higher functioning disabled children, who have been trained at the institute, have been absorbed into employment (usually sheltered), and contribute economically to the family. Many have also married with the support of the institute as well as family members. Interestingly, former students are often instructed by their family members not to publicly acknowledge the staff of Arpan Institute for fear of stigma. The kin network, thus, devises strategies to manage the 'discreditable' identity (Goffman 1963) of its intellectually disabled members.

In urban areas of Haryana, the disabled are being recognised as a distinct social category with special needs. There are attempts to integrate them into the social mainstream through special schools and training centres. The situation is different in rural areas, where they are not considered a specific group in need of special intervention, largely because they often continue to function as 'normal' members of society (Mehrotra 2006). Hardly any encouragement is given to intellectually disabled children to obtain an education and vocational skills, as the local community finds ways of negotiating with the disabilities on their own terms. There is very little information about special schools, which are largely concentrated in urban areas. The few schools that exist remain out of reach of the majority of children with intellectual disabilities. Since caste, class and gender determine access to resources, male children from higher landowning castes and upwardly mobile middle-class families have greater access to the limited services and facilities available for the disabled in the state. There is still a great deal of resistance to sending girls to residential schools, largely, though not solely, on account of security concerns. Further, sending them away would deprive the household of their participation in household chores.

Action for Autism: The case from Delhi

Autism as a syndrome was first described by the Austrian psychiatrist Leo Kanner in his landmark paper 'Autistic Disturbances of Affective Contact' published in 1943. A year later, working independently, his compatriot, the physician Hans Asperger, published a dissertation concerning 'Autistic Psychopathy' in childhood (1944/1991). Over the next few decades, autism or autism spectrum disorder came to be recognised as a psychiatric condition, and subsequently, as a neurological developmental disorder. The prominent characteristics of the disorder include the absence of a theory of mind, failure in interrelatedness, failure to establish an experiencing self, and executive function deficit, that is, inability to plan, monitor and direct activities and achieve goals (Jordan 1997).

In India, as in many other countries, knowledge about autism amongst medical and mental health professionals, and awareness among laypersons are of a low order. Very few professionals are familiar with its symptoms and diagnostic criteria (Daley 2004). Although no epidemiological studies have been carried out in India, the estimates suggest that 1.7 million individuals may be afflicted with the disorder. Only a miniscule number of the affected are correctly diagnosed. Many persons with autism are either regarded as 'mentally retarded' or 'mentally ill'. Over 85 per cent of persons diagnosed are males.

The pioneering organisation in Delhi that brought autism to public attention is Action for Autism (AFA). It was set up in 1994 by Merry Barua, herself a mother of an autistic child. It has grown over the years and provides a range of services. In addition to running a school, AFA offers diagnostic facilities, a training programme for mothers, conducts an annual workshop for parents and professionals, runs a Diploma in Special Education (Autism), and is involved in awareness-building among the general public, and advocacy with medical professionals. Open Door, a model school for autistic children, which started with one child, Barua's son Neeraj, now has 55 children, 46 of whom are boys.

The AFA also runs *Aadhaar* (meaning 'support' in Hindi), a centre for young adults with autism. It provides training in work skills to 10 persons ranging between the ages of 18 and 30 years; at present, there are seven men and three women. Under the supervision of a teacher and an assistant, they undertake activities like weaving, block printing, envelope-making, painting, and decorating pots, cards and other items. Their work sessions are punctuated with tea breaks and recreational activities. The trainees make tea for themselves and the office staff, and are encouraged by their teachers to socialise. As autism is a spectrum disorder, the young people at the centre display a wide range of abilities. Some are highly verbal and socialise easily, while others may be less so, and may appear disinterested in the world and people around them.

Conversations with the families of some of the male attendees reveal that coming to the centre gives them 'something to do'. They are provided with a routine; they spend the day in surroundings that are congenial, respectful of their differences and amidst peers. In addition to vocational activities, the centre is the fulcrum around which many of their social and recreational activities revolve. They participate in school activities, be it fancy dress or theatre, Christmas parties or picnics. The school ambience is not judgemental; a 25-year-old man in fancy dress may share the stage with children between six and seven years of age, a sight that may jolt the uninformed outsider.

The following case study highlights the role played by the organisation in shaping a meaningful life for its young people:

Prateek[11] is a 24-year-old man who attends Aadhaar. He was diagnosed with autism when he was 12. Prateek's milestones were within the normal range, and he started to attend a regular school at the age of four. His parents noticed nothing conspicuously odd about his behaviour during the early childhood years. However, as he went to higher classes, he began to find the schoolwork increasingly difficult. His interactions with his classmates also became stressful. He could not understand their jokes and pranks and was often the butt of ridicule. His parents were at a loss and sought psychiatric help. They were referred to the then nascent Action for Autism, where Prateek finally received a diagnosis of autism. Since then, he has been a regular client of the organisation. He comes to the centre every morning, accompanied by one of his parents, and spends the day there. He is extremely particular about his routine, which, according to his parents, gives purpose and meaning to his life. Prateek has good self-care skills and communicates quite effectively — he can read, write, count and has good work skills. However, there are other life activities and social situations for which he will require assistance throughout his life. Money management, interacting with service providers like shopkeepers, and negotiating the nitty-gritty of everyday life in a city like Delhi pose enormous challenges for him. Prateek's parents say that AFA is the only place where their son is really understood and accepted for what he is. Relatives, neighbours and the wider community regard some of his behaviour with a mixture of amusement and embarrassment, and subject his parents and siblings to unwanted pity. Within the organisation, however, the family has found a space where his personhood is valued and his oddities accommodated. Furthermore, amidst a community of other families with disabled children, Prateek's family realises that they are not alone. A major preoccupation of such families is the care of their disabled family members after the death of the primary caregivers.

One of the major future goals of AFA is the provision of group living facilities to autistic adults. Now that the first batch, so to speak, of children diagnosed and brought within the ambit of the organisation are adults, issues of employment (sheltered or otherwise), sexuality, need for companionship, independent living, etc., have assumed salience. With the shrinking of kinship bonds in the urban context and the absence of social security and welfare provisions, families and NGOs have to devise strategies for the care of disabled children after the death of their parents. It is interesting to note that while in the West the last two decades have seen a shift from institutionalisation to family- and community-based support of the intellectually disabled, in urban India the reverse seems to be taking place. Traditional family and community support structures are withering away and there is no social security net provided by the state. NGOs and voluntary organisations have thus assumed a magnified role. To what extent they will manage to mediate between family, community and state is an issue worth examining.

In the context of the discussion on masculinity and adulthood, there is a paucity of opportunities for young men like Prateek at AFA to interact with other 'normal' men, with the exception of their fathers, brothers and other male relatives. Non-disabled age-mates consider it stigmatising or a waste of time to hang out with or participate in activities with their autistic counterparts, activities that may appear infantile to them at their age — for example, playing with toys, colouring with crayons, or watching cartoons on TV. Their relative lack of awareness about sexuality in general, and their inappropriate sexual behaviour in particular, may lead to teasing or other forms of abuse. We heard of the case of a very able autistic boy studying in a mainstream school, who was goaded by his 'normal' peers to touch the breasts of his class teacher, so that the other boys could have fun at his expense and witness the teacher's outrage and anger. The gender bias in favour of women in professions like special education results in a paucity of male teachers and therapists in care settings. This adversely affects male autistic persons' access to peer relationships outside the family, and the possibility of finding role models for emulation.

Enacting the female role is also problematic for autistic girls and women. Unlike girls with milder intellectual impairments, their core deficits in social skills, communication and imagination make it hard for autistic girls to understand social codes and expectations, including those associated with proper feminine behaviour. Sitting 'modestly', modulating one's voice, not staring at or touching strangers, and understanding 'improper' touch are skills that need to be carefully taught in order to help them maintain sexual safety, and avoid being exploited or ridiculed. The onset of menarche and associated issues of privacy and personal hygiene also need to be handled with great understanding and sensitivity.

The young people at Aadhaar have moderate to severe intellectual disabilities, making it difficult to conceal their disabled status in the outside world. However, there are numerous individuals inhabiting the autism spectrum (formally diagnosed and undiagnosed) and considered odd or eccentric at best, who have been incorporated into society — people who hold normal jobs, marry and raise families. But due to their core difficulties in social skills, imagination and communication, they often find it hard to cope with or adequately understand the demands of 'normalcy' and, in particular, the controlling, instrumental discourses of masculinity and femininity. The availability of the internet to ever larger sections of the population and the growing awareness of autism and associated conditions through the mass media have led many individuals to seek help for themselves and their children. The awareness, that defective personhood or 'madness' could well be nothing but a medical condition (albeit one that does not have a known cure), has brought relief to many people who would, otherwise, have suffered in silence on account of not knowing what was wrong with them.

Concluding Observations

The two institutions discussed above, namely, Arpan Institute and Action for Autism, working in different locations and contexts, have certain commonalities: first, they assist in identifying certain deficiencies in biomedical terms, so that the stigma of difference and defective personhood may be mitigated. Second, they open up spaces, whereby individuals affected by these conditions may avail of appropriate education and training in order to gain a measure of autonomy and self-reliance. Last, they involve families and the wider community in understanding, empathising with and seeking care for persons identified as being intellectually disabled.

The main differences between Arpan Institute and the AFA may be located in their genesis. While Arpan is the product of an NGO initiative supported by the state, AFA is a parent-driven and parent-administered organisation. Arpan was formed as a result of a top-down initiative to educate parents of the intellectually disabled about the nature of their children's difficulties and the need to bring them under the umbrella of state-sponsored welfare initiatives. A disability that was dealt with, howsoever adequately or inadequately, within the ambit of the family and kin group, was thus named, medicalised and its management taken over by experts. The AFA arose as a result of the denial of social space for autistic children and the struggle of a handful of parents to become the voices and advocates of the rights of their disabled children. While the former represents an attempt by state and civil society to sensitise the community and train such children, the latter is an attempt by affected families to secure recognition and respect by the state and civil society for their autistic children. Indeed, the AFA had to lobby very hard with the government to accord recognition to autism as a disability, which was finally achieved in 1999 with the passing of the National Trust Act for the Welfare of Persons with Autism, Cerebral Palsy, Mental Retardation and Multiple Disabilities. The Act is based on the premise that people with the above disabilities are likely to need lifelong support and care. It recognises the need for independent living within the community and capacity-building, so that intellectually disabled persons may contribute meaningfully to society.[12]

The degree of familial involvement in the two institutions also varies. The staff at Arpan has to work very hard to elicit some measure of co-operation and involvement from the families of their students. AFA, being a parent-driven organisation, is seen by the parents of the students enrolled there as 'their own' organisation. Many parents regard it as the only place where they and their children are 'understood'. Students and families at Arpan, however, attempt to shake off the stigma of being branded disabled, in the event of their securing employment or getting married, by deliberately not recognising their former teachers and therapists. On the other hand, the AFA is viewed by families as probably the only social space where their identities are not stigmatised. Parents remark that within the four walls of the organisation, their children can 'be themselves', where their oddities are not met with social opprobrium or ridicule. Here, teachers and therapists do not actively seek to iron out seemingly inappropriate behaviours for the purpose of normalisation or in an attempt to make these individuals 'pass' (Goffman 1963) in the outside world; rather, they strive to understand whether such behaviours perform a specific function for the affected individual per se. For example, echolalia (repeating verbatim the utterances of others), a common behaviour associated with autism, is now acknowledged to aid autistic persons in communication and, thus, is not discouraged or sought to be suppressed by therapists. Acknowledging different embodied experiences and unique modes of being are viewed as an essential step in recognising the personhood and agency of all individuals, irrespective of their status as disabled or not.

Our discussion has sought to open up the category of intellectual disability by focusing on its variability across space and time. We have emphasised the need to view disabled individuals not merely as aggregates of impairments but as gendered beings who face the same pressures as 'normal' individuals to enact age and gender appropriate roles. While acknowledging the multiple discrimination faced by disabled women, we have also argued that negotiating with masculinity is equally problematic, particularly in the context of an increasingly competitive society where, seemingly, only the fittest are able to survive. The role played by the state, NGOs and civil society in making the category of intellectual disability a part of ordinary parlance, and their efforts at enhancing the life opportunities of the disabled, cannot be underestimated.

We argue for sustained sociological and anthropological enquiry into the embodied, lived understandings of the world in which the intellectually disabled find themselves. These lifeworlds are influenced by changing cultural and structural contexts. Constructs of 'personhood' prevalent within different sociocultural milieux have an impact on the spaces and opportunities available to disabled people, and in the way 'normal' society views them.

Notes

* This essay first appeared in the *Indian Journal of Gender Studies*, 15 (2): 317–40, 2008, New Delhi: SAGE Publications. Editorial changes have been made to the original published chapter with permission from the Centre for Women's Development Studies, New Delhi.
1. In anthropology, liminality refers to the threshold period, the transitional phase between two phases. It was introduced into the discipline by Arnold van Gennep (1909/1960) in his studies of rites of passage, such as coming of age rituals and marriage that mark points of transition between different life cycle stages.
2. Sir Francis Galton coined the term 'eugenics' in 1865. The eugenics movement (whose historical roots can be traced to Plato) is a social philosophy, which advocates the perpetuation of 'culturally' valued hereditary traits (health, fair colour, intelligence) through interventions like selective breeding and genetic screening, so that only desirable traits are allowed to be transmitted. Eugenics was operationalised by the Nazis in Germany during World War II in their quest for a super Aryan race. Since then, it has been discredited as a justification for coercive State-sponsored discrimination and a violation of human rights.
3. Reification of intelligence in the context of eugenics implies that intelligence is a universal category that is inborn, heritable, invariable and measurable through an IQ protocol. The IQ score is considered permanent and stable for an individual throughout life.
4. The Fragile X syndrome (FXS) is a genetic disorder caused by the mutation of a particular gene on the X chromosome. Symptoms include physical characteristics like elongated face, large or protuberant ears, flat feet and large testicles in men. Behavioural characteristics include atypical social

development, speech delays and mental subnormality. Persons with Fragile X in family histories are advised to seek genetic counselling to assess the likelihood of transmitting it to their offspring.
5. Community-based rehabilitation (CBR) is a strategy for rehabilitation, equalisation of opportunities and social inclusion of people with disabilities, by focusing on the community as the agency that provides services and opportunities for integration.
6. India adopted the Persons with Disabilities (Equal Opportunities, Protection of Rights and Full Participation) Act in 1995 (see http://socialjustice.nic.in/pwdact1995.php?pageid=3); and also ratified the United Nations Convention on the Rights of Persons with Disabilities (UNCRPD) on 1 October 2007 (see http://www.un.org/disabilities/convention/conventionfull.shtml).
7. The ethnographic research for the Haryana case was carried out by Nilika Mehrotra from May to August 2002, and in June 2006 as part of a larger study on disability in Haryana (Mehrotra 2004a, 2004b, 2006). The Delhi case study is part of Shubhangi Vaidya's doctoral fieldwork conducted during 2005–6 (Vaidya 2008).
8. These are caste-based organisations that have no legal legitimacy, but which, nevertheless, attempt to impose caste rules. Caste or *khap panchayat*s in Haryana have played a particularly nefarious role in violently breaking up marriages between members of different caste and lineage groups.
9. Due to the rampant practice of female foeticide, Haryana has one of the lowest sex ratios in the country. From 865 females for every 1,000 males in 1991, the sex ratio has declined to 861 females for every 1,000 males in 2001.
10. See http://socialjusticehry.nic.in/Website/DisabilityWelfare.pdf (accessed 20 May 2012).
11. Pseudonyms have been used to protect the identities of informants.
12. The important provision of the Act pertains to guardianship, wherein an individual or an institution is granted legal guardianship of the disabled individual. The National Trust is expected to monitor whether the guardian is adequately discharging the assigned duties and, in the event of abuse, neglect or exploitation, is authorised to divest him/her of guardianship. For recent discussions, see Mehrotra (2011). Also see http://www.thenationaltrust.co.in/nt/images/stories/list/ntact%201999.pdf.

References

Armstrong, Derrick. 2003. *Experiences of Special Education*. New York: Routledge and Kegan Paul.

Asperger, Hans. 1944/1991. '"Autistic Psychopathy" in Childhood', in Uta Frith (ed.), *Autism and Asperger Syndrome*, pp. 37–92. Cambridge: Cambridge University Press.

Baron-Cohen, Simon. 1997. *Mindblindness: An Essay on Autism and Theory of Mind*. Massachusetts: MIT Press.

Chowdhry, Prem. 2005. 'Crisis of Masculinity in Haryana: The Unmarried, the Unemployed and the Aged', *Economic and Political Weekly*, 40 (49): 5189–98.

Dalal, Ajit K., Namita Pande, Nisha Dhawan, Deepa Dwijendra and John W. Berry. 2000. *The Mind Matters: Disability Attitudes and Community Based Rehabilitation*. Allahabad: University of Allahabad Publications.

Daley, Tamara C. 2004. 'From Symptom Recognition to Diagnosis: Children with Autism in Urban India', *Social Science and Medicine*, 58 (7): 1323–35.

Das, Veena and Renu Addlakha. 2001. 'Disability and Domestic Citizenship: Voice, Gender, and the Making of the Subject', *Public Culture*, 13 (3): 511–31.

Devlieger, Patrick J. 1998. '(In)competence in America in Comparative Perspective', in Richard Jenkins (ed.), *Questions of Competence: Culture, Classification and Intellectual Disability*, pp. 54–75. Cambridge: Cambridge University Press.

Dube, Shyama Charan. 1990. *Tradition and Development*. New Delhi: Vikas Publishing House.

Edgerton, Robert B. 1967. *The Cloak of Competence: Stigma in the Lives of the Mentally Retarded*. Berkeley: University of California Press.

Fine, Michelle and Adrienne Asch (eds). 1988. *Women with Disabilities: Essays in Psychology, Culture, and Politics*. Philadelphia: Temple University Press.

Foucault, Michel. 1967. *Madness and Civilization: A History of Insanity in the Age of Reason*, trans. Richard Howard. Cambridge: Cambridge University Press.

Gill, Carol J. 2001. 'Divided Understandings: The Social Experience of Disability', in Albrecht, Gary L., Katherine D. Seelman and Michael Bury (eds), *Handbook of Disability Studies*, pp. 351–72. Thousand Oaks, CA: SAGE Publications.

Gilmore, David D. 2001. 'The Manhood Puzzle', in Caroline Brettel and Carolyn Fishel Sargent (eds), *Gender in Cross-Cultural Perspective*, pp. 207–20. Englewood Cliffs, NJ: Prentice-Hall.

Goffman, Erving. 1961. *Asylums: Notes on the Social Situation of Mental Patients and Other Inmates*. Chicago: Aldine Publishing Company.

———. 1963. *Stigma: Notes on the Management of Spoiled Identity*. Englewood Cliffs, NJ: Prentice-Hall.

Ingstad, Benedicte. 1995. 'Public Discourses on Rehabilitation: From Norway to Botswana', in Benedicte Ingstad and Susan Reynolds Whyte (eds), *Disability and Culture*, pp. 174–95. Berkeley: University of California Press.

Ingstad, Benedicte and Susan Reynolds Whyte (eds). 1995. *Disability and Culture*. Berkeley: University of California Press.
Jenkins, Richard. 1998. 'Culture, Classification and (In)competence', in Richard Jenkins (ed.), *Questions of Competence: Culture, Classification and Intellectual Disability*, pp. 1–24. Cambridge: Cambridge University Press.
Jordan, Rita R. 1997. *Education of Children and Young People with Autism*. Paris: UNESCO.
Judge, Cliff. 1987. *Civilization and Mental Retardation: A History of the Care and Treatment of Intellectually Disabled People*. Mulgrave: Magenta Press.
Kanner, Leo. 1943. 'Autistic Disturbances of Affective Contact', *Nervous Child*, 2 (1): 217–50.
Kleinman, Arthur. 1980. *Patients and Healers in the Context of Culture: An Exploration of the Borderland between Anthropology, Medicine, and Psychiatry*. Berkeley: University of California Press.
Klotz, Jani. 2003. 'The Culture Concept: Anthropology, Disability Studies and Intellectual Disability'. Paper presented at the Symposium on Disability at the Cutting Edge: A Colloquium to Examine the Impact on Theory, Research and Professional Practice, 12 September, University of Technology, Sydney, and Disability Studies and Research Institute (DSaRI).
Lang, Raymond Paul. 2000. 'Perceiving Disability and Practising Community-Based Rehabilitation: A Critical Examination with Case Studies from South India'. Unpublished Ph.D. dissertation, University of East Anglia, Norwich.
Leicester, Mal. 1999. *Disability Voice: Towards an Enabling Education*. London: Jessica Kingsley Publishers Ltd.
Lin, Tsung-Yi and Mei-Chen Lin. 1980. 'Love, Denial and Rejection: Responses of Chinese Families to Mental Illness', in Arthur Kleinman and Tsung-Yi Lin (eds), *Normal and Abnormal Behaviour in Chinese Culture*, pp. 391–401. New York: D. Reidel Publishing Company.
Mehrotra, Nilika. 2004a. 'Understanding Cultural Conceptions of Disability in Rural India: A Case from Haryana', *Journal of Indian Anthropological Society*, 39 (1): 33–45.
———. 2004b. 'Women, Disability and Social Support in Rural Haryana', *Economic and Political Weekly*, 39 (52): 5640–44.
———. 2006. 'Negotiating Gender and Disability in Rural Haryana', *Sociological Bulletin*, 55 (3): 406–26.
———. 2011. 'Disability Rights Movements in India: Politics and Practice', *Economic and Political Weekly*, 46 (6): 65–72.
Murphy, Robert F. 1987. *The Body Silent: The Different World of the Disabled*. New York: W. W. Norton and Company.
Nirje, Bengt. 1992. *The Normalization Principle Papers*. Uppsala, Sweden: Centre for Handicap Research, Uppsala University.
Nuttall, Mark. 1998. 'States and Categories: Indigenous Models of

Personhood in Northwest Greenland', in Richard Jenkins (ed.), *Questions of Competence: Culture, Classification and Intellectual Disability*, pp. 176–93. Cambridge: Cambridge University Press.

Oliver, Michael. 1990. *The Politics of Disablement: A Sociological Approach.* London: Macmillan.

Parmenter, Trevor R. 2001. 'Intellectual Disabilities — Quo Vadis?', in Gary L. Albrecht, Katherine D. Seelman and Michael Bury (eds), *Handbook of Disability Studies*, pp. 267–96. Thousand Oaks, CA: SAGE Publications.

Scheff, Thomas J. 1966. *Being Mentally Ill: A Sociological Theory.* Chicago: Aldine Publishing Company.

Shakespeare, Tom. 1999. 'The Sexual Politics of Disabled Masculinity', *Sexuality and Disability*, 17 (1): 53–64.

Stiker, Henri-Jacques. 2000. *A History of Disability*, trans. William Sayers. Ann Arbor: University of Michigan Press.

Thomas, Gary and Andrew Loxley. 2001. *Deconstructing Special Education and Constructing Inclusion.* Buckingham and Philadelphia: Open University Press.

Thomas, Maya and Maliakal Joseph Thomas. 2002. 'Status of Women with Disabilities in South Asia', in Maya Thomas and Maliakal Joseph Thomas (eds), *Disability and Rehabilitation Issues in South Asia: Selected Readings in Community Based Rehabilitation*, *Asia Pacific Disability Rehabilitation Journal* (special issue), Series 2, http://www.aifo.it/english/resources/online/apdrj/selread102/thomas.doc (accessed 20 October 2007).

Tomlinson, Sally. 1982. *A Sociology of Special Education.* London: Routledge and Kegan Paul.

Trent, James W. 1994. *Inventing the Feeble Mind: A History of Mental Retardation in the United States.* Berkeley: University of California Press.

Vaidya, Shubhangi. 2008. 'A Sociological Study of Families of Autistic Children in Delhi'. Unpublished Ph.D. thesis submitted to Jawaharlal Nehru University, New Delhi.

van Gennep, Arnold. 1909/1960. *Les Rites de Passage.* New York: University of Columbia.

West, Candace and Don H. Zimmerman. 2000. 'Doing Gender', in Michael S. Kimmel (ed.), *The Gendered Society Reader*, pp. 131–49. Oxford: Oxford University Press.

Whyte, Susan Reynolds. 1998. 'Slow Cookers and Madmen: Competence of Heart and Head in Rural Uganda', in Richard Jenkins (ed.), *Questions of Competence: Culture, Classification and Intellectual Disability*, pp. 153–75. Cambridge: Cambridge University Press.

Wolfensberger, Wolf. 1972. *The Principle of Normalisation in Human Services.* Toronto: National Institute on Mental Retardation.

World Health Organization (WHO). 1980. 'International Classification of Impairments, Disabilities and Handicaps'. Geneva: WHO Press.

7

Corporeality, Mobility and Class: An Ethnography of Work-related Experiences in Urban India

AMIT UPADHYAY*

Introduction

Disability rights are presently competing for space alongside various other social issues in civil society in India. As an evolving interest group in challenging able-normativity, it is now firmly entrenched within the human rights discourse, both in the academy and in civil society. Disability rights features, if perhaps self-consciously, both in the Government of India's interventionist policy agendas as also in the work of non-governmental organisations. In addition, it appears to have regained popular culture's mandate, what with the renewed spate of films foregrounding disability, or disabled persons as a social category being any indication. Scuffling for a vantage point from which to orchestrate its politics, disability rights activism is contending for visibility and legitimacy where earlier it was variously shunned (if not summarily dismissed) as being liberal–humanist, diversionary for social movements, or for not having a radical enough agenda for social transformation. Whatever its variously hued avatars may have implied in the past, it now seems squarely back and animates civil society's normative–cognitive interests.

In this chapter, I begin by providing the theoretical landscape within which issues pertaining to disability are usually recounted. This involves a theoretical engagement with the medical model, its critique by the social model, and the payoffs of employing the sociology of impairment perspective as a useful departure from the preceding frameworks. Drawing upon the Indian Census of 2001, I will seek to contextualise the employment experiences of people with disability. Subsequently, I will discuss the findings of a research study on a cohort of locomotor disabled employment seekers carried out in Bangalore in 2004.

The academic terrain is preponderant with reactions to the medical and the social models of disability. The medical model fortifies the standpoint that an individual is 'handicapped', regardless of the built environment and its role in producing disability (Michailakis 2003). The clinical status of an individual, and not social practices, determines impairment. Attaining autonomy is considered compromised by the absence of certain capacities that are necessary, and that therapies 'cure' the body of its impairment (ibid.: 209). The social model offsets the excessive medicalisation of the impaired body within the medical model. It takes into account, among other things, 'economic, political and social forces' that act upon the individual (ibid.: 210). It argues succinctly, in keeping with the finest constructivist oeuvres, that disability is produced in society with able-normativity as its organising algorithm. It offers a tempting corrective to what is arguably an undersocialised conception of disability within the medical model. The social model of disability inflects the focus off the body and its experiences. However, as a result of privileging the social over the biological, the body and its experience are rendered discursively invisible within the social model (Hughes and Paterson 1997). While emphasising the social forces attendant on people with disability, it leaves out descriptions of the everyday experience of the impaired body (Shakespeare and Watson 1995).

The sociology of impairment is evocative of the sociology of the body recommended by Bryan Turner, who asks for a critical combining of 'ontological foundationalism with cultural constructionism' (2001: 255). Embodiment in everyday life becomes the lynchpin of analysis (Nettleton and Watson 1998; Turner 1998). Indeed, the sociology of impairment perspective has a legacy going back to Maurice Merleau-Ponty's phenomenology (1962), and has been reinvigorated by feminist scholarship such as Wendy Seymour (1998). Furthermore, organic linkages between the sociology of impairment and feminist scholarship on the body and lived experiences are unmistakable, considering Dorothy Smith's views (1987) about how existing social scientific practice devalues women's experience of the everyday. Renu Addlakha (2008) demonstrably delivers a similar ethnographic feel for the everyday pertaining to gender and mental health in an urban Indian context. Susan Wendell (1989) reminds us that impairment issues and implications of chronic illness must not be elided within disability studies. Similarly, a section of feminist disability studies scholarship has sidestepped impairment in stating it as a biological given, and justifies calls for understanding both impairment and disability in 'mutually constitutive terms' (Corker 2001: 36).

The impaired body and its experiences are important not only because the body is acted upon as a passive recipient of social forces. Indeed, it is considered a vital register because people with disability, like most people but with significant differences, interact with their environment at a much more heightened bodily level. The social model of disability, conversely, renders the impaired body acquiescent and lacking agency. The sociology of impairment recognises that to speak of the body and its experiences has been difficult, since the disabled body as a field of study has featured primarily within the rubric of the medical model. This has meant that treatment and rehabilitation of the impaired body are overemphasised and considered exhaustive of the bodily terrain. While the social experience of disability was not considered worthy of academic investigation within the medical model, the social model, in offering a sociological corrective, has occluded the body and its experiences.

In answering the question about barriers to employment for people with disability, the social model would offer a convincing social–structural explanation. Indeed, the international literature is replete with references to discrimination and prejudice as related to spinal cord injury (McMahon, Shaw, West and Waid-Ebbs 2005), multiple sclerosis (McMahon, Rumrill, Roessler and Fitzgerald 2005), and cerebral palsy (Lowman, West and McMahon

2005). But in making the valid political point that follows from highlighting discrimination, the consequent focus on physical experiences and the body becomes imperceptible. In resisting the medicalised body as the unit of analysis — and this is surely an act of political resistance — it is cautious in acknowledging the body as a register and repository of everyday experiences that justify academic inquiry. Experiences of fatigue and pain, or how people struggle, strategise and compensate are passed over, since they do not find a theoretical space within the depersonalised cultural explanations of the social model. To understand the experiences of the impaired body and its interaction with the built environment has been the agenda of the sociology of impairment. It is this perspective that informs of the attempt here to bring together the experiences of people with locomotor disability in seeking market integration.

The Research Problem: An Ethnography of Work-related Experiences

In documenting the experiences of people with locomotor disability in finding a job in an Indian urban metropolis like Bangalore, the focus is on what prospective jobseekers identify as obstacles in looking for employment. Most studies on employment experiences of people with disabilities originate in the West against the backdrop of a largely formal economic structure (Elwan 1999). There is an absence within the literature on the experiences of looking for work in urban spaces from the developing world. Research concerns in India, till date, have largely tended to be about the connections between poverty and disability, particularly in rural areas (Harriss-White and Erb 2002). Since two-thirds of India's population is estimated to be living in villages (NSSO 2003), the bias in studies focusing on rural India is indeed justified. But such a bias does not obviate the need for research in urban contexts.

According to the Census of India 2001, of the 22 million persons with disability, 16 million live in rural India and 5.5 million in urban areas. The National Sample Survey Organisation (NSSO 2003) estimates that they form about 1.8 per cent of the national population,[1] and that 57 per cent of them are people with locomotor disabilities.[2] The available evidence seems to indicate that these are conservative estimates. The *Encyclopaedia of Disability* puts the number at 70 million people with disability in India (Ghai 2005). The discrepancy between these sets of statistics is probably due to the deployment of varying definitions of disability. Anita Ghai critiques the 'unwillingness of the government to include the domain of disability in the 2001 census to obtain a conclusive idea about prevalence' (ibid.: 440), a measure that would perhaps inaugurate a wider national debate on modalities of arriving at numbers and definitions pertaining to disability.

According to the Census, 29.5 per cent of all people with locomotor disability were employed. The general employment rate for the entire population is, however, 40 per cent. This is likely to be a conservative estimate, given that the Census employs a narrower definition of locomotor disability than the NSSO (Mitra and Sambamoorthi 2006). There are no cash benefits under any disability or social security insurance schemes from the Indian government in the event of unemployment, although there is a scheme for disability pensions as a welfare measure.

Sampling

Quotes that embellish this study are drawn from 24 interviews conducted in Bangalore between July–September 2004.[3] Data collection was achieved mainly through one-to-one interviews in English, Kannada and Urdu, with individuals who had registered with an Indian NGO that provides vocational training and career counselling to people with disabilities. Bangalore is at the heart of India's burgeoning IT and manufacturing industries. The sample was collected from the NGO database using the following criteria: (1) people with locomotor disability only, excluding those with multiple disabilities; (2) excluding respondents younger than the age of 16; (3) residing in Bangalore's urban area; and (4) having some experience with the employment market. The database revealed that 15 per cent, that is, 467 of the total 2966 persons registered with the NGO during 1996–2004, had provided their phone details.

Using phone numbers to select a sample introduces bias as poorer people have fewer phones. However, of the 467 phone numbers in the database, 84 (18 per cent) were not owned by the potential respondents. Low-income families not owning telephones were, therefore, less likely to be excluded from the study. Of the 14 men in the sample, six were in the lower salaried class, one in the petty business class, and seven in the skilled and semi-skilled manual labourer class. Of the 10 women in the sample, seven were in the upper salaried class, two in the petty business class, while one woman was in the skilled and semi-skilled manual labourer class. The sample was classified using the Erikson–Goldthorpe Class Schema (Erikson and Goldthorpe 1992).[4] The demographic seemed to be split largely between working class men and middle class women.

Among the 16 Hindus in the study, a majority are from the dominant castes of South India. Only one person each from the Scheduled Castes and Scheduled Tribes forms a part of the sample. There are five Muslims who come from different castes as well. In addition, there are three Roman Catholics in the sample. However, there are too few members of each caste and religion represented in this sample to be able to meaningfully separate what the respondents may have said about employment experiences and their social location. In retrospect, a larger study within each constituent group could better reveal internal differences on the basis of caste and community on employment prospects among people with locomotor disability, if any.

None of the interviewees had availed of jobs through state intervention. There are certain low-end jobs, such as STD (subscriber trunk dialling) booth workers, telephone operators, horticulturalists, mechanics, shop vendors, shop assistants, etc., that have historically been handed out to people with disability in India. Some of these jobs, such as telephone booth operator, are state-sponsored, in that phone booths are commissioned for people with disability. There is also a moral imperative from within the IT industry to hire a diverse workforce under the overarching framework of corporate social responsibility, since the 1995 Persons with Disabilities (Equal Opportunities, Protection of Rights and Full Participation) Act only applies to public sector industries (Friedner 2009: 39). The findings of this study illustrate the experiences of a diverse group of respondents not restricted to the above job categories.

Transport and transfer experiences

> The fact that I have to travel so much in the city is a problem for me. I can't move around the city a lot. My heart starts to hurt with too much exertion. Hands and legs start to ache, I feel fatigue and that's why I don't try to roam around a lot. Still I tried in quite a few places. Because I got tired looking for work, it had become a kind of violence. That's why I don't roam around anywhere. So I try to find out from home, here. (23-year-old male, formerly lottery-stall attendant, currently unemployed. Interview in Kannada.)

Finding a job is a corporeal experience, albeit with varying degrees of exertion. It places ineluctable demands on the body. It involves checking with prospective organisations about vacancies by visiting offices, keeping the relevant human resource (HR) departments in the know and enquiring of small-scale establishments. Making such 'cold calls' go side by side with scanning newspapers, navigating the internet, accessing noticeboards of establishments and relying on word-of-mouth communiqués from friends.

Information, transport and employment

Information about vacancies is critical in determining the level of effort required in finding work. Those with access to better quality information seem to display more favourable results in their search (Granovetter 1995), and with lesser physical strain.

Middle class respondents use job portals on the internet more frequently in their endeavour. They can cast the net wider, rather than going to offices and dropping off resumes, or trying to meet HR managers. The latter, more physical approach is preferred by working class respondents for both corporate companies and working-class enterprises. They, however, have to make strategic calculations about how far and how expensive each search attempt is likely to be. This is evaluated against the likelihood of getting an interview call.

Looking for a service-class job as a tailor, carpenter, beauty parlour assistant or STD booth operator involves following up word-of-mouth communiqués. Potential employers gauge the mobility of the person vis-à-vis the intrinsic job functions. A desk job for a person wearing callipers at a courier company, for example, which doubles as an STD booth, requires lesser mobility than a beauty parlour assistant having to bend painfully to thread eyebrows. Candidates are often asked to demonstrate their ability to perform the designated skills for a day or two before being given the job. The commuting distance between residence and workplace is also factored into the final decision. The whole ordeal is more arduous for poorer people with locomotor disability because it involves a lot of pain and fatigue.

Getting to a bus stop and boarding the bus

The commute to the office involves negotiating staircases at home, followed by a walk to the nearest bus stop. Bus stops are seldom located at the doorstep of any residence, and the physical effort it takes to cover a distance of over 50 metres poses specific kinds of problems. At the bus stop, bus drivers often stop their overcrowded buses five metres before or after the actual stop, resulting in a 'race' among commuters competing to board the already crowded bus. Not everyone is successful, as the bus often has 12–15 people perched on the footboard, hanging on to the railings. In the bus, there are two seats earmarked for the 'physically handicapped', but getting to them involves wading through 50 people. This is not to say that everyone else manages to use a bus easily; the point is that people with locomotor disability have to exert more to derive the same utility as non-disabled commuters.

Interviewees identify other structural constraints in boarding the bus: the entrance is too high to climb; the passageway leading into the aisle is too narrow, involving bending and straightening of the knees at an angle, which results in pain for someone wearing callipers. While newer low-floor buses with automatic doors have lower and wider entrances with a less steep angle for mounting, there are no handrails on both sides to propel oneself diagonally and upward into the bus. Crowded buses do not stop at bus stops. Often during rush hour, they stop further away from a stop, which ensures that passengers can only alight, and none can board. In the words of one respondent:

The biggest problem is they (the buses) don't stop; that's why I am trying to get a vehicle. Everywhere I go, the bus is a problem; if the buses are a little overcrowded, no one helps us at all. They just get angry with us. I know I can get a job that is far away — I can work there too — it is just the travelling to and fro that's a problem. (23-year-old male, formerly lottery-stall attendant, and currently unemployed. Interview in Kannada.)

So, why do people with locomotor disability use the bus? What payoffs do they see in travelling by this mode of transport? The same reasons as everyone else who uses a bus — it is the cheapest way of getting from one place to another. Besides, government-provided bus passes for disabled people subsidise the cost of travelling by bus even further. Commuting by autorickshaw costs 10 times as much as a bus ticket, although it allows approximately as much flexibility, accessibility and comfort as a modified two-wheeler or car. Respondents who own cars and modified two-wheelers report significantly reduced transfer obstacles. This is identical to the group that uses autorickshaws on a daily basis. Those who cannot afford autorickshaws use it sparingly, often after a thorough cost–benefit analysis, especially if it involves a loan for the fare for a job interview. If the respondent feels that s/he does not stand a chance, s/he will not travel for the interview. The benefits appear limited in comparison to the cost and effort involved in commuting for it.

Everyone calculates the cost–benefit of their job-seeking endeavours. However, people with locomotor disabilities have more variables to contend with in terms of effort expended. A cheaper means of transport is not available for every job application attempt. As one person says, 'You are able-bodied, you spend two rupees by bus and you are on your way. Where should the disabled go?' Expenditure on travel, and the effort expended per application, are higher.

Comparing public transport with self-driven transfer

Some respondents disagree that private transport is the answer, especially if it is self-driven. One respondent had had an accident after losing control over his two-wheeler. He says:

> Nowadays it's (travelling in the city) become a problem. If I go on my own vehicle, and huge traffics (sic), I'll be unable to control the vehicle. That's the problem. Otherwise I'll go by bus. But if I go by bus, I have to walk a distance to the bus stop. It'll take some pain in the leg. I have to walk almost a kilometre to get to a bus stop. (24-year-old male accountant trainee, formerly market research data collector. Interview in English.)

The volume of peak-hour traffic is difficult to negotiate as it requires control and skill over the vehicle. Going by bus, on the other hand, involves a long walk to the bus stop, although the interviewee feels that it is a safer mode of transport. On being asked if he prefers a bus or a two-wheeler, he says:

> Both I can't prefer, because if I go by bus it takes a long time. If I go by vehicle, I am unable to cope with the traffic. Safer is bus, but the distance matters . . . walking a long distance makes me tired. Going by bus makes me more tired, because I have to walk from my home to the bus stand, and again get into the bus and again I have to stand in it for an hour, and then walk from the bus stop (to destination). Each walk takes 15 minutes. (Interview in English.)

Travelling by bus makes respondents more tired, and recovery time has to be factored into their itinerary. The trade-off is between the dangers of riding a two-wheeler in unruly traffic to the autonomy and mobility that personal conveyance offers. The relative safety of a bus is offset by the difficulties in getting to the bus stop, boarding it and having to endure an arduous journey. Travelling by car and autorickshaw affords the most convenience and comfort, but is also the most expensive. Once the journey is surmounted, the workplace poses other problems.

Workplace-related barriers

Staircases and railings

> I face many problems when I go to a building. Wherever I go, I need assistance. I need a hand so that staircases do not become a problem for me. I use support when I am climbing stairs. I don't climb a lot, I stop climbing by the 1st floor or the 2nd floor. It takes me half an hour to climb ten steps, one by one. So it is difficult. (23-year-old unemployed male, looking for a call-centre job in accounts. Interview in Kannada.)

Staircases having a steeper angle of incline are more difficult to negotiate — the resultant angle produces a higher gravitational force to climb against. It requires more effort to propel oneself vertically. There is also the danger of falling backwards due to the incline of the staircase. For this interviewee, a half-hour climb of 10 steps involves gripping the railings for support, pivoting and propelling oneself upward. This fatigues the hands and shoulders resulting in acute pain. A recovery period is necessary after such an activity.

Staircases with railings make climbing easier. However, most respondents say that railings are often absent, especially at the street-level entrances of buildings. The type of railing also makes a difference to the staircase climbing experience in a particular building. They are described as being 'slippery', 'easy to hold' and even 'unmanageable'. Some are too ornamental and smooth to grasp for someone using it to pivot and propel oneself forward, whereas some are considered too wide for the hand to hold for support. Interviewees feel that railings in most buildings serve an aesthetic function rather than lend climbing support. However, even railings serving an ostensibly aesthetic purpose provide more traction than a staircase with no railings at all.

Respondents cite a correlation between staircases with railings, age of the building and their accessibility. They readily approach buildings with easy-to-manage railings alongside staircases. Establishing beforehand with a telephone call whether a building is 'old' or 'new' appears to be a general strategy.[5] Older buildings tend to have staircases with steeper inclines or a lack of railings. They are also less likely to have elevators, and respondents are least inclined to enter such buildings. Consequently, meticulous preparation is required to ensure accessibility to the built environment.

Restroom access

> Because urinals and all during work and all tension, you have to go. Because that long hours you cannot control [the urge to use the restroom]. This can be solved during lunch hour, but if it is a room type, we can use it; can't use a public space. Controlling urinals and all she feels tired. We cannot use it in public; we feel just because of female we

cannot. Just because of this reason, she is not able to go to good jobs what she wants to do it [she cannot do the kind of work she would like to]. Especially for female, we have to take care of this one mainly. The office timings was 9 am to 6 pm, and it takes one hour to go and one hour to come [home from office]. So she has to leave by 8 am, and if you have to be half an hour later in the office, one cannot tell what time you will leave. 6 to 7 — one hour she has to come back. From 8 am to 7 pm, how she has to manage? So, that was the problem. So, for urinals and all we cannot depend on colleagues or somebody else. She will be comfortable with us (only). (Interview with the sister of a 26-year-old female engineer. Interview in English.)

Only women in the sample speak about accessible restrooms at the workplace. Men report using the streets to relieve themselves, if none are available at the workplace. The lack of accessible restrooms makes the office environment intolerable for women. Since the theme of restroom accommodation is intertwined with issues of shame and body image, especially for women, it is rarely brought up before the management. Being perceived as weak and incapable of coping with the workload acts as a deterrent to voicing even legitimate needs. The pain and discomfort of controlling bodily functions cannot be overemphasised. Respondents mention having coped with the pain for years, often leading to health complications. In the words of another respondent who operates an STD phone booth adjoining a major hospital:

Yeah, we are coming back [home] by 10 pm or 10.30 pm by night. Till my other colleague comes [I can't leave the STD booth]. Till then, I can't go to toilet and all. It takes me 15 minutes to walk there [to the restroom located in a hospital], and 15 minutes to walk back. I have to control from morning till night. (22-year-old female STD booth operator, formerly beauty parlour assistant. Interview in English.)

Gender and class differences influence access to lavatories. Some middle class women in this study say that their offices have accessible restrooms, having earlier been residential apartments. This subset of respondents had consciously waited to find an accessible workplace, i.e., one that is located on the ground floor, closer home and with an accessible restroom. The differences in the experiences on the basis of socioeconomic status are critical. The under-representation of women with disability in the urban labour market begins to intuitively make sense. The women in this sample are over-represented from the middle and higher classes. Consequently, generalisations drawn from these interviews cannot be universalised, since the sample is preponderant with working class men and middle class women.

Fatigue: Its Experience and Management

Although the experience of pain is variable, fatigue is a ubiquitous category across interviews. Walking, climbing stairs and using public transport require management of acute pain and fatigue. While both are universal experiences, they have specific connotations for people with locomotor disability. A lot of energy is frittered away in engaging in activities that are obstructed by the built environment. Providing accessibility significantly reduces levels of fatigue. In fact, the effort expended to overcoming physical obstacles may well influence persons' view of whether it is worth their while in going through with this experience in the first place.

Wheelchair and calliper users report finding it difficult to operate these assistive aids. Callipers are a hindrance in bending the knees while climbing staircases. Wheelchair users are generally averse to using their wheelchairs where accessibility is uncertain. They are comfortable in using wheelchairs only where they are sure of minimal circumstantial barriers — or the presence of dropped kerbs, curb cuts [US] or ramps. The gradient of the road is particularly difficult to negotiate. Many wheelchair owners have even packed them away. Wheelchairs appear to be technologically geared for a particular spatiocultural setting in developed countries, which is unavailable in other national contexts. A minority of respondents try to straddle both of these worlds; one respondent keeps a wheelchair at his workplace and another one at home. He has also employed an attendant who assists him in boarding his car, packs the collapsible wheelchair into the boot and travels with him to his workplace, where the entire process is repeated in reverse. Managing fatigue on a day-to-day basis requires this sort of strategising.

More affluent respondents appear to report better fatigue management strategies. There are vehicles, kinship networks, supportive educational institutions, hired personal assistants and kind friends, who always appear to be available to provide assistance. No one in this helpful reference group is under any obligation to supplement the family income. Circumventing barriers in the built environment proves too onerous a task for those who cannot afford alternatives.

There is also hesitation among respondents in attributing causality to fatigue, or indeed, even talking about it. Feeling tired, though privately felt, is never publicly acknowledged especially at the workplace. There is a fear of being appraised as unable to cope with the workload due to one's impairment. This inhibits people with locomotor disability from publicly admitting exhaustion. One respondent walks to her office, climbs the stairs up to the third floor and then does not move between floors till closing time. When asked if she thinks this posed obstacles to her workday, she says:

> Look, I really don't want to show that I can't do particular work. Even if I am tired, I never used to express it. I used to do that [never express] no matter how difficult it is. I never used to express to anybody. (24-year-old female, former secretary at a chit finance company, currently pursuing a company secretaryship correspondence course. Interview in English.)

Consequently, employees with locomotor disability are apprehensive of demanding workplace accommodations, such as an elevator in the above instance. Not in a single interview is the dynamic posed in the language of workplace accessibility that the employers have to provide these facilities. Recruiters are known to evaluate potential employees as neat receptacles of human capital. The less 'encumbered' they appear, the more effortless the employment experience (including recruitment) is likely to be. This issue requires more research, not just into recruitment practices, but also into why people with disability do not pose the access question. Why are they not forthcoming in asking for workplace accommodations? What kind of a moral universe informs their being unable to deploy a rights-based language in making their demands in the workplace? This leads directly to the theme of the employer's attitude towards people with disability.

Employer's Attitude: The Negation of Human Capital

> The first question ... they [employers] feel that there is a doubt in a normal person's performance, how can a disabled person be trusted on the job? They doubt the abilities. As an institution, they feel what benefits will I get out of this person who can't be wholly independent, who needs support. Will I be spending more on him than he'll be able to contribute to the organisation? The moment I mention disabled, they question to what extent they are able to perform their job. She can't type [fast], right hand not as strong. Slow in performing things. So, in comparison to normal people, she can't bargain. She can't take down 120 words per minute in the secretarial position. (Sister of a 26-year-old unemployed female respondent looking for work as a secretary and/or beautician. Interview in English.)

The foundation for a supportive work environment is directly linked to employers' understanding and attitudes towards disabilities (Scheid 2005). Often, these gatekeepers of employment opportunities make assumptions about what people with disability can or cannot do. Neither employers nor recruiters offer any workplace accommodation to respondents. Abilities of disabled persons to perform blue- and white-collar jobs seem to be subject to negative assumptions. As one respondent says:

> I asked for a job at Manipal Hospital (as an STD booth operator). They said, 'You can't get up fast, you can't do this work. No job for you.' They shouldn't say things like that; they should try to improve us. If they put us down, we'll also think like that: 'Oh, what they say is true'. In parlour also, they say, 'You can't stand for a long time. You handicapped people can't do anything.' They should give us a chance to do, then we'll also feel like doing. Otherwise, if they say we can't do means we *can't do*. (22-year-old female STD booth operator, formerly beauty parlour assistant. Interview in English.)

Such assertions by employers can become self-fulfilling prophesies as indicated by this respondent. Most interviews are shot through with the employers/recruiters referencing 'inability' as a bargaining point. Dealing with questions about how s/he would hypothetically accomplish certain tasks is a mandatory part of the unpleasant interview experience. Some respondents mention employers' obvious discomfort in having people with disability representing or being the public face of the company. Other respondents explain that employers are often not open about their bias in hiring employees, choosing to appear politically correct. However, one respondent notices avoidance strategies used by some employers:

> Sometimes, they may avoid me by seeing from the door when I walk towards the interviewer. That time they'll come to know I'm handicapped person, since I have not mentioned in my resume, so they'll give me some negative ranking. They might. Even though I am capable of doing it, they may not be knowing it. (24-year-old male accountant trainee; formerly a market research data collector. Interview in English.)

More affluent respondents in the study do not consider access issues as important in finding work and keeping it. They think employers' attitudes are more explanatory in being denied promotions, and not so much in looking for work. As one respondent says:

> I did my master's degree, yet they were not willing to promote me to the higher post. And the people who held this post earlier had just finished their 10th standard and PUC (Intermediate). I find this degrading. Whenever I asked the HR officer, he'd say that I cannot give you that position because that position requires a lot of movement. HR requires movement, but only in a limited way. It's not a technical job where you have to sit and do [work] all the time. I know that, and it's not like that. You have to move, you have to meet the employees personally, only then you come to know what problems the company is facing, which I have done, but people are not ready to accept that I can do it. (27-year-old female recruitment consultant looking for a HR managerial position. Interview in English.)

This respondent had earlier managed the HR segment of a firm of 1500 employees on her own. When it came to promotions and career advancements in her next job, she was reminded of her impairment. It was the employer's assumption of inability to work that made the difference in her not getting promoted. She feels it is degrading that another colleague, with lesser experience and education, was promoted to the job. The literature on discrimination by employers in the West is echoed within the urban Indian corporate experience (Shier, Graham and Jones 2009).

By all accounts, employers' perception of a person's disability plays a part in determining their quality of experience in getting a job. A vocabulary of normal–abnormal has entered corporate discourse in pigeonholing individuals as capable or incapable. As gatekeepers to employment, they negate human capital when denying a job to people with disability. Seldom are job accommodations offered whereby the workplace is rendered accessible. Doing so would enable employers to distinguish between skills intrinsic to a job and the disabling conditions of an inaccessible workplace that produce a perceived incapacity in the first place. Maintaining this distinction would be a more equitable method of evaluating the capabilities of individuals. With global capital making its presence felt in the developing world, there is a view that a transformed work culture for people with disability will correspondingly establish itself. The next section voices the experiences of people with disability within corporate work environs.

Globalising the equal opportunity imperative

There is significant body of literature on how neo-liberal transformation and its consequent economic restructuring would reorder techno-governed subjectivities (Harvey 2005; Rose and Miller 2008). Newer market exigencies have demanded an unmaking of the self and a resizing of subjectivities to correspond with the newly arrived work culture of the global economic process, often with mixed results. In the experience of people with disability, recruiting practises appear unaffected by the avowed global equal opportunity imperative displayed by many corporate and government entities. Few companies display an equal opportunities policy, and, in the words of one respondent:

> People say now it is BPO (business process outsourcing) environment, IT companies follow American policy, and that some per cent of handicap[ped] people are employed. Really, when you go to the company, they don't recruit handicaps. I had gone for an interview, beforehand I had clarified to them I am a handicapped person, will it be a constraint to work in your company? I always clarify, only then I'll go for interview. They said no, no problem. But when I went there I felt some discomfort on their part. Then, they came back and told me that

they are looking only for male candidates. They had said before that they use only American policies and (that) we see that there are some percentage for handicaps. I said ok. Why only on paper is it mentioned? I am not asking for reservation. We only need equal opportunities. We don't need anyone's charity (gets angry). (27-year-old female recruitment consultant looking for a HR managerial position. Interview in English.)

There is a strong belief that in an interview, one is not evaluated on the basis of the intrinsic skill/s required by a particular job. Recruiters are forced to pay lip service to political correctness about equal employment opportunities. But there appears to be a tacit understanding within HR departments that acts like a glass ceiling for people with disability. People with disability believe that their applications are not rejected on merit alone. One seemingly discordant voice has this to say:

> These jobs are mentally cope-up jobs, so I don't find any problems. Moreover, they adopt MNC (multi-national corporation) culture in the office, so I don't find any discriminations, anything like that, all those things. MNC companies have policies: 'no discrimination against people with disability'. Previous company I worked in was not an MNC. There, I faced and heard some unwanted things. I did not feel like giving up work, but I decided to look for another job, and I got this job. (28-year-old male engineer employed in an IT firm. Interview in English and Kannada.)

The spirit of equity displayed by MNCs in the developing world is debatable. Comparing the disabled-friendly work cultures between MNCs and Indian companies might be warranted, but is clearly out of the purview of this essay. However, there appears to be differences in the work culture *between* companies, but not necessarily across the MNC–non MNC binary. Companies are not in favour of hiring people with disability or in maintaining a diverse employee profile. The neo-liberal vision of suitably crafted and pliant workers does not seem to include people with disability. An industry-level policy, however, now exists to standardise what is and is not acceptable behaviour towards people with disability, both at the workplace and in recruitment interviews (DEOC 2009). The effect of the Confederation of Indian Industry (CII) policy document on employment and recruitment practises remains to be seen. Having seen the experiences with corporate companies, it would be useful to look at experiences with the government.

Government offices and the disabled-friendly imperative

> Recently, when I applied for a job in the post office, they asked me for a physically handicapped certificate. I had every qualification that the post office required. I only didn't have a medical certificate as I had submitted it elsewhere. So, I wanted to make the new certificate, so I had gone to Bowring Hospital. There is a 'broker' (tout) in Bowring Hospital. He is also a handicapped person. He introduced me to the doctor who makes the medical certificate. I was asked to pay the doctor 300 rupees and the broker 200 rupees. I didn't have the money, and I had to call my cousin who brought the money. And then I got my certificate. And if you don't pay bribe, they make us come 101 times to the place. They don't know the value of our time, our effort. (26-year-old male MCA graduate training in J2EE programming. Interview in English.)

A medical certificate is crucial in applying for jobs reserved for people with disability. Authorities meant to dispense services convert their duties into illegal money-making ventures. Around three per cent of all jobs in public sector industries in India are reserved for people with disability. There is a lot of paperwork and red tape involved in availing this reservation. Anybody, regardless of disability, is made to run from pillar to post in securing the relevant signatures and revenue stamps. These are often located on multiple floors of government buildings. It is not clear from the interviews whether a bribe would yield a more enthusiastic response from the authorised signatories. According to one respondent:

> Government employees treat me as a not-normal person. If I go to the post office: 'What do you want, you go there. Go to 2nd floor and go do this thing'. They won't take my form, fill it and take it to 2nd floor and bring it down. They very well know I cannot go there, climb the stairs, submit the form, come down again. There are procedures. They've to sign one place, stamp one place, submit one place. Someone should help us to get all this work done. Five minutes before lunch, they'll close. So we've to wait for lunch hour to get over — after that, they'll say go get this signature, that stamp, and that will take one more hour.

We've to do this for routine things like handicap certificate, ration cards. (26-year-old male MCA graduate training in J2E programming. Interview in English.)

When procedural complexities are combined with inaccessible buildings, the process of applying for a job meant for a person with disability is exhausting. Governmental imperatives mean that all procedures have to be satisfied, however inaccessible the building within which it is housed. This respondent suggests that a mobile kiosk carrying the relevant officials, doctors, forms and revenue stamps should travel within the city to reduce cumbersome commutes for the target group. IT professionals interviewed ask for these procedures to be available online. Travelling to avail these government-led reservations and subsidies can be especially harrowing for the poor. In the words of a young mother:

> The employment exchange will send me to a second place for interview, and they will send me to a third place. And I'll lose all my money in travelling from one place to another. From Kalasipalyam[6] to faraway places. And they would disappoint me. Now, I don't want to go looking. I'm tired. I'm fed up. No guarantee I'll get the job. At least this way (staying at home) I can save up for my daughter's education. Maybe these reserved jobs go to those who bribe. There should be a single window for medical certificate, railway concession, bus passes, pension, job counselling, ID card. It should be area-wise, so that travelling isn't there. They should sell shoes, callipers, wheelchairs, sticks, aids at concessional rates there. Can we go to Lingarajapuram[7] every time? Disabled people can man this single window. Able-bodied can go work anywhere. This is not the case with disabled people. (30-year-old female B.Com. graduate with computer diploma, currently unemployed. Interview in Dakkani Urdu.)

Clearly, there is great dissatisfaction with the government. It takes a heavy toll in terms of fatigue, pain, and costs in running from pillar to post for essential documents to avail of state-sponsored policy benefits. There are also the psychological concomitants of mobility with a disability, specifically in the above instance where avoidance of travel, anxiety and fear are manifested. Much thought and work appear necessary across the public–private enterprise divide (Schur, Kruse and Blanck 2005). Corporate entities appear as ill-equipped as the government in the accounts provided by people with disability seeking employment. Only a handful of middle class respondents seem to be in the best position to utilise the limited employment opportunities available to them in the public and private concerns.

Role of social class

An explanation gesturing towards why people with locomotor disability give up their jobs can now be forwarded here. Some themes keep recurring among the findings, and it is increasingly evident that middle class respondents manage to circumvent the barriers experienced by more impoverished respondents. Such variables as the cost of education, job applications, travelling by autorickshaws, being unable to afford one's own vehicle, and disability-specific costs are subsumed under the rubric social class for purposes of this essay.

Middle class respondents

Middle class respondents have the financial cushioning to wait and look for work requiring manageable physical barriers. They can thereby focus on the exertion expended professionally, as opposed to making extra effort only to travel. They can afford to delay entry into the job market for that much longer than someone whose choice of entry into employment (as opposed to, say, studying further) is dependent on his/her financial situation. They can avoid travelling to work by bus, since they can afford a mode of travel that does not cause them fatigue or pain. Family support is also visible where relatives drive disabled respondents to work, thereby circumventing transport-related barriers.

Planning an architectonic ascent requires careful calculations. It often involves the physical support of a family member. Middle class respondents report taking family members to assist them in overcoming architectural barriers such as staircases without railings. They (family members) carry them to different floors all through school and college, apart from providing transfer between home–school–home. It means making prior arrangements to ensure availability of someone within the family to provide (possible) assistance within a building. In the following instance, family support is not forthcoming because of financial difficulty:

> The distance was far for me. Then, my father has to take care of his work, he couldn't pick me up and drop me. Buses were not so good at that time from Lingarajapuram. Nobody was there to pick me up and drop me. I don't have any elder brothers or younger brothers. I have only sisters. So, they can't pick me up and drop me because they have to take care of their education. Most of the time I sat and cried because of this problem. (23-year-old male, formerly lottery-stall attendant, currently unemployed. Interview in Kannada.)

In the case of family support, relatives who provide this logistical assistance are under no economic obligation to contribute to the household income. Socioeconomic status of the family allows the possibility of being able to afford a car, a two-wheeler or an autorickshaw. The relative's time spent in picking up and dropping a person off cannot be assumed to be 'free' in a monetary sense. It is an opportunity cost, and is also often a hidden cost. Ferrying (or not) a person with disability to the workplace, or school and college, appears dependent on the extent of the family income. Middle class respondents have organised and reliable family support, whereas the opposite case prevails further down the socioeconomic ladder. Impecunious disabled people do not attend as many job interviews, appointments and meetings. Being late or absent is, therefore, an endemic feature of their employment experience.

Working class respondents

Interviews in Bangalore reveal that it is indigent families that cannot spare a relative for caregiving to tide over the physical barriers of staircases for people with disability. These families feel the pinch of the income foregone from that relative. Insolvent families cannot afford private transport to overcome travel-related barriers in their search for employment. Travelling by autorickshaw is accessible but expensive, and, therefore, out of the reach of more impoverished respondents. Not owning a two-wheeler or not being able to maintain one is also cited. The cost of applying for jobs is a heavy burden. Getting a biodata written in English, getting it typed or printed, making photocopies, getting photographs for application forms, buying application forms, attaching demand drafts of ₹100–200, and mailing the applications can eat into a poor household's savings. One respondent acknowledges that his father takes loans to pay for these applications, whereas another respondent has spent ₹10,000 on applications. Consider the following quote:

> No, I have left applying. For each (job) application, it costs me 1000 rupees. My father is a driver, and we are four children. Everyone in the house has to be taken care of (not just me). Right now he is looking after all, alone. He took a lot of interest and he gave me good amount of money continuously. But there was no results, he would have pity and bring me money for application. He would borrow money outside and give me the money. So it was a problem for him too. (23-year-old male trainee tailor looking to set up his own tailoring shop. Interview in Dakkani Urdu.)

Tired of applying for government jobs, this respondent has started an apprenticeship for ₹15 a day at a tailor's shop near his house. Given that the sample in the Bangalore study has more middle class respondents, the impact of these barriers on poorer people with locomotor disability is likely to be more pronounced.

Deploying class to overcome inaccessibility of the built environment

Respondents with the advantage of socioeconomic class convert that advantage to manage fatigue better. That they consequently perform better at education and at their workplace is expected. People with locomotor disability travel by bus because it is cheap, and would much rather prefer to travel by autorickshaws or their own vehicle, if only they can afford to. Those who can afford their own means of transportation stop using public transport as soon as it is financially feasible. Connected to means of transport is the level of exertion that different respondents feel. Those who have to walk more and take buses more often are more likely to be tired than those who are dropped off by family or friends in vehicles. Not only does it affect the level of exertion they feel, but it also changes their professional aspirations and goals. They report fewer barriers at the entry level of the employment market, and obstacles reported have more to do with not being considered for office promotions. Dropping out of jobs in all probability is lower for this group.

Respondents who cannot use a bus or afford any other mode of transport are likely to have the poorest occupational outcomes. Owners of vehicles report fewer barriers than the subset that have to use buses for getting around the city. Interestingly, the subset of respondents, who use autorickshaws, also report fewer barriers to employment. Their experiences in transfer appear to mirror those of the vehicle owners. The question of being able to afford one's own vehicle, or travelling by autorickshaw, is important here. Socioeconomic class appears to mitigate the harsh experience of travel by public transport.

Conclusions

While this chapter has specifically looked at mobility in connection with employment through the prism of class, a similar analytic frame may be deployed in other domains of life such as education and everyday activities like shopping, paying bills, entertainment, etc. They entail a similar kind of cost–benefit analysis as involved in mobility pertaining to occupation-related transfer. The present study does not ask respondents about the effects of everyday activities in other spheres of life. In retrospect, this appears to be a critical future path for research given the findings in this study.

The attempt in this chapter is not to supplant one structural explanation for another, i.e., moving from a social model explanation into a class-determined one. Neither is this an indulgent attempt to resolve the intransigent dialogue between structure and agency governing the sociology of disability. Respondents who can afford to do so appear to knowledgeably manoeuvre between social structures that inform their everyday, in this case, offsetting the disabling built environment with socioeconomic class. In fact, respondents tended to draw on their social class habitus to inflect the effects of a disabling environment. Focusing on the body and its experiences, following from the sociology of impairment, yields a class-enmeshed explanation that thickens our exploration of the disability experience with employment, and describes the basis for internal differences within those experiences.

This essay does not frame the access question from within a prescriptive, human rights axis. Rather, it has focused primarily on emphasising the lack of barrier-free environments. This is in order to detail the contours of the disability experience with the built environment, to underscore an 'an ethnography of physicality' (Shakespeare and Watson 1995). I contend that accessibility to the built environment is more critical for poor people with locomotor disability. They cannot subsidise means of managing fatigue and the inaccessibility of the built environment, a factor crucial in the relative educational and occupational success of middle class respondents with disability. What an affluent respondent could sidestep by virtue of travel, an uninterrupted education, avoidance of public transport and finding an accessible workplace, is not available for an impoverished person with locomotor disability. This is the import of making the built environment accessible for urban India. It would render equitable access to services that are, otherwise, the exclusive preserve of more affluent respondents who tend to buy their way out of inaccessibility of the built environment and transport. Perception of barriers change depending on the socioeconomic class of the respondents. This would necessarily alter the view that people with locomotor disability are a homogenous category. Of course, I would hesitate to pronounce this generalisation across disabilities.

However, one cannot de-emphasise the explanatory effects of disability in favour of socioeconomic class. The latter cannot explain everything about the disabled experience of employment. We could also agree that the inaccessibility of the built environment at the workplace produces the alleged inability of people with disability. And that those who can afford to dodge these structural exigencies, indeed, have the best occupational outcomes among people with disability. But even if socioeconomic class determines the quality of transfer, it would be difficult to explain employers' perceptions at the recruitment stage as also a function of economics. Clearly, the answer appears intertwined given the explanatory variables revealed by the study. The transfer explanation is premised on the lack of an accessible environment, along with the lack of policy enforcement, that maintain an inaccessible built environment.

Notes

* The present essay has evolved from an M.Phil. dissertation submitted to the Department of Social Policy and Social Work at the University of Oxford in 2005. A version of this essay was presented at the Critical Disability Studies Conference, University of Hyderabad, in October 2007. I would like to thank Renu Addlakha for detailed comments on an earlier draft. Responsibility, however, for any inaccuracies remain solely mine.

1. Different definitions of disability are used by the Census and the NSSO leading to discrepancy in results (Mitra and Sambamoorthi 2006). For a critique of the official statistics pertaining to disability and the census, see Harriss-White and Erb (2002).

2. The National Sample Survey Organisation defines locomotor disability as 'a person with (a) loss or lack of normal ability to execute distinctive activities associated with the movement of self and objects from place to place and (b) physical deformities, other than those involving the hand or leg or both, regardless of whether the same caused loss or lack of normal movement of body — was considered as disabled with locomotor disability. Thus, persons having locomotor disability included those with (a) loss or absence or inactivity of whole or part of hand or leg or both due to amputation, paralysis, deformity or dysfunction of joints which affected his/her "normal ability to move self or objects" and (b) those with physical deformities in the body (other than limbs), such as, hunch back, deformed spine, etc.' (NSSO 2003: 43). The NSSO, by employing a wider definition of locomotor disability to 'include people with paralysis, amputation, deformity, dysfunction of joints and dwarfism' (Mitra and Sambamoorthy 2006: 4024; NSSO 2003: 8), has higher prevalence rates (10.6 million people or 57.5 per cent of all disabled people) than the Census (Mitra and Sambamoorthy 2006: 4023, NSSO 2003: 43). The Census definition only covers 'the absence of all toes, all fingers, deformity, the ability to move without aid, the inability to lift and carry any small article' (Mitra and Sambamoorthy 2006: 4024), which, therefore, pegs the number of people with locomotor disability to 27.9 per cent of all disabled people, or 6.1 million people (ibid.).

3. Submitted to the Department of Social Policy and Social Work, at the University of Oxford, as an M.Phil. thesis in 2005.

4. The Erikson–Goldthorpe class schema is a 'categorization which allocates individuals and families into social classes', which would enable comparison between an individual's market situation (degree of economic security, chances of advancement) and their work situation

(their location within systems of authority governing the processes of production) (Marshall 1998).
5. There appears to be no consensus about the timeline implied when respondents distinguished between old and new buildings. Some respondents seem to suggest that buildings built over 30 years ago qualify as being 'old', whereas for some others, the figure is closer to 70 years. It is difficult to arrive at a uniform cut-off time period for assessing what is being referred to as an old building or a new one. But ascertaining if it is old or new is important in estimating how accessible it is likely to be.
6. Kalasipalyam is a busy commercial area in central Bangalore.
7. Lingarajapuram, a middle income suburb in northwest Bangalore, also houses a few NGOs working for people with disability.

References

Addlakha, Renu. 2008. *Deconstructing Mental Illness: An Ethnography of Psychiatry, Women and the Family*. New Delhi: Zubaan.
Corker, Mairian. 2001. 'Sensing Disability', *Hypatia*, 16 (4): 34–52.
DEOC (ed.). 2009. *A Values Route to Business Success. The Why and How of Employing Persons with Disability*. Bangalore: Confederation of Indian Industry.
Elwan, Ann. 1999. 'Poverty and Disability: A Survey of the Literature', *Social Protection Discussion Paper Series*. Washington, DC: The World Bank, http://siteresources.worldbank.org/DISABILITY/Resources/280658-1172608138489/PovertyDisabElwan.pdf (accessed 13 July 2012).
Erikson, Robert and John H. Goldthorpe. 1992. *The Constant Flux: A Study of Class Mobility in Industrial Societies*. Oxford: Oxford University Press.
Friedner, Michele. 2009. 'Computers and Magical Thinking: Work and Belonging in Bangalore', *Economic and Political Weekly*, XLIV (26, 27): 37–40.
Ghai, Anita. 2005. 'Disability in Contemporary India', *Encyclopedia of Disability*. Thousand Oaks, CA: SAGE Publications.
Granovetter, Mark S. 1995. *Getting a Job: A Study of Contacts and Careers*. Chicago: University of Chicago Press.
Harriss-White, Barbara and Susan Erb. 2002. *Outcast from Social Welfare: Adult Disability in Rural South India*. Bangalore: Books for Change.
Harvey, David. 2005. *A Brief History of Neoliberalism*. Oxford: Oxford University Press.

Hughes, Bill and Kevin Paterson. 1997. 'The Social Model of Disability and the Disappearing Body: Towards a Sociology of Impairment', *Disability and Society*, 12 (3): 325–40.

Lowman, Dianne Koontz, Steven L. West and Brian T. McMahon. 2005. 'Workplace Discrimination and Americans with Cerebral Palsy: The National EEOC ADA Research Project', *Journal of Vocational Rehabilitation*, 23 (3): 171–77.

Marshall, Gordon. 1998. *A Dictionary of Sociology*. New York: Oxford University Press.

McMahon, Brian T., Phillip D. Rumrill, Richard T. Roessler and Shawn M. Fitzgerald. 2005. 'Multiple Sclerosis and Workplace Discrimination: The National EEOC ADA Research Project', *Journal of Vocational Rehabilitation*, 23 (3): 179–87.

McMahon, Brian T., Linda R. Shaw, Steven L. West and Kay Waid-Ebbs. 2005. 'Workplace Discrimination and Spinal Cord Injury: The National EEOC ADA Research Project', *Journal of Vocational Rehabilitation*, 23 (3): 155–62.

Merleau-Ponty, Maurice. 1962. *Phenomenology of Perception*, trans. Colin Smith. London: Routledge and Kegan Paul.

Michailakis, Dimitris. 2003. 'The Systems Theory Concept of Disability: One is not Born a Disabled Person, One is Observed to be One', *Disability and Society*, 18 (2): 209–29.

Mitra, Sophie and Usha Sambamoorthi. 2006. 'Disability Estimates in India: What the Census and NSS Tell Us', *Economic and Political Weekly*, 41 (38): 4022–26.

Nettleton, Sarah and Jonathan Watson (eds). 1998. *The Body in Everyday Life*. London and New York: Routledge.

NSSO. 2003. *Disabled Persons in India: NSS 58th Round, July–December 2002*. New Delhi: National Sample Survey Organisation, Ministry of Statistics and Programme Implementation, Government of India.

Rose, Nikolas and Peter Miller. 2008. *Governing the Present: Administering Economic, Social and Personal Life*. Cambridge: Polity Press.

Scheid, Teresa L. 2005. 'Stigma as a Barrier to Employment: Mental Disability and the Americans with Disabilities Act', *International Journal of Law and Psychiatry*, 28 (6): 670–90.

Schur, Lisa, Douglas Kruse and Peter Blanck. 2005. 'Corporate Culture and the Employment of Persons with Disabilities', *Behavioral Sciences and the Law*, 23 (1): 3–20.

Seymour, Wendy. 1998. *Remaking the Body: Rehabilitation and Change*. St. Leonards, NSW: Allen & Unwin.

Shakespeare, Tom and Nicholas Watson. 1995. 'Defending the Social Model', *Disability and Society*, 12 (2): 293–300.

Shier, Michael, John Graham and Marion Jones. 2009. 'Barriers to Employment as Experienced by Disabled People: A Qualitative Analysis in Calgary and Regina, Canada', *Disability and Society*, 24 (1): 63–75.

Smith, Dorothy E. 1987. *The Everyday World as Problematic: A Feminist Sociology*. Toronto: University of Toronto Press.

Turner, Bryan S. 1998. 'Foreword', in Wendy Seymour, *Remaking the Body: Rehabilitation and Change*, pp. v–viii. London and New York: Routledge.

———. 2001. 'Disability and the Sociology of the Body', in Gary L. Albrecht, Katherine D. Seelman and Michael Bury (eds), *Handbook of Disability Studies*, pp. 252–66. Thousand Oaks, CA: SAGE Publications.

Wendell, Susan. 1989. 'Towards a Feminist Theory of Disability', *Hypatia*, 4 (2): 104–24.

PART III
Gender and Disability

8

Bhalo Meye: Cultural Construction of Gender and Disability in Bengal

NANDINI GHOSH

Gender has been conceptualised as a power relationship based on perceived differences between the sexes, expressed through social structures and institutions. Gender uses culturally given and accepted ideologies to distinguish between activities, behaviour, norms and representations accorded to the two socially constructed genders, and to legitimise the sexual distinction between men and women in society. Similarly, disability has been conceptualised as a power relationship between people with impairments and non-disabled people that devalues and excludes disabled people from mainstream society by constructing different acts/people as deviant (Abberley 1987). Attitudes, discourses and symbolic representations are critical to the reproduction of disablement, but are themselves the product of the social practices which society undertakes in order to meet its basic material needs (Gleeson 1997; Oliver 1996).

Feminist disability scholars posit an alternate understanding of disabled women, in order to understand how bodies — marked by gender and disability, and by impairment and sex — are formed in, created by, and acted upon by society, as also act within and impact society (Morris 1998; Schriempf 2001). Feminist disability studies attempts to understand the ways in which the representational systems of gender, race, ethnicity, ability, sexuality and class mutually construct, inflect and contradict one another, and intersect to produce and sustain ascribed, achieved and acquired identities. The simultaneous experience of gender and disability highlights the ways in which bodies interact with socially engineered environments, including the natural environment, the built environment, culture, the economic system, the political system and psychological factors to conform to or depart from social expectations (Thomson 1997).

This chapter looks at the ways in which the simultaneous experience of gender and disability influences the lives, of Bengali women and structures their daily lives to create uniquely gendered and disabled identities. The essay looks at the daily lives of a cohort of women with orthopaedic disabilities and explores the multifarious ways in which gender and ability affect the play of power in their lives, both within their home and outside. Using a life cycle approach, the essay reveals the experiences of disabled Bengali women at different stages of their lives, such as childhood, adolescence and adulthood in their natal and affinal families. It specifically explores the subjectivity of the disabled female body in structuring notions of femininity, desirability and sexuality.

Over the last three centuries, there has been a complex process of construction of gender in India through cultural symbols, social ideologies and invoking of the so-called indigenous belief systems. According to Bagchi (1995), Indian womanhood is based on a multi-layered accretion of myths that serves patriarchy in both its global and local manifestations. In Bengal, gender ideologies, developed and accepted by the upper middle classes during the Nationalist struggle, recast women as mothers, with the Nation being projected as a Mother to be obeyed, protected and revered. However, the same ideologies also posited a separation between the realms of operation of men and women, with the outside, or *bahir*, seen ideally as the men's domain and the inside, or the *ghar*, being the women's domain. The *bahir* was seen as the domain of practical considerations and dominated by the profane activities of the material world, while the home was posited as the representation of one's true identity, one's spiritual self; and women became the representation and repository of this inner/spiritual domain. This ideological distinction between the public/private, the *bahir/ghar* and the material/spiritual led to the specification of social roles by gender and the differential spheres of operation of men and women in Bengali society (Chatterjee 1999). The strict segregation of private feminine spaces from the public male areas led to the formulation of two completely different worlds of physical experience and quality of life, governed by varying norms and expectations, which not only created distinct spheres of functions and influence but also affected the relationship between the sexes. Although these ideologies were mostly put into practice in the upper middle class homes, they were accepted and internalised by most sections of Bengali society.

In Bengal there are two dominant representations of femininity for women to follow, one for young unmarried girls and the other for married women who are expected to model their lives on those of their mother or mother-in-law. There is no model associated with spinsterhood in this society. The life of a woman can be divided into two parts: one, before her marriage spent at her *baper bari* (father's home) and the other, thereafter, at her *sasur bari* (father-in-law's home). In Bengal, with its stress on motherhood as the only goal for women, the domestic arena is recognised as the most suitable for them. Bengali girls are trained by female relatives and kinswomen from a very early age to fulfil their future roles as wife and mother (Bagchi 1993; Chakraborty 1998; Roy 1972). Within the family, girls learn to help with the household chores, are familiarised with their domestic duties and obligations, and are trained to modify their expectations and adjust their behaviour accordingly (Bagchi, Guha and Sengupta 1997; Cormack 1953).

Methodology

Feminist ethnography emphasises that knowledge is contextual and interpersonal, based on women's experiences within the concrete realms of everyday reality. It offers opportunities for the documentation of women's lived experiences in a way that they are not rendered subsidiary to men's lives (Bryman 2001). This study is exploratory and has been conducted in the cultural context of Bengal concentrating on women with orthopaedic disabilities. Feminists recognise that the category 'woman' is not universal across space and time, and that cultural differences, social divisions and power relations lead to varied experiences for women. Thus, selection of the research participants has taken into account differences among disabled women themselves based on degree of disability, type of residential setting (rural/urban), religious affiliation, and varied status positions, for example, working/not working, married/single, young/middle-aged, etc. Being primarily ethnographic in nature, the study uses different qualitative techniques for data collection and contextual analytic tools for data analysis.

The research was conducted in two districts of West Bengal — Kolkata, which is urban, and 24 Parganas (South), which is rural. Most of the disabled women were identified and approached through NGOs working in the area, but were subsequently contacted personally to enlist them in the research. Fieldwork was completed in a period of 12 months, which involved a pre-study visit, data collection and a backup visit to all the women to get their feedback about the findings. Multiple methods of data collection were used, including observation and in-depth interviewing. Local people in the field sites, such as heads of *panchayats* or the *gram panchayat* representatives, school teachers and other people in the community were contacted to gain a better understanding of the specific gender/disability ideologies operating in the areas.

Of the 16 women who participated in the study, eight have a severe disability. While four have mild physical impairments, the remaining four have moderate disabilities. Their ages vary between 24 and 40 years, with most of them falling in the age range of 30–40 years. Among the participants, 10 live in villages, while six stay in the city. Only five of the mildly disabled women have been married — at present, one is widowed. Five of the single women stay with their natal families, while two stay away from their homes due to employment factors. Twelve of them either work or are between jobs. Most of the women living in the rural areas belong to the poorer socioeconomic group and to the lower caste groups like the *Mahisya*.[1] The predominant occupation in these areas is agriculture and agro-based enterprises, with most of the (predominantly extended) families growing paddy and meeting their annual need for rice from their harvest. The land holdings are small, fragmented by continuous division over generations. The villages are located off the major roads in the area, with the *paras*[2] in which these women reside often being even more inaccessible in the interiors. In contrast, the women living in the city belong to the upper castes, like the Brahmins and Kayasthas, and to upper and middle class families.

The Bhalo Meye: Contradictions and Constraints

Patriarchy in Bengal works in a benevolent fashion, concealing the rigid control that is exercised over the daughters and womenfolk in the family through mechanisms like coercion and persuasion. The cultural strategy used is that of an image, an ideal type of a 'good' woman towards which all women must aspire or be relegated to the image of a 'bad' woman (Bandyopadhyay 1995). A *'bhalo meye'* refers to a good woman, which, in common parlance, means a morally upright woman with all the positive feminine attributes, primarily one who is the pivot of an ideal family. A *bhalo meye* is one who gets married and adheres to the cultural stereotype of being a wife and mother. With respect to disability, a *bhalo meye* symbolises a woman with an unimpaired body and optimum capabilities, one who is seen as potentially capable of taking on increasing responsibilities to cater to the needs of her natal and affinal families, one whose productive and reproductive capacities blossom from adolescence to adulthood.

Disabled girls are socialised within their families and the community to accept and live according to gendered/disabled norms that govern their entire lives, leading to the creation of differences that underpin their identities. As women's primary roles are of wife and mother, they have to be capable of doing household work. Women have the responsibility of maintaining the *sansar*[3] once they grow up. In such a cultural context, the onset of disability is seen as a catastrophe for the young daughter who becomes flawed and physically less capable than other girls. Perceiving that their disabled daughters would have to struggle against a social order that values women's productive and reproductive capabilities, parents make all efforts to ensure that the impairment is 'cured', or its impact minimised, so that the affected girl would at least be able to lead a life as 'normal' as possible. The paramount concern, especially in the minds of the mothers, is that she should at least be able to take care of herself, if not of the other members of the family. One strategy is to reduce the visual impact of the disability, which many parents feel would give a semblance of normalcy and also enable their disabled daughter to be more independent. Here the effect is twofold — helping their daughter to overcome or minimise the effects of her disability, which would reduce the visual impact of the disability, thereby 'normalising' her and, thus, enabling her to live a more independent life.

Childhood

Disabled girls in the study experience the processes of gender socialisation like other girls in Bengali culture. Their impairment is seen as something that interferes with such socialisation in a variety of ways. Within the family, disabled girls live a protected and pampered life, cared for by their mothers and sisters and cosseted by their fathers and other extended family members. They forge close bonds with their siblings and cousins, and participate in family and community activities like other children. Differences are created subtly between them and their siblings — differences that are not always negative, but which may reinforce their 'special status' in the family. These differences are based on perceptions about the impairment, pain and insufficiencies associated therewith, and the possible medical rehabilitation of the condition. The impact of the impairment, both actual and constructed, is linked to the construction and performance of gendered abilities. Such processes serve to concretise and consolidate the gender identity of disabled girls, while at the same time underlining her distinctiveness and marking her as different from the other children around her.

While loved and cared for in their families, the socialisation of disabled daughters is characterised by startling similarities and subtle differences between them and their brothers and sisters. Perceived by the sociocultural ideologies as imperfect and flawed, parents and extended family members often create a distinct difference between the disabled girl and her siblings by granting special privileges, like pampering her more than the other children and excusing her from household chores. Although the degree of disability influences such behaviour, parental cosseting reveals the nature of the sociocultural ideologies that construct the disabled girl as weak and in need of protection. Fathers, in particular, were found to be more protective and pampering of their disabled daughter, while mothers sought to reinforce the fact that the disability notwithstanding, their daughters were still subject to a gender-based socialisation. Siblings are made to realise and accept that their sister is special and needs extra support and help from them. The exemption of disabled girls from household work, or assignment of work that is considered to be 'light', serves to highlight differences with other siblings and reinforces ableist ideologies that decree disabled people as unfit to participate in familial and social processes. The creation of such differences, in the form of special privileges between the disabled girl and her siblings, sometimes leads to strained relations among them. A majority of the study participants feel that being perceived as special and different meant that they are excluded from the activities that their siblings could engage in. Disabled girls come to realise and accept that they are different from their non-disabled sisters, and that they cannot aspire to achieve what is subsumed in the ideological construct of the *bhalo meye*, meaning the good girl, implying, at least in theory, a girl with a functionally perfect body.

Adolescence

During late childhood and early adolescence, disabled girls are more sharply made aware of differences between them and their other siblings, especially their sisters and female cousins. Interviewees feel that in childhood there was greater equality among them because they were unaware of the social construction of disability and disabled people, and hence developed a relationship of deep affection, of sharing of daily activities like bathing, eating and playing. They felt more comfortable and less self-conscious about moving by crawling or limping, as they had not yet internalised social perceptions that deem crawling as degrading. Thus, going out of the house crawling to the playground with siblings, friends and cousins was not perceived as humiliating, particularly in rural areas. During adolescence, disabled girls, who feel the differences between themselves and their able-bodied female counterparts most sharply, also experienced feelings of jealousy towards the latter.

Training in household work usually begins for all girls in late childhood, with mothers assigning different tasks like fetching water, washing utensils, peeling vegetables, cleaning the house, etc., that are aimed at preparing them for their adult roles of wife and mother. From the age of six or seven years, a girl starts helping out with the work at home in the rural areas. Girls with the most severe disabilities, like cerebral palsy affecting all limbs, are the only ones exempted from this kind of gendered training. The girls with mild to moderate disabilities find themselves being assigned household work, although the imperative of taking up the responsibility varies from family to family. All girls, disabled or not, are expected to take some responsibility for household work, but differences are created between sisters with regard to the kind of work assigned to them — the lighter or easier tasks being assigned to disabled girls, especially if there are elder sisters or sisters-in-law in the family. For disabled girls, the ability to engage in and efficiently perform household chores is one way of lessening the differences constructed and enacted between them and their female siblings.

As they grow up and widen their spheres of interaction, disabled girls increasingly come to realise the extent of their difference from other people and the wider ramifications of their impairments, which are accompanied by feelings of anger, bitterness and deep resentment. On seeing them crawling or walking with a very different gait on the road, people stare, point towards and tease them. This difference is devalued and makes the girls objects of ridicule. Informants recall how boys were more derisive of them and their impairments. The social valuation of perfect bodies not only accentuates visible differences but, when coupled with teasing comments and taunts, also gives rise to feelings of inferiority and humiliation. Girls who are unable to walk feel a sense of shame because of the way in which they move, either by crawling or by dragging their hips, which makes them the objects of mockery and pity in public. These feelings get crystallised during adolescence, and coping strategies, such as leading a reclusive existence, may be used to deal with them.

The internalisation of difference is further reinforced in school in the face of different physical and material realities, and from the way in which a non-disabled strange world looks at and treats them. The nature and extent of disability influences this experience. For girls with mild to moderate disabilities, parents stress the need for education, because they realise and accept the fact that their daughter has to be made capable of supporting herself financially, as gender roles available to other women might be closed off to her. Some interviewees report how teachers used to encourage them to study further, because they had implicitly accepted and wanted the girls to also accept that the lifestyle options available to other girls would most likely be denied to them. However, most girls drop out of school at the secondary level because high schools are located in faraway villages. For disabled girls, it becomes nearly impossible to traverse such distances given the difficulties of mobility.

Given the material reality of the impairment, disabled girls learn to struggle against, accept and manage their bodies according to gendered constructions decreed by the culture. The performance of a feminine self becomes central as they grow up, especially in public spaces where they encounter the 'gaze' more fiercely than in familiar surroundings. Disabled girls become most aware of differences in gait and ability during adolescence, and experience a sense of failure at not being a *bhalo meye*. They seek to minimise the visual impact of their impairment by adopting a gait that appears more 'normal' in order to gain greater acceptance. For instance, notions of femininity internalised through socialisation may influence the use of mobility aids. Some prefer to use the aids only outside the home, as they feel it confers more dignity in public spaces. Other girls feel that the metallic aid attached to leather boots diminishes their sense of themselves as women.

Adulthood: Living the difference

Wanting to be identified and accepted as 'women', interviewees, particularly those with mild to moderate disabilities, wear feminine clothes reflecting feminine norms of beauty in order to prove their equality with other women. Although the popular attire for growing girls is the *salwar kameez*, a long tunic with loose trousers, it is the degree of disability that determines the choice of clothes to a great extent; and women, who earlier wore skirts and blouses, continue to do so, citing convenience of movement in such clothes. Notions of modesty are tailored to the needs of their impaired bodies and different gaits, but the adherence to adolescent dress codes is suggestive of arrested womanhood and a slightly different code of modesty that allows them to wear pre-pubescent types of clothes for reasons of convenience. Some of the women downplay their femininity by dressing conservatively, so as not to call any extra attention on themselves than what they are already subjected to on account of their impairments.

Ableist ideologies and the actuality of their impairments deem that these women are represented as dependent and incapable of dealing with increased responsibilities. Household work given to women includes cooking, cleaning utensils, washing clothes, sweeping and swabbing the rooms, and taking care of young children and elderly people; in the rural areas, additional tasks like fetching drinking water, collecting firewood and tending to animals are also part of their daily chores. Disabled women, however, experience this process differently depending on their bodily deficits, the milieu in which they are located and individual familial perceptions regarding the capacities of women with disabilities. Disabled women are considered incapable of engaging in most of these tasks. Interviews with both parents and the women themselves reveal that they feel that the impairment is the main source of difference between them and their sisters. In adolescence, disabled girls are seldom asked to help with the household chores, even while their younger sisters are coached carefully. Mothers are afraid to assign tasks to their disabled daughters that involve moving around or carrying heavy loads, as they feel they would harm themselves or, in poorer homes, lead to spoiling of expensive articles.

In Bengali culture, household chores are divided into *gharer kaaj* (housework) and *sansarer kaaj* (household work). While the *ghar* signifies only the home, *sansar* is conceptualised as the entire family and household, with social and cultural importance, and entailing an entirely different set of responsibilities. While a disabled woman may be assigned *gharer kaaj*, she is deemed unfit for *sansarer kaaj*, which includes taking care of the entire family. Assumed to be less capable and often treated at par with children, disabled women are seen as incapable of shouldering the *sansarer kaaj*, though she may be capable of dealing with some of the work within the home. Although families have a tendency to treat the disabled daughter differently in terms of giving her a lighter workload, yet they also tend to undermine the capabilities of the women and negate their efforts citing the inability of the women to do the work independently, and without assistance, in completing tasks. This happens even in cases when the women are actually shouldering many of the household responsibilities, including cleaning utensils and washing clothes of the entire household.

Families devalue and question the capacity of disabled women to engage in productive work like other women. Disabled women themselves also internalise such ideas of devaluation and doubt their own abilities. Due to the travel and physical stress involved, disabled women are perceived as particularly incapable of engaging in agricultural activities in rural areas. However, we know that degree of impairment and availability of opportunities are the major factors. Ideologies of work posit mild and moderately disabled women as capable of handling income-generating work outside the home. Interviewees were found to be engaged in different kinds of work that entail hard labour, despite the connotations of incapability associated with disability and weakness associated with both gender and disability. Indeed, the awareness that most people expect that they will not be able to fulfil work responsibilities impels these women to take on their jobs as a challenge.

Sexuality

The notion of a *bhalo meye* dominates the minds of disabled women as someone who is physically unimpaired, and hence a 'complete' woman. Socialisation into patriarchal ideologies results in internalising notions of feminine beauty, attractiveness and appropriate feminine behaviour where there is no space for deviation from fixed norms. Patriarchal/ability systems specify the visual nature of desirability in women, which, for disabled women, depends not only on their physical features in general but also on the kind and degree of disability. They come to realise that although they are expected to conform to other 'feminine' norms, they are excluded from gendered notions of sexuality. This affects the ways in which disabled women experience, adapt to and deal with culturally valued notions of femininity, desirability and attractiveness. While severely disabled women in the research accept such exclusion more or less passively, women with mild and moderate disabilities find it more difficult to accept and negotiate such exclusion, because of the semblance of 'normality' that they have or experience in their lives.

In the public domain, disabled women are more openly confronted with dominant ideas regarding femininity and ability and stereotypical representations that cast them as dependent, incapable and weak. Within the neighbourhood, despite evidence of the work that they engage in on a daily basis, their condition may be described as 'legs are bad' (non-functional) and 'cannot do any work'. Seeing them in the public domain amounts to transgression of norms of acceptability, which are gendered and ability-centred. Prevalent ideologies posit them as 'incomplete' women, who do not need any form of ornamentation, as against 'normal' women, who have to adhere to acceptable notions of dressing and adornment. Disabled women, regarded as unfeminine and unattractive, are relegated to the sidelines of femininity and made to feel that they need not attempt to beautify themselves as objects of male pleasure.

Like other young persons, respondents discuss boys — and what they find attractive in other girls — with their sisters and friends, but they hesitate to reveal their feelings regarding men for fear of ridicule and rejection as women by both men and other women. Women in the study feel that men do not consider them attractive, because they do not match the feminine requirements of beauty, grace and physical perfection. During adolescence, norms of appropriate behaviour, applicable to women in general, are also extended to disabled women, curbing their freedom of movement outside the home for fear of losing their reputation as a *bhalo meye*. However, there is a denial of sexuality, as even mothers opine that their daughters are less at risk of sexual abuse and assault on account of being disabled.[4] They express less anxiety for the safety of their disabled daughters in comparison to their non-disabled daughters. On the other hand, mothers will ask their disabled daughters to avoid male attention in order to protect their reputation as the onus is on them as single women to guard the family honour.[5]

Disabled women are not expected to get married due to the sociocultural constructions of marriageability for women. Disabled women, located beyond definitions of sexuality, desirability and marriageability, live in the liminal space of not being a *bhalo meye* and, yet, also not being a *baje meye* (bad girl). Hence, they fear being labelled a loose woman as also being shamed for being disabled and having sexual urges. This is observed more in the case of women living in rural areas, comprising closed communities, where every action is noticed and commented upon. The onus of maintaining their reputation as a *bhalo meye* in the moral sense is doubly important for disabled women, as they feel that they have already lost status as physically and functionally perfect women. Despite the denial of their sexuality, disabled women report fearing repercussions, both physical and social, on account of any sexual attention that they might receive.

From adolescence, these girls are given subtle messages and come to accept the impossibility of the idea of marriage in their lives. While families rarely tell the girl directly, silence conveys equally loudly the message that she is not considered marriageable. Asha says that at her home, no one ever talks of her marriage even though she is the oldest of the sisters. Her grandmother would tell her: 'You stay in this house like a son. Other girls will get married and leave but you will stay here always.' Asha adds, 'My mother also says I am like her son as I will never leave home. I am their elder son, and my brother, their younger son.'

Such messages are used to condition the young disabled girl to accept her 'fate' by comparing her to the sons of the family, who never have to leave their natal homes. This desexing of disabled girls not only further denies their femininity and sexuality, but also underscores the fact that she will never get married like her sisters.

The notion of the *bhalo meye*, a woman who is physically unimpaired, beautiful and capable of physical labour, plays an important role in the representation of disabled women as unmarriageable. The association of marriage for a woman with the ability to engage in household work is uppermost in the minds of parents. Families, people in the community and the women themselves accept that their impairments would make it impossible for them to assume household responsibilities and perform all the tasks expected of a married woman — functional incapacity becomes one of the primary reasons for not being considered fit for marriage. Inability to cope with household work and caring for the affinal family are the most common reasons cited for the lack of marriage prospects for disabled women. Families also fear that disabled daughters would be subjected to physical violence for not being able to cope with the responsibilities of marriage.

Aspirations for marriage vary with age as well as severity of disability. Girls with severe disabilities come to accept at an early age that marriage is an impossible proposition for them. As they grow older, women with moderate to severe disabilities reconcile themselves to the fact of remaining single throughout their lives. Older women express fears of being deserted by men after marriage, especially if they were lured with the promise of dowry. Younger girls struggle against societal and familial ideologies that deem that they cannot get married. Notions of heteronormativity and social acceptability dominate their perceptions. The women stress the need for fulfilment of their husbands' desires and consider the shame and rejection that non-disabled men would face for having a disabled wife. The fear of social ridicule works in a reverse manner also, when women with mild to moderate disabilities contemplate marriage with a disabled man.

Judged against the imaginary norms of femininity and the ideal of *bhalo meye*, disabled women feel that they are considered incapable of having relationships that allow women to express their sexuality. Ideologies of feminine attractiveness represent impaired bodies and disabled women as undesirable, unfit for attracting the attention of potential partners and incapable of entering relationships that require women to assume the roles of wife, mother and carer of families. Encounters with men in the public sphere reaffirm these beliefs and representations, with rejection and negation of their femininity being the habitual responses.

Marriage is cited as one of the least possible options for disabled women — proposals are received at an older age mainly from disabled men, reinforcing their sense of devaluation as women. Such marriage proposals are received only by women with mild to moderate disabilities. Most disabled women, however, prefer to have non-disabled partners. The idea of social acceptability is internalised by them, too, and they prefer men who will be able to support them financially and whose impairment is not visibly severe. Offers of marriage from non-disabled men are not only few and far between, but also come with (unacceptable) clauses and conditions attached to them. The family of one of the women having mild impairment had found a suitable match for her — a boy from another district, who was living and working in their own village. He agreed to the marriage on the condition that he would be allowed to live with her family till he was able to construct a house for both of them. Just a week before the marriage, he laid down another condition — part of the natal home of the disabled woman would have to be legally transferred in his name before the marriage. For yet another woman, the groom's family demanded enough money to build the second floor of their house, which they claimed would be given to the new couple. On being asked by the woman's family to transfer part of the house in the name of the disabled girl and her husband, the groom's family refused and cancelled the arranged marriage.

Disabled women face both denial of their sexuality as well as sexual abuse. Men in public spaces often treat them not only as objects of pity and ridicule, but also as available for sexual favours. The same ideology that deems disabled women as sexually unattractive works in favour of men who treat them as objects of pleasure without fear of repercussions since, they reason, 'who would ever think of doing anything to a girl like her?' The 'gaze' for disabled women is constituted not just by the way men look at and objectify women, but also by the way in which the non-disabled world looks at disabled people. Disabled women simultaneously feel the pressure of feminine and able-bodied bodily norms and expectations that contribute to their exclusion and exploitation in society.

Conclusion

Gendered socialisation is one of the basic processes through which identities are constructed and maintained by learning of sociocultural ideologies regarding appropriate behaviour and practices in daily life contexts. It is evident that all girls, able-bodied or disabled, are socialised into gender identities, but for the latter the socialisation process is tempered by the ways in which their impairments are interpreted within their families and the wider society. Bengali gender culture, which attributes the essence of womanhood to being a wife and mother, treats the disabled girl benevolently, almost as if compensating her for her imputed inability to attain such socially valued roles. Parents' reaction to the onset of disability reflects the way in which women are constructed as potentially productive and reproductive beings, spurring them to seek measures that will restore the girl to minimum standards of 'normality'.

Disabled girls are pampered, cosseted, protected and cared for within the family, creating differences between them and their brothers and sisters, sometimes in subtle and sometimes in not so subtle ways. Some of the women expressed rage at such gender-laced ideologies and practices, and felt that their parents could have challenged such perceptions instead of devaluing them with assumptions of incapability. Neighbourhoods, schools and other public spaces were experienced as oppressive and degrading, where one was judged solely by the prescribed standards of idealised normality, and not by one's actual capacities and capabilities. Though cultural ideologies negate the capacities of disabled women, their lived realities often differ as they experience, negotiate and tailor the needs of their impaired bodies to the performance of the ideal feminine self.

The cultural meanings attributed to 'different' bodies exert a great influence on the formation of gendered identities, which are also deeply coloured by ableist ideologies. For women with disabilities, the body becomes the sole point of both similarity and difference between them and other women, and determines the ways in which they perceive and experience the difference in their everyday lives. They strive to adhere, as far as possible, to the socially acceptable ideal of a *bhalo meye* by performing a feminine self in gait and bearing, and in dress and comportment. Normative femininity is accepted, endorsed, and negotiated with through the impairment. Disabled femininity is constructed, nurtured and contested by a strategic management of the impaired body, sociocultural devaluations of disability in general, and the pervasive normative social expectations of women. In the process, women with disabilities redefine the ideal of a *bhalo meye* in the private and public domains of their daily lives. At a psychological level, the weight of perceived differences may lead them to accept their impaired bodies as devalued and 'wanting' in comparison with other women. However, in everyday practice, the impaired body engages in and manages almost all the activities that govern their daily lives, although there will be variation depending on the degree of the disability. Disabled women redefine existing norms, a process which is viewed in a paternalistic fashion by family and community, because the modified behaviour is accepted subject to the overt rejection of expressions of sexuality and femininity. In other domains, especially in the sexual division of labour within and outside the home, disability is thrust upon them regarding work appropriate for women who are considered to have reduced physical capacities. This is most profoundly realised in the way disabled women are represented as engaging in *gharer kaaj*, while other 'normal' women are seen to assume the responsibility for *sansarer kaaj*.

Normative feminine norms of beauty have no space for impaired female bodies, which are regarded as lacking, unattractive and unfit for sexual relationships. The process of negation and denial of the sexuality of disabled women proceeds from suppression within the household to encounters in the public sphere, that serve to reinforce the asexual ideologies and lead to withdrawal of disabled women, sometimes reluctantly, from the arena of sexuality. But again, this process varies according to the degree of disability as well as the family contexts in which the women are located and the aspirations they are allowed to harbour from childhood.

In the public sphere, disabled women feel most conscious of their impaired bodies and are made acutely conscious of their failure to live up to the expectations of 'normal' female bodies. Interactions outside the home, whether in the school, workplace or neighbourhood, almost always reinforce the differences and highlight the deficiencies of the impaired feminine body. The realisation that their bodies are different from the socially constructed physical norms impels disabled women to draw as little attention upon themselves as possible in public; yet they find themselves at the centre of attention in their public encounters, with people focusing only on their impairments and ignoring their presence as women. Moreover, these stigmatising encounters also convey messages about the ways in which disabled female bodies arouse public sympathy but are rejected and discriminated against, not only because they are disabled, but also because they are female. The 'gaze' constructs and devalues impaired female bodies that occupy public spaces, and pushes them further onto the margins of society. The real tragedy is that it seems as if society cannot bear the sight of the disabled female self that dares to exercise agency in any way.

Notes

1. Name of a peasant OBC caste.
2. Neighbourhood, cluster of houses.
3. *Sansar* literally means 'household' in (Hindi or) Bengali, but is conceptualised as the entire family and household with social and cultural importance, and entailing an entirely different set of responsibilities.
4. Research in different countries has pointed to the abuse of women with disabilities within the home, at the institutions they may be living or working in, by medical professionals, and within the community. Disabled women are liable to be subjected to physical, sexual and emotional abuse regardless of age, class and type of disability. A study conducted by an NGO in Orissa (*Aaina* 2006) revealed that women with disabilities tend to be more vulnerable to exploitation of various kinds, such as domestic violence, whether from the parents, siblings or husband and his family. Furthermore, their social isolation usually acts as a barrier to seeking help. As disabled women are in a state of physical, social and economic dependence, they experience abuse for longer periods and are likely to be abused by a greater number of perpetrators, with increased risk for those living in the cities. They also tend to be relatively easy targets of sexual exploitation if intellectually disabled. The violations against disabled girls go unreported as they and their families do not have the courage to approach the legal and police systems (Baquer and Sharma 1997; Maqbool 2003).
5. In the symbolic world of Hindu society, the moral codes that structured the position of women varied in each stratum of the hierarchy. However, in almost every situation, the burden of maintaining the honour of the community and family rested on women. Bengali girls are trained by female relatives and kinswomen from a very early age to fulfil her future role as a good wife and mother (Bagchi 1993; Chakraborty 1998; Roy 1972).

References

Aaina. 2006. 'Women with Disabilities Status Report — An Analysis of Data Collected from 8 Districts', http://www.aaina.org.in/Resources/Publications/WWDstatusreport.pdf (accessed January 2008).

Abberley, Paul. 1987. 'The Concept of Oppression and the Development of a Social Theory of Disability', in Len Barton and Michael Oliver (eds), *Disability Studies: Past, Present and Future*. Leeds: The Disability Press. http://www.leeds.ac.uk/disability-studies/archiveuk/Abberley/chapter10.pdf (accessed 9 September 2010).

Bagchi, Jasodhara. 1993. 'Socialising the Girl Child in Colonial Bengal', *Economic and Political Weekly*, 28 (41): 2214–19.

——— (ed.). 1995. *Indian Women: Myth and Reality*. Kolkata: Sangam Books.

Bagchi, Jasodhara, Jaba Guha and Piyali Sengupta. 1997. *Loved and Unloved: The Girl Child in the Family*. Calcutta: Stree.

Bandyopadhyay, Sekhar. 1995. 'Caste, Widow Remarriage and the Reform of Popular Culture in Colonial Bengal', in Bharati Ray (ed.), *From the Seams of History: Essays on Indian Women*, pp. 8–36. New Delhi: Oxford University Press.

Baquer, Ali and Anjali Sharma. 1997. *Disability: Challenges versus Responses*. New Delhi: Concerned Action Now (CAN).

Bryman, Alan. 2001. *Social Research Methods*. Oxford: Oxford University Press.

Chakraborty, Sambuddha. 1998. *Andare Antare: Unish Shatoke Bangali Bhadramahila*. Calcutta: Stree.

Chatterjee, Partha. 1999. 'The Nation and Its Fragments', *The Partha Chatterjee Omnibus*, pp. 116–57. New Delhi: Oxford University Press.

Cormack, Margaret Lawson. 1953. *The Hindu Woman*. New York: Columbia University Press.

Gleeson, Brendan J. 1997. 'Disability Studies: A Historical Materialist View', *Disability and Society*, 12 (2): 179–202.

Maqbool, Salma. 2003. 'The Situation of Disabled Women in South Asia', in Asha Hans and Annie Patri (eds), *Women, Disability and Identity*, pp. 188–98. New Delhi: SAGE Publications.

Morris, Jenny. 1998. 'Feminism, Gender and Disability'. Paper presented at a seminar, February, Sydney, Australia. http://www.leeds.ac.uk/disability-studies/archiveuk/morris/gender%20and%20disability.pdf (accessed 5 June 2005).

Oliver, Michael. 1996. *Understanding Disability: From Theory To Practice*. Basingstoke: Palgrave Macmillan.

Roy, Manisha. 1972. *Bengali Women*. Chicago/London: University of Chicago Press.

Schriempf, Alexa. 2001. '(Re)fusing the Amputated Body: An Interactionist Bridge for Feminism and Disability', *Hypatia*, 16 (4): 53–79.

Thomson, Rosemarie Garland. 1997. *Extraordinary Bodies: Figuring Physical Disability in American Culture and Literature*. New York: Columbia University Press.

9

Body Politics and Disabled Femininity: Perspectives of Adolescent Girls from Delhi

RENU ADDLAKHA*

The point of departure for the disabled identity is an impaired body (or mind).[1] Revulsion is programmed into the non-disabled social order against impaired bodies. Abnormality defect, deficit and deficiency are the epithets used to describe such bodies, since they appear to depart from both a 'natural' normal sexed body and a socially mediated and acceptable body. Feminists with disabilities like Susan Wendell, Mairian Corker, Simi Linton, Jenny Morris, and Anita Ghai, among others, have recognised the centrality of the body and impairment in the personal experiences and social reactions to disability. Written into able-bodied normative femininity is the near total invisibility of the woman with a disability. In addition, feminist disability scholars have also recognised that the neglect of the body is one of the manifestations of the masculinist bias of the male-centric disability movement all over the world. The first section of this chapter presents a synoptic view of the main concepts of feminist disability studies as it has emerged in the past two decades.

For the individual person/woman with disabilities, the disabled body is a source of shame and embarrassment. Even sensorily deprived persons such as the visually or hearing challenged often harbour a negative body image, regarding it as defective, diseased, ugly and repulsive. Depending upon the nature and degree of the impairment, the disabled body is more often than not subjectively perceived as uncomfortable, painful and burdensome. It contributes to a sense of ill-being and alienation with the environment. More graphically, it is 'the spectre of incontinence, leakages, smells and spillages, that engenders anxiety and fear in society as a whole' (Seymour 1998:19). Such negative perceptions of impairment and disability are internalised both by persons with disabilities and non-disabled persons, and influence their behaviour and self-concepts. Yet, as Michel Foucault (1980) has highlighted, even within seemingly impenetrable hegemonic structures, individuals manoeuvre, subvert and offer resistance within existing cracks and crevices to exercise agency. Using ethnographic data gathered as part of a larger study[2] to map the relationship between sexuality, disability and youth in India, the essay will highlight how individual young women with different types of disabilities in Delhi negotiate a sense of embodiment that both incorporates and challenges prevailing aesthetic standards of feminine appearance and behaviour.

The argument that I seek to advance is that the embodied female self of the disabled subject is primarily constructed through a formal allegiance to the sexual and aesthetic norms and values of the non-disabled patrifocal world. Agency emerges in the choice of areas of relative focus and appropriation, which is critically dependent on the specific experience of impairment. For instance, visual disability may predispose affected individuals to develop a non-visual aesthetics of the body, while mobility impairment may push the affected to construct a politics and aesthetics of the body that shifts the focus away from dynamics of physical grace and movement. Furthermore, in the wake of a 'dys-appearance'[3] of subjective corporeality in the face of disability, notions of beauty and attractiveness that accentuate mental abilities and moral rectitude may be highlighted in place of physical characteristics in the presentation of the self. The chapter explores how young women with different disabilities conceptualise and articulate a sense of self that straddles the slippery terrain between normative and disabled femininity.

Feminism and Disability: Belated but Inevitable Rapprochement

In order to put into perspective the relationship between feminism and disability, it is important to bear in mind a number of conceptual distinctions stemming from both disability studies and feminist theory. For instance, core themes of impairment and disability,[4] as they crystallised within the medical and social models of disability, have for a long time had the impact of obscuring the importance of the disabled body in both theory and advocacy. From another perspective, feminist concerns with objectification of the female body and the critique of conventional familial roles of women, combined with the physical absence of women with disabilities from the women's movement, resulted in the almost total exclusion of disability as a fundamental axis of oppression from the feminist agenda.

Disability has historically been conceptualised almost exclusively in terms of biological abnormality or dysfunction necessitating medical intervention and rehabilitation. The medical model looks at impairment as personal tragedy and at the individual through the lens of patienthood. Through self-advocacy by persons with disabilities, the concept of disability was redefined not as personal tragedy necessitating therapy but as collective oppression necessitating political action. In the social model of disability, the focus shifts from the inability of persons with disabilities to adapt to the so-called 'normal' environment to the failure of the social and structural environment to adapt to the needs and aspirations of persons with disabilities. Interestingly, the social model of disability has also contributed to the invisibility of the disabled body with its overwhelming emphasis on disabling environments and barriers to social integration. The fear of yielding to the medical model, embedded in concepts of impairment and rehabilitation, resulted in the near total ejection of corporeality from the social model. In their zeal for advocating for accessibility and rights, proponents of the social model overlooked the fact that even impairment takes shape within a politico-economic and sociocultural context.

While the invisibility of women with disabilities in the male-dominated disability movement is, to some extent, understandable, their absence from the women's movement cannot be so easily overlooked. While ethnicity, race, class and caste gained importance as hierarchies of inequality within the women's movement, disability and non-normative sexuality have only recently been explicitly acknowledged as axes of women's oppression. Women with disabilities did not figure in international conventions and policies till the Beijing Declaration (Platform of Action) in 1995, which clearly mentions women with disabilities as one of the groups facing barriers and suffering violations of basic human rights. Even in the case of abortion debates within the women's movement, the right to survival of foetuses with disabilities has not figured in the discussion. The ethical implications of the pro-choice stance promoting antenatal testing for elimination of defective foetuses feeds into prevailing notions of bodily perfection. Unfortunately, the women's movement also ceded to the negative attitudes and representations of disability that the medical model has so successfully promoted.

Notwithstanding the ideological vortex generated by second wave feminism and the emerging social model of disability, women with disabilities continued to remain an invisible constituency. It was mainly during the 1990s that the theoretical innovations and social activism of feminists with disabilities catapulted women with disabilities as a separate identity category. Consequently, it is only in the course of the past two decades that the masculine bias in disability theory has been questioned, and the exclusion of women with disabilities from feminist theory and praxis highlighted primarily by women with disabilities themselves (Corker 1999, 2001; Meekosha 1990; Morris 1991, 1993a, 1993b, 1996, 2001; Thomas 1999; Wendell 1996).

Feminist discourses on the body have overwhelmingly focused around issues of reproduction, sexuality and violence. It is ironic that while the body has been a major site of contestation in feminist theory, yet the disabled body has been until recently marked by its absence in such debates. This is partly due to the hegemony of the medical model, which naturalised disability taking it out of the realm of socioeconomic, political and cultural configurations. Deriving from conventional feminist principle that the body is a site of ideological contestation, feminist disability scholars and activists enunciated the premise that experiences of impairment are central in women's lives.

As a logical corollary, the imperfect body comes to signify absence of femininity and social unacceptability, since female subjectivity is so deeply intertwined with embodiment in patriarchal society, the simplistic chain of association being that since women with disabilities do not look like normal women and their bodies do not function like normal bodies in some respects, they cannot take on the roles of normal women and hence are less than women. According to Michele Fine and Adrienne Asch (1988), this situation turns conventional feminist wisdom on its head in two striking ways. First, at an experiential level, the social obscurity and annulment of femininity signalled by a defective body prompt women with disabilities to long for the roles of wives and mothers that their able-bodied feminists decry and critique as oppressive. Second, sexual objectification gives way to asexual objectification, frustrating normal sexual needs and aspirations, and consigning the woman with a disability to a life of social isolation. Last, a core component of normative constructions of femininity is the woman as caregiver in procreative and maternal roles, but the woman with a disability is herself in need of care.

Men with disabilities do not become victims of such total 'rolelessness' that is the fate of their female counterparts, though disabled masculinity poses challenges for men with disabilities as well (Shakespeare 2000). According to Jenny Morris (1991), the powerlessness of women with disabilities has arisen, either due to their being treated as invisible or having their needs and experiences predefined for them by non-disabled feminists or by men with disabilities. Although a level of freedom may be associated with asexuality, it is an insignificant gain in comparison to the perception of oneself as physically unattractive and sexually undesirable. Thus, asexual objectification and pervasive rolelessness differentiate the operations of patriarchy on disabled female bodies, creating unique oppressive practices of exclusion and personal devaluation.

Just as gender is socially constructed from the biological differences between men and women, disability is similarly constructed from the biological differences between persons with disabilities and non-disabled persons. Susan Wendell (1996) situates the marginalisation and low self-esteem of women with disabilities on the disabled or what she calls 'rejected body'. She argues that the celebration of the female body by feminists like Adrienne Rich (1976) as a source of pleasure and empowerment has strengthened processes of idealisation and objectification of women's bodies. There is an underestimation of bodily frustration and suffering engendered by difference. Consequently, women with disabilities may consider themselves an embarrassment to feminism (Wendell 1996). Wendell identifies age as a specific type of disability giving rise to the concept of the 'temporarily able-bodied person', demolishing the barriers of otherness that separate the able-bodied from persons with disabilities, since ageing is a universal experience of the human condition. She also questions the unitary concept of women with disabilities, highlighting the variability introduced by type of disability, gender, age, race, ethnicity, etc. Similarly, Mairian Corker (1999) highlights the dangers of applying a universalising disability norm or discourse overwriting the diversity among persons with disabilities. She critiques the categorisation of disability into sensory, physical and mental impairments, leading to a certain essentialisation of disabled identity. People with different disabilities have different notions of limitation. There is a need for exploring different forms of anomalous embodiments in the project of emancipation from oppression.

According to Helen Meekosha (1990), impairment is a variable process that challenges the fixity and permanence of a socially constructed corporeality. Like Wendell, she questions the notion of an unproblematic normal female body, and in this process, highlights the constant change and flux of the body in negotiating the disabled identity. Urging for a feminist interrogation of science, technology and medicine, she underscores the need to understand disabled embodiment within historical, cultural and class contexts. Women with disabilities have as much a right to womanhood and selfhood as non-disabled women. Social and gender justice demand that the disabled women's self and experiences be valorised within a refined notion of autonomy as interdependence.

Bringing a strongly postmodernist perspective, Janet Price and Margrit Shildrick (1998) argue that the experience and knowledge of disability are situated and positional. We need to move beyond simple binaries of health and illness, normal/abnormal, and disabled and non-disabled, because silencing the categories that don't fit, '. . . may acquire in their dislocation an accumulative force that returns to inhabit the moments of fracture' (ibid.: 241). The ethics of care need to be reformulated to move beyond issues of caring (Hillyer 1993) to issues of being cared for, vulnerability and uncertainty in the caring relationship (Price and Shildrick 2002).

Some omissions and points of contention notwithstanding, disability feminists also share the basic premises of feminism in general, such as questioning the validity of universalising norms, challenging the politics of appearance and naming and actively working towards the creation of positive identities. As Carol Thomas points out: '. . . the forms and impacts of disablism are always refracted *in some way* through the prism of gendered locations and gender relations' (1999: 28). Both feminists and disability advocates are opposed to a norm assumed to be innately superior — patriarchy and ableism, respectively, are the ideologies that they oppose. Then, in keeping with the credo of plurality, heterogeneity and identity politics of second wave feminism, feminist disability studies not only challenges the universal category of woman, but also the unitary category of disabled woman or woman with a disability.

The beginnings of a critical feminist analysis of disability in a multidisciplinary perspective has been initiated in the Indian context by feminist scholars like Renu Addlakha (1998, 1999, 2001, 2005; [Addlakha and Das 2001]), Bhargavi Davar (1999, 2001), Amita Dhanda (2000), Anita Ghai (2003), and Asha Hans and Annie Patri (2003), among others. Historically, the Indian women's movement has focused on issues like poverty, caste inequalities, employment, social practices like sati and dowry, population policies and reproductive technologies, female foeticide, sexuality and domestic violence, but disability-based oppression has not featured in its agenda. Again, while women's mental health and distress have been explored by some researchers (Davar 1999, 2001; Dhanda 2000), the situation of women with physical or sensory disabilities has not found a separate discursive space. While dalit women, women workers, agricultural labourers and minority status groups are highlighted as marginalised groups, women with disabilities are only now being recognised as a distinct marginal category. The use of genetic screening for aborting foetuses with disabilities is not discussed in the female foeticide and infanticide debates, which have been critical pillars of the Indian women's movement. This is a serious lacuna in the feminist and women's studies circles. Anita Ghai (2002) points out that the reason given for such exclusion by representatives of the movement is the non-participation of women with disabilities; but the same invisibility that marks their lives in their families and the community has prevented them from taking part in meetings and other actions. To say that their invisibility is the cause of their non-participation reflects a lack of understanding of the existential reality of their lives, wherein moving out of the home and using public transport are tortuous goals often beyond their reach. On the other hand, we know that choice of issues in advocacy is dependent on the perceived needs of participants; and a majoritarian logic more often than not operates in such selection processes.[5]

The remainder of this chapter attempts to examine how urban adolescent girls that the author met in the course of fieldwork conducted in Delhi constitute their femininity in the context of different disabilities. It needs to be remembered that adolescents with disabilities must cope with the same physical changes, emotional anxieties and social conflicts that adolescents face in general, in addition to those produced by their disabilities. They experience the same physical changes and sex drive that are part of normal biological development, but have greater concerns about their bodies than their able-bodied counterparts. These concerns may be both realistic and irrational, but they influence their behaviour and identities in significant ways. Negotiations of selfhood with a disabled body may produce an alternative aesthetics with a selective focus on ability-based and moral ideals of selfhood. Pervasive experiences of sexual harassment, particularly in the public sphere, create both affinities and ruptures with normative notions of womanhood. While abuse is indisputably a form of violence, yet in the overriding context of asexual objectification and rolelessness that configure the lives of women with disabilities, it may at times be self-perceived as the only sign of a precarious femininity.

Anomalous and Normative Embodiment[6]

Absence of a sense of self-assurance and confidence in the functioning and attractiveness of the body is one of the major stumbling blocks in the lives of persons with disabilities. Disabled bodies do not fit the cultural ideal of the healthy, strong, independent and beautiful body. Persons with disabilities may be dependent on others for activities of daily living, and their bodies may be deformed and aesthetically unappealing in more ways than one. The disabled body is not valued as a source of pleasure or value — it cannot work, reproduce or be attractive, according to normative standards. Subjectively, these perceptions may contribute to development of a poor body image, which not only refers to appearance but also encompasses the whole range of perceptions about bodily sensations, abilities and functions. Even persons with sensory disabilities, such as blindness and deafness, may experience such devaluation even though they may have no other physical abnormalities.

Disability may lead to the loss of sense of self as a sexually attractive and sexually functional person. Comparisons with the normal body emphasising physical beauty, bodily fitness and sports attainment, so abundantly projected in the popular media, may lead to feelings of frustration and annoyance at having a disabled body. Such negative attitudes and perceptions are internalised, leading many persons with disabilities to avoid looking at themselves in the mirror. They may also avoid social interaction and intimacy with others, and further recede into isolation.

Health, normality, physical attractiveness, sexuality, and self-esteem are interdependent variables in the construction of gender identity. Persons with disabilities are encouraged to enact a form of desexualised subjectivity that is not regarded as threatening to the non-disabled majority (Price 2005). They may not take the risk of communicating sexual interest out of fear of being ridiculed, ignored or outright rejected. Psychological barriers in the form of low self-esteem and poor body image combine with the lack of physical and social opportunities for developing relationship skills. Seclusion in institutions or being policed at home by their own families further exacerbates their social isolation.

A sexual double standard also pervades this domain. If a woman with a disability even voices sexual desire, she is considered a freak, morally corrupt and socially dangerous, because sexuality in women with disabilities is perceived as more threatening than sexuality in women without disabilities or men with disabilities. For many women with disabilities, the message is clear — their bodies are neither acceptable nor desirable. To be non-disabled is the ideal. Disability is seen as a 'deficit'. For women with disabilities, the challenge often lies in being legitimately identified as a female in the first place.

Nonetheless, there is a vast terrain of possibility between stereotype and reality. While acknowledging the existence of the disability and the limitations it imposes on their everyday lives and overall life chances, many young women with disabilities contest the social stereotypes that cast aspersions on their capacity to be sexual partners, homemakers and mothers. They regard themselves and others like them as completely capable of performing household chores efficiently, having meaningful sexual relationships and producing and rearing healthy children. Whether this affirmation is primarily an expression of actual perception of reality, a politically correct articulation or an opportunity for momentary self-assertion, is open to debate.

Interviews with female adolescents with different kinds of disabilities and belonging to different socioeconomic strata in Delhi reveal to a large extent an agreement with, and endorsement of, prevailing standards of female beauty and behaviour. While physical appearance and bodily functioning, especially with regard to mobility, are strategically underplayed, there is often overcompensation in focusing on non-physical aspects of female personhood, such as intelligence, modesty, loyalty and moral uprightness. For instance, Anita,[7] a mobility-challenged 17-year-old girl residing in a low income neighbourhood of Delhi, voices the opinion of many women with disabilities. She says:

A good girl should be well educated and good at her work. She should be interested in everything and should speak well to everyone. She should obey her parents and respect her elders. I don't know about beauty, but it is important nowadays.

According to Priya, a 17-year-old visually challenged girl:

A good girl should study, should be hard working, should obey her parents and not tell lies. Beauty is also important, but 'nature'[8] is more important. Long black hair and fair complexion are nice also. People say Aishwarya Rai[9] is very beautiful. Personally, I don't think I am either beautiful or ugly. I am ok; that is what my mother and the girls, who can see, say.

A recurrent sentence in interviews on the topic was that a 'person should be "beautiful by nature"' — strategically shifting the focus of the discussion from visible physical attributes to psychic characteristics of moral qualities.

The configuration of the ideal of physical beauty and optimum bodily functioning is linked to a corresponding de-emphasis on those organs and functions connected to the experienced disability. For instance, in their formulation of the feminine ideal, visually challenged women may emphasise non-physical (read non-visual) behavioural and personality traits. Continual feedback about our own bodies, and of those around us, provides us with a well-integrated sense of female and male physiques that visually impaired persons do not share. Consequently, personal appearance is created with the active assistance of sighted persons, be they family members or peers. Priya's predicament is illustrative of the dilemma faced by many visually challenged young persons:

I am not that beautiful. I am ok. People at home say the face cut of Priya is the best, but I don't think that is true. I think my mother is just saying it to make me happy. Fact is fact, but since I cannot see this, I feel doubtful.

Veena, another visually challenged young woman, says she relies on perceptions of the sighted and the partially sighted. For instance, her sister told her that such colours as pink and brown suit her complexion, so she buys outfits in these colours when she goes shopping. Furthermore, while she does not use visible cosmetics like lipstick and eye makeup, she uses olfactory items like deodorants and perfumes, and skincare products like creams. She also prefers to keep her hair short because it is easier to manage.

For persons with disabilities, the body often emerges as a productive rather than an aesthetic object. This is highlighted by Priti, a partially sighted girl just out of school: 'So, if by being slim, you are more energetic, can do more work and become faster, then it is good. It should not just be for looks.'

A key characteristic of femininity in the Indian context is efficiency in housework. While most girls with disabilities are called upon to make some contribution to household chores, a pervasive enforced invalidism and control by family members (often cloaked in the guise of benevolence) result in them developing a poor sense of competence in household tasks. In this connection, Savita voices the views of many differently-abled girls when she says, 'My mother does not let me do any housework when I go home. They [family members] say, "Why do you want to do this? You will do it when the time comes. Now you focus on your studies".'

In a similar vein, Anita says:

> My mother tells me to work, but then she says, 'Let it be; I'll do it'. I can cook, but I can't wash clothes; I can sweep, but can't mop; I can make rotis,[10] but I don't know how to knead the flour. I can also look after my young niece and nephew when my sister-in-law is doing the housework.

Most of the young women interviewed showed a strong interest in developing competence in the whole gamut of tasks related to domesticity.

Comparatively speaking, interviews with young male adolescents reveal strivings for freedom, autonomy and economic independence. Interestingly, female informants also report an equally strong striving for economic self-sufficiency, followed by having intimate nurturing relationships and overcoming loneliness. For the young woman with a disability, economic empowerment is critical, since it is envisaged as a kind of insurance against possible future penury after the death of parents or significant caregivers. In addition, gainful employment can also serve as a bargaining chip for negotiating her status both within her natal home and for her marriage. In the Indian context, disability often automatically translates into exclusion from marital roles. With the lack of pressure for marriage, families, especially poor ones, may not actively scout for matrimonial alliances, especially if the girl is employed, because it would mean the loss of an income for the natal family. In such a scenario, a natal family can be just as oppressive towards a girl with disabilities as a marital family towards a non-disabled girl.

Veena narrates how her elder brother wanted her to forgo higher education and look for a job through the reservation quota.[11] Interestingly, while her mother and brothers were not opposed to her seeking employment, her father, a man with more traditional views, was not in favour of women going out of the house to earn a livelihood. Earlier, she says, he would not even allow her sisters to go to the market alone. Nonetheless, Veena says, 'I want to study, do a job and stand on my feet. I want to be independent.'

Chetna, an 18-year-old partially sighted girl in her final year in a school for the blind, underscores the necessity of employment in no uncertain terms:

> I don't want to be a burden on my parents. It is not definite whether I will get married or not, and that will be much later. In the meanwhile, I should be *independent*. Firstly, I am disabled and it won't be good if I depend on my parents. Every girl wants to do a job. My father is not working. Only my elder sister is working.

Not surprisingly, a direct connection is established between economic self-reliance and marriage in the perceptions of young women with disabilities. This is clearly summed up by Chetna:

> I want to get married and I also don't. Through marriage, one gets support; but then if I have a job, it is also not necessary to get married. If I were a boy, it does not matter if I don't get married, but because I am a girl, marriage is necessary. In the end, it is one's fate. If it is not in my fate to get married, it won't happen. It is not like even if I don't want it, it won't still happen.

Marriage is a highly valorised and sought-after status for the woman with disabilities, which society denies to her. Motherhood is also a forbidden aspiration. Her capacity to be a good mother, physically and psychologically, is challenged by social stereotypes that paint women with disabilities as incapable of taking on caring roles. None of the young women interviewed explicitly agree with this formulation. Their adherence to an alternative perspective may also be interpreted as resistance to such social prohibitions. The consensual opinion of interviewees with total loss of vision or hearing is that disability is not in itself an obstacle to marriage or motherhood, but with a rider that the partner should also have a disability — only then will it be successful. Priya, who studies in a residential school for the blind in Delhi, says, 'Well I have really not thought about marriage, but if I do get married, it will be to someone like me. Only a blind [person] can understand our problems.'

Similarly, Savita does not want to marry a sighted person because she fears betrayal/abandonment. On the other hand, Kajol, a 16-year-old mobility challenged girl studying in an integrated school, says, 'I want to get married, but not to someone with the same problem as me. That won't look good.'

In this connection, the perceptions of the partially sighted/hard of hearing are more blighted than those of the totally blind or deaf. Total disability appears to provide a sense of security in the sense of complete alterity or difference, which is diminished as the barriers with normal society become more permeable. Chetna says she only wants to marry a fully-sighted person even though she is partially sighted. Her depiction of the ideal female is also more visual-based:

> An ideal girl should be beautiful. She should have good features and brown complexion. I don't like too much fair colour. She should have a pretty nose, big eyes, nice lips and long hair. Her nature should also be good. She should be frank. She should respect her parents, and she should be educated.

Some women with disabilities openly challenge the perceptions of the ideal of the beautiful body but continue to adhere to the ideal of the perfect body with capacity for peak performance, the disability notwithstanding.

Regarding parenting with a disability, Chetna is equally categorical in her views:

> All persons with disabilities should get married and have children if they want to because everyone has a heart. God has created everyone

alike. If he has given someone a disability, does that mean s/he does not have a heart? Even if a person is less beautiful, even that person has a heart. It is not that because He has given us a disability that our hearts are also dead. Everyone's heart is the same. It is not necessary that the disability of an individual will also come to the child. Mostly, it is not necessary. I have seen many cases where the parents are blind, but the children are absolutely fine. In fact, if the parents are disabled, in some cases the children are even more intelligent.

Even though women with disabilities are perceived to be asexual, yet they are at greater risk of being sexually abused. This makes sense when sexual abuse is understood to be more about power than about sex. Offenders generally do not violate persons who are well respected or equal to them. Consequently, it is not the disability per se which renders these women more vulnerable to abuse, but the negative social perceptions and stigmatisation that reduce them to positions of powerlessness and dependence. Not only are women with disabilities less likely to resist, but their general lack of social and economic power also makes them easy targets for abuse. In addition, need for assistance renders them vulnerable, be it at home, on the road or in institutions, and unable to defend themselves even in routine situations. Persons with developmental disabilities may be too trusting of others and, hence, easier to trick, bribe or coerce. They may not understand differences between sexual and non-sexual tactile behaviour. Those with speech and hearing difficulties may have limited communication skills to report abuse. Furthermore, since persons with disabilities are often taught to be obedient, passive and to control their behaviour, this renders them easy victims.

The plight of the challenged child is the asexual perspective that their families inculcate in him/her. There is a tendency to treat the child as innocent of sexual thoughts and feelings; yet, at the same time, there is an extreme fear of sexual involvement leading to overprotective behaviour. Both are counterproductive because one may lead to sexual exploitation and the other may lead to dependency, isolation, anger and resentment. The purpose of institutions, including educational institutions for the blind and the deaf, is to provide residents with a safe and respectful environment. Nonetheless, placement in a residential institution puts the disabled at risk of physical and sexual abuse. Some hostels are sites of abuse, with houseparents, caretakers and peers themselves taking on the role of perpetrators. Institutions are places of unequal distribution of power where staff fiat runs supreme and, hence, inmates may not report abuse out of fear of being disbelieved or labelled deviant. They are often isolated from the wider society and reduced to a state of complete dependence and powerlessness.

Although the interviews with adolescent girls in residential schools do not reveal explicit experiences of abuse,[12] many instances of sexual harassment on the roads and in public transport are reported by the informants. For instance, Priti, a visually challenged girl, says that on the roads she is compelled to ask for assistance from men, simply because there are more men on the roads than women. She recounts an incident when a man, whom she had asked directions from in a bus, started up a conversation with her and actually visited her several times at the hostel. This incident frightened her so much that she consulted her friends on how to handle the situation.

Regarding sexual harassment of persons with disabilities, Kajol says:

> It can definitely happen more to disabled persons because they can't do anything, they can't even run nor can they scold them. The boys also suppress the girls, so it can happen more. In the bus, boys misbehave with the girls who are 'smart' and dress up well. Many girls have also have given them slaps. Here, boys can just catch you and take you away. Many boys have taken away girls like that at our place. Then, the police have been called in. I have heard about it.

Veena feels that girls sometimes invite trouble. Echoing the patriarchal logic of victim-blaming that she has internalised, she says:

> Makeup and fashion are a matter of personal choice, but the girls who wear very short clothes give me irritation. They should know their limitations, because there are some differences between males and females. Wearing short clothes encourages rape. It raises a lot of curiosity in people's minds, especially in India where sex education is not given properly. Girls wear such clothes because they think they look

pretty and boys get attracted to them. If they knew the dangers, they would not wear them. There is nothing wrong in being modern, but being modern is in thoughts, not in clothes. Maybe I am old-fashioned, but I believe it.

Disability challenges all notions of perfection and beauty as defined by popular culture. Constructing a positive view of the disabled body as beautiful is still rare at an experiential level; yet a 20-year-old hearing challenged girl studying in a vocational centre being run by an NGO says, 'I do think I am somewhat attractive. I don't like wearing jewellery or cosmetics on my skin because I like the natural look, but I do like to wear nice clothes.'

Conclusion

Women with disabilities are perceived not to measure up to the physical standards of non-disabled women, nor does society expect them to take on the normative roles of wife and mother that are expected of the latter. The chapter has shown that women with disabilities do not quietly acquiesce to such characterisations. As individuals, they struggle to diminish such negative stereotyping in an attempt to develop a positive sense of self within the parameters of some physical deficit and a patriarchal cultural ethos. However, celebration of difference and pride in one's individuality are almost non-existent in such self-configurations.

Discussions of the body within feminism have, till recently, neglected the materiality and cultural representation of the disabled body. Conventional feminist thinking regards being a woman as a form of disability and utmost oppression, but this similarity, to my reading, is superficial. Disability undermines the self in irredeemable ways. While disability politics can use feminist theoretical devices like 'the personal is political', and strategies for emancipation like consciousness-raising and self-advocacy, the point remains that everyday forms of pain and impairment that obstruct basic vegetative functions like eating and sleeping, sensory functioning like seeing, hearing and listening, and physical movement, cannot be compared to the socially instituted gender-based oppression like absence of inheritance rights or lack of participation in public life. However, it is the overarching category of violence that brings the concerns of women with disabilities directly into the agenda of mainstream feminism, creating the necessity and possibility for a more inclusive feminism and disability discourse.

Such an inclusive feminist project must affirm the rights of women with disabilities to self-expression, agency and desire. Three main features of disability feminism are that gender needs to become an integral part of disability advocacy and research; second, disability identity needs to be iteratively asserted; and third, disability is not a unitary concept but embraces many different kinds of experiences and realities. There is a need to reclaim what has been traditionally viewed as 'negative' and accentuate the reality that 'differentness' carries with it exciting and creative opportunities for change. This is only possible when the existential reality of women with different disabilities is explored, challenged and redeemed. Disabled bodily experience must become an intrinsic part of feminist discourse. Conditions that enable them to exercise their rights to womanhood and bodily status beyond that of personal suffering and social burden must be created.

Disability as social construction overlooks the materiality of the impaired body, while disability as impairment overlooks the extent to which the environment disables individuals. The two need to be brought together so that that we recognise the pain and discomfort of the material disabled body, as also the fact that physical differences do not automatically imply deficiency or defect. Indeed, negative attitudes and stereotypes of disability are embedded in power relations (including gender relations) and social institutions that systematically work in tandem to exclude, isolate and disempower persons with disabilities, more particularly women with disabilities.

Notes

* An earlier version of this essay was presented at the conference 'A World in Transition: New Challenges for Gender Justice' organised by the Gender and Development Network (GADNET), Sweden, and the Centre for Women's Development Studies, New Delhi, at the India International Centre, from 11–15 December 2006.

1. Classifications of disability into physical and mental are derived from the Cartesian dualism that underlies post-Enlightenment scientific rationality.
2. The research was supported by a grant from the MacArthur Foundation in India as part of their Programme for Leadership Development 2003–5.
3. Following up Drew Leder's phenomenological analysis (1990) of the absent body, Simon J. Williams (1998: 61) notes that 'the body seizes our attention most strongly at times of dysfunction, 'it dys-appears' that is, it appears in a dysfunctional state: and this contests the 'normal' bodily state of disappearance. The normal disabled binary primarily rests on the notion of impairment or dysfunction.
4. I am using the distinction between impairment and disability proposed in 1976 by the Union of the Physically Impaired Against Segregation (UPIAS) that underscores how society disables impaired persons. Impairment refers to anatomical and/or functional abnormality and is defined as 'lacking part of or all of a limb, or having a defective limb, organism or mechanism of the body'. Disability, on the other hand, refers to the social and cultural reactions to such impairment and their impact on the life of the individual. It is defined as 'the disadvantage or restriction of activity caused by a contemporary social organisation which takes no or little account of people who have physical impairments and thus excludes them from participation in the mainstream of social activities' (UPIAS 1976).
5. Ironically, the forced hysterectomies of inmates of a home for the mentally disabled in Pune district of Maharashtra (India) in 1994 did not elicit any response from the disability rights movement in India, which, as Ghai (2003) points out, has continued to be the preserve of elite men with disabilities. It did, however, ignite a debate around disability in the women's movement and the medical profession in the country, but it was a discontinuous engagement that ended as abruptly as it had begun.
6. The phrase is taken from Price and Shildrick (2002: 65).
7. Pseudonyms have been used to maintain confidentiality of interviewees.
8. The reference is to personality or psychological profile.
9. A well-known Bollywood actress.
10. Unleavened flatbread made from wheat flour, which constitutes the staple cereal diet in North India.
11. The Persons with Disabilities (Equal Opportunities, Protection of Rights and Full Participation) Act, 1995, stipulates 3 per cent reservation for the disabled in government jobs.
12. I was only allowed to conduct short interviews with informants who were quite hesitant to talk about living conditions in the special schools for fear of the information getting back to school authorities. Consequently, the

absence of data in this regard can be attributed more to the limitations of the interview context rather than the absence of the experience of abuse per se.

References

Addlakha, Renu. 1998. 'Nisha: Who would marry someone like me?', in Abha Bhaiya and Lynn F. Lee (eds), *Unmad: Findings of a Research Study on Women's Mental and Emotional Crisis: The Voice of the Subject*, pp. 100–113. New Delhi: Jagori.
———. 1999. 'An Ethnographic Account of Family Burden and Coping Strategies in Chronic Schizophrenia', *Indian Journal of Psychiatry*, 41 (2): 91–95.
———. 2001. 'Lay and Medical Diagnoses of Psychiatric Disorder and the Normative Construction of Femininity', in Bhargavi V. Davar (ed.), *Mental Health from a Gender Perspective*, pp. 313–33. New Delhi: SAGE Publications.
———. 2005. 'Affliction and Testimony: A Reading of the Diary of Parvati Devi', *Indian Journal of Gender Studies*, 12 (1): 63–82.
Addlakha, Renu and Veena Das. 2001. 'Disability and Domestic Citizenship: Voice, Gender, and the Making of the Subject', *Public Culture*, 13 (3): 511–31.
Corker, Mairian. 1999. 'Differences, Conflations and Foundations: The Limits to "Accurate" Theoretical Representation of Disabled People's Experiences', *Disability and Society*, 14 (5): 627–42.
———. 2001. 'Sensing Disability', *Hypatia*, 16 (4): 34–52.
Davar, Bhargavi V. 1999. *Mental Health of Indian Women: A Feminist Agenda*. New Delhi: SAGE Publications.
———. 2001. *Mental Health from a Gender Perspective*. New Delhi: SAGE Publications.
Dhanda, Amita. 2000. *Legal Order and Mental Disorder*. New Delhi: SAGE Publications.
Fine, Michelle and Adrienne Asch (eds). 1988. *Women with Disabilities: Essays in Psychology, Culture and Politics*. Philadelphia: Temple University Press.
Foucault, Michel. 1980. *Power/Knowledge: Selected Interviews and Other Writings, 1972–1977*, ed. Colin Gordon. New York: Pantheon Books.
Ghai, Anita. 2002. 'Disabled Women: An Excluded Agenda of Indian Feminism', *Hypatia*, 17 (3): 49–66.
———. 2003. *(Dis)embodied Form: Issues of Disabled Women*. New Delhi: Shakti Books.
Hans, Asha and Annie Patri (eds). 2003. *Women, Disability and Identity*. London; Thousand Oaks; New Delhi: SAGE Publications.

Hillyer, Barbara. 1993. *Feminism and Disability*. Norman and London: University of Oklahoma Press.
Leder, Drew. 1990. *The Absent Body*. Chicago: University of Chicago Press.
Meekosha, Helen. 1990. 'Is Feminism Able-bodied? Reflections From Between the Trenches', *Refractory Girl*, (August): 34–42.
Morris, Jenny. 1991. *Pride against Prejudice: Transforming Attitudes to Disability*. London: The Women's Press.
———. 1993a. 'Feminism and Disability', *Feminist Review*, 43: 57–70.
———. 1993b. 'Gender and Disability', in John Swain, Vic Finkelstein, Sally French and Mike Oliver (eds), *Disabling Barriers — Enabling Environments*. London: SAGE Publications.
——— (ed.). 1996. *Encounters with Strangers: Feminism and Disability*. London: The Women's Press.
———. 2001. 'Impairment and Disability: Constructing an Ethics of Care that Promotes Human Rights', *Hypatia*, 16 (4): 1–16.
Price, Janet. 2005. 'Connecting Bodies through Space and Time: Disability, Feminism and Globalisation', Women's Global Network for Reproductive Rights newsletter, 86: 12–15.
Price, Janet and Margrit Shildrick. 1998. 'Uncertain Thoughts on the Dis/abled Body', in Margrit Shildrick and Janet Price (eds), *Vital Signs: Feminist Reconfigurations of the Bio/logical Body*, pp. 224–49. Edinburgh: Edinburgh University Press.
———. 2002. 'Bodies Together: Touch, Ethics and Disability', in Mairian Corker and Tom Shakespeare (eds), *Disability/Postmodernity: Embodying Disability Theory*, pp. 62–75. London: Continuum.
Rich, Adrienne. 1976. *Of Woman Born: Motherhood as Experience and Institution*. New York: Norton.
Seymour, Wendy. 1998. *Remaking the Body: Rehabilitation and Change*. London; New York: Routledge and Kegan Paul.
Shakespeare, Tom. 2000. 'Disabled Sexuality: Toward Rights and Recognition', *Sexuality and Disability*, 18 (3), 159–66.
Shildrick, Margrit and Janet Price. 1996. 'Breaking the Boundaries of the Broken Body: Mastery, Materiality and ME', *Body and Society*, 2 (4): 93–113.
Thomas, Carol. 1999. *Female Forms: Experiencing and Understanding Disability*. Buckingham: Open University Press.
UPIAS. 1976. 'Fundamental Principles of Disability'. Summary of discussions between the Disability Alliance and UPIAS, held on 22 November, London. http://www.leeds.ac.uk/disability-studies/archiveuk/UPIAS/fundamental%20principles.pdf (accessed 2 May 2012).
Wendell, Susan. 1996. *The Rejected Body: Feminist Philosophical Reflections on Disability*. London: Routledge.
Williams, Simon J. 1998. 'Bodily Dys-Order: Desire, Excess and the Transgression of Corporeal Boundaries', *Body and Society*, 4 (2): 59–82.

10

Identity Formation and Transnational Discourses: Thinking beyond Identity Politics

MICHELE FRIEDNER*

> Disability in Europe and North America exists within — and is created by — a framework of state, legal, economic and biomedical institutions. Concepts of personhood, identity, and value, while not reducible to institutions, are nevertheless shaped by them. Notions of citizenship, compensation, and value lost through impairment and added through rehabilitation are institutionally reinforced constituents of disability as a cultural construct . . . In countries of the South, where this kind of institutional infrastructure exists only to a very limited degree, disability as a concept and an identity is not an explicit cultural construct (Ingstad and Whyte 1995: 10).

Susan Reynolds Whyte and Benedicte Ingstad's work (1995) on disability and rehabilitation in the developing world discusses the ways that disability is a cultural construct associated with the global North and its particular institutions. The specific model of disability that they are referring to is the cultural model, which states that disability can be the source of a positive and empowering identity. Indeed, according to this model, disability possesses its own culture, and individuals with disabilities can manifest disability pride in the same way that ethnic or cultural groups can. Eventually, it is society and its attitudes and physical barriers that create disability. This model exists relationally with and is juxtaposed with the medical model, which looks at the specific ways that individuals with disabilities are medically impaired. Whyte and Ingstad make the important point that the cultural model is specifically Northern, since in the global South, disability is not thought of as a distinct culture. However, over the last 20 years, we have witnessed a massive surge in Northern-created rehabilitation institutions and organisations, which bring their particular model of disability to the South. This paper is an attempt to grapple with the increasingly important question: What happens when these Northern institutions, and their specific views and discourses about disability, spread to the global South, and to India in particular? In what ways is disability, and for the purposes of this article, Deafness,[1] as a culture and an identity, actualised and enacted in a Deaf women's organisation like DFDW (Delhi Foundation of Deaf Women) in urban India?

This article is based on fieldwork conducted at multiple sites: at DFDW, an annual nationwide Conference of Deaf women, and visits with Deaf women associated with DFDW and their families. Through paying close attention to the discourses utilised by my informants, I hope to track transnational discursive flows around Deafness and explore how they play out within different spaces. While I draw upon the analytic of public and private spaces — in the form of institutions and non-governmental organisations (NGOs) for the former, and the domestic sphere for the latter — in order to examine how the domestic sphere might be a space of contestation between multiple identities and meanings, I am also aware how this analytic might be limited for my informants, for whom public and private spaces constantly overlap and intertwine — some of my informants have Deaf family members, while others frequently bring their hearing family members to Deaf events and functions.

Therefore, it is important to look at how places and spaces are produced, both in relation to and in contestation with each other. This analytical methodology critically engages with Arjun Appadurai's call for a shift from 'ethnographies of locations' to 'ethnographies of circulations' through which we can examine 'horizontal, global networking' or the sharing of knowledge and information regardless of space and place (and seemingly regardless of power dynamics) (2001: 25). Appadurai's claim that one must look at multiple sites in order to see how discourses circulate and are utilised is important for this work, as I am engaging with discourses that are seen by certain activists, academics and rehabilitation professionals to be universal and unfettered by place and space.

While I find this analytic productive in thinking about Deaf women in urban India and their relationship with Northern Deaf activists and rehabilitation technocrats, I am also reminded of the critiques of global feminism by post-colonial feminist writers. Notions of a universal global sisterhood ignore uneven power dynamics and access to resources. Perhaps most importantly, such totalising views of the global also ignore locally-situated practices and knowledges (Nagar and Sangtin Writers 2006). Against the backdrop of such critiques, I would like to begin to speculate on what I call 'global Deafness'[2] — the emergence of a normative set of understandings through the practices of international rehabilitation institutions and organisations that disseminate a highly specific concept of Deafness based upon ideas of a universal Deaf culture and community. Discourses flow from Northern Deaf organisations to Deaf organisations in India as a result of visits by Northern Deaf individuals and organisations and electronic communication. However, is this discursive flow horizontal? What are the effects and manifestations of hidden power relations? How can we carve out a space for understanding locally-situated practices and knowledges in the face of what seems to be an overpowering 'global Deafness'?

This essay is an attempt to engage with a body of academic work written on Deafness known as Deaf Studies. Through engaging with the universalised 'global Deafness' that Deaf Studies produces, I hope to show that its focus on the privileging of Deaf identity through contentious identity politics and a framework of transnational discursive flows does not apply to locally-situated practices of Deaf women in urban India. In addition, I hope to show that just as these women cannot be seen as being constituted exclusively by transnational discursive flows, they cannot be viewed through a purely localised lens either. As Doreen Massey states, 'What we need, it seems to me, is a global sense of the local, a global sense of place' (1994: 156). For the women of DFDW, meaning is produced through creating and traversing multiple spaces, including both the public space of rehabilitation organisations and the domestic space of their homes and families. By exploring themes of kinship, Deaf culture, and Deaf identity, I attempt to track how meaning is created in two particular spaces, the public and the domestic, and how these spaces, in turn, overlap.

A Rupture in the Façade

Between 10 and 14 February 2005, I attended the 6th National Conference of Deaf Women/2nd Deaf Cultural Festival of India held in New Delhi and hosted by the DFDW. Approximately 70 women from all over India attended this public conference, held at the Vishwa Yuvak Kendra in New Delhi.[3] While Delhi and Maharashtra were the two most highly represented states, participants travelled from as far away as Assam and Orissa. The conference was a mix of leadership training, drama workshops and dance performances. A 'Miss Deaf India' beauty pageant was planned, but it was cancelled in the wake of the 26 December 2004 South Indian tsunami tragedy. Despite communication difficulties,[4] participants were most excited about meeting and socialising with other women. In fact, due to the high priority that they placed on socialising, presentations and performances were often delayed as women lingered over meals and congregated outside during breaks, sharing information and ideas.

Presenters at the conference included highly regarded Deaf educators and activists from both India and abroad. A senior official from the Scandinavian-based World Federation of the Deaf (WFD) attended, as did a well-respected Gallaudet University[5] professor who himself is a member of the Indian Deaf community. In addition, throughout the conference a steady stream of members of the Indian business community arrived, delivered presentations of varying levels of relevance, accessibility and quality, and then left. These presentations ranged from information on microcredit loans to guidelines on how to establish and run a small business. Participants, unable to read lengthy PowerPoint slides and uninterested in the nitty-gritty of entrepreneurial endeavours, signed amongst themselves and paid little attention to the sign language interpreters and relay interpreters. A façade of (dis)interested politeness was maintained: Deaf women performed their roles of obedient and respectful conference attendees, standing when presenters arrived and clapping after presentations were finished.

However, this façade cracked when the Chief Commissioner for Persons with Disabilities in New Delhi arrived to deliver his presentation. A new and enthusiastic member of the Indian bureaucracy, this official is committed to 'doing' outreach to different disabled populations. As such, he accepted an invitation to speak at this conference and arrived armed with detailed PowerPoint slides highlighting government schemes to uplift and improve the lives of people with disabilities in the country. While many of the women were unable to read these slides due to their low levels of literacy, the Commissioner's high status captured their attention and side conversations ceased. And here is when the 'rupture' occurred. The Commissioner enthusiastically shared some of his office's plans to eradicate deafness by reducing the incidence of babies born with hearing disabilities. Immediately after he uttered this statement, there was shocked silence in the room. Then, one of the women defiantly yelled out (in sign language, via an interpreter), 'We want *more* Deaf babies. We love Deaf babies. There should be more Deaf in the world.' The other 60 or so women in the room cheered and signed their support for her words. The official looked momentarily shocked (and aghast), although he quickly regained his composure and demurred, moving on to another topic. Order was instituted and side conversations resumed.

I call this event a 'rupture' because an otherwise seamless (and mundane) presentation turned into a site of contestation between two competing epistemologies. The conference participants' strong response to the Commissioner's well-intentioned comment about eradicating deafness was motivated by a sense that being Deaf is something to be *proud* of, that it is something to be embraced, cherished and appreciated. The official, on the other hand, saw Deafness as a medical impairment to be eradicated. He, like most Indian government officials, does not see Deafness as a culture or source of identity, but rather as an unfortunate condition that must be prevented. It should be noted that this expression of Deaf pride by conference participants was not an isolated incident. Throughout the conference, I frequently heard comments such as: 'Deaf can do everything that hearing people can'; 'Deaf need Deaf teachers'; 'Deaf should marry other Deaf'; and 'I want to have Deaf children'. Participants with Deaf husbands spoke proudly of them, and pointed out that they were Deaf. One woman named Pushpa,[6] a member of DFDW, about whom I will discuss in further detail later, was upset that she was married to a man who is not Deaf. She expressed feelings of admiration for friends with Deaf husbands.

Such sentiments and thoughts sounded almost uncanny coming from Deaf Indian women. As a Deaf person who has spent a significant amount of time in Deaf schools, institutions and social gatherings, largely in the United States, I had heard *all* of these things before — nothing that I heard was novel. The only thing that was different was the *place*. I was no longer in the global North, where the disability-as-culture paradigm prevails. Instead, I was in India, a place where scholars have noted that a certain focus on family, caste and religion remains strong (Cohen 1998; Das and Addlakha 2001). So, what does one make of this *doppelgänger* of Northern Deaf discourse?

Deafness, Deaf Culture, and Travelling Discourses

The Northern discourse around Deafness, which I contend constitutes 'global Deafness', is propelled by a body of scholarship known as Deaf Studies, an emerging academic discipline concerned with exploring the 'Deaf experience'. The Deaf Studies canon is mostly dominated by Deaf academics who largely adhere to a cultural universalism in their work (Ladd 2003; Lane, Heifmeister and Bahan 1996; Padden and Humphries 2006); that is to say, the discipline uncritically embraces the concept of a monolithic and universal Deaf culture, although this might slowly be changing. As Harlan L. Lane, Robert Hoffmeister and Benjamin J. Bahan (1996) show us, Deaf written with a capital 'D', is distinct from deaf written with a lower case 'd'. A Deaf individual is a member of Deaf culture, the Deaf community, and s/he communicates using sign language; s/he sees the world through Deaf eyes and possesses Deaf pride. In contrast, someone who is deaf has a medical condition or impairment. S/he does not identify with Deaf culture, and most likely does not use sign language. Deafness is an identity, a culture and a community for those who identify with it, and along with this identity comes a certain conception of rights and entitlements.[7]

What are these rights and entitlements? The Deaf community in America (and in other Northern democracies) has, by most accounts, successfully organised to secure access to education provided in sign language, sign language interpretation, appropriate telephone technology, and other services and technologies. In addition, the Deaf community has tried to create Deaf-run institutions and spaces. In one particularly memorable and precedent-setting incident in 1988, Deaf students and activists at Gallaudet University staged a successful mass protest, later named Deaf President Now (DPN), to demand a Deaf president for their school. DPN and its victorious aftermath resulted in a Deaf empowerment movement and the creation of significant collective cohesion and unity.

The DPN event and the subsequent Deaf empowerment movement ushered in an age of identity politics in which Deaf identity trumps *all* other identities and kinship ties, including, most significantly for the purposes of this article, family identity. It became impossible to be Deaf 'plus something else'. Within this discourse, Deafness is a Deaf individual's primary identity (Breivik 2005). It should also be noted that the Deaf identity movement has become a powerful framing tool for making claims upon the state (Nakamura 2006; Padden and Humphries 1988; Shapiro 1994). The boundary between culture and politics can appear quite blurred, since culture permeates politics and vice versa. However, the driving force behind this perspective is a distinct idea of what it means to be a Deaf individual with rights and entitlements predicated upon this Deaf identity.

How are these discourses around Deafness spread? International development organisations, the UN, the World Bank, and NGOs such as the WFD, Rotary Club and Lions Club International, through their programmatic efforts, have played a major role in disseminating such discourses and creating new forms of identity formation and personhood in Deaf people, and in people with disabilities in general.[8] In particular, over the last 30 years, significant international attention has been devoted to the situation of individuals with disabilities in the developing world (Kohrman 2005). The UN designated 1981 as the International Year of Disabled Persons; in 1982, it enacted the World Programme of Action Concerning Disabled Persons; 1983–1992 was the UN Decade of Disabled Persons; in 1992, 3 December was designated as an international disability awareness day (International Day of Disabled Persons); and finally, in 1993, the UN passed the Standard Rules on the Equalization of Opportunities for Persons with Disabilities. In June 2003, the General Assembly voted to draft 'a comprehensive and integral international convention to promote and protect the rights and dignity of persons with disabilities' which was ratified and adopted in December 2006.[9]

As alluded to in the quote from Benedicte Ingstad and Susan Reynolds Whyte (1995) at the beginning of this essay, rehabilitation programmes that are instituted by international development organisations and NGOs have resulted in new opportunities for identity formation and self-definition by Deaf people and other individuals with disabilities in the developing world. There is a certain conception of distinct comportment and a sense of self that individuals with disabilities are expected to actualise, one that is associated with core Western political liberal characteristics and concepts such as autonomy, independence and empowerment. Documents such as the United Nations Declaration of Human Rights, as also the more recent Convention on the Rights of Persons with Disabilities, simultaneously encapsulate this highly specific and universal view of the 'human'.

To turn to my own situation, I have received tremendous benefits as a result of my identification and affiliation with the American Deaf community. I have benefitted from discourses surrounding ideas of Deaf pride and Deaf rights. I feel proud, not stigmatised, when signing in public. The idea of a Deaf culture, a Deaf community, is empowering and positive. I recognise the salience and productivity of this in terms of identity and self-image, and in making claims upon the state. And, of course, everyone *should* have access to such a culture and community, especially in the face of vast societal discrimination against Deaf people — or should they? At the risk of entering anthropology's tired old battleground of cultural relativism and contrasting global and local spaces, I would like to issue a call for an 'anthropology of circulation' that, while appreciating sameness, also allows for an awareness of power-laden practices as well as an understanding of *difference*.

Now turning to the members of DFDW, my question is how are their hybrid identities constituted, since they are exposed to both the transnational (sameness) and the local (difference) discourses on disability and Deafness which exist relationally to each other?[10] I am interested in carving out a space for the exploration of the ways that these Deaf Indian women are *particularly* situated in relation to 'global Deafness'. The discourse used by the Deaf women at the National Conference was identical to discourses heard in the North. Yet, this conference, which took place in the public sphere, was only one of the myriad spaces that these women occupy. They also exist within a particular conjuncture of forces and relations — social, material and political — that are not explained by the totalising discourse surrounding 'global Deafness'. It is my contention that a close exploration of the different spaces (domestic, professional, public) that they negotiate in an ongoing fashion is crucial to tracking and highlighting the relationship between Northern discourses around Deafness and the local.[11]

The (Public) Field Site

The Delhi Foundation of Deaf Women (DFDW) was founded by three Indian Deaf women on 25 January 1973 as an offshoot of the All India Federation of the Deaf (AIFD). The latter was formed on 22 December 1955, and is affiliated with, and receives technical support from, the World Federation of the Deaf. DFDW was started on the premise, according to a history sheet provided by the organisation, of 'Help Them to Help Themselves'. According to the organisation's Secretary, there was a need for an association that specifically met the needs of deaf women within the Delhi metropolis, providing them with vocational and social development opportunities. Vocational programmes include batik-making, leather craft; tailoring, toy making, bookbinding, typing, computer training and English (sign) language teaching.

Deaf women are trained by fellow Deaf women, who are artisans, and successful students can become teachers and mentors to other students. Perhaps more important than its rehabilitation functions, DFDW organises a host of cultural and social events, such as beauty pageants and talent competitions that promote Deaf awareness and pride. DFDW also hosts an annual marriage programme called *Pranay Milan Sammelan* (gathering for matrimonial purposes), where Deaf women have the opportunity to meet and socialise with Deaf men in a structured setting. DFDW often hosts an annual nationwide leadership and cultural conference of Deaf Women, such as the one that I attended in 2005. In addition, it works closely with the All India Sports Council of the Deaf and helps organise Deaf sports tournaments. As such, DFDW is a rehabilitation and social organisation, providing both skill development and cultural and identity-building opportunities.

It should be noted that DFDW not only serves Deaf women but also provides Deaf young men with computer and typing training. In addition, some of the computer and tailoring teachers are men. There are occasionally programmes for children from schools for the Deaf around Delhi. In addition to linkages with national-level organisations for the Deaf, DFDW also has connections with the US-based Rotary Club, Lions Club and the Church of Jesus Christ of Latter-day Saints among others. By most accounts, DFDW is a well-connected organisation within the Delhi Deaf community and the larger northern Indian Deaf community. There are frequent visitors from other organisations, who come to meet with the administration and visit the workshop. DFDW has also served as a role model for organisations in other states where Deaf women, with either informal or formal support from DFDW, have started similar organisations.[12]

It is unclear where the bulk of DFDW's funding comes from, as the organisation's administration is not at all transparent about this, citing a need to guard its funding sources from competing organisations (Kiyaga 2003). However, it is clear that DFDW receives some government funding, in addition to revenue generated from selling the handicrafts made in the workshop. DFDW's organisational structure is extremely hierarchical. There is a ruling class of Deaf women, some of them with advanced degrees and financial resources, and they do not appear to be at all accountable to the bulk of the women who work there or receive services. As a result, there is considerable tension within the organisation with some of the more outspoken women calling for an ousting of the ruling class, financial transparency, and a more democratic structure.

DFDW occupies a floor in a battered community hall down a small lane in Paharganj, a commercial area located close to the New Delhi Railway Station. On a routine day, approximately 30 women report for work and classes at DFDW. These women range in age from 18 years to their late 60s; and most of them can be found in DFDW's rectangular-shaped workshop, painstakingly working on leather wallets, batik paintings, and fabric coin purses to be sold to tourists and at state emporia. DFDW's Secretary and Office Manager have their own offices, and the tension between the administration and workers is palpable.

While working, the women sit facing the windows and rarely speak, except to ask for guidance from lead instructors, or during tea and lunch breaks. An air of camaraderie and affection exists among them, which is heightened during breaks when they joke, confide in each other and share their food.[13] There are two lead instructors and one manager, who is also an instructor. All three have been with DFDW for over 20 years. These three senior women have extremely close relationships with the other younger women for whom they function as mentors and confidantes, in addition to being teachers. DFDW is open five days a week for eight hours a day, and on Saturday for a half day. Pay is on a sliding scale depending on seniority and position, and by all accounts, is quite meagre.

When positioning DFDW within the wider disability rehabilitation apparatus in Delhi, and India at large, it is important to note that through its focus on Deaf women's empowerment, in the absence of a direct connection to either the larger international rehabilitation apparatus or the women's movement, it has managed to carve out a space for itself that is unique. All its board members and governing body are Indian, and it seemingly prides itself on being an *Indian* organisation. This is especially obvious at cultural pageants which feature classical Indian dance, in DFDW's workshop which features 'traditional' Indian crafts, and at marriage pageants in which caste is factored in. As such, while it does benefit from interactions with transnational organisations and discourses, it has created a more or less protected space that at times lends to contestation and conflict with other more 'Western' NGOs like the recently formed National Association of the Deaf (NAD) that are recruiting DFDW's younger members with the lure of Western-style identity politics.

The Domestic Sphere as a Space of Transnational Difference: *Which Family*?

While interviewing members at DFDW, I became increasingly aware of the importance that they placed on the domestic sphere (family and home), an importance that a focus on Deaf identity and culture elides and misses. They travel between the domestic sphere and the public sphere, occupying multiple spaces and identities. They are simultaneously wives, mothers, daughters-in-law, sisters and (Deaf) teachers and artisans. Deafness has not trumped their other identities and affiliations. Here, I turn to and extend the work started by Veena Das and Renu Addlakha in which the authors call for a return to the domestic sphere. Noting that current work on disability, which locates its subjects firmly within a liberal political regime (and the public sphere), misses what happens in domestic spaces, they state:

> In this essay, we propose to analyse notions of impairment and disability through a reconfiguration of the domestic sphere. We hope to show that the domestic, once displaced from its conventionally assumed reference to the private, becomes a sphere in which a different kind of citizenship can be enacted — a citizenship based not on the formation of associational communities, but on notions of *publics* constituted through *voice*. The domestic sphere then is always on the verge of becoming the political (Das and Addlakha 2001: 511–12).

While recognising the importance of Paul Rabinow's concept (1996) of biosociality — the emergence of associational communities around shared biological characteristics like deafness — Das and Addlakha are also entreating us to remember the domestic sphere. DFDW is biosociality in action, in that it is an intergenerational organisation run by and for Deaf women in Delhi. If I were to focus my research *only* on this biosocial configuration, I would be missing the importance that the domestic sphere holds for these women. And as DFDW is, in some respects, a product of Northern discursive flows (through its multiple affiliations with the All India Federation of the Deaf, which is associated with the World Federation of the Deaf and other international rehabilitation organisations such as the Rotary and Lions Clubs), I would also be missing the tension between the global and the local.

In order to understand what their participation in DFDW means to its members and to their families, I interviewed[14] DFDW's three senior workshop teachers, all three of whom are married with children and can be broadly classified as middle-class. I chose these women because they have been with DFDW the longest and they play multiple roles within the organisation — they are teachers, mentors and friends. In addition, their status as middle-aged women (between the ages of 40 and 60 years) means that they have been married for a long period of time, ostensibly allowing for the creation of significant spousal and family bonds. In particular, I was interested in how they negotiated their obligations to their families with their work at DFDW, and if they felt that their relationship with other Deaf women in DFDW usurped their family relationship in importance. I was interested in these issues in the light of Northern discourses around Deafness which, as noted above, require that Deaf identity be first and foremost in importance. These women and other members of DFDW have had much exposure to these discourses through meeting members of the international Deaf community at sporting events, cultural conferences and visits from international organisations. Through interviews, I found that these three women viewed *both* the public and the domestic spheres as spaces of meaning and identity. As Meenakshi, who has been with DFDW since 1986, states:

> No, they [the women at DFDW] do not feel like family because family means blood tie relations, and I have none with any of the women at DFDW. Our relationships are different but beneficial, because we are

able to share things about our lives, as the communication is easy between us. Perhaps as a second family, yes, because I feel an obligation, a duty to educate and advise the younger women who come to DFDW. I am attached to them and feel concerned about their lives and future, because we experience the same life challenges. I feel an important part of their lives and the young ones also come to me for advice about any problem. I feel good to be able to help and support them, because at home they may have no family relations to confide in.

We can see that while Meenakshi feels affection and concern for the younger women at DFDW, she states unambiguously that her conception of family still depends on bonds created by and through blood. Yet, the plot thickens when we add the fact that Meenakshi lives with her Deaf husband and his hearing parents. Her daughter, who is also Deaf, attends a school for Deaf girls in Chennai.[15] Meenakshi's mother-in-law does not sign, but is often present at social events for the Deaf held at Meenakshi's house.

Similarly, Pushpa, who has been involved with DFDW since 1981, says:

No, they are not like my family, but we get along well together, and are able to support one another in many ways. We share news and love the atmosphere we work in because we feel equal and are all Deaf. I learnt many skills from this organisation. But most of my values I learnt from my family.

Then, Anuradha, who has been involved with DFDW since 1973 and is one of the founding members, endorses her colleagues' viewpoints:

I enjoy the company of the women with whom I work. We communicate easily and cooperate with one another. If a person has a problem, we are all involved in trying to find solutions to family or personal problems.[16]

Through my interviews with Meenakshi, Pushpa and Anuradha, it was clear that these women possess love and affection for each other and enjoy being mentors to younger women. What was not so clear, however, was whether they had engaged in the creation of new kinship forms (Rapp and Ginsburg 2001). It appears that boundaries between the public sphere of work and the domestic sphere of home become blurred when these women and their families spend their precious day off socialising among themselves; in fact, they and their families spend significant time together outside of DFDW's working hours.

In order to explore further how these women negotiate the domestic and public spheres, I asked them how their families viewed DFDW. All of them reported that their families were happy that they had found a women's only workplace that was 'safe' and 'positive'. For the most part, there is no conflict with their family members over their occupying multiple spaces. As Meenakshi says:

> Yes, my family likes DFDW because they can see that it has had a positive influence on my life. It has given me opportunities to be progressive, and promotes Deaf women's issues, giving us possibilities of leading interdependent/independent lives. It gives us economic independence, so our families don't have to worry that we'll depend on them for money. It is a women's only organisation, which makes our families feel secure knowing that we are safe and won't get spoilt by bad people (that is, men). Our families trust us and know that we are brave women, which gives a positive image about each one of us.

Pushpa is the only one among the three with a hearing husband; she is also the eldest of the three and lives the farthest away from DFDW. Her commute takes over an hour each way in a crowded city bus in which she is often forced to stand. Her husband is retired, and he spends his days chatting with other retirees in the courtyard of the middle class housing colony in which they live. In the past, her husband volunteered at DFDW and attended Deaf functions quite often. While he recognises the importance of DFDW for Pushpa, he has entreated her to retire as well, so that she would not have to endure such an arduous commute each day. However, as she tells me:

> I must continue going to DFDW as it is at DFDW where I am able to meet with others like me. If I were to stay at home, I would just sit around and be bored. At DFDW, I have my friends and I am always learning new things. If I do not go to DFDW, I will not have other Deaf people to talk to.[17]

For Pushpa, Meenakshi and Anuradha, DFDW is not their family, but it is more than just a job. It is a place where they can go to meet others who are *like them*. When I asked them what they talk about when they were at work, responses included 'family problems and conflicts', 'mother-in-law problems', 'money problems' and 'the future'. As Meenakshi says:

> We talk about the future, personal problems, family conflicts (harassment), job challenges and low pay. We are able to advise one another and try to solve our problems. Sometimes, a woman will talk about how her family wants to jail her in the house and not let her go outside. When young women come to DFDW with such problems, I tell them to bring their parents, and I am able to advise them and put some sense into their heads!

While I was only able to conduct in-depth interviews with these three senior functionaries of DFDW, I also spent time during the summers of 2003, 2005 and 2006 with younger women receiving training. One young woman named Anjali goes to a government school for the Deaf during the year and attends DFDW during her summer vacation to train for a possible career as a tailor. She told me that DFDW taught her about 'Deaf pride' and that she 'feels comfortable and happy being Deaf now'. When I asked her what 'Deaf pride' meant, she said that she 'is happy that she is Deaf and that Deaf people can do anything and should have confidence'. Another young woman, 26-year-old Prachi, told me that the older women at DFDW were wonderful mentors to her, and that she learned a great deal from them. She said that she is much more 'responsible and confident now thanks to help from her teachers'. It should be noted that the younger women, especially those who are unmarried, do spend some time socialising with each other after DFDW closes for the day and on weekends. However, they tend to spend much more time with their families.

It is important to note that presently the field of rehabilitation and political organisation around Deafness in Delhi is changing; and this shift is specifically affecting youths. There is an organisation called the National Association of the Deaf (NAD), which focuses on contentious politics and making demands upon the State. Its motto is 'Let us come together, know our rights and claim them', and it specifically targets young Deaf adults with a focus on identity politics and the formation of new kinship bonds by members.

An increasing number of Deaf youth are joining this group and are articulating Northern-style discourses around Deafness. These young adults spend significant amounts of time together, discussing ways to form new Deaf kinship groups ('families') with their peers. Additional research is needed to determine how this organisation is changing the terrain of identity politics among young Deaf women.[18]

Conclusion: Sameness and Difference/ Public and Domestic Spaces

I would like to conclude by returning to the issues of difference and sameness with which I began this essay, in particular, the idea that Deaf culture is something that is homogeneous and monolithic regardless of where it is found; space does not matter and Deaf identity and culture trump all other possibilities for self-identification (Breivik 2005; Wrigley 1996). Jan-Kåre Breivik (2005) writes about space in order to stress the transnational and translocal nature of the Deaf community. 'Home', and the domestic sphere, are often troubled concepts for Deaf people, as spatial *closeness* might mean emotional and personal *distance* (due to inadequate communication between hearing persons and Deaf sign language using members). In writing about the ways that Deaf people tend to feel alienated around their family members, Breivik discusses the ways that spatial closeness can often confirm or emphasise difference. In contrast, spatial distance can imply sameness — as in the case of Deaf people meeting each other at the Deaf Olympics or World Deaf Congress meetings. Due to communication barriers and cultural differences, Deaf individuals seek out new forms of kinship that are not confined by space. He contends that Deaf people must be understood beyond a familial and national territorial framework. By focusing on the ways that Deaf people across the globe are similar, Breivik identifies his scope as a *global* one. As he writes: 'Deaf people are thus potentially and actually members of a transnational and translocal framework that overrides any local or national loyalty they may additionally possess' (ibid.: 12). Indeed, Deafness is most productively thought of in terms of *routes* rather than *roots*. While he recognises the subtle tensions for Deaf persons as they negotiate multiple senses of belonging and identity at the local level, his overriding emphasis is on the transnational and translocal contexts. While this story might work for Breivik's Norwegian and other Scandinavian Deaf informants, it does not work for thinking about similar questions of identity, belongingness and home among the women of DFDW. A different story needs to be told about them, a story that does not dismiss the domestic sphere, but specifically accounts for the ways that identities and spaces can be overlapping sites of belonging and contestation.

The preliminary research that I have conducted at DFDW shows that these women of multiple generations, while participating in both national and international conferences and sporting events, still identify their primary kinship ties as being with their families. At the same time, they do feel a sense of affinity, affiliation, and closeness towards other Deaf women. My informants can be seen to be inhabiting multiple and contesting spaces, including the space of 'I am Deaf, you are Deaf, we are the same' and the space of being a member of a particular family, caste, religion and nation marking out sites of difference.

I return here to Das and Addlakha's call for a return to the domestic sphere, as my ethnographic research has shown that it is quite impossible to disentangle public space from domestic space. The women of DFDW and their families are actively involved in the creation of overlapping spaces. The fact that some of Meenakshi's blood family is deaf/Deaf, and that Pushpa's hearing husband used to volunteer at DFDW, points out how spaces can overlap. While it is important to retain the domestic sphere as an analytic space of kinship and identity formation, we must also be careful not to create unnecessary analytic boundaries between public and domestic spaces.

It is important to note that for members of DFDW, the closeness that they feel towards other Deaf women does not translate into identity politics or new forms of kinship based on identity politics. In fact, when I sat down with some of the younger women in DFDW's workshop to discuss identity politics in the summer of 2006, identity as a concept did not resonate with them immediately, and initially, they thought that I was asking them to tell me what was written on their government-issued identification cards certifying that they were disabled. While they eventually did get the drift of my query, they were quite clear that there were several identities that they *also* cared about, apart from and in addition to being Deaf: their gender, religion, caste, family background and geographic place of origin were equally important for them. While many of them had internalised Northern discourses around Deafness, these discourses had not necessarily translated into new forms of identity. Further research will need to be done in order to see how newer organisations such as the NAD, based more specifically on identity politics and assertion of rights, might change this.

Notes

* This essay first appeared in the *Indian Journal of Gender Studies*, 15 (2): pp. 365–85, 2008, New Delhi: SAGE Publications. Editorial changes have been made to the original published chapter with permission from the Centre for Women's Development Studies, New Delhi. I would like to thank Renu Addlakha, Gillian Hart, and the members of the Spring 2007 Geographies of Development Seminar at Berkeley for their generous feedback and comments. In addition, and most importantly, I would like to thank Nassozi Kiyaga and all the wonderful women of DFDW for their time, patience and unyielding support.
1. Here and throughout this article I have chosen to write 'Deaf' using a capital 'D' in order to stress that I view the medical condition of deafness as providing the conditions of possibility for distinct ontologies and epistemologies to emerge (Friedner 2010). While 'Deaf' is often used to represent Deafness as a culture, and Deaf people as a linguistic minority, I do not see 'culture' or 'linguistic minority' as wholly appropriate frameworks for analysing the experiences of my informants in India. I, therefore, want to stress that I use 'Deaf' (with a capital 'D') with hesitation and ambivalence as I am unsure of its applicability to the lived realities of the d/Deaf women with whom I worked in India.
2. In this chapter, 'global Deafness' and Northern discourses around Deafness are being used synonymously.
3. Vishwa Yuvak Kendra is a leading NGO in youth training established in 1968 and supported by the Indian government. It is based in New Delhi.
4. As there is currently no national standardised Indian Sign Language (ISL), participants struggled to understand each other. Throughout the conference, communication was an ongoing issue and it was only

through the help of relay interpreters — deaf women who were able to interpret one form of ISL to a 'simpler', pared down form — that communication was established.
5. Gallaudet University, the world's oldest and only liberal arts college exclusively for the Deaf, is located in Washington, DC in the United States. Since 1864, it has been a highly cherished institution by Deaf people all over the world. In fact, when travelling in foreign countries and meeting Deaf people, the first question that I am often asked is 'Did you go to Gallaudet?'
6. All names have been changed to protect the identity of informants.
7. It goes without saying that this Deaf culture movement has been most successful among middle and upper class urban individuals in the global North, who have access to education in sign languages as well as social and cultural opportunities to meet and interact with other Deaf individuals.
8. As noted previously, the Deaf community sees itself as a linguistic minority and *not* as a disability group. As such, significant tension exists — how to benefit from the legal protections and services that the category of disability offers, and yet, how to define oneself as not a part of this community.
9. From the United Nations Enable website: http://www.un.org/esa/socdev/enable/ (accessed 30 October 2007). Since this article was written, India signed and ratified the United Nations Convention on the Rights of People with Disabilities (UNCRPD) in October 2007. The UNCRPD has resulted in increased attention to disability rights and the proliferation of what I call 'disability capital': increased funding available to NGOs and governments to focus on disability. It should also be noted that the UNCRPD puts forth the concept of deaf people as a linguistic minority and sign language as d/Deaf peoples' language. As such, it adopts (and imposes) a Western-centric idea of what it means to be d/Deaf.
10. This is not to say that the categories of 'sameness' and 'difference' are pure ones. They are contested in their own right. Thanks to Catherine Guimond (personal communication) for pointing this out to me.
11. While I recognise that recent scholarship has shown that 'the local' is a reified and problematic concept (Mohan and Stokke 2000) that obscures more than it actually reveals, here I hold on to it more as a homogeneous concept in an attempt to salvage a space for difference.
12. These other organisations are barely functioning at the moment, possessing few programmes and limited number of members. The DFDW's Delhi branch is the most active.
13. While the atmosphere is generally collegial and friendly, some social/professional hierarchies exist. For instance, women responsible for cleaning are not invited to sit with the others and share their food during lunchtime.

14. As I am not fluent in Indian Sign Language, interviews were conducted with the help of Nassozi Kiyaga, a community activist who worked in DFDW in the early 2000s for five years.
15. One could argue that because members of Meenakshi's family are d/Deaf, she does not need to redefine kinship — that, for her, public and domestic spaces are completely overlapping and indistinguishable. This is possibly true as well for other members of DFDW who are married to Deaf men and/or have Deaf children.
16. Since the writing of this article, Anuradha has left DFDW in order to take care of her grandchildren. She initially moved to Bangalore, in south India, to take care of one grandchild and then moved to Gurgaon, a suburb of New Delhi, which is far enough from DFDW to make commuting there rather unfeasible. When I met her in Bangalore in the summer of 2009, she was not so happy about this situation, and told me that she missed the women at DFDW and did not enjoy being in Bangalore. However, she said that she felt a sense of responsibility to help her children and grandchildren.
17. Since the writing of this article, Pushpa's husband died. As her family was worried about her living alone, Pushpa went to spend some time in Vietnam with a son who lives in that country. She reported to me that she felt extremely bored and isolated there and wished to return to India and to DFDW. Since returning, she continues to commute to DFDW each day.
18. Many of the young women at DFDW have attended the NAD's programmes, but they say they feel alienated by the organisation's 'Western' approach, as one informant puts it. She expresses concern that most of the young women who attend NAD's programmes wear 'Western-style clothing' and eat in McDonalds and other American-style restaurants. To this informant, as well as to many others, this choice of clothing and food represents a departure from Indian culture, and is a sign of potential moral decline.

References

Appadurai, Arjun. 2001. 'Deep Democracy: Urban Governmentality and the Horizon of Politics', *Environment and Urbanization*, 13 (2): 23–44.

Breivik, Jan-Kåre. 2005. *Deaf Identities in the Making: Local Lives, Transnational Connections*. Washington, DC: Gallaudet University Press.

Cohen, Lawrence. 1998. *No Aging in India: Alzheimer's, the Bad Family, and Other Modern Things*. Berkeley: University of California Press.

Das, Veena and Renu Addlakha. 2001. 'Disability and Domestic Citizenship: Voice, Gender, and the Making of the Subject', *Public Culture*, 13 (3): 511–32.

Friedner, Michele. 2010. 'Biopower, Biosociality, and Community Formation: How Biopower Is Constitutive of the Deaf Community', *Sign Language Studies*, 10 (3): 336–47.

Ingstad, Benedicte and Susan Reynolds Whyte (eds), 1995. 'Introduction', in *Disability and Culture*, pp. 1–32. Berkeley: University of California Press.

Kiyaga, Nassozi B. 2003. *Deafness in the Developing World: A Case Study*. Washington, DC: Gallaudet University.

Kohrman, Matthew. 2005. *Bodies of Difference: Experiences of Disability and Institutional Advocacy in the Making of Modern China*. Berkeley: University of California Press.

Ladd, Paddy. 2003. *Understanding Deaf Culture: In Search of Deafhood*. Clevedon: Multilingual Matters Ltd.

Lane, Harlan L., Robert Hoffmeister and Benjamin J. Bahan. 1996. *A Journey into the Deaf-World*. San Diego, CA: DawnSignPress.

Massey, Doreen B. 1994. *Space, Place, and Gender*. Minneapolis: University of Minnesota Press.

Mohan, Giles and Kristian Stokke. 2000. 'Participatory Development and Empowerment: The Dangers of Localism', *Third World Quarterly*, 21 (2): 247–68.

Nakamura, Karen. 2006. *Deaf in Japan: Signing and the Politics of Identity*. Ithaca, NY: Cornell University Press.

Nagar, Richa and Sangtin Writers. 2006. *Playing with Fire: Feminist Thought and Activism through Seven Lives in India*. Minneapolis: University of Minnesota Press.

Padden, Carol and Tom Humphries. 1988. *Deaf in America: Voices from a Culture*. Cambridge, MA: Harvard University Press.

———. 2006. *Inside Deaf Culture*. Cambridge, MA: Harvard University Press.

Rabinow, Paul. 1996. *Making PCR: A Story of Biotechnology*. Chicago: University of Chicago Press.

Rapp, Rayna and Faye Ginsburg. 2001. 'Enabling Disability: Rewriting Kinship, Reimaging Citizenship', *Public Culture*, 13 (3): 533–56.

Shapiro, Joseph P. 1994. *No Pity: People with Disabilities Forging a New Civil Rights Movement*. New York: Three Rivers Press.

Wrigley, Owen. 1996. *The Politics of Deafness*. Washington, DC: Gallaudet University Press.

11

The Inner World of Adolescent Girls with Hearing Impairment: Two Case Studies

SANDHYA LIMAYE*

Adolescence has been recognised as an important phase in human development. It is a transitional stage of the life cycle between childhood and adulthood when individuals acquire the specific skills and emotional commitment necessary to participate as adults in society. In addition to negotiating with many physical changes, an adolescent is expected to acquire interpersonal, technical, vocational and participatory skills with the aim of broadening his/her range of social contacts, exercising new behaviours and developing future life goals. Robert James Havighurst (1972) considers adolescence as a specific stage when particular developmental tasks must be mastered. These tasks define healthy, normal development at different stages of the life cycle in a particular society. Biological, social, cultural and individual personality factors structure the nature and management of these developmental tasks. Every individual has to confront them at different stages of his/her life. In addition to their universality, the tasks are sequential and cumulative — success in learning the appropriate tasks during the early years leads to greater chances of success in subsequent tasks undertaken in later years. Failure in mastering the necessary tasks in the early years can lead to negative outcomes later in life (ibid.). They form the ongoing step-by-step process by which a personality matures and becomes productive.

The major developmental tasks of adolescence are awareness and acceptance of the changing body, internalisation of gender role expectations, development of peer relationships, acquisition of autonomy, training for economic independence, marriage and family life, and the development of a distinct personal identity. How these tasks are perceived by adolescents and by society are influenced by the culture, subculture, lifestyle, beliefs and practices, and geographical location of the individual (Mattessich and Hill 1987). According to Betty Carter and Monica McGoldrick, 'the successful accomplishment of the developmental tasks in adolescence is also in part dependent on and contributes to the successful accomplishment by other family members of their appropriate tasks' (Carter and McGoldrick [1980] in Greene [1986: 121]). This is of particular importance when the adolescent is disabled.

In addition to the limitations imposed by the particular impairment, the environment to which adolescents with disabilities are exposed, including the attitudes of their own family members, may not be conducive to normal development. While adolescents with hearing impairment face the same developmental challenges that confront all hearing adolescents, their passage through this stage is more difficult, since the basic deprivation due to deafness is more than sensory as basic communication skills are seriously affected.

Hearing impairment or deafness is one of the most severe of all disabilities because it strikes at a basic human function — communication. Richard G. Brill (1974) has defined the deaf as those in whom the sense of hearing is non-functional for the ordinary purposes of life. The *Gallaudet Encyclopedia of Deaf People and Deafness* (Van Cleve and Gallaudet College 1987) defines deafness as an inability to hear and understand speech through the ear alone. As deafness is both a sensory defect and a communication disability, the affected child finds it difficult to communicate clearly about his/her own needs, thoughts and experiences. Parents also find it difficult to communicate with their child adequately (Meadow 1980). A hearing aid does not completely compensate for the hearing loss but only enables the child to make as full use as possible of the residual hearing s/he has. Thus, it is difficult for such a child to learn naturally what is expected of him/her, and to obtain satisfaction of his/her needs in socially acceptable ways. For a deaf child, the development of speech, language, and verbal abstraction is a continuous struggle, which affects his/her cognitive, social, emotional and psychological development and self-concept. This invisible disability tends to foster greater misunderstanding (Fitz-Gerald and Fitz-Gerald 1987). It has been said that blindness separates people from things, whereas deafness separates people from people (Bishop 1979). As the environment is normally brought to the child through the medium of spoken language, the hearing impaired child, with no alternative means of communication, will be at a disadvantage. If the parents are not deaf, the major problem will be the absence of effective communication, which will adversely affect the parent–child relationship. This situation can manifest itself in behavioural problems, including throwing temper tantrums in response to frustration (Freeman, Carbin and Boese 1981).

Since the understanding of the world and meaning construction may be adversely impacted by hearing impairment, parents may misunderstand the behaviour, motives, fears and anxieties of hearing impaired adolescents. It is, in fact, not an easy job for the parents to help them cope with their life situation and grow into well-integrated young adults. Then, similar to non-disabled adolescents, not all adolescents with hearing impairment want to talk to their parents about their private thoughts, as they fear being criticised or misunderstood by them. This makes it all the more necessary to understand their specific concerns regarding the developmental tasks that they have to manage. It is the aim of this article to understand the thoughts, feelings, fears and aspirations of two young persons with hearing impairment as they work through this process.

The main criteria for selection of deaf adolescents as respondents were their ability to understand the researcher, as well as to express their feelings in such a way that she could understand them as well. Thus, language usage and communication capacity were two important factors considered while selecting interviewees. In addition, care was also taken to ensure that they did not have any other disability apart from hearing impairment, in order to understand its particular influence on the comprehension and performance of the developmental tasks of adolescence. The sources of data were the adolescents themselves. In addition, interviews and discussions were held with collaterals such as their parents, teachers, siblings and friends. The researcher used a mix of communication methods — oral and sign languages, gestures and writing. Simple sentence construction, reiteration through repetition, and short duration interviews marked the research strategy. The researcher had to repeatedly explain and check to make sure that the interviewees understood the questions clearly. It was a trying experience, but it gave her insights into the frustration and tension that hearing impaired adolescents feel when trying to understand other people, and their struggle to respond to them. Since the respondents had not had the experience of being asked about their feelings, attitudes and desires, they were unfamiliar with many words and concepts taken for granted in a hearing world. Due to the high level of concentration required for such communication, interviews could not exceed one and a half hours; thereafter, respondents became tired and lost concentration. Three sessions were required per respondent to complete the interview schedule. Many other issues were revealed once the respondents found that the researcher was sincerely making an attempt to understand their feelings.

Names of the informants have been altered to preserve confidentiality. The article does not claim that the information received from them is in any way representative of *all* deaf adolescents. It is an attempt to throw light on the impact of deafness on the developmental tasks of two female adolescents with hearing impairment. It is hoped that such research, rather than confirming deafness as a personal tragedy, will encourage both the deaf community and the hearing world to be more constructive and positive in their approach to deaf adolescents and their families, so that young deaf people may realise their full potential and participate as meaningful individuals in society.

Radha

Radha is a 15-year-old girl residing in Mumbai. She is the only child of educated parents from the upper socioeconomic strata. She is tall, fair, slim and good-looking and studies in the 10th standard in an English medium school for the deaf. Her father has a business in electronic goods in Cochin in the state of Kerala. He travels frequently between Cochin and Mumbai for business purposes. Earlier, with her mother working as an officer in the Reserve Bank of India in Cochin, Radha resided with her paternal grandmother and studied in a regular school in the neighbourhood. Then, when her grandmother fell ill, Radha's mother resigned from her job and came to Mumbai to look after them. After a few days, her grandmother passed away. When her mother found that Radha could not cope with the curriculum in a regular school, she was admitted into the school for the deaf in the 7th standard. In this school, Radha is comfortable and feels a sense of inclusiveness amidst a group of deaf children. Her mother plans to return to Cochin after Radha's matriculation, since their relatives live there. Radha, however, does not relish the idea of shifting there. Her mother tongue is Malayalam, but she does not know the language. She visits Kerala often during the holidays, but feels very lonely and bored there due to the language barrier. When in Cochin, her mother pressurises her to mix with relatives. However, no one tries to communicate with her in English, which is the language she can understand. Therefore, she gets very anxious at the thought of going back to Cochin permanently. She has tried to discuss the matter with her parents, but her mother refuses to reconsider this issue, and insists that Radha should learn to adjust anywhere. Worried about her daughter's future, she feels that once Radha learns to adjust to the family, she will get continual support from them even after their (her parents') death. She thinks that Radha is too young to understand the importance of the family support system.

Radha's parents had noticed her deafness before she was a year old. In addition to an Rh incompatibility,[1] Radha's mother had a difficult pregnancy. Radha was diagnosed with bilateral profound sensorineural hearing loss, and she has used BTE (behind-the-ear) hearing aids regularly at home and at school. She and her parents communicate orally, which is quite stressful for all of them. The couple is aware of the risk of disability due to the Rh incompatibility, and have, therefore, decided not to have any more children.

Radha does not have any friends in the neighbourhood. She hates the school holidays as she feels lonely at home. Her mother does not allow her to visit her school friends since they stay far from her house. Radha reveals that her mother begins vomiting and has dizzy spells, if she comes home late from school or visits her friends on her own. She is tired of her mother's overprotective attitude. She realises that she needs her mother's emotional support, but at the same time fears her. She maintains little communication or interaction with her father, who stays in Cochin for long spells, and she gets very tense when interacting with him.

Hasina

Hasina, an 18-year-old girl from an orthodox Muslim family, studies in the 8th standard in a Hindi medium school for the deaf. She is a tall, thin and smart girl. She is an extrovert, talkative and likes to help others. She is very sensitive about her deafness; and she gets angry with her mother who looks down on her deaf friends. Hasina has accepted her deafness and wants to be a part of the deaf world. While she argues with her mother, she admits being afraid of her father.

Hasina is the second among four siblings in a nuclear family. Her family belongs to the lower socioeconomic class — her father is a tailor who earns ₹500 a month, and her mother is a housewife. Her parents are second cousins. They are from the Saurashtra region of Gujarat and speak Gujarati. Three generations ago, the family migrated to Mumbai in search of employment. According to her mother, Hasina was born with normal hearing. When she was 7-years-old, she had typhoid and tuberculosis, and '126 injections of streptomycin' were given to her. As a result, she gradually developed hearing loss and her speech was also affected. After consultations at the Jamshedji Jeejeebhoy Hospital and the Nair Hospital in Mumbai, she was diagnosed as having bilateral severe sensorineural hearing loss. At the age of eight, she was admitted to a school for the deaf. She wears body level hearing aids, which she finds beneficial. She communicates through a mix of verbal speech (incomplete sentences) and sign language. She takes a little time to understand what is said to her, but she loves to respond. It is not difficult to understand her speech, provided one makes a little extra effort. Hasina feels frustrated when her family fails to understand her — she is convinced that they do not pay enough attention to her.

Negotiating with the Developmental Tasks of Adolescence in a Hearing World

This section looks at how Radha and Hasina work towards fulfilling their developmental tasks. It is an attempt to understand their views regarding the developmental tasks, difficulties faced by them as hearing impaired young persons, expectations from parents and other adults in the hearing world, and the coping skills that they have devised to negotiate the challenges.

Awareness of the changing body

Adolescence is marked by a spurt in physical growth and the development of secondary sexual characteristics. Radha started menstruating at the age of 12. She came to know about the menstrual cycle from her friends who were a few years older than her. When many of them started menstruating around the age of 10, Radha was upset — she felt excluded from her group of friends when they discussed periods. After her transfer from the regular school to the school for the deaf, Radha noticed changes in her body, like the development of breasts and growth of pubic hair. She made new friends with whom she would discuss menstruation, which enabled her to be mentally prepared for its onset. Hasina began menstruating at the age of 14. She was not tense but curious about it, because she had been told about it by her seniors at school. All the girls in her class started their periods at around the same age.

Radha and Hasina say that their mothers had talked to them about menstruation, emphasising what they could not do during their periods, such as not going to the temple, not coming home late, not mixing with boys, not allowing boys to touch them, not talking to any strangers, and sitting properly. When they first started menstruating, they noticed that their mothers were happy. Both the girls were also excited and discussed it with their friends. Though they did not initially like the fact that they would have to go through this every month, after a while they accepted it as something natural. They noticed that their mothers checked regularly every month whether they had had their periods; but they never answered any questions that their daughters posed about the topic. Radha and Hasina were interested in knowing why menstruation occurred. Hasina said that her mother was not comfortable discussing it. Her elder sister explained to her that it was related to childbirth. Radha's mother gave her the same explanation. Both girls were dissatisfied with the inadequate information provided to them. When they tried to discuss the matter with their friends, they found that their friends did not know much either.

Radha and Hasina were acutely aware of their bodily changes and felt a mixture of curiosity and shame about them — they tried to walk in such a way that nobody would notice that they were growing up. Both girls often looked at themselves in the mirror and were aware of their attractiveness. They were pleased when other people, especially boys at school, complimented them on their appearance. They understood the impact of their physical attractiveness on others, and tried to enhance their looks by wearing good clothes and sporting different hairstyles.

Radha was concerned about her oily hair and facial blemishes like pimples and blackheads. She watched television advertisements for pimple treatment and other beauty products, and received beauty tips from her friends, but her mother did not allow her to experiment. Radha says, 'I wanted to remove my pubic hair and apply ointment on my face to remove pimples, but my mother gave me a lecture.'

Hasina does not have pimples or blackheads, but she is concerned about the size of her breasts. She is sure that she is smart and good-looking, but she has a complex about not having well-shaped breasts. Her friends have advised her to wear padded brassieres, but she does not have the courage to ask her mother to buy them for her.

Both Hasina and Radha expected their mothers and schoolteachers to tell them about the biological changes they were experiencing, as also about childbirth, attraction to boys, the male reproductive system and family planning methods. Since parents and teachers are loath to address such issues and their friends are not well informed, they feel that a sex education counsellor or an adult deaf person should give them proper information related to sexuality. Otherwise, they feel, they will be exposed to incorrect information from unreliable sources.

Gender roles

Every society designates specific modes of behaviour for males and females. Radha and Hasina are well aware of gender role expectations in their social milieu. Apart from performing household tasks themselves, observing their parents, other family members and neighbours has enhanced their understanding of appropriate gender-based behaviour. They are advised, from time to time, by adults about appropriate behaviour, language use and dress codes. Their families want them to gain proficiency in housework so that their self-confidence is boosted. Neither Radha nor Hasina feels that their deafness has adversely affected their gender role performance. They subscribe to stereotypical images of how boys and girls should behave.

Both the girls do routine household chores such as sweeping and washing utensils. In addition, Hasina looks after her younger brothers. She enjoys these tasks. She says that her mother places higher value on her ability to work at home than on her education. Radha observes that despite having a full-time job, her mother manages everything at home as well. Hasina's mother is a housewife, but her own role model is a teacher at the special school for the deaf. Hasina does not want to work outside, but plans to sew and embroider at home in order to earn and contribute to the family income. She observes that many men drink and beat their wives. While accepting the fact that men drink, Hasian feels that they should treat women with respect. Both girls expect their future husbands to not only shoulder financial responsibilities but also take on some household and childcare responsibilities. They also expect to be treated equally by them.

Peer relationships

The influence of peers in moulding the behaviour and attitudes of adolescents is critical for personality development at this stage of the life cycle. Adolescents with hearing impairment, who have both some ability and the desire to communicate, find it easier to establish companionable relationships with friends who are not deaf. However, when the topic under discussion becomes abstract, ease of communication diminishes. The failure to share complex ideas with hearing friends leads to unsatisfactory relationships. Although they enjoy chatting with their hearing friends, Radha and Hasina say they do not have the knowledge or the desire to discuss complex issues with them. Often, they are left out of conversations because they cannot understand the topic being discussed. Radha says, 'Friends who can hear suddenly change topics; it takes too much time for me to understand what is being said.'

Hearing impaired persons find that most of their hearing friends are impatient while communicating, often ignoring what the deaf person is trying to get across. In this regard, Hasina comments, 'I always felt left out when they ignored us.' In a similar vein, Radha says, 'In the end, I turned away from hearing to deaf friends. The former never had time for us. If I did not understand and I asked them, they never offered any explanation as they did not want to disturb their conversation.'

Radha feels that her hearing friends speak too fast and use big words. She does not like their way of talking loudly with hearing impaired persons. She also feels that the negative attitude of others affects the hearing impaired person's efforts to be a part of the circle of hearing friends. Expressing a feeling of separation between the hearing and hearing impaired persons, Hasina adds, 'Friends who can hear say "hi" and then run away. Sometimes they took me into their friends' circle, but they forgot about me and began speaking with the others. I felt left out and bored.'

The girls report that their parents advise, even pressurise, them to be friendly with people who can hear normally, but when they discuss the practical difficulties in this regard, their parents do not have any suggestions on how to improve communication. Radha and Hasina say that although they still maintain limited contact with their hearing friends, they feel more comfortable with their deaf friends from school with whom they share common interests. Radha feels lonely during school holidays as she is not allowed to visit her deaf friends who live far from her home. Being an only child, she is overprotected by her mother, which she finds very frustrating. Hasina faces similar problems — she comes from an orthodox Muslim family and is not allowed to travel alone anywhere, not even to visit her friends during the school holidays. She says that her mother does not want her to develop relationships with other deaf children as she looks down on them.

Radha and Hasina have friends of the opposite sex at school. Their parents allow them to be friends with boys only in the school and during school hours. They admit that they like to spend time with their male classmates, and ensure that their parents and other family members do not come to know much about these relationships to avoid conflict at home.

Both girls have arguments with their parents, especially their mothers, over restrictions on their social lives. Contentious issues include going to the movies, eating out and spending time with friends. Hasina explains:

> My mother is always furious with me because I talk with my deaf friends [both male and female] while walking home from school. She warned me not to touch anyone. I touch only to get attention, and am not doing a bad thing. She should learn to trust me.

Similarly, Radha says, 'My mother is suspicious. She always tries to listen to what we say. Luckily, she does not understand sign language, and we can maintain privacy through the use of sign language in front of her.' Radha wishes that her mother would allow her to visit her friends. She feels that she has the right to decide how to spend her leisure hours, and that her parents should understand her feelings of loneliness and boredom. Hasina wishes her mother would welcome her deaf friends rather than criticise them. She says, 'They are my friends, not their friends; and they should learn to respect them.'

Hasina and Radha admit that in the end they have no choice but to listen to their parents. This makes them angry, sometimes pushing them to acts of rebellion — they resort to withholding information from their parents regarding their social interactions.

Autonomy

In common parlance, autonomy means self-determination or freedom of action. For hearing impaired persons like Hasina and Radha, personal autonomy is embedded in their network of social relationships. They discuss personal problems, such as feeling hurt when people make nasty remarks, arguments with friends, and problems with mothers and teachers. At times, Hasina approaches her eldest sister to talk about issues that she cannot discuss with her mother. The girls are afraid of their fathers — neither do they approach their fathers to talk about their problems, nor have the latter ever tried to understand them. They, instead, turn to their deaf friends whose advice they find more useful. On the whole, the girls feel that their mothers understand their situation better. The generation gap, however, often results in heated arguments.

Radha and Hasina feel anger at their exclusion from important family events and matters. They resent not being consulted when important decisions are made, especially on matters directly concerning them. Radha says, 'My parents have decided to shift to Kerala permanently after my matriculation. They did not even bother to consider my opinion.' Hasina reveals that several days had passed before she learned that her sister was engaged to be married. She feels unhappy at not being included in this important family matter. She says:

> I asked my mother why I was not informed about it. She told me that I was too young to understand. On the other hand, she gives me a lecture about not taking up responsibility as I am a grown-up girl. Why such differences?

Radha and Hasina also fail to understand why they are excluded from family discussions about money. They feel that they have a right to know such things as they are also a part of the family.

Radha wants to open her own bank account, but says her mother is suspicious of her motive, not believing that she just wants to have an account like her friends. She also complains that her schoolteacher does not consider her opinion on the selection of the optional courses that she is to take, but prefers to discuss them with her mother. Radha finds her mother's controlling and overprotective nature a major cause of irritation. The opposition from her mother and neglect by her father make her feel lonely and unloved. She sometimes retaliates by ignoring her mother, not talking to her and refusing to eat, leading to more tension between them.

Hasina's situation is not very dissimilar. She also complains that her mother does not allow her to visit her friends' homes, forbids her to talk to boys, and insists on her coming home immediately after school. These restrictions lead to heated arguments between mother and daughter. Hasina notices the partiality shown towards her brothers who are allowed to go anywhere without permission and to come home late without being questioned. Like Radha, she is afraid of her father and avoids talking to him.

Both girls perceive their mothers to be the dominant authority figures who govern their schooling, social activities, household responsibilities and discipline issues. They hate being ordered to do things without being given an explanation. Consequently, they direct their pent-up anger and frustration at their mothers by sulking, not talking for long periods, refusing to eat, crying and being uncooperative.

Marriage and family life

With the onset of puberty, life partner selection and procreation take on a salience in the minds of adolescents. Radha and Hasina have definite plans in this connection. Radha hopes to marry her deaf Muslim classmate when she turns 23 or 24-years-old. She knows that his being from a different religion will be a major obstacle to obtaining her parents' approval. She says, 'My mother always asked me, "Why does the boy want to marry you? Because he loves you or your father's money?" I hated her.'

Being the only child of a well-off family, her mother counselled her to think about the boy's motives in wanting to marry her. Her comments have upset and confused Radha, making her wonder how to find out the boy's true motives. Although she is ready to leave home for love, not taking a penny from her parents, she is not sure about her boyfriend's plans. Being from an orthodox Muslim family, they also expect opposition from his parents. Radha feels that once she becomes economically independent, she can marry him. She has only a vague idea about the complications of an interreligious marriage, such as the impact of parental opposition, the possibility of social boycott and other adjustment problems. She knows that her parents would prefer to have a hearing son-in-law from their own community. If they do not respect her decision, then she will leave them, she says. Radha expects her mother to support her and explain to her what is expected of her after marriage. She also expects her prospective mother-in-law to understand and support her. She knows that her boyfriend has a deaf brother, but she does not believe deafness would affect her offspring. She says, 'Nobody in my family is deaf, but I am deaf. It is fate. Nobody can change such things. The only solution is to pray to God.' She has strong faith in God and believes that things will go well for her. She also reports meeting a few deaf couples whose children are not deaf.

After matriculation, Hasina also wants to marry a deaf classmate, who is a Muslim like her. She has already met his family. She reports that his mother approves of her, and they look forward to welcoming her as their daughter-in-law. She knows that her parents, especially her mother, will not approve of such a relationship even though they are from the same community. Her mother looks down on deaf people, always makes fun of them, and says that she does not want a deaf son-in-law. Hasina plans to run away from home after the completion of her studies to marry her boyfriend. She is confident of being accepted into his family. Even though, initially, it would create problems at home, she feels that with time her parents will come to accept her relationship. Like Radha, she is not clear about the responsibilities and adjustments required of her after marriage, but she expects her mother-in-law to guide her.

Both girls feel that their deafness will not adversely affect their chances of finding life partners, as they want spouses who are deaf themselves. What is most important to them is ease of communication, understanding and support from their future spouses. They say, 'It is best deaf with deaf. There is more to talk about with each other.' They feel that their future mothers-in-law would understand them better as they themselves would have had the experience of raising deaf sons. They do not believe that their offspring will be deaf, as they have met some deaf couples who have hearing children. They want their school to invite these couples for discussions regarding jobs, sexual life and childbirth, as these couples are ideal role models for them.

Economic independence

Adolescence is a time for developing knowledge and skills for economic self-sufficiency. Radha is a good student and she wants to go abroad for higher studies. She wants to do a postgraduate course in business administration and join her father's business. Her parents, however, want her to go to a college in Kerala, where they plan to move permanently after her schooling in Mumbai. If she finds it difficult to cope with college studies, they plan to enrol her in a computer course and help her find a job as a bank clerk. Radha says:

> I do not want to go to Kerala. I prefer to study in Mumbai up to standard 12 in commerce, and then join Gallaudet College for the Deaf, USA, for further study in business. My mother is well aware of my ambition, but she does not want me to go there. She feels that there is nothing wrong with our educational system. But I want to go abroad like many deaf youth to get more exposure. At the same time, I will also get a lot of freedom from my mother once I go to USA.

Radha and her classmates often discuss the jobs that are open to them. Besides, many former students of the school, who have been abroad, visit the school and give information about various vocational courses and job opportunities in the US. She is impressed by their achievements, confidence and independence. She asks, 'If they can do it, why can't I?'

Radha feels that her parents, especially her father, should have faith in her, and explain to her how the business is run. She is sure that women can run businesses successfully if they have the interest and the will to do so. She does not see deafness as a barrier. She explains:

> You know your potential and limitations. Keeping this in mind, you should learn to find ways to achieve your goals. Why [does] everybody,

including parents and teachers, tell us that we cannot do anything? They are the real problem, not deafness. I do not think deafness is an obstacle to achieving my goal. It depends on your interest, hard work, strong will power, guidance and support from the family. Nothing is impossible.

Besides, she argues, 'Why should I get a job outside as a clerk, when my family has our own business? You can work at your own pace; you are the boss. This is a very different job compared to a nine-to-five job.' Radha knows that it is not going to be an easy task, but she is prepared to give it her best shot. The discouraging attitudes of her family, teachers, relatives, and even some friends, really annoy her.

Being an average student, Hasina has more modest plans. She wants to complete her matriculation and get married. She desires to be a housewife and to supplement the family income by taking up tailoring and embroidery, if required to earn. Being from an orthodox Muslim family, her parents do not want her to work outside the home. They want her to acquire a minimum level of education and skills to equip her for marriage. As she says candidly, 'I am not interested in a job. I like to cook at home and chat with the neighbours. This is the life, without financial trouble, that I want.'

Personal identity

Developing a stable self-concept is one of the main aims of adolescence. For persons with disabilities, the impairment constitutes a core component of the self. Radha got to know that she was deaf around the age of 9 or 10 years. Hasina realised she was deaf at the age of 7, when her parents admitted her to the special school for the deaf. Both girls had wanted to know the reasons for their deafness; they asked their mothers. Radha learnt that her deafness was due to an Rh incompatibility. She says, 'I do not know what exact problems my mother had during pregnancy. I only know that there is something wrong in her blood; so I became deaf.' Saying this, Radha becomes very emotional and bursts into tears.

Hasina knows that an episode of typhoid resulted in her hearing loss. She says, 'I do not remember what it was like to hear before I got typhoid. I got many injections for the illness.'

Although both Radha and Hasina have come to accept their deafness and build a life and future around it, they still feel sad and hope for a cure that will restore their hearing. The causes and treatment for deafness are a major topic of discussion with teachers and classmates. Their teachers have told them that it is nobody's fault that they lost their hearing and, therefore, they should not blame their parents.

The girls are aware of the differences between themselves and those without the disability — use of hearing aids, inability to hear clearly, and absence of clarity in speech. Hasina realised she was 'different' when she was admitted to a special school located at a distance from her home, while her friends in the neighbourhood went to nearby schools. Radha initially went to a regular school where she was the only one wearing a hearing aid. She envied her schoolmates their ability to speak fluently. Despite her efforts, many children did not want to communicate with her; some did not understand her speech, while others made fun of her. However, there were some classmates who helped her adapt. About them, she says:

> Everyone is nice to me, but I feel that they behave nicely to me out of a sense of responsibility. There are many things that they are not sharing with me. For example, talking about a particular girl, I ask them her name, they do not tell me. They ignore me or tell me not to poke my nose into the conversation.

However, she does not want to blame these friends, because they have also helped her a lot.

Radha's transfer from a regular to a special school came as a relief, and she feels a deep sense of belonging among the deaf community. She says, 'I feel that I am at home. Everyone shares everything with me. The thought of my contribution to the group gives me confidence.' Radha does not underestimate her interactions with people without her disability. She says she has learnt a lot from them. Her family does not discourage her from socialising with deaf persons. Therefore, she has been able to adjust to both worlds. Although she still feels bad about being deaf, especially when people make nasty remarks, she accepts it as her fate. She has learnt to be comfortable with her disability and to mix with others without a major inferiority complex.

Conclusion

The case studies show two young people with hearing impairment trying to participate in society. They express their opinions related to the difficulties they face, their ways of coping and the expectations of their parents and adults who are not deaf. The researcher is impressed by their positive attitude, their enthusiasm for life, their resilience, and their attempts at coping with the misunderstandings and marginalisation that they encounter as they try to take control of their lives.

The main problem for Radha and Hasina is not hearing loss per se. It is, in fact, the communication bottlenecks that arise as they try to cope with the demands of a hearing world, and the insensitivity and lack of understanding of hearing persons, including their own families, teachers and friends. Both the girls feel the pressure to fit into a view of themselves and the world that excludes their unique experiences as belonging simultaneously to both the hearing and deaf worlds. For instance, their resentment at being excluded from family matters and their preference for socialising with other hearing impaired persons reflect this difficult predicament. In other respects, they have the same aspirations, family conflicts and misgivings that characterise non-disabled adolescents. For instance, physical attractiveness is as important to hearing impaired adolescents as it is to their hearing counterparts, since it plays a key role in both self-esteem and social acceptance. It is, therefore, important to underscore the similarities rather than highlight the differences between the hearing impaired and hearing persons, if we are to create an inclusive society.

Notes

* This essay first appeared in the *Indian Journal of Gender Studies*, 15 (2): pp. 387–406, 2008, New Delhi: SAGE Publications. Editorial changes have been made to the original published chapter with permission from the Centre for Women's Development Studies, New Delhi.
1. Rh incompatibility occurs when the pregnant mother and her child have opposite Rh blood types. Consequently, the mother's body begins to

produce antibodies that attack the foetus's blood cells, which may result in various types of disabilities.

References

Bishop, Milo E. (ed.). 1979. *Mainstreaming: Practical Ideas for Educating Hearing-Impaired Students*. Washington, DC: Alexander Graham Bell Association for the Deaf.

Brill, Richard G. 1974. *Education of the Deaf: Administrative and Professional Developments*. Washington, DC: Gallaudet College Press.

Fitz-Gerald, Max and Della Fitz-Gerald. 1987. *Sexuality and Deafness* (Pre-College Programme). Washington, DC: Gallaudet College Press.

Freeman, Roger D., Clifton F. Carbin and Robert J. Boese. 1981. *Can't Your Child Hear? A Guide for Those Who Care about Deaf Children*. Baltimore: University Park Press.

Greene, Roberta R. 1986. *Social Work with the Aged and Their Families*. New York: Aldine de Gruyter.

Havighurst, Robert James. 1972. *Developmental Tasks and Education*, 3rd edition. New York: David McKay.

Mattessich, Paul and Reuben Hill. 1987. 'Life Cycle and Family Development', in Marvin B. Sussman and Suzanne K. Steinmetz (eds), *Handbook of Marriage and the Family*, pp. 437–70. New York: Plenum Press.

Meadow, Kathryn P. 1980. *Deafness and Child Development*. London: Edward Arnold.

Van Cleve, John V. (ed.) and Gallaudet College. 1987. *Gallaudet Encyclopedia of Deaf People and Deafness*. New York: McGraw-Hill.

PART IV

Assertion of Difference through Art and Communication

12

Body/Text: Art Project on Deafness and Communication

José Abad Lorente*

Plate 12.1: *Disability Rights* (2008). Interpreted by Bahar Alan, Rishikesh Anand, Karan Kumar and Pravesh Behl.

This chapter describes a collaborative and interdisciplinary art project conducted by the author with the Deaf community in New Delhi in 2008. It explores disability and representation through contemporary visual art practices. In most societies, people with different behaviours and bodily functions are often subjected to considerable discrimination resulting in stigma. One feature of stigma in India is the ongoing battle for Indian Sign Language (ISL) to be recognised as a natural language of the Deaf. The project was aimed to prompt discussion of this stigma by representing the language corpora of the deaf minority. It illustrates how the Deaf community uses ISL as their natural language.

Using participatory techniques, the project aimed to map the qualities or abilities that Deaf people have developed as a result of using their whole body as a natural medium of communication. The goal is to represent the endeavours of disabled people to reach independence, depicting abilities and responding creatively to the challenge posed by the hearing world.

Introduction

> In general the history of disability and representation is one of 'negative' forms and that this has happened is precisely because disabled people are excluded from the production of disability culture and excluded from the dominant 'disability' discourse (Hevey 1993: 118).

As a way to represent disabilities from a positive perspective incorporating my own experiences, I created 'Life Bricolage', a photographic and auto-ethnographic project. Through the project I sought to explore my own bodily movements and ways of doing things in everyday life as someone without the use of one hand. Rather than focusing on social barriers encountered as a person with body impairment, I chose to represent instead 'body abilities' in order to explore how the impaired body creates solutions to overcome daily obstacles.

In picturing myself in 'Life Bricolage' (Plate 12.2), I applied the concepts of Chinese calligraphy to represent body movements as lyrical compositions. Chinese calligraphy is one way of representing the body, which is given voice by a cosmic and spontaneous energy called 'qi'. This energy is produced at the very moment of executing the performance or writing. In this way, Chinese calligraphy is a representation of the artist's physical actions translated into pictograms or characters at the time of writing. Therefore, this conceptual 'Body Calligraphy'[1] celebrates diversity and questions what constitutes normal behaviour and movement.

Body/Text ✦ **287**

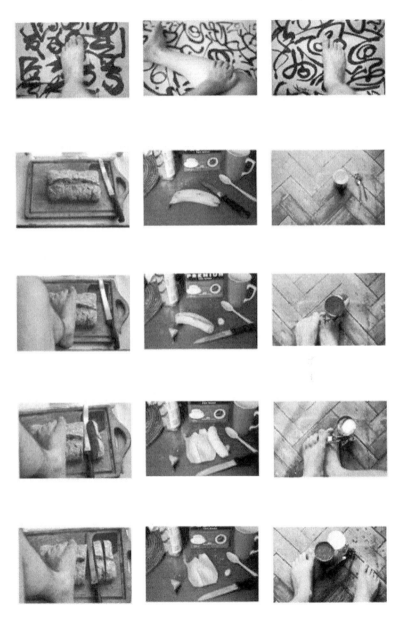

Plate 12.2: *Life Bricolage* (2006). Performance and photography by José Abad Lorente.

For most deaf individuals, 'SPOKEN/WRITTEN is a burden to be tolerated or a barricade to be broken, rather than an imaginative, creative means of self-expression' (Rose 1996: 427). Prelingually deaf children find it very difficult to learn sound-based languages. Education for the deaf has historically been oralist in nature, being based on the assumption that persons without oral language cannot think normally. Hearing or oral dominated education systems emphasise use of hearing aids, written language and lip reading. Oralism depicts hearing deficit as a disability, and suppresses sign language, which is seen to be an obstacle to the integration of the deaf person in society. It emphasises spoken and written language as a means of integration. In oral schools, speech therapy and English teaching become the main focus of children's education, leaving them unacquainted with other subjects. Most adult deaf persons end up reading and writing only at a third or fourth grade level (Lane 1992).

Sign linguists contest the oralist paradigm. The underlying assumption of sign language is that the deaf habitually acquire a real language. These veridical languages are vernaculars endemic to deaf people and not just an amalgam of manual versions of oral languages of the surrounding hearing world. Sign language has a distinct grammar, syntax and morphology. It operates spatially and visually: for instance, standardised handshapes have been evolved to represent sizes, shapes and movement of objects. The fact that it does not have a written form can be overcome through audiovisual technology which can inscribe and preserve its articulations.

Sign linguists emphasise the essential similarity between oral and sign languages. As Washabaugh points out, they are '. . . doubly structured, syntactically coded, socially acquired and shared linguistic systems' (1981: 238). Children of deaf parents progressively acquire them without tutoring. But even though they may be similar in many ways, sign languages also differ from oral languages on a number of counts, most importantly their multidimensionality of communication. Since most deaf persons are born and brought up in hearing families (only 10 per cent of deaf children have deaf parents), sign language is acquired by deaf persons, not as a mother tongue, but when they are youths in residential schools or when they are adults in their workplaces. In addition to deaf acquaintances, deaf language may also in some cases be acquired from deaf siblings.

In the light of the distinctiveness of sign language and the advocacy and scholarship in the area, a distinction is made between deaf and Deaf. Lower case d (in deaf) connotes the hearing deficit as a disability, an audiological condition that may be ameliorated through hearing aids and cochlear implants. Upper case D connotes deafness as a distinctive culture and linguistic community with sign language as a defining characteristic. This essay takes the perspective of Deafness as a distinctive linguistic and cultural category, a perspective that is at present in a rudimentary state of development in India (Jepson 1991).

Although historically there is hardly any material on sign language or on the lives of deaf people in India, symbolic hand gestures, known as *mudra*s, have been employed in religious contexts in Hinduism and Buddhism. Unfortunately, these religious traditions have often excluded deaf people from participation in rituals or religious membership. Classical dance and theatre often employ stylised hand gestures with particular meanings. Documented deaf education in India began with welfare services, mission schools and orphanages from the 1830s. Later in the 19th century, residential Deaf schools were established, and they tended (increasingly) to adopt an oralist approach over the use of sign language in the classroom. These schools include the Bombay Institution for Deaf and Mutes, founded in the 1880s, and schools in Madras and Kolkata which opened in the 1890s. Other residential schools soon followed in different parts of the Indian subcontinent.

While a few students, who were unable to learn via the oralist method, were taught with signs, many students preferred to communicate with each other via sign language, sometimes to the frustration of their teachers. The first study of the sign language of these children, which is almost certainly related to modern Indian sign language, was done in 1928 by H. C. Banerjee, a teacher. She visited three residential schools for deaf children — at Dhaka, Barisal and Calcutta — observing that 'in all these schools the teachers have discouraged the growth of the sign language, which in spite of this official disapproval, has grown and flourished' (Banerjee 1928: 70). She compared sign vocabularies at the different schools and described the signs in words in an appendix.

Indian sign language shares grammatical features with many other deaf sign languages, including the use of space and simultaneity and the five meaningful parameters of handshape, location, orientation, movement, and non-manual features such as body position, head movement and facial expression. The website www.ethnologue.com claims that sign languages across urban India appear to share about 75 per cent of their vocabularies, and that the Mumbai–Delhi dialect is the most influential.[2] Ethnologue identifies the following regional dialects within India:

a. Mumbai–Delhi Sign Language (or separately: Delhi Sign Language, Bombay Sign Language)
b. Calcutta Sign Language
c. Bangalore–Madras Sign Language (or Bangalore–Chennai–Hyderabad Sign Language)

While the sign systems in ISL appear to be largely indigenous, elements in ISL are derived from British Sign Language. For example, ISL does not have signs for the Devanāgarī script, and finger-spelling is based on the Latin alphabet. In addition, a small number of the Deaf persons near Bangalore sign in American Sign Language (ASL) owing to a longstanding ASL deaf school there.

The Rehabilitation Council of India and the Ishara Foundation are also involved in ISL training, English through ISL, and interpreter training. A number of vocational schools, e.g., ITI Secunderabad, use ISL for teaching. Other institutes, such as the All India Institute of Speech and Hearing in Mysore, remain exclusively focused on oralism. In 2005, the National Curriculum Framework (NCF) gave some degree of legitimacy to sign language education by hinting that sign languages may qualify as an optional third language choice for hearing students.

The art project under discussion was undertaken among a group of urban Deaf youths who are members of The Deaf Way, an organisation working for the welfare of Deaf youths in different parts of the country. As already mentioned, most urban deaf persons come together as adolescents or adults when they begin formally acquiring sign language. They come from diverse castes, religions, ethnic backgrounds and geographical areas. Urban Indian Sign Language (UISL) is a unified and relatively standardised language used by members of the educated urban middle class Deaf community. It transmits information by way of a syntactic code and a conventional standardised lexicon. According to Jepson (1991), UISL is probably indigenous to India and is pan-Indian in scope.

With this brief overview of the Deaf community and sign language in India, we now turn to the actual articulation of sign language by a group of urban youths as a means of giving expression to their everyday experiences of the world mirrored through signs and bodily performance.

Body, Sign Communication and Art in Process

Sign language involves gestures, body movements and spacing. Not only is it a medium of communication, but well developed sign languages, such as American Sign Language and British Sign Language, also have a literary repertoire. Themes common to deaf traditional literary forms include tensions between the Deaf and hearing worlds, affirmation of sign language and development of Deaf identity. Other themes include deaf–hearing miscommunication, struggle for autonomy and self-expression in a hearing dominated world, triumph over ignorant and authoritarian figures, Deaf pride and unity, etc. Sign languages, like oral languages, provide scope for individuals to innovate and be creative using multi-channelled communication involving the whole body. For Deaf persons, creating and performing in sign language is like a rite of passage allowing them to negotiate their place in the Deaf community (Rose 1996).

As a way to look at disability, the project started with the concepts of normality/abnormality and social behaviour. The sociologist Michael Oliver (1996) has a radical critique of the subject. According to him, 'society's narrow definitions of physical normality lead it to ignore and marginalize those who do not fit within that definition'. In many societies people with different behaviours and bodily functions are often subjected to considerable discrimination.

Body/Text

This project explores sign language as the natural language of the Deaf and focuses on how the body is used as a medium of communication through expressing, representing and performing sign language. The process of conceptualising and implementing the art project was an interesting and illuminating challenge in itself. The workshop was held twice a week for about three months, in the Deaf Way centre. At the beginning, I had little idea about Indian Sign Language, so I was prepared to start a new journey working with a group of 10 Deaf participants. The content of the workshop was an introduction to visual poetry. I set up all the explanations in PowerPoint presentations, using images as words. Since the participants knew English as a second language, it made communication easier. With the help of a notebook, our main medium of communication was written English, but at the same time I was learning Indian Sign Language.

Within the workshop, we first explored visual poetry as a way to look at the relationship between words and images. To open up the creative process, the participants were encouraged to express their own ideas. Participants then used a collage of signs, words and images to play with their ideas. To explore their own natural sign language, they signed while I photographed them. Using visual ethnography techniques as a way to collect different data, the participants were also provided with photo cameras. The goal was to get an overview of the different means of communication used by the Deaf community. The resulting photographs and poems were discussed within the group to identify a range of communicative modalities.

The group then moved to Khoj art studios to work more intensively on creative language and alternative communications. First, during these eight days of experimentation, the work of Spanish poet Federico García Lorca (1898–1936) was introduced; later, the participants created their own poems for further visual representation.

The photo sessions explored ways of using the body as a site for text and representation. In doing this, we used multiple reference points from different cultures — on the one hand, embracing and interpreting Lorca's poems with ISL, and on the other, appropriating Indian aesthetics such as Hindu and Buddhist iconography. We saw cultural appropriations go in different directions — using both cultural points and transforming them into a new embodied image. Simultaneously, the author explored his own view with focus and out-of-focus images.

Plate 12.3: *Making the Way* (2008). Interpreted by Navneet Kaur, Bahar Alan, Rishikesh Anand and Pravesh.

The creativity of the group moved from using iconography of multiple-limbed Gods to photographs that have much in common with sculpture. Each photograph represents the culmination of a dynamic performance, which creates a visual text. These photographs act as a linguistic photo-album of the deaf community exploring the manual and corporal form of 'voice' and aesthetics. In addition, it expresses their thoughts, and projects a positive message about the Deaf community and their language.

The following images combine body and text with a particular verbal message, such as 'I feel independent with sign language' (*Signs for Living*, Plate 12.8) or 'Mobile phones help us to communicate with SMS and bring us together' (*SMS Boon*, Plate 12.6).

Plate 12.4: *Cyber Connections* (2008): 'Computers and the internet mean communication.' Interpreted by Bahar Alan.

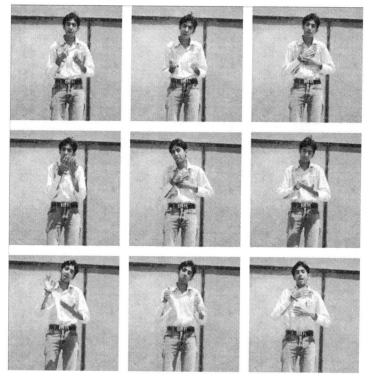

Plate 12.5: *Expressions of Learning* (2008): 'I want to read and write. These make me feel good.' Interpreted by Karan Kumar.

Plate 12.6: *SMS Boon* (2008): 'Mobile phones help us to communicate. SMS brings us together.' Interpreted by Mohod Haroon, Pravesh Behl and Hira Singh.

Plate 12.7: *Definition, Discrimination, Debilitation* (2008): 'We don't like to beg, cry or get beaten because of our disability.' Interpreted by Mohod Haroon, Pravesh Behl and Hira Singh.

Plate 12.8: *Signs for Living* (2008): 'I feel independent with sign language. It helps me to work and succeed in life.' Interpreted by Rishikesh Anand, Navneet Kaur, Bahar Alan and Sudesh Kumar.

Plate 12.9: *Variegations* (2008): 'Justice for the disabled. Red, black, yellow, and white people. Learning equals prosperity. Our flag is orange, white, and green.' Interpreted by Bahar Alan, Rishikesh Anand, Karan Kumar and Pravesh Behl.

In other images, aesthetics plays the main language reflecting the creativity and body expressions underlying the live art process, and creating an art genre denominated by the artist as 'Body Calligraphy' (Plates 12.10–12.13).

Plate 12.10: *Body Calligraphy: Lotus I* (2008). Interpreted by Rishikesh Anand, Bahar Alan and Sudesh Kumar.

Plate 12.11: *Body Calligraphy: Lotus II* (2008). Interpreted by Bahar Alan, Navneet Kaur, Rishikesh Anand and Sudesh Kumar.

Body/Text ✦ **297**

Plate 12.12: *Body Calligraphy: Cobra* (2008). Interpreted by Navneet Kaur, Rishikesh Anand, Sudesh Kumar and Bahar Alan.

Plate 12.13: *Body Calligraphy: I Love You x 8* (2008). Interpreted by Bahar Alan, Rishikesh Anand, Karan Kumar and Pravesh Behl.

In order to explore their own natural sign language in relation to photography, participants also signed in the same rhythm as they were photographed creating a visual text imaginary. This offers an overview of the different means of communication used by the Deaf community. The resulting photographs and visual poems were discussed within the group to identify a range of communicative ways. In general, the photographs show, on the one hand, the important advantages of new technologies such as SMS, mobile phone and the Internet. On the other hand, more basic methods, such as body language, gesture, popular signs, and hand-writing on paper and on their hands, were used more spontaneously as forms of communication.

Plate 12.14: *Salute Colors* (2008). Interpreted by Bahar Alan, Rishikesh Anand, Karan Kumar and Pravesh Behl.

The cultural appropriations went in different directions using both cultural points and transforming them into new embodied images. The group developed and created this new corpora and visual text images through the adaptation of two poems from Lorca: 'It's True' and 'Goodbye' (Plate 12.15). Both poems belong to 'Canciones' and 'Romancero Gitano' (Gypsy Ballads) and describes the Spanish gypsy culture, which originally comes from north India. The gypsy minority, a marginalised community in Spain, inspirited Lorca in this literary work. With this point of connection, the project intends to show how the participants use the creative and poetic language to represent their own community. The group developed and created new body and text imagery to interpret the poems — from using iconography of multiple limbed gods to photographs that have much in common with sculpture.

Body/Text ✦ **299**

If I die

Let the balcony open

The boy is eating oranges

From my balcony I can see him

Plate 12.15: *Goodbye* (2008): Fragment from the poem 'Goodbye' by Federico García Lorca. Interpreted by Guruvendra Jhar, Mohod Haroon, Akshay Bhatnagar and Hira Singh.

Ay, the pain it costs me
to love you as I love you!
For love of you, the air, it hurts,
and my heart, and my hat,
they hurt me.

Plate 12.16: *It's True* (2008): Fragment from the poem 'It's True' by Federico García Lorca. Interpreted by Guruvendra Jhar, Kalaparthi Sudhir, Kara Kumar, Akshay Bhatnagar and Hira Singh.

Conclusion

It is not incorrect to assume that hearing persons hold negative attitudes towards deaf persons and, by extension, towards sign language. These attitudes are not random but systematically structured into prevailing social institutions and practices including the family, the education system and the general community. This leads to inescapable denigration challenging not just the hearing capacity of the Deaf but the very social identity of the person. According to Washabaugh (1981), negative attitudes are formed through communication between the hearing and the deaf. Such communication is distorted by misreadings and miscues, which lead to mutual dislike and distrust of the other's communicative system. Such repeated distorted communications result in typification of the other as incompetent and untrustworthy, which in turn culminates in mutual negative stereotyping. Over time, such negative attitudes become entrenched and difficult to dislodge.

Even though used by a number of Deaf persons, Indian Sign Language is still in the process of being standardised. Official recognition is only half-hearted. For instance, it is not recognised in the Census even though the National Centre for Education, Research and Training (NCERT) makes it a part of the curriculum. The upshot of this situation is that the Deaf community still has a long way to go before it is recognised as a distinctive cultural and linguistic entity. Projects, such as the art-cum-photographic initiative discussed in this essay, are an attempt in this direction.

Notes

* The project has been made possible in part by sponsorship from the cultural department of the Spanish Embassy in New Delhi, and support and guidance from KHOJ International Artists' Association. Both sponsors and supporters believe in promoting disability art culture and encouraged me to develop it further. I want to express my gratitude to The Deaf Way with whose co-operation the project could be operationalised. Special thanks to Rishikesh Anand, Pravesh Behl,

Guruvendra Jhar, Sudesh Kumar, Karan Kumar, Akshay Bhatnagar, Kalaparthi Sudhir, Navneet Kaur, Mohod Haroon, Bahar Alan and Hira Singh. This project would not have taken shape without their active and creative collaboration.
1. 'Body Calligraphy' is a conceptual style of calligraphy where a group of people sign words or phrases all at one time, and aesthetics plays the main role of language reflecting creativity and body expressions.
2. 'Indian Sign Language: A Language of India', *Ethnologue: Languages of the World*, http://www.ethnologue.com/show_language.asp?code=ins (accessed May 2007).

References

Banerjee, H.C. 1928. 'The Sign Language of Deaf-Mutes', *Indian Journal of Psychology*, 3: 69–87.
Hevey, David. 1993. 'The Tragedy Principle: Strategies for Change in the Representation of Disabled People', in John Swain, Vic Finkelstein, Sally French and Mike Oliver (eds), *Disabling Barriers — Enabling Environments*, pp. 116–21. London: SAGE Publications.
Jepson, Jill. 1991. 'Urban and Rural Sign Language in India', *Language in Society*, 20 (1): 37–57.
Lane, Harlan. 1992. *The Mask of Benevolence: Disabling the Deaf Community*. New York: Knopf.
Oliver, Michael. 1996. *Understanding Disability: From Theory to Practice*. London: Macmillan.
Rose, Heidi M. 1996. 'Inventing One's "Voice": The Interplay of Convention and Self-Expression in ASL Narrative', *Language in Society*, 25 (3): 427–44.
Washabaugh, William. 1981. 'Sign Language in its Social Context', *Annual Review of Anthropology*, 10: 237–52.

13

Blind With Camera: Photographs by the Visually Impaired

PARTHO BHOWMICK

When we think of sight, we think of light; and when we think of blindness, we think of darkness. This binary is taken for granted because the dichotomy between people with sight and people with blindness is deeply rooted in our historical, psychological and sociological worlds. Our cultural emphasis on eye-centeredness for interpretation of knowledge, truth and reality, makes it even more difficult for us to imagine living without sight. Consequently, photography by the visually impaired appears inconceivable to us. In fact, most of us are unaware of the long history of visual expression by the blind.

This essay offers interpretations of a collection of photographs taken by a group of visually impaired persons in Mumbai (India) as part of the Blind With Camera Project initiated by the author. The project explores what they (blind) see differently from what we (sighted) see, and how 'learning to see' in the blind is cultivated and translated into visual art. While exploring the relationship between the 'seeable' and the 'unseeable' worlds, the essay encourages readers to conceptualise forms of creativity and media of communication that challenge taken-for-granted notions of vision, reality, knowledge and power. Such enterprises also expand the borders of visual art by interrogating the monolithic vision of sight and, in the process, lead both the sighted and blind to find their 'own' light.

What do the Blind See?

Able-bodied ideology posits a universal relationship between the categories of vision, power, knowledge and subjectivity by virtue of which the blind are seen as diminished and helpless figures. Photography by the visually impaired disturbs this presumption of the sighted world. The photographs presented in this essay make a case for alternative ways of visualising the world, different ways of apprehending reality and other ways of valorising selfhood.

Apart from the universally acknowledged genius of such renowned figures as Homer (around 9th century BCE), Surdas (1478–1581) and John Milton (1608–1674), several thinkers have written profound meditations on art and blindness to suggest that sight and blindness are complimentary and inextricable concepts, and that in blindness, pure art exists. For instance, in Orhan Pamuk's book *My Name Is Red* (2001 [1998]), sight and blindness have a common lineage embedded in memory. He elaborates how in the 15th century, the older generation artists in Persia grow blind in their obsessive dedication to the art of miniature painting. Yet the memory was so profound, and the techniques so perfectly mastered, that they continued to not only practice but even refine their art after they lost their vision. Supported by the ruling Sultans, blind miniaturists played an important role enriching the artistic tradition in Persia. Today's miniaturists stand on the shoulders of their blind predecessors; while some were mere copyists, others shifted to different styles of miniature art.

From another perspective, the French philosopher Jacques Derrida (1993) has written on art and blindness. With his revolutionary deconstruction philosophy, Derrida posits that the origin of art is actually localised in the experience of blindness, because the act of drawing/painting recalls only memory of a sight in the absence of the gaze. Memory intervenes in that moment between the eye's observation and the brush's application. In *Memoirs of the Blind* (ibid.), he explores the theme of truth, desire, loss, and memory in the paradox of art and blindness.

Photography by the visually impaired raises a fundamental issue — what do the blind see? I would in turn ask: while being so unself-conscious about what we see, we, who see, do not even know how it is that we see; we are also unaware of how we 'learn to see'. The well-known neurologist Dr. Oliver Sacks (2003) describes an interesting case to highlight this point:

> A man born blind, in adulthood got his sight restored by miracle of medical science. At that point he can 'see' but he cannot interpret the visual data at all. A set of stairs which were familiar to him by touch, is now a jumble of lines and shadows, and the jumble utterly changes with the viewing angle and shift of light. He literally could not recognize them as stairs. He leans to see his cat in 'visual' profile, but if the cat shifted posture he could no longer differentiate the cat's shape from that of his room. Unexpectedly, the world of sight becomes a nightmare for him. Eventually he again loses his sight, and it was a relief for him. He returns to a world where everything makes sense by touch and sound. Stairs become stairs and his cat becomes once more a cat.

Seeing is learned and the blind man in this case has never learned to see. This raises another interesting question: if a sighted person has to undergo the process of 'learning to see', what is the parallel for 'learning to see' for a blind person. We normally think of seeing the visual reality through our eyes. Seeing is as much touching and hearing, but because vision is so overwhelming, we are unaware of other sensations and perceptions that contribute to seeing. When a sighted person sees a cup, he is also feeling it with his mind's hand. The blind can arrive at mental pictures of the visual realities around them through touch, sound, the warmth of light, visual memories of sight and other cognitive abilities. A mental representation is a lot like seeing, only less powerful. When a blind person touches a cup, he is also seeing it with his mind's eye. A cup is both a 'visual' cup and a 'tactile' cup.

To get more insight into tactile perception, let's take a more complex case. Imagine a blind person examining a table. A few touches reveal that the table is set for four, the table is rectangular in shape, and the top is smooth and partly covered by a thin oval tablecloth. Further tactile exploration reveals that the table is neatly arranged with thick round plates between knives and forks — the knives are sharp and the forks have four teeth. Beside each knife is a wineglass — the glasses are full and the surface of the fluid is fuzzy. There are also rough, rectangular mats laid, with covered hot serving dishes on them. The table and the objects on it are as much tactile as visual. A blind person can tell the shapes of each object by touch, a process analogous to a sighted person seeing the same table. While the eye can see the table and objects on it as 'all-at-once', the hand uses a 'step-by-step' approach, builds layers of memory of touch and finally adds them to create a 'whole' mental image.

According to Dr. John Kennedy (1993), an authority on Art by the Blind, the geometry of direction is common to vision and touch, and where a sighted person looks out, a blind person reaches out, and they will discover the same things. Similarly, what you see is also what you hear.

It is well established by medical science that the visual cortex of the brain, which processes all visual inputs in a sighted person, is reallocated in a blind person for processing touch and sound. The same region is also highly active during visual thinking in the blind. 'Learning to see' is common for both the sighted and the blind; only the vehicle and route of seeing are different. The blind person has to work much harder than the sighted person to be visually aware and translate that awareness into mental pictures.

Blind With Camera Project

All our knowledge has its origins in our perceptions; but perception is successful at its work if it gives accurate knowledge. In philosophy, psychology and art, questions have been asked about the role of our senses in building our perceptual system, and how perception stimulates an understanding of form, shape, pattern, texture, depth and space. Perception occurs only when a chain of events is complete. The chain starts with an object and an observer or perceiver — between them there are many links as object, medium, receptors, nerves, brain receptions and cognition. Our sense of representation evolves as we gain knowledge of the physical world through use of our senses. Perception-building process in blind people is similar to that of sighted people. Pictures from the Blind With Camera Project give us a better understanding of perception and sense of representation in blind people in particular, and vision in general.

My research on visual art by the blind finds much 'sight' at the core of blindness. In 2004, I accidentally picked up an old issue of a photo magazine from a pavement vendor in Mumbai, and came across an article on Evgen Bavčar, an accomplished blind photographer based in Paris. I contacted him over the Internet and was totally overawed by his work. Subsequently, I engaged in self-study on blindness and visual art, and in the process, came in touch with several blind photographers and blind artists around the world such as Evgen Bavčar (Paris), Michael Richard (Los Angeles), Kurt Weston (California), Gerardo Nigenda (Mexico) and a group named Seeing With Photography Collective (New York), as also others working on artistic expression by the blind.

I decided to start a workshop on photography for the blind, but it was not easy to get around endless queries and doubts from both sighted and blind persons. Finally, after months of trying to get participants, the workshop started in January 2006 with just two participants. It aimed to show that since photography is as much an issue of mental representation as of visual perception, there is no reason why those without vision could not engage in it. Till date, more than 80 visually impaired participants have taken part in the workshops, and the numbers are steadily growing. Blind With Camera Project is the first of its kind in India, and has culminated into 'Beyond Sight', a travelling inclusive exhibition on visual art by the visually challenged.

Blind With Camera is based on the belief that disability is a diverse human condition, people with physical or mental limitations are 'differently abled', and art by them is an invaluable expression of creative diversity. 'Arts by all and for all' can lead to an equitable society.

Objectives of the Blind With Camera Project

a. To promote photography in the vocational curriculum in schools for the visually impaired;
b. to execute workshops on photography with the visually impaired;
c. to showcase work of visually impaired photographers through 'inclusive' exhibitions;
d. to provide financial support through sale of photographic works;
e. to facilitate empowerment of visually impaired persons and their social inclusion through the art of photography.

Workshop format

Visually impaired persons learn the art of photography at the workshop. Participants are between 15 to 50 years, with varying ages of onset of blindness. The visual impairment ranges from complete congenital blindness to low vision later in life. They come from various socioeconomic and cultural backgrounds; none of them have any formal training in photography or the arts.

The workshop introduces the camera as the 'functional' eye to the visually impaired, an extension of 'self' to explore the visual world and gain deeper insight. During the workshop sessions, participants learn the basics of camera optics, how to handle a camera (there is no special camera for the blind), its functions, and how to take a picture. Various tactile, audio clues, visual memories of sight, the warmth of light and cognitive skills are used by the visually impaired to create mental images in order to take a picture.

How do the Blind take Photographs?

This is the central and most obvious question in the minds of both sighted and visually impaired persons. There is no straightforward answer to the question. Blind With Camera Project demands an alternative approach to photography, free from the techniques and rules followed by sighted photographers. The project takes a holistic approach that is realistic and closer to the experiences of life of the visually impaired to highlight the nature of visual impairment — different life experiences trigger different kinds of visual thinking, which translates into different expressions. My research on Art by the Blind helped me to design the workshop that would take a creative journey and explore ways to reach new visual destinations.[1] Some guidelines that emerged in the course of the Project are presented here:

Assessment of visual connections

The workshop begins with the participants sharing with me their biography of vision loss. Intense 'visual talking' and deep 'inward' interactions with them help me to understand the extent to which they are connected with visual reality, their experiences with disability and how challenges of life are handled. By 'challenges of life', I mean how they handle daily activities, including how they understand the visual realities around them. Over a period of time, visual imagery becomes a part of the conversation.

There is no better way to learn about blindness than to engage in conversation with a blind person. I consciously use 'visual' content while interacting with my students, asking them to describe their home, school or workplace, the faces of their loved ones, the new places they last visited, their favourite movie stars, cartoon characters and TV shows. I inquire from those not born blind what they remember most from their sighted life — do they remember the colour of the sky, grass, roses, etc.? I find 'visual' talk opens up the floodgates of blind persons' mysterious and intriguing world, where time and space seem to blend into a new dimension, where concepts of relevant and irrelevant are turned upside down, where minute details of the surroundings, such as insignificant puffs of air, hardly audible sounds and changes in the tone of one's voice, are crucial for moving around and for interpreting the world. These intensive sessions help me understand their sensitivity towards non-visual clues, and how closely or remotely they are connected to the visual realities around them. This exercise serves to define the training needs of each participant.

Learning session

The workshop is designed to both trigger systematic visual thinking in the visually impaired and enhance their mental image formation, as also impart skills to translate mental into meaningful visual expressions. To explore new visual languages by the visually impaired, I rarely share with my students the rules of photography — the way we, the sighted, know it; or what makes a photograph good or bad — the way we judge it. Instead, the focus remains on their life experiences in relation to visual realities that can be captured to communicate new meanings. I share with them the philosophy behind works of art of the great masters, take them to art galleries and try to conceptually convey what the works depict. We also go to the theatre and movies to understand the relational harmony between dialogues and visuals on stage and on screen.

In the process of photographing, participants are asked to spend time feeling the space, sensing the layout of objects in the space, touching them (if within reach) or using their judgement. They are asked to listen to the detailed descriptions provided by sighted companions and other accompanying sounds, feel the warmth of light entering the space to identify the direction of light and contrast, search for visual memories of sight (if not born blind) and correlate the visual memories with the external visual conditions. This process triggers visual thinking in the visually impaired, leading to the first version of the abstract mental image. By seeking more clues, a more refined version of the mental image is created. Then, by touch and judgement, they measure the distance from the object and the space around it, place the camera in relation to the object, assess space and light, and finally 'click' a photograph. Such synchronisation of mental and physical processes may take hours or sometimes may be accomplished in minutes. I help participants conceptualise images to a point, giving them enough independence to develop and crystallise their own mental images and take a considered decision in clicking the photograph.

Dominance of senses

The synchronisation is guided sometimes by touch, sometimes by sound, sometimes by a mix of both touch and sound, and sometime by memory of sight. The dominance and mix of the senses are usually caught in the photographs. Interestingly, each photograph is unique as it depends on the visually impaired photographers' life experiences, the extent of their blindness, clarity of visual memories, attentiveness and sensitivity to non-visual senses, cognitive abilities and, most importantly, their involvement with the subjects to be photographed.

Seeing what they click

After a picture is taken, the next challenge is how to make the visually impaired person 'see' what s/he has clicked. It demands yet another approach, I have one-to-one sessions with the students to discuss in detail and help them connect to the pictures taken by them. Raised pictures are made from the normal photo prints, so that the visually impaired photographer can touch it to get a feel of the object(s) and its orientation in the picture. Through touch and description/discussion, participants are transported to the same state of mental imagery, which s/he had while clicking the picture. Students with low and partial vision can see the photographs taken by them by bringing the photo print close to their eyes or by using visual aids such as a magnifying glass.

Plate 13.1: A visually challenged person experiences a 'touch & feel' raised photograph at an exhibition by Blind With Camera. Tactile 'touch & feel' photographs, Braille and Large Print footnotes, and recoded audio descriptions (AD) that accompany the photographs are some of the adaptive methods used to aid the visually impaired to access and enjoy the photographs, while also offering a whole new experience for the sighted. Photograph by Harsh Vyas (2011).

How to 'Read' these Pictures?

Photography by the visually impaired opens the critical gap between what we 'see' in the photograph and what we are supposed to 'read'. It invites the viewer to visit the question — how do we read these photographs? Some would view the work of the visually impaired photographers in the context of their disability rather than in the content of their work. Others might find the idea too paradoxical and reject it. Some purists might critically rate such photographs as mere snapshots.

Without getting swayed by sympathy, viewers should 'read' these pictures by penetrating the surface images to explore the interplay of conscious and unconscious perceptions and experiences, present and past time, certainty and uncertainty in the construction of reality, etc. Imagining the 'visual synergy' between mental representation and the visual reality in front of the camera would enhance our understanding of the expressions and the feeling anchoring the photographic images.

The experience of sight is structurally idiotic; we end up seeing what we are trained to see, what we want to see. This is the politics of seeing. Sight-centred interpretations of knowledge and truth fail to value other senses, resulting in narrowing our sensibility, flattening our experiences, eventually leading to perceptual poverty. Interestingly, sighted companions describing places and objects in great detail to visually impaired photographers may make the sighted persons see details they would not otherwise notice. This is an example of a reciprocal process that is mutually enriching.

Seeing through the mind's eye of visually impaired photographers is the purest way of looking at the visual realities around us, away from the influences of visual history and modern visual culture, away from the conscious struggle for control, away from formalistic rules of perfection, away from notions of visual literacy and, most importantly, away from our expectations from a photographer.

The hand has eyes

'Memory of Touch' (Plate 13.2) is a series of pictures by Bhavesh Patel (born blind), which is taken as he goes up the staircase of his college. He feels the space, uses his mental judgment to position himself before taking the series of pictures. The abstractness in these pictures is due to the unorthodox position of the camera during his physical movements and effective summation of layers of imagery formation based on memory of touch.

Plate 13.2: *Memory of Touch* by Bhavesh Patel (2009).

By touch, I am familiar with this space of my college. I am familiar with this space by touch. The challenge was to photograph it as I went up the staircase. In this series of pictures, I understand from sighted friends that the space has turned out to be 'visually' unfamiliar to them, but in my 'touch memory' it is just the same space.

In 'Chair and Door' (Plate 13.3) Rahul Shirshat (born blind) takes a simpler approach. Rahul feels the space and objects within the space. He measures the space from the left bottom corner to the right bottom corner (say 10 steps) and positions himself at a distance of four or five steps from the right to take this picture.

Plate 13.3: *Chair and Door* by Rahul Shirshat (2006).

By touch, I am aware of old and new furniture and fittings at the school. The contemporary designed chair next to an old styled, big wooden door interested me to convey the coexistence of the old and new in our lives.

In another perfectly composed picture called 'Light and Shade' (Plate 13.4), Satvir Jogi (low vision, silhouette-like vision) has made maximum use of his residual sight to understand the range of the space, supplemented by touch, and the warmth of sunlight.

Plate 13.4: *Light and Shade* by Satvir Jogi (2009).

I measured the space by touch and placed myself in relation to the space above.

Mahesh Umrrania's 'Closed Door by Closed Eyes' (Plate 13.5) is made by touch, expressing his agony of finding an object that bears resemblance to his sightless eyes. Both are closed.

Plate 13.5: *Closed Door by Closed Eyes* by Mahesh Umrrania (2006).

The ear has eyes

'Sound is My Eye' (Plate 13.6) by Rahul Shirshat (born blind) and 'Clapping Hands' (Plate 13.7) by Sujit Chaursia (born blind) reflect the dominant use of sound.

Plate 13.6: *Sound is My Eye* by Rahul Shirshat (2006).

Plate 13.7: *Clapping Hands* by Sujit Chaursia (2006).

'Cycling By The Sea' (Plate 13.8) by Ravi Thakur (born blind) is a picture that every sighted photographer would dream of taking.

Plate 13.8: *Cycling by The Sea* by Ravi Thakur (2010).

I was initially confused to hear the sound of a cycle from the seaside. Accompanied by a sighted companion, I followed the sound to take this picture.

'Maths Teacher' (Plate 13.9) by Nikhil Mundhe (low vision) reduces vision under low light and captures the decisive moment.

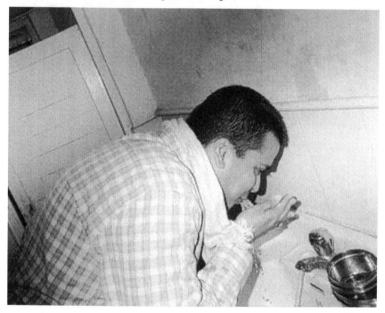

Plate 13.9: *Maths Teacher* by Nikhil Mundhe (2006).

During lunch I followed my Maths teacher to take his picture. I took some random 'clicks', but this one I was sure I will make it. The feel of his presence and sound of the running tap and water in his mouth guided me to point the camera.

Both images (Plates 13.8 and 13.9) are based on sound and are appropriate examples of the photographer being in the right place at the right time, and making the most of an opportunity.

'Subway' (Plate 13.10) by Rahul Shirshat is the outcome of a rare combination of touch and sound, one supplementing the other, and their overlap results in a highly intuitive picture.

Blind With Camera ✦ **317**

Plate 13.10: *Subway* by Rahul Shirshat (2006).

> I had taken the underground subway at the Churchgate Railway Station many times, but was unaware of an indicator inside the subway at a touchable height. By touching the indicator, I could feel the bulbs as Braille dots with the warmth of glowing bulbs of the indicator. On hearing people talking inside the subway from the same direction as my touch, I pointed the camera towards that direction to take this photograph.

Bhavesh Patel (born blind) makes the 'Pigeon Series' (Plate 13.11) by randomly pointing the camera in the direction of sound, resulting in a blurring effect and giving a feeling of a painting.

Plate 13.11: *Pigeon Series* by Bhavesh Patel (2009).

I heard lot of sound around me and pointed the camera. These are some random clicks.

'Building' (Plate 13.12) by Ravi Thakur (born blind) highlights another interesting approach to photography by the visually impaired based on descriptions provided by sighted companions. It bears resemblance with the drawing of criminals by specialised artists based on descriptions by witnesses or people who knew the suspect.

Plate 13.12: *Building* by Ravi Thakur (2009).

Based on the description by sighted companions, I could see the beauty of the architecture in my mind's eye.

'Big Life' (Plate 13.13) by Kanchan Pamnani (early complete blindness) is taken by asking a person to hold the magnifying sheet in front of his face and say 'Hello'. The picture may not be aesthetically rich, but it reflects the photographer's personal and untiring spirit.

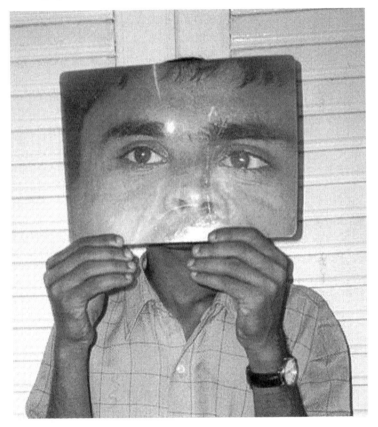

Plate 13.13: *Big Life* by Kanchan Pamnani (2006).

Life is bigger than it appears.

Memory has eyes

Late blind persons use non-visual information to create an abstract mental picture, and then scan through their 'inventory' of past memories to find one that reconciles the mental picture before taking a shot. The process of reconciliation between the mental image and the one locked in memory gives an edge to the picture; better the reconciliation, better would be the photographic disclosure, and more effective the message.

'Designer Shadow' (Plate 13.14) by Mahesh Umrrania (late, complete blindness) illustrates that memory has eyes, and the reconciliation of visual memory and visual reality.

Plate 13.14: *Designer Shadow* by Mahesh Umrrania (2006).

> I could manage to touch the lower branches of the tree and feel the warmth of the summer sun over my head. By imagining the 'designer' shadow on the footpath, I took this picture.

Mahesh's 'Self Portrait' (Plate 13.15) expresses a desire to retain his memory of faces of his close and dear ones.

Plate 13.15: *Self Portrait* by Mahesh Umrrania (2006).

I was made aware of a mirror in the toilet. I have no memories of faces after losing complete sight; taking a self-portrait may help me to remember the lost faces.

In 'Visual Handshake' (Plate 13.16), Dharmarajan Iyer (late blindness), who had a long sighted life, uses the sound of hands tapping against photographs fixed on the wall. Before losing his sight, he had wielded the camera and had knowledge of photography.

Plate 13.16: *Visual Handshake* by Dharmarajan Iyer (2006).

I was made aware of the photographs on the wall. I followed the tapping sound made by the hands of the visually impaired touching these photographs and took this picture. This image is the 'handshake' between the visible and the invisible world and reflects philosophy of my life to convert negative into positive.

'Mumbai' (Plate 13.17) by Raju Singh (low vision, depth of field problem) is a result of mental images created by foggy vision. Raju's 'Mumbai' is similar to Evgen Bavčar's 'Paris'[2] and Michael Richard's 'San Francisco'[3]. These blind photographers have used skilful 'inward' reconciliation of mental images and memories of the city they live in. Raju, Evgen and Michael share a common background of losing sight late in life and taking up photography after becoming blind. Interestingly, their common biography of visual loss has resulted in creating multi-layered images — a 'visual puzzle' that conveys the mysterious quality of our postmodern city, both as an experience and as a physical place.

Plate 13.17: *Mumbai* by Raju Singh (2006).

> It may be interesting to dream this image with 'closed eyes', but it was even more exciting to create it with traditional multiple exposures by imagining it with my open eyes with limited sight.

The visual construction of these three images reflects artistic excellence and makes them eligible to join the struggle of mainstream artists to show the city in a new order of space and scale, to find answers to what Charles Dickens (1852) had asked in his book *Bleak House* — 'What does the city mean and how can one represent it?' — and to demonstrate that the mind's eye can see more than the physical.

324 ✦ Partho Bhowmick

The eye has new eyes

Photographers with different types of visual impairments, such as low vision, depth of field, blurring peripheral vision, outline vision and light sensitive vision, make advantageous use of their limitations for capturing different subjects and environments. For instance, Raju Singh has low vision with depth of field issues. While looking through the viewfinder, he sees the first two pillars (in Plate 13.18) clearly, but beyond that, all looks foggy. In the print, he can see all the pillars clearly as the three-dimensional world has turned into a flat two-dimensional one. For Raju, photography helps him to see more.

Plate 13.18: *Pillars* by Raju Singh (2006).

I was learning ways to judge the size of objects. By moving around and touching them, I came to know the magnitude of the architectural structure. By refreshing my sense of geometry, I took this picture.

By getting closer, Raju can clearly see through the viewfinder Mahesh playing the sitar. In 'Getting Close' (Plate 13.19), he takes advantage of the camera going out of focus to show us what he actually sees.

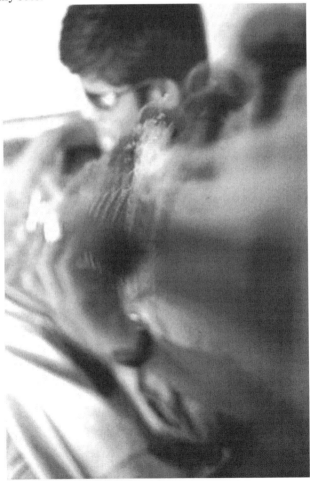

Plate 13.19: *Getting Close* by Raju Singh (2006).

I get very close to objects to see them 'somewhat' clearly. My limited sight makes the normal sighted people see the abstractness they wouldn't see otherwise.

'Pointing Fingers' (Plate 13.20) by Vaibhav Girkar (low vision, issues with peripheral sight) reflects on the issue of access to art for the blind.

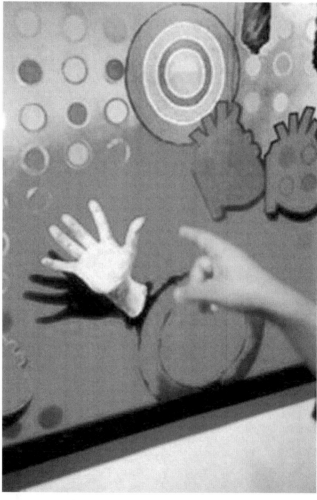

Plate 13.20: *Pointing Fingers* by Vaibhav Girkar (2009).

I am trying to be in 'touch' with our art, culture and heritage.

In 'The Face' (Plate 13.21), Vaibhav can see the raised mural between silhouettes of viewers. He has foggy and dark peripheral vision with funnelling clear vision as the picture depicts.

Plate 13.21: *The Face* by Vaibhav Girkar (2009).

> We were not allowed to touch at the art gallery. Instead of touch, I took this picture.

'This is My Sight' (Plate 13.22) by Nikhil Mundhe (low vision, outline vision in dim light) conveys an impression of his 'detail-less' vision.

Plate 13.22: *This Is My Sight* by Nikhil Mundhe (2006).

Similarly, Satvir Jogi's 'Puddle' (Plate 13.23) depicts his silhouette-like sight.

Plate 13.23: *Puddle* by Satvir Jogi (2009).

Reflections on puddle of water look similar to the silhouettes that I see in real life due to low vision.

Conclusion

Able-bodied ideology presumes equation between reality, knowledge and the gaze; what you see is what is real. Photography by the blind challenges this blind faith in the certitudes of visual perception. It illustrates a critique of the taken-for-granted binaries of presence, visibility and identity as given. It contests sightedness as the sole and principal mode of access to the world. In Georgina Kleege's words (1999), photography by the blind is a kind of 'practising blindness, which decentres sightedness as the primary mode of perceiving and situating oneself in the environment.'

Photography by the blind has developed in the past quarter century and is an integral part of the new field of disability art culture.[4] Curators in Europe and the US are showcasing works of disabled artists through exclusive exhibitions, and also displaying works of disabled artists along with their non-disabled peers. Many disabled artists are themselves putting up shows, and several are invited to exhibit, one instance being the exhibition of a blind Singaporean artist at the UN Headquarters in May 2005. Blind With Camera is the first step towards promoting disability art culture and lending voice to the view that: 'The blind are not totally blind. Reality is not totally real'.[5] In India, many would wonder about the rationale and utility of such a project. Apart from the intrinsic fascination that such an issue would arouse, art critics and historians of art would agree that art is to be enriched by another approach, by another gaze. This essay aims to interrupt the monocular vision of sight and liberate visual art from the monopoly of the sighted people.

Art opens up the mind to unexpected ways of viewing the world. In addition to the aesthetics embedded in art, its vital functions as an instrument of change, a reminder of diversity, and as a source of healing and development cannot be overlooked. Every human being has the creative potential to be an artist. Art programmes can help individuals express themselves, develop their confidence, use their imagination and ignite their creativity. Support for art education and practices should be accessible to all as a basic right without prejudice to class, language, gender, religion, and physical or mental limitations.

Notes

1. My research involves the history of art by the blind, how it has evolved with time, the process being adapted by blind artists for different art media, how touch and sound work in the blind to understand art, like touch, including an audio tour conducted in museums in the UK, France, Italy, USA and Japan. I continue to remain in touch (over the internet) with several blind artists around the world.
2. See http://www.zonezero.com/exposiciones/fotografos/bavcar/bavcar 33.html.
3. See http://www.blindatthemuseum.com/richard.html. Also see 'Sight Unseen: International Photography by Blind Artisits', p.82, http://cmp.ucr.edu/exhibitions/sightunseen/_pdf/SIGHTUNSEEN_Catalog.pdf.

4. In 1985, the then Japanese Emperor organised an annual photo competition-cum-exhibition for the Blind. The winning photos are published in a book called *Invisible Power*. The Aperture Foundation in New York has published an exclusive coffee table book *Shooting Blind*, having photographs taken by visually impaired photographers in collaboration with sighted photographers. 'Senses and Sensuality' is an annual show organised by Blind Art, a UK-based organisation that celebrates visual art by the visually impaired for the last 10 years. The VSA Art, a US-based organisation with a global network, has been engaged in art education for the disabled for the last 30 years and promotion of disabled artists through exhibitions. The University of California, Berkeley, hosted an international seminar 'Blind at the Museum' in 2005 and 'Sight Unseen' in 2009 to showcase work, of blind artists across the world. The Massachusetts Institute of Technology runs projects where disabled artists make use of technology to create art.
5. Inspired by a quote by Walker Evans (1903–1975), an American photographer. See http://www.masters-of-photography.com/E/evans/evans_articles2.html.

References

Derrida, Jacques. 1993. *Memoirs of the Blind: The Self-Portrait and Other Ruins*, trans. Pascale-Anne Brault and Michael Naas. Chicago and London: University of Chicago Press.

Dickens, Charles. 1852. *Bleak House*. London: Bradbury and Evans.

Kennedy, John Miller. 1993. *Drawing & the Blind: Pictures to Touch*, 1st edn. New Haven, CT: Yale University Press.

Kleege, Georgina. 1999. *Sight Unseen*. New Haven, CT: Yale University Press.

Pamuk, Orhan. 2001 (1998). *My Name is Red*, trans. Erdağ M. Göknar. New York: Alfred A. Knopf.

Sacks, Oliver. 2003. 'The Mind's Eye: What the Blind See', *The New Yorker*, 28 July, pp. 48–59.

PART V

Contesting Marginality at Micro- and Macro-levels

14

From Mental Illness to Disability: Choices for Women Users/ Survivors of Psychiatry in Self and Identity Constructions

BHARGAVI V. DAVAR*

This chapter aims to describe the engagement of the women's movement with mental illness (or what is presently named as psychosocial disability) through the 1990s, articulating the contested areas vis-à-vis feminist politics and psychiatry. The essay traverses a piece of this history in order to highlight the paucity of concepts necessary to bring clarity and sensitivity to our understanding of mental disability. It is also a self-reflection of a user/survivor of psychiatry,[1] as she engages with the women's movement as a political agent, against patriarchy. Terms such as 'madness', 'mental illness', 'mental distress', etc., which one has applied to oneself through this political process, not only create new possibilities in the construction of self and identity, but also pose poignant questions. The paper asks if there is personal hope in the concept of psychosocial disability for users of mental health services and survivors of psychiatry.

To my mind, three phases can be discerned in the Indian women's movement's engagement with mental illness, disability and psychiatry: the first phase was one of radical intellectual disbelief about the existence of madness.[2] Mental illness was seen sometimes as a tool used by women to question patriarchal norms and expectations. Critiques of psychiatry came, not so much from feminism, but from other human and social science disciplines, such as law or anti-psychiatry.[3] In the second phase, mental illness as an experienced reality was underscored. The general neglect of gender relations by mainstream psychiatry, and the punishment of individual mentally ill women for violation of normative feminine roles in clinical contexts were the focus of attention. And the right to care was articulated as the need for the creation of 'gender-sensitive' theories and scientific practices for helping women suffering from mental illness. In the third, present phase, the paper interrogates the paths taken towards the creation of 'gender-sensitive' sciences and practices, particularly situating the discourse within the context of globalisation, the relentless influence of psychopharmaceuticals[4] on psychiatry or psychopharmacracy (Szasz 2001), and the creation of 'prozac nations' (Wurtzel 1999). There is a need to look at other paradigms of thought to recover the rights to life and liberty of persons (labelled) mentally ill. This essay then explores the possibilities of conceptualising mental health in terms of psychosocial disability. Future courses of action are opened up by making this timely linkage.

A Question about Language

The notion of mental illness will always remain a medicalised one linked to psychiatric labelling determined by law (Dhanda 2000), and imbued with negative social consequences alienating women from themselves, their minds, bodies, and their life worlds. The gender discourse could look at disability as an alternative way of constructing the identities of persons and women who experience psychological distress. The gains of using a language of disability over a language of mental illness in order to remain close to personal experience of psychological suffering are explored in this paper.

There is a need to theorise psychological distress, hitherto called mental illness, in terms of psychosocial disability. Not much definitional literature is available. Women-centred compendiums on disability in India do not include topics related to mental health (for example, Hans and Patri 2003). Das and Addlakha's (2001) paper, one of the few available providing case studies of psychiatric disability, assumes that the two, that is, mental illness and psychosocial disability, are co-terminus. Fitting mental disability within a social analysis of the overall popular notion of bodily defect, the paper elides the all-important question of definitions: whether mental illness and psychosocial disability are simply substitutable, and whether we simply interchange depression or schizophrenia with depressive disability and schizophrenic disability respectively. This substitution will carry forward all the problems of psychiatric labelling and undermine the empowerment values embedded in the disability discourse. There is a need for an intervening sociopolitical discourse theorising the relationship between these constructs. This paper is an attempt in this direction, using a historicising approach that examines what all these concepts have meant for women users/survivors of psychiatry.

Madness as Patriarchal Protest

Since Phyllis Chesler's (1972) classic work about women in institutions, Western feminist critiques of madness and psychoanalysis have had a long and well-established place in the political and theoretical developments of Western feminism. However, the development of a critical discourse, addressing the legitimacy and foundation of madness and psychiatry, has had a much shorter history in India.

The women's movement in India as a mental health movement

Many insiders are of the view that the women's movement in India itself is a mental health movement (Shatrughna 1999; Uberoi, Shirali and Sadgopal 1995). It has given scores of women safe spaces, support and belongingness, much required resources for self-recovery and healing. 'Feminism itself is therapy for much of women's disease', wrote some feminists (Uberoi, Shirali and Sadgopal 1995: 61). The women's movement gave 'mad' women a chance to locate their lives within patriarchy, understand their powerlessness, and engage with re-scripting their identities from a political perspective. If we see personal struggles, the loss of identities and living amidst privations and violations as the causal factors for psychological and emotional distress, then the women's movement, supporting major values such as social justice, equality and empowerment, was, in fact, a mass-based intervention to cure and prevent mental problems and promote the emotional well-being of many women. The therapeutic value of political activism was evident as women became empowered, using feminist spaces for the reconstruction of personal identities and expanded their orbit of personal actions and affirmations. Whether this attempt to psychologise the women's movement, and ascribe healing properties to it, takes away or adds to the political content and agendas of the movement, is a debatable question. The difference in theory and practice, the tensions and the negotiations between personal and group identity, between personal well-being and political life, and between being a mental health professional and social activist, have been discussed (Davar 2001). Newer and nuanced responses to this question are necessary.

Legal writings on women and mental health

Indian feminism was silent on the question of mental health among women until the 1990s. An early report on medico-legal intrusion into women's lives was brought out in connection with the campaign contesting hysterectomies forcibly performed on 11 women with mental handicap in the state-run Shirur Home for Mentally Handicapped Women in Pune (Maharashtra) in February 1994 (Women's Studies Centre 1994). Writings on women who were oppressed and punished by psychiatry came more from the legal discourse (Dhanda 1987). This pioneering article on the issue, marking out the line where gender intersected with psychiatry, predated much interrogation in Indian feminist literature. Written even while the Mental Health Act, 1987, went into print, this paper did not align itself with gender politics. It questioned the values and foundations of psychiatry, especially diagnostic practices. It interrogated the proximity between patriarchal constructions of femininity and insanity. Where insanity was alleged, particularly in the context of divorce, more women came before the courts as the recipients of such allegations. An early warning was issued in this paper:

> The dangers of the psychiatric naming process need to be especially realized today when women are trying to break away from their deeply entrenched role functions and are attempting to evolve personalities distinct from their societal moulds (ibid.:190).

Dhanda's paper highlighted the collusion of the state with psychiatry in protecting patriarchy through the psychiatric labelling of assertive women. It presented case after case — wherein 'insanity' was consistently applied to diminish, discard, divorce or incarcerate women — of the bigamous husband getting rid of an inconvenient first wife; of brothers deserting an unmarried sister; and case after case of men filing for divorce ascribing insanity to the wife who refused to consummate the marriage on the wedding night, the woman who 'acted familiar with strangers despite being warned', the Brahmin woman who did not bathe daily, the woman who put too much salt and pepper in food, the woman who cried during a sacred ceremony before guests, and to the woman who did not properly receive the relatives of her husband.

That dissenting women are still being punished with the label of insanity is evident from a *Tehelka* exposé, in 2004, wherein a psychiatrist from the Agra Mental Hospital was caught issuing false certificates to husbands wanting to relieve themselves of their wives at the rate of ₹5,000 per certificate (*Aaina* 2004: 1). Another report described the connivance of a brother with the magistrate in order to institutionalise his sister for trying to marry a man not approved of by her family (Indian Social Institute 2005).

Mental health is a sector driven totally by law (civil laws, criminal laws and the Mental Health Act, 1987). Among the major weaknesses of our laws is the placing of legal sanctions upon the lives of those labelled mentally ill. Legal researchers like Amita Dhanda, working on constitutional jurisprudence and human rights, willy-nilly encounter serious barriers to constitutional rights in the Mental Health Act and other Acts, which determine the lives of people labelled as mentally ill.

In the health sector in general, the gap between a medical intervention and a legal intervention is large: not every medical issue is a legal issue. A healthcare user does not automatically come within the purview of the law because of his/her medical condition. A provider is not automatically called upon to validate his/her clinical decisions before the law; nor is s/he called upon to pronounce on the life capabilities of the user. In the mental health sector, every clinical action automatically has a legal implication. Law and social practice determined by the law regularly pronounce upon the 'incapacity' and 'incompetence' of persons diagnosed with a mental illness, and can be applied in various civil contexts.

Also, since most mental health work has taken place within custodial institutions, legal professionals have had to engage with the laws governing those institutions. Policy discussions regarding service delivery, such as the National Mental Health Programme (NMHP) launched in 1982, have been — and continue to be — sidelined, as much of the sectoral reform work happened within medico-legal institutions. Since the 1970s, lawmakers and psychiatrists were involved in re-examining the Indian Lunacy Act of 1912. The 1980s saw the beginnings of an age of public interest litigations (PILs) demanding better living conditions in mental institutions in different parts of the country: for instance, the Shahdara Mental Hospital in Delhi and other mental hospitals in the north and northeast. In addition, the illegal detention of mentally ill persons in various jails in West Bengal[5] also came up for scrutiny (reviewed in Dhanda 2000). Human rights violations in custodial institutions were challenged through PILs before the Supreme Court. Legal researchers were quick to utilise these opportunities to explore areas where the judiciary needed to intervene for the protection of human rights of the incarcerated, the mentally ill, the poor, women and other vulnerable groups.

Law played a leading role in the interrogation of psychiatry. In the legal data was found incontrovertible evidence on the patriarchal underpinnings of the lives of women carrying a label of 'insanity', and to whom personhood and citizenship were totally denied.

The personal or political?

Law, however, stopped short of interrogating the philosophical validity of insanity, with intent being more on saving the 'normal' from the realm of the 'mad' using a social justice discourse. It did not deal with identity questions of users/survivors of psychiatry and experiences of personal fragility and vulnerability. For example, Dhanda (1987) expressed the apprehension 'that the protestors (women) may be dubbed insane and their dissent reduced to the incoherent rambling of the mad' (ibid.: 190). Herein is the assumption of a real difference between feminist protestors, political dissenters and the rambling insane. Working on the thin line between protest and insanity, Dhanda saw the latter as the risk and the limit of the former, a risk that was avoidable. The integrity of the protestors would be compromised if we could not distinguish them from the insane; and protest would lose its potency if the protestors turned insane.

For feminism,[6] 'abnormality' is both patriarchal and psychiatric labelling leading to the exclusion of women. All women's behaviour not conforming to patriarchal norms, including insanity, was to be understood as protest. Evident in collections of women's stories, writings and archives, the emotional subtext was totally patriarchal. Women's spaces for personal anger, anguish, suffering or disability were politicised in the women's movement. These personal spaces were seen as socially constructed and instrumental for political ends, namely, the challenge to patriarchy. As in the legal writings, here too there was the tendency to frown upon the personal and personal vulnerability per se. 'I' references and statements were to be externalised and matched with patriarchal actions. Integrity was defined in terms of political agency and madness as a dissenting subversive route to challenge patriarchy. The women's movement seemed to be saying to those who were experiencing psychological disability and periods of profound personal vulnerability that: 'We are political agents first and that we should unpack our inner experiences in order to explicate that agency'. The social justice and empowerment discourses did not allow legitimate personalised conversations about intense experiences of psycho-physical well-being, vulnerability and disability.

Mental health professionals played an important role in questioning their own gendered assumptions, albeit with a view to improving the quality of their services. Interventions were made

(Kapur and Shah 1992; Raghavan, Murthy and Lakshminarayana 1995) on gender discrimination in epidemiological studies and in the provider–client interaction. These researches highlighted the questionable nature of professional claims to value neutrality.

An interesting clinical position was that through the therapeutic process, women gained identity consolidation and psychological empowerment to deal with and make choices about the violations and privations in their lives. This perspective gave credibility to the realm of the personal, acknowledged vulnerability and disability, and allowed for the possibility of personal growth. That there can be an inner movement of personal construction from disability to growth, based on insights about personal fragility, was not allowed for in the prevailing legal activist and feminist discourses. You were expected to be always strong. And if you were not, someone had to help you with the intellectual tools of social empowerment (law, feminist theory). The elite rhetoric in all these discourses had to be contended with by women with psychosocial disabilities.

Writers have dwelt upon the (left-inspired) politics of Indian feminism leading to the erasure of all kinds of questions having an aura of the 'personal', be it sexuality, disability or psychology (Vindhya 2001). Indian feminism reflected the dominant critical rationalist thinking of the time that material issues of immediate political and economic import were more worthy of a studied interrogation than a befuddling philosophical realm of the private. The disability discourse affirms the expertise of experience. The women's movement did not address the issue of women's fragility, the real experience of disability, the possibility of insight into the disability, and the desire for healing, recovery, joy and growth.

The experiences of individuals in the movement, who went through psychosocial disability and a recovery process, pointed to the fact that patriarchy directed not only the material world, but also the mental world of women. Depressed women knew from direct experience how real patriarchy was, because it affected their mood by the minute. But we needed to talk about moods in an experience-friendly personal language. Omitting the mental world from feminist interrogation vested patriarchy with heightened power over our internal spaces, as the psychological, untouched by the feminist-political, was left wide open for exploitation. That the mental world, with its own language, could also become a part of women's repertoire of vulnerabilities, agencies and dynamic movements of selves, too, needed to be addressed.

Privacy

At the level of fundamental assumptions, there were clear dissonances between the feminist political process and the therapeutic/healing process. While privacy is a notion deconstructed in general by feminism, it is at the core of any ethically practised healing. Establishing a private and safe space for disclosure of personal stories is the first step on which any healing work is built and recovery is made possible. Indeed, women's ways of telling their stories, politicised in the women's movement through personal letters, poetry, etc., are methods of recreating private spaces for themselves. They are not just means to an end, but satisfy a need for connecting with the self. Women in emotional distress experience vulnerability when they find themselves denied or even robbed of the realm of the personal, where their most intimate belief systems, thoughts, emotions and embodied experiences are challenged or otherwise denied legitimacy. While having an enduring 'self' may be a myth, coherence and continuity in everyday life are tied to having at least momentary experiences of a consolidated self. In many mental illnesses, there is a sense of loosely hanging together, not hanging together at all, of not owning your body or thoughts. You lose a sense of being able to predict what you are about — something that so-called 'abled' or 'normal' persons take for granted. In fact, it is this threat to the *personal* which probably led to the distress in the first place. Women are socialised into co-dependent relationships for their self-validation. They do not have personal spaces where they can experience themselves as they are. In denying the possibility of the personal, there is an undermining of disabled women's needs for their own inner spaces. Recovery-oriented healing traditions aim to restore this realm of the *personal*, to enable women to experience at least a small degree of control over scripting their selves all over again.

The personal risk of public disclosure, involved for women in emotional distress, considered politically empowering by movements, leads to the thorny ethical issue of the breach of privacy in the process of such disclosure, that is, 'giving voice to your story'.[7] It was at the same time also necessary for us to highlight abuse of female patients in male-dominated psychiatric settings, where they were taken by their families in secrecy for treatment.

Thus, the issue of privacy needs an interrogation and a conceptualisation that preserves a woman's experience and articulation of the personal, while not leaving unscrutinised the problematic clinical practices — such as electroshock, a controversial form of treatment — that are used to keep women within the norms of patriarchal society. Restoring a woman's sense of the personal, while rejecting the patriarchal/psychiatric abuse of the private, is necessary.

Activism or healing?

Political *activism* and *healing* of whatever sort require different perspectives and strategies — this has been a personal anguish for me, as I traverse both the terrains and see other activists struggling with this as well. The former requires the emotional stamina, qualities and boundary closures to participate in or even inspire conflict, while *healing* requires openness to work towards emotional resolution in a loving, compassionate or empathetic way. This is a tiring struggle between reason and emotion, between political logic and individual experience, between the collective and the individual, and between the public and the personal. Whether political movements can include values promoting well-being — such as love and compassion — is not just an abstract spiritual question, but an urgent one situated in one's existential quest and agency. The metaphors of war, commonly sourced in political communications ('fight', 'struggle', etc.), do not offer discursive spaces for another kind of language for activism. Is it at all possible for us to create political movements which are less angry and filled more with love?

The cognitive–rational part of human consciousness directs political activism, while the heart/emotional/spiritual realm drives the healing process. Healing discourses that are aimed to nurture the spirit are built on a philosophy of unconditional *love*, whereas political activism is built on finding suitable channels for women's rage. We can get by, calling the softer, feminine and healing parts of interpersonal interactions as 'support', instead of 'intimacy', a taboo word given the historical fact that patriarchy draws mileage from it at every step. Since challenging patriarchy involved suspicion of all places where 'care' is provided, caring for self was not granted any legitimacy either. However, we have yearned for interpersonal intimacy and for a sense of personal well-being. The sexuality and disability discourses in the women's movement today are a response to this yearning. It is a desire for intimate human connection and bonding.

We may not gain too much by stretching this dichotomy between *activism* and *healing*, given that all dichotomies are artificial and set up by the categorising rational mind. But the point is that while political agents may see healing traditions as 'anti-political', healers may see the political process as 'anti-therapeutic'. Women with disabilities and those who need care fall through the cracks in the tensions wrought by these different worldviews. One of the early lessons learnt by us was that women with psychosocial disabilities may *not* be forcibly pushed into one or the other of these positions, either to become political agents or to seek care through therapy and that, to do so, in whichever direction, is coercive.

Not every user/survivor of mental health services pursues an identity or an occupation as a political agent. Experientially, many women seeking healing come away singed when touched by the dogged logic and rationality of political activism. We, who have been labelled as 'difficult', 'emotional', 'disturbed' women, or 'not feminists', by fellow agents in the political process, also experienced with disbelief the incongruence of being initiated into 'empowerment', when what was urgently needed was an immediate, loving, healing conversation (Davar 2002, 2003). Being silent on the issue of mental illness did not and cannot bring inner peace and a sense of stability to the women, and it has been remarked that 'silence can be oppressively powerful' (Davar 2000: 62), undermining one's deepest experiences.

It was also remarkable that, except for a few scattered voices that drew emotional power from theology (Chawla and Pinto 2001), the women's studies literature paid little attention to theorising love, pleasure, desire, pride, joy, devotion, the sacred and other positive emotions driving women's lives. For emotionally depleted women, the hope of experiencing oneself through positive emotions and psychological states was a very important personhood issue that was not discussed.

Right to Care

It is necessary to articulate this existential concern in order to reconcile the experiences of women suffering from psychosocial disabilities with the intellectual, rational and masculine power driving all political movements.

An alliance between 'mad women' and 'queer women' within the feminist movement has formed. Both were united by their marginalisation and involvement with questions of personal identity. Further, lesbian women and 'mad' women were often found among the people accessing psychiatric care, had suffered the disability caused by psychiatric labelling, and had shared experiences of coercion being meted out as treatment. These were women who, while they believed that the personal was political, also desired that the political should be personal, healing and therapeutic, leading to recovery from inner hurts. The inner space, a cauldron of mental events rich in promise as well as peril, was an experienced space, irreducible to a patriarchal or to a psychiatric construct. An everyday language of disability, healing and recovery, based on our self-identity as sufferers needing care, had to be created (Davar 2000). What peers in the movement saw in the 'myth of mental illness' as *empowering*, was experienced as *neglect*. While mental illness could be a myth, the suffering and disability were not. We wanted to talk about feeling sick and the right to ask for support and to be cared for.

Mental illness as experience

For many of us who were in the thick of depression or other forms of emotional turmoil, the personal suffering and resulting disability were an experienced reality. If it was a patriarchal protest, we should have felt enabled and not disabled. Disappointingly, the reality did not match. We felt vulnerable, fragmented, lonely, hopeless, sad, powerless, angry, and unable to function. Our bodies often gave up long before, or along with, our minds. The body was reduced to overwhelming pain, fatigue, bizarre experiences and overall sickness. We also had an acute sense of our own responsibility in destroying relationships and feeling alone. We did not rule over the depression, nor did we use the depression in our own interest. It seemed overwhelming in its power over us. It was an equally bad, if not worse, situation for the women who were 'cutters' (self-harmers), jumpers, wanderers, etc. They were typically picked up and put away in institutions in the name of treatment.

Perhaps the disability gave us the necessary reprieve from monotonous domestic chores. It gave us the chance to shout and scream at our oppressors in a depressive rage, or the space, hitherto absent, to be violent, and to escape. In being mentally ill, we did have the chance to defy social norms, and we placed an expectation of tolerance and acceptance upon our families and the community. But these were trifles, hardly signifying power. The real oppressor was within. No amount of public protest against patriarchy affected the internal oppressor. One did not necessarily come out of such disabling episodes feeling good. It fractured the natural sense of self even more, as we neither recognised nor understood the experiences of anger and violence, and even less, the fears, the obsessions, the visions and the voices. Sure enough, this confusion about our own internal experiences came from patriarchy. But we had to deal with the subjectivity of this experience: how these disturbing emotions hung together inside and moulded our perceptions about our selves. Such episodes stunted self-consciousness, took away awareness about our selves, our bodies, the power to confidently make choices and to establish boundaries, resulting in self-doubt and leading to a yearning for a lost, confident, joyful, non-violent, relaxed and firm self.

It is not as if a psychiatric diagnosis is always misguided. As Davar has pointed out elsewhere:

> A radical anti-psychiatric position that mental illness is just convenient money making construct made by some unscrupulous male professionals is not favoured by those who have been psychiatrically diagnosed (2002: 478).

In Western literature, becoming mentally ill as a dynamic process of personal identity formation has been discussed (Estroff, Lachicotte,

Illingworth and Johnston 1991). The diagnosis is a site for the women to root their identities, a temporary and fragile site, but as legitimate a site as all other sites of self and identity construction. It gives one the space to mark oneself as a 'mad' subject (Davar 2000: 70), while beginning the process of recuperation and self-recovery. In so far as the psychiatric label helps in explaining the disorganisation of the experience of the self and developing an understanding about it, however limited, it is useful. However, this is not to suggest a naturalist position. In an earlier article (ibid.), the author has questioned the validity of biomedical language, and talked about the need to build a phenomenology of (mental) illness, described as a '... self-expressive, experiential and personal language, untreated by analysis' (ibid.: 56). Our choice is to reconstruct our experiences as one of distress and disability, and not rule out the possibility of personal vulnerability.

The issues of representation and political participation of the mentally ill became important. Emotions were also spent on the stakes issue, as to who should be the real participants in an interrogation of psychiatry (Davar 1998). Some of us felt that only those who have experienced mental disability, have used, or have survived psychiatric treatments, should set the tone and the pace for such an interrogation. While the earlier paradigm linked madness with unreason and political action as the cure, this paradigm saw women with psychosocial disability saying: 'We may be *ill*, but we are not *mad*'.

There were also issues concerning economic security and the responsibility of the state in providing care — 'naming mental distress invites the responsibility of care' (ibid.: 62). The situation of women in state-run mental hospitals showed that we needed to explore these areas in more detail. If mental illness is a myth, it becomes impossible to talk about service guarantees, right to care or to policy/programme benefits. Mental health needed to be promoted (Astbury 1999) as a gendered agenda requiring policy initiatives.

Reasons for the recognition of mental illness

There are many political and historical reasons for this new engagement between mental health, feminism and the state, including the crumbling of communism as a viable political tool for intellectual criticism and governance: Marxism was dismissive of the mental (Vindhya 2001). Another reason could be the formulation of new economic policies, leading to greater and newer forms of oppressions and inequities and, consequently, newer experiences of personal miseries in the development process. We may also mention the increasing privatisation of business and the lure of profit of the 'wellness' industries.

Another reason for the emergence of this issue is perhaps the movement of feminism from a nihilistic philosophy of pain and victimisation into a more positive theorising of the personal, emphasising pleasure, sexuality, embodiment, well-being and agency. The 'right to mental health' emerged as an important right in this time, pressing upon the state to articulate its responsibilities.

There is also a need to remark on the fact that mental health is a subject which can be used with facility in converting a social deprivation issue, which is justice-linked, into a softer service or healthcare issue. This has surfaced repeatedly in the case of farmer suicides,[8] the Gujarat carnage,[9] and various other social justice situations. It has been easier for public health actors, including policymakers and NGOs, to go into these situations with a mental health (suicide prevention) service package rather than take on the formidable task of restoration of peace and justice environments. The concept of mental health converts structural barriers and crimes into mental healthcare relief measures, minimising the responsibility of the state and legitimising its power. With increasing human disorganisation and disasters brought about by the recent socioeconomic changes and the development process, mental health is increasingly standing in for or substituting for social justice.

A call for 'gender-sensitive' mental health sciences

By the mid-1990s, psychiatry was prised open for much critical interrogation, especially about the true nature of mental illness and the most appropriate and effective ways of studying and treating it. We turned to advocacy for real-time, good quality services for mental healthcare which would address women's needs. We were asking to be included as potential and legitimate beneficiaries of the mental health system, little realising the dangers of doing so.

A flurry of meetings and conferences happened in this phase.[10] Safe spaces were created for personal disclosures, as women with similar experiences found each other and shared their stories. More personal stories of users and survivors of psychiatric services appeared in print. Trips were made to visit Sihaya Samooh, in Pune, a collective of men and women labelled mentally ill, struggling to help and support each other (Sadgopal 2005). Discussion forums were created, wherein mental health professionals and feminists thrashed issues and harvested likely reconciliations or plainly disagreed. Linkages between violence and mental health, and the 'ethics' of the encounter with women who have experienced and survived mental suffering were enunciated (IFSHA 1999).

The objective at the time was to examine gender bias within the mental health profession, to question diagnostic practices relating to women, to understand mental illness as a form of suffering as against a form of protest, to reconstruct women's mental health experiences using feminist phenomenology, and to reform mental health services to empower women, rather than to control them (Davar 1999a).

A new language was needed to describe the experience, and vaguely, we described it as 'emotional distress' or 'psychological ill health' trying to resist psychiatric labelling. An offensive against psychiatry was launched by studying the research of the discipline in the post-colonial era (Davar 1999a, 2001; IFSHA 1999; Purewal et al. 1999; Uberoi, Shirali and Sadgopal 1995). These writings established that mental illness referred to suffering of some form, that it was neglectful of women to romanticise it, and that there was a clear need for political discourses of distress and healing. There was a need to speak about psychological *suffering* and the *right to care* in the health sector. A call was made for an everyday phenomenological discourse about 'madness', an experiential, existential language that persons suffering from emotional problems could own and speak confidently with. While we rejected psychiatry and its abusive practices, we needed to understand the reality of our own suffering and have an ordinary language to talk about it.

There was a call to create 'gender-sensitive' sciences and practices. Psychiatric survey type methodologies and policy formulations were questioned, and gender bias in psychiatric practices was marked and counted. Such inquiries probing a 'gender-sensitive evidence base' also pointed to the fact that psychiatry was *not* a healing discourse (Davar 1999a; Purewal, Bhuyan, Ganesh and Sanyal 1999). It was a discourse of exclusion, systematically marginalising women who deviated from the norm as 'abnormal', damaging their brains and erasing their minds through various inhuman and degrading treatments — sometimes amounting to torture — such as solitary confinement in asylums and shock treatment.

A careful reading of the Indian psychiatric literature showed that psychiatry was not about healing, and that Indian psychiatrists, at least those who were writing in the *Indian Journal of Psychiatry* and other professional journals, were not healers (Davar 1999a). We had fits of rage about how *they* described *us*: the medical elite, mostly men, defining 'sanity', describing mentally ill women as having 'weak egos', being 'suggestible', 'dependent', 'maladjusted', 'neurotic personality', 'hysterical', 'emotional', 'somatising', etc. Many professionals also wrote about the inferior mental lives women had to lead because of their inherently sick bodies that were subjected to hormonal changes during menstruation, childbirth and menopause. Brahminical values, brought into the evolution of psychiatric evaluations during the colonial period and sustained in the post-independence period, were very much part of these assumptions (Davar 1999b).

A search for valid data ensued, data that would reflect the correct situation about women with mental disease, a quest that a fellow traveller warned was doomed from the start (Hegde 2001), as all quests for the 'real' are. The statistical relationships in Indian surveys pointed to the over-representation of women in some categories of psychiatric disorders, namely, depression, anxiety, trauma, phobias, and other such common mental disorders (CMDs). Other surveys authenticated these early suggestions, based on a review of secondary literature, also extensively found in Western literature (Dennerstein, Astbury and Morse 1993). A language to locate women's miseries within the realm of 'distress' rather than 'illness' was pursued, and CMDs seemed to be a comfortable space in psychiatric science for talking about distress.

What were the gains offered by using a language of CMDs? First, it normalised experiences by bringing psychological suffering within a spectrum of everyday experiences. Ill-health in the psychological realm was validated. A continuum from well-being to ill-health, intersected by social structural vulnerability, was offered by the CMD discourse. Psychiatry was questioned for not taking into account the social determinants in clinical practice, especially violence. Clinical data was reported (John 1999) at a meeting on violence and mental health in Delhi. The report described how insensitive psychiatrists are to the issue of the low status of women, and the impact of violence on their mental health (IFSHA 1999). The findings were truly startling.[11]

Fuelled by rationalism and challenging culture, we saw women who visited traditional healing centres as superstitious, backward and forcibly driven by cultural norms into acceptable spaces from where they would be pushed back into their feminine roles through the use of religious discourse and morality. A range of Western readings of cultural practices supported this interpretation (Skultans 1991; Thompson 1983). Women visiting traditional healing centres, and those who professed to be healers, trancers or possessed, were seen as victims of patriarchy. They were seen as not having the spaces to overtly negotiate their problems. An attack on the cultural *maya* of possession and trancing was offered in Davar (1999a), while psychiatric labels such as hysteria, which these practices commonly elicited, were rejected. These women were seen as social victims on the lowest rung of the feminist movement, who needed 'empowerment' and 'social therapy'. The embodiment of women in these practices as an expression of their cultural entrapment was described by feminist anthropologists (Ram 2001). There was no engagement with the question whether spirituality — defined here simplistically as access to the emotions of the sacred — had a role to play in self experience, healing and recovery (Seligman 2005).

As a part of the right to care, other domains of health, such as reproductive and maternal health, were also interrogated (Davar and Wayal 2004). Psychiatric work on women's bodies and reproductive health experiences were challenged. The creation of a cadre of NGOs providing psychiatric services was initiated (Pathare 2005). The life of women living on the streets, in beggars' homes, in mental hospitals and in jails was documented and their right to care and treatment was reiterated (Anand and Davar 2005; Murthy et al. 1998; Shankardass 2001). In a philanthropic mood, women's rights organisations were rescuing wandering mentally ill women and bringing them in for care and treatment within their NGO setups. The National Mental Health Programme (NMHP) was questioned for its gender bias, and a demand made that mental health policy should prioritise CMDs.

While not questioning the very existence of mental illness, a path pursued earlier, there was a push for gender-sensitive clinical practices and more clinical services for the CMDs. The sexual abuse of female clients in clinical settings was highlighted, and the responsibility for developing a 'sexual ethic' was placed on psychiatrists, a responsibility yet to be fulfilled at the time of writing this essay.

Creating good sciences also creates profit markets

The rationalist approach cannot be missed in all this — that there was enough evidence to show that the psychiatric sciences and practices were gender-biased. So, if we are all reasonable people, then it is assumed that psychiatrists would come around and 'correct' the sciences for the bias. Women who approach the medical sciences for help, then, would receive nurturing care; their voices and stories would be heard in the clinics; the hands that deliver psychotropic medicines and the electroshock would be loving and empathetic. Many years down the road, I am disappointed with the results and find the very possibility of this correctional approach questionable. There is the harsh reality that we ended up creating a market for the psychiatric/psychopharmaceutical industry.

The whispering doubts turned into an uproar when doctors became allies in putting together evidence on gender. Research based on gender started pouring out of psychiatric journals (Chandra, Venkatasubramanian and Thomas 2002; Chandran, Tharyan, Muliyil and Abraham 2002; Patel, Rodrigues and deSouza 2002a, 2002b; Rodrigues, Patel, Jaswal and deSouza

2003). Looking at these researches (reviewed in Davar and Wayal [2004]), it will be appropriate to call the year 2003 the Year of PPD (Postpartum Depression)! Women's reproductive health was medicalised. Umpteen papers have been printed in the last few years in the Indian, Asian, African and Western contexts on postpartum depression and menstrual problems, the need for screening at the primary care level, and to start preventive and curative medical interventions. Citing improved clinical and economic outcomes, doctors have advocated the use of antidepressants such as fluoxetine (Prozac) in general healthcare (Patel et al. 2003).

There have been policy recommendations that essential psychiatric drugs should be freely available in primary healthcare centres, and that people other than psychiatrists, managing care at the primary level, should be allowed to prescribe (Pathare 2005). It has been said (Patel et al. 2003) that in poor countries such as India, counselling is not as effective an alternative as medication. There is a colonial flavour in this view, that natives somatise (Davar 1999b), and this view is much to the benefit of the pharmaceutical companies.

A review of the PPD literature (Davar and Wayal 2004) showed that often trials testing the safety of a drug in the post-delivery phase consisted of minute sample sizes such as 12 tablets. They reported only short-term results, for example, a few weeks of drug use following delivery. They did not consider its larger impact on the maternal or infant physiological systems; neither did they consider the effects of drugs on the woman's caregiving functions and other aspects of her life.

When seen in light of the rising tide of pharmaceutical lawsuits in the West, and the Food and Drug Administration (FDA) warnings in 2005 on popular antidepressants (Menzies 2004) and the equally popular antipsychotics (*Aaina* 2005), this trend of 'psychiatrising' communities and women's empowerment programmes is very worrying. Popular drugs, such as Prozac, have been associated with an increased risk of violence and suicide. Antipsychotics, such as olanzapine, and other newer drugs which have now flooded the Indian market, are highly associated with obesity, diabetes mellitus and risk of serious cardiovascular problems. These, being full blown diseases, go way beyond the benign notion of side-effect (Breggin 1993).

Adding a further twist to the postpartum discussion, Prabha S. Chandra, Ganesan Venkatasubramanian and Tinku Thomas (2002) talk about women who turn violent in this period, reinforcing certain stereotypes about dangerous mentally ill women and the need for forced care. When we ask for the right to care, the women's empowerment NGOs will have to grapple with the ethical issue of whether low cost antidepressants should be made available at the community level, or whether we should think about creating effective healing methods that are non-drug oriented (Pavri and Balsara 2005; Segal, Williams and Teasdale 2002).

From Mental Illness to Disability

The language of mental illness has not helped, and using terms such as distress and ill health, while keeping the language tied to experience, has also not been satisfactory. Such linguistic modifications have not led to the development of culturally-validated gender-sensitive psychosocial tools or a clear language of articulation to operationalise healing in the field of women and mental health. On the other hand, it has led to greater medicalisation of women's minds, bodies and self experiences. By reason of medicine and law essentially subsisting together in mental health, medicalisation has also meant a serious threat to citizenship and personhood. Core issues of self and identity were erased for persons labelled mentally ill.

Whether medicine is at all the best panacea for mental disorder needs to be examined in detail. There are no biological markers for the spectrum of mental disorders. Psychiatry, unlike medicine, is a statistical and infant science, developed only in the 1940s. The first tentative version of the *Diagnostic and Statistical Manual of Mental Disorders* (DSM) of the American Psychiatric Association was published in 1952. There are correlations of symptoms with populations (for example, higher incidence of anxiety and neurotic disorders in women), but no biological or aetiological research to explain those correlations in a biologically comprehensive way.[12]

There are no hormone assays, blood tests, urine analysis or other tests which can conclusively prove mental disorder.

Recent researches in integrative psychiatry (e.g., neurology, neuro-endocrinology, nutrition, biological psychology) have led to the view that many psychological/psychiatric symptoms are medical, metabolic, nutritional or otherwise physiological, and not purely psychological. Psychiatric evaluations often do not check for common confounding medical problems, particularly relevant in the context of women, such as temporal lobe epilepsy, hypothyroidism, anaemia or nutritional deficiencies (Arem 1999; Klonoff and Landrine 1997). Also, the specificity of drug action taken for granted in medical care, for example, chloroquinone for malaria, is a utopian dream yet to be fulfilled in psychiatry. For these reasons, psychiatry, and the mental and behavioural sciences in general, can be accused of working with a lower burden of proof as compared to the natural or medical sciences. Some humility is warranted from the medical community, contrary to the enthusiastic promotion of magic drugs.

We may also have to look at cultural practices in a different way than we are used to — as experiences of healing rather than symptomatically. Recent advances in psychobiology and in cultural healing practices (Csordas 1983; Raghuram, Venkateswaran, Ramakrishna and Weiss 2002; Seligman 2005; West 2000; Winkelman 2000) describe the positive, curative, neuroendocrine changes effected by traditional healing, possession, trancing and meditative states. Such practices are being seen not as a part of a syndrome, but rather as a part of a healing solution developed by women and by communities. A full understanding of this will have to include an exploration of the possibility and dimensions of *spirituality* in human consciousness as a part of the human brain/consciousness/intelligence system. A sense of the sacred satisfies an important dimension of human consciousness, and there is something psychobiological about this experience.

The questions, herein, are no more whether psychiatry can be reformed from the gender perspective, but how much of the present science must be thrown out to make way for a more mind–body integrated, psychosocial and spiritual knowledge on well-being and disability.

The final, but perhaps the most important, reasons for the medicalisation rife in the mainstream and developmental mental health sectors are the barriers in law explicated in detail by Dhanda (2000). The barriers are overarching, leading to deprivation of rights of all kinds — civil, political, social, economic and health rights. The impingement on the lives of men and women on the basis of 'imputed' disability also needs to be recognised: Disability is not only about having a disability, but also about being constantly attributed a disability by societal forces. Such discriminatory and deprivatory practices have led legal writers to question the constitutionality of laws regulating the lives of men and women diagnosed with a psychosocial disability in India, and advocating reformulations from a disability perspective, as envisioned in the United Nations Convention on the Rights of Persons with Disabilities (UNCRPD).

Are people labelled mentally ill also persons with a psychosocial disability? Do users and survivors of psychiatry identify with 'having a psychosocial disability'? Is psychosocial disability a condition, like mental illness, and will it lead to labelling of another sort? The UNCRPD offers a framework for legal, normative systems around the world to make way for a non-coercive system of psychosocial care. For the first time, the user/survivor world, struggling hitherto to have the UN's 1991 Standard Principles for the Protection of Persons with Mental Illness removed from normative discourse, has access to a legal instrument which may be interpreted as non-coercive.[13] It acknowledges the right to positive self-identities of users/survivors as well as their full rights to personhood and legal capacity.

The mental health system is built on a regime of coercion based on the view that users do not have insight. The UNCRPD accommodates the view that users/survivors may have *more* insight, and not less. Many users/survivors of psychiatry, like other disabled people, claim that because of their disability experiences, they are in a position to provide a spiritual outlook and a vision for the world in general, an aspect embedded in the Convention. They, like persons with other kinds of disabilities (Ghai 2002), offer a more life-affirming imagination about care and well-being. As a user writes, the world changed for her when she decided, 'I had to make the difference in others' lives and not them in mine. I had to move to move others' (Val 2007: 13). Some users/survivors have found that connection with the sacred within the self, leading to recovery and also giving strength and capacities to lead others into recovery (Clare 2006; Houston 2006; Nichols 2006).

Due to the coercion involved in the provision of care, the mental health system has led to further user deskilling, slowly draining out whatever insight a person may have had to begin with (Minkowitz and Dhanda 2006). The UNCRPD mandates systems of care which will allow for personal freedom of expression, insight and self-understanding, as well as opportunities for building upon these. For users/survivors of psychiatry, reference to psychosocial disability names that aspect of nameless suffering which they have carried in their lives without the stigma. Disability normalises the experience with respect to humanity as a whole, and does not set up a regime of exclusion.

The UNCRPD has been, and remains, a global legal instrument; and the fact that it was built upon the collective vision of disabled peoples' organisations around the world has ensured its proximity to subjective experiences. It gives a universal framework for disability thinking. There is a need for the legal instrument to make the necessary and primary linkages with women with psychosocial disabilities through sustained feminist work. While bringing the disability discourse into mental health thinking is promising and prominent in public policy today, substituting the notion of mental illness with psychosocial disability would be nominal and will once again result in mirroring errors from the past. To anchor psychosocial disability and make the UNCRPD relevant to users and survivors of psychiatry, it is important that we directly address the personal identities of women who experience mental pain and suffering.

Notes

* This essay first appeared in the *Indian Journal of Gender Studies*, 15 (2): pp. 261–90, 2008, New Delhi: SAGE Publications. Editorial changes

have been made to the original published chapter with permission from the Centre for Women's Development Studies, New Delhi. An earlier version was also submitted as a background paper for the International Women's Health Meeting held in New Delhi in September 2004.

1. The terms 'users and survivors' of psychiatry are used by human rights activists around the world struggling to reform the psychiatric system. See www.wnusp.org.
2. Just like the 'Gay Pride' movement, worldwide human rights activists and mentally ill people now talk about 'Mad Pride'. Mad Pride events are organised in the month of July in many Western countries. Rather than stigma, 'madness' is associated with self-identity, self-pride and dignity when seen within the context of marginalised identities. Broadly referred to as the 'users and survivors of psychiatry', many people having an identity as 'mentally ill' prefer the term 'madness' to mental illness or mental disorder, since the latter are pale and overly medicalised descriptions of their intense experiences.
3. Anti-psychiatry developed as a stream of thought within psychiatry during the 1960s and 1970s. It espoused a radical critique of the medical approach to mental illness, which was reconceptualised more as problems of living and rebellion against social institutions and practices, especially the medical profession and the family. The main exponents of this perspective were Ronald David Laing (1961, 1965) in the UK, and Thomas Szasz (1971, 1974) in the US.
4. Psychopharmaceutical refers to the range of psychiatric drugs used in clinical practice, such as hypnotics, tranquillisers, antipsychotics, antidepressants, and antiepileptics.
5. During 1993–94, more than 300 male and female mentally ill persons — referred to as non-criminal lunatics — were released from jails in West Bengal on the directive of the Supreme Court. Many of them had been in prison for more than 10 years; their only crime was that they were mentally ill.
6. This chapter has not attempted to take in the whole field of Indian feminism. There is also no comprehensive review of Indian feminist psychology — this chapter is an attempt to do this. I myself have worked within the context of Indian left-inspired feminism.
7. In a national seminar organised by the Anveshi Research Centre for Women's Studies in 1996, users/survivors who spoke against psychiatry were victimised by the doctors who were present, both in formal sessions and informal spaces. This led to further distress after the meeting.
8. The reference is to a spate of suicides by farmers in different parts of the country due to indebtedness arising out of structural adjustment programmes that have adversely affected the agricultural economy.
9. The reference is to a communal genocide in the state of Gujarat, India, during February 2002, in which over 2,000 persons were killed.

10. Jagori, a women's NGO in New Delhi, organised a small study circle in Shimla (Himachal Pradesh), in October 1995, called Unmad, which went on to collect stories of women labelled 'mad'. Anveshi organised a national seminar on women and mental health in 1996. A pre-Beijing meeting was organised by Priti Oza in Shimla, during the summer of 1995. Reports, bibliographies and advocacy notes were circulated in these meetings. IFSHA (Interventions for Support, Healing and Awareness) organised a meeting on violence and mental health in Delhi in 1999.
11. Only 54 per cent of those interviewed acknowledged the low status of women; 12 per cent routinely checked for abuse histories of their clients. Further, a meagre 8 per cent checked for child sexual abuse, seeing it as a 'Western problem'. Of the sample, 52 per cent said that women did not require a different approach in treatment, citing the commonly held, but scientifically invalid, view that medication was necessary and sufficient, and that psychotherapy was only an additional support. For treatment of depression, a syndrome known to be effectively managed/cured by the use of cognitive behavioural psychotherapy, 85 per cent of the doctors favoured medication.
12. There are very few studies which show that schizophrenia, anxiety or depression are related to any 'brain abnormality'. It is well accepted even by mental health professionals that psychiatry, being an infant medical science, has yet to figure out the physiological and biological pathways. There is demographic data, but no biological pathways backing up the demographic data and the diagnosis. There are complex interactions between bodily conditions and psychological states that defy the simplistic mind–body dualism.
13. See http://www.wnusp.net.

References

Aaina. 2004. 'Editorial', 4 (2): 1.
———. 2005. 'Atypical Antipsychotics: A Research Review', 5 (2): 9–10.
Anand, Ramya and Bhargavi V. Davar. 2005. *Life Behind Walls: Human Rights Within Institutions.* Pune: Bapu Trust.
Arem, Ridha. 1999. *The Thyroid Solution: A Mind–Body Program for Beating Depression and Regaining Your Emotional and Physical Health.* New York: Ballantine Books.
Astbury, Jill. 1999. 'Gender and Mental Health', Working Paper Series No. 99. Cambridge, MA: Harvard Centre for Population and Development Studies.

Breggin, Peter Roger. 1993. *Toxic Psychiatry: Drugs and Electroconvulsive Therapy: The Truth and the Better Alternatives*. London: Harper Collins.

Chandra, Prabha S., Ganesan Venkatasubramanian and Tinku Thomas. 2002. 'Infanticidal Ideas and Infanticidal Behaviour in Indian Women with Severe Postpartum Psychiatric Disorders', *The Journal of Nervous and Mental Disease*, 190 (7): 457–61.

Chandran, Mani, Prathap Tharyan, Jayaprakash Muliyil and Sulochana Abraham. 2002. 'Post-partum Depression in a Cohort of Women from a Rural Area of Tamil Nadu, India: Incidence and Risk Factors', *The British Journal of Psychiatry*, 181 (6): 499–504.

Chawla, Janet and Sarah Pinto. 2001. 'The Female Body as the Battleground of Meaning', in Bhargavi V. Davar (ed.), *Mental Health from a Gender Perspective*, pp. 155–80. New Delhi: SAGE Publications.

Chesler, Phyllis. 1972. *Women and Madness*. New York: Doubleday.

Clare, Dana. 2006. 'Clare', in Tina Minkowitz and Amita Dhanda (eds), *First Person Stories on Forced Treatment and Legal Capacity*, pp. 47–52. Odense: World Network of Users and Survivors of Psychiatry; and Pune: Bapu Trust.

Csordas, Thomas J. 1983. 'The Rhetoric of Transformation in Ritual Healing', *Culture, Medicine and Psychiatry*, 7 (4): 333–75.

Das, Veena and Renu Addlakha. 2001. 'Disability and Domestic Citizenship: Voice, Gender, and the Making of the Subect', *Public Culture*, 13 (3): 511-31.

Davar, Bhargavi V. 1998. 'Of Schizophrenic Mothers and Depressed Daughters', *Indian Psychologist*, 3 (1): 5–8.

———. 1999a. *Mental Health of Indian Women: A Feminist Agenda*. New Delhi: SAGE Publications.

———. 1999b. 'Indian Psychoanalysis, Patriarchy and Hinduism', *Anthropology and Medicine*, 6 (2): 173–93.

———. 2000. 'Writing Phenomenology of Mental Illness: Extending the Universe of Ordinary Discourse', in A. Raghuramaraju and Sultan Ali Shaida (eds), *Existence, Experience and Ethics*, pp. 51–82. New Delhi: DK Printworld.

——— (ed.). 2001. *Mental Health from a Gender Perspective*. New Delhi: SAGE Publications.

———. 2002. 'Dilemmas of Women's Activism in Mental Health', in Renu Khanna, Mira Shiva and Sarala Gopalan (eds), *Towards Comprehensive Women's Health Programmes and Policy*, pp. 460–82. Pune: SAHAJ for Women and Health, Maharashtra.

———. 2003. 'Sexuality, Trafficking and Women in Prostitution', *Psychological Foundations: The Journal*, 5 (1): 13–18.

Davar, Bhargavi V. and Sonali Wayal. 2004. *Mental Health, Pregnancy and Childbirth: Evidence*. Pune: Bapu Trust.

Dennerstein, Lorraine, Jill Astbury and Carol Morse. 1993. *Psychosocial and Mental Health Aspects of Women's Health*. Geneva: WHO Press.

Dhanda, Amita. 1987. 'The Plight of the Doubly Damned: The Mentally Ill Women in India', in P. Leelakrishnan, G Sadasivan Nair and Srimandir Nath Jain (eds), *New Horizons of Law*, pp. 187–98. Cochin: Cochin University of Science and Technology.

———. 2000. *Legal Order and Mental Disorder*. New Delhi: SAGE Publications.

Estroff, Sue, William S. Lachicotte, Linda C. Illingworth and Anna Johnston. 1991. 'Everybody's Got a Little Mental Illness: Accounts of Illness and Self among People with Severe, Persistent Mental Illnesses', *Medical Anthropology Quarterly*, 5 (4): 331–69.

Ghai, Anita. 2002. 'Disabled: An Invisible Minority', *Psychological Foundations: The Journal*, 4 (2): 11–16.

Hans, Asha and Annie Patri (eds) 2003. *Women, Disability and Identity*. New Delhi: SAGE Publications.

Hegde, Sasheej. 2001. 'Further Considerations on Women and Mental Health', in Bhargavi V. Davar (ed.), *Mental Health from a Gender Perspective*, pp. 99–120. New Delhi: SAGE Publications.

Houston, James. 2006. 'Houston', in Tina Minkowitz and Amita Dhanda (eds), *First Person Stories on Forced Interventions and Being Deprived of Legal Capacity*, pp. 60–66. Odense: World Network of Users and Survivors of Psychiatry; and Pune: Bapu Trust.

IFSHA. 1999. *Report of a Meeting on Women, Violence and Mental Health*. New Delhi: IFSHA.

Indian Social Institute. 2005. 'Madly in Love, Couple ends up in Mental Asylum', *Human Rights News Bulletin* (ezine), 29 June, Bangalore.

John, T. 1999. 'Spouse Abuse and Depression in Women: An Aetiological Approach to Depression in Women', *Report of a Meeting on Women, Violence and Mental Health*, pp. 7–8. New Delhi: IFSHA.

Kapur, Ravi L. and Anisha Shah. 1992. 'A Psychosocial Perspective of Women's Mental Health', *Women in Development III: Gender Trainer's Manual*. Bangalore: Sakti.

Klonoff, Elizabeth A. and Hope Landrine. 1997. *Preventing Misdiagnosis of Women: A Guide to Physical Disorders That Have Psychiatric Symptoms* (*Women's Mental Health and Development*, Volume I). Thousand Oaks, CA: SAGE Publications.

Laing, Ronald David. 1961. *Self and Others*. Harmondsworth: Penguin Books.

———. 1965. *The Divided Self: An Existential Study in Sanity and Madness*. Harmondsworth, Middlesex: Penguin Books.

Menzies, Karen Barth. 2004. 'The Rising Tide of Pharmaceutical Lawsuits: What the Practitioner Needs to Know about the Future of Psychiatric Drug Litigation. Non-Pharmaceutical Approaches to Mental Health', *Conference III: A Continuing Medical Education Program*. Los Angeles: Safe Harbor.

Minkowitz, Tina and Amita Dhanda (eds). 2006. *First Person Stories on Forced Interventions and Being Deprived of Legal Capacity*. Odense: World Network of Users and Survivors of Psychiatry; and Pune: Bapu Trust.

Murthy, Prathima, P. S. Chandra, S. Bharath, S. J. Sudha and R. S. Murthy. 1998. *Manual of Mental Health Care for Women in Custody*. Bangalore: National Institute of Mental Health and Neuro Sciences (NIMHANS).

Nichols, Grace. 2006. 'Nichols', in Tina Minkowitz and Amita Dhanda (eds), *First Person Stories on Forced Interventions and Being Deprived of Legal Capacity*, pp. 14–17. Odense: World Network of Users and Survivors of Psychiatry; and Pune: Bapu Trust.

Patel, Vikram, Daniel Chisholm, Sophia Rabe-Hesketh, Fiona Dias-Saxena, Gracy Andrew and Anthony Mann. 2003. 'Efficacy and Cost-Effectiveness of Drug and Psychological Treatments for CMDs in General Health Care in Goa, India: A Randomised, Controlled Trial', *The Lancet*, 361 (9351): 33–39.

Patel, Vikram, Merlyn Rodrigues and Nandita deSouza. 2002a. 'Gender, Poverty and Postnatal Depression: A Study of Mothers in Goa, India', *The American Journal of Psychiatry*, 159 (1): 43–47.

———. 2002b. 'Postnatal Depression (PND) and Infant Growth and Development in Low Income Countries: A Cohort Study from Goa, India', *Archives of Diseases in Childhood*, 88 (1): 34–37.

Pathare, Soumitra. 2005. 'Less than 1% of Our Health Budget is Spent on Mental Health', *Infochange Agenda*, 2: 29–30.

Pavri, Nafeeza S. and Zubin Balsara. 2005. *Building Musical Bridges: A Report on Drum Circle Therapy with Autistic Children at Prasanna Autism Centre, Pune*. Pune: World Centre for Creative Learning Foundation.

Purewal, Jasjit, D. Bhuyan, I. M. Ganesh and S. Sanyal. 1999. *In Search of Her Spirit: A Report on Women, Violence and Mental Health*. New Delhi: IFSHA.

Raghavan, K. S., R. Srinivasa Murthy and R. Lakshminarayana. 1995. *Symposium on Women and Mental Health: Report and Recommendations*. Bangalore: Astra-IDL.

Raghuram, R., A. Venkateswaran, J. Ramakrishna and M. G. Weiss. 2002. 'Traditional Community Resources for Mental Health: A Report of Temple Healing from India', *British Medical Journal*, 325 (1): 38–40.

Ram, Kalpana. 2001. 'The Female Body of Possession: A Feminist Perspective on Rural Tamil Women's Experiences', in Bhargavi V. Davar (ed.), *Mental Health from a Gender Perspective*, pp. 181–216. New Delhi: SAGE Publications.

Rodrigues, Merlyn, Vikram Patel, Surinder Jaswal and Nandita deSouza. 2003. 'Listening to Mothers: Qualitative Studies on Motherhood and Depression from Goa, India', *Social Science and Medicine*, 57 (10): 1797–1806.

Sadgopal, Mira. 2005. 'Sihaya Samooh: A Mental Health Self-Help Support Group in Pune', *Psychological Foundations: The Journal*, 7 (2): 41–42.

Segal, Zindel V., J. Mark G. Williams and John D. Teasdale. 2002. *Mindfulness-Based Cognitive Therapy for Depression: A New Approach to Preventing Relapse*. New York: Guilford Press.

Seligman, Rebecca. 2005. 'Distress, Dissociation, and Embodied Experience: Reconsidering the Pathways to Mediumship and Mental Health', *Ethos*, 33 (1): 71–99.

Shankardass, Rani Dhavan. 2001. 'Where the Mind is Without Fear and the Head is Held High: Mental Health and Care of Women and Children in Prison in Andhra Pradesh'. Hyderabad: Penal Reform and Justice Association (PRAJA); Penal Reform International (PRI); and Andhra Pradesh Prisons Department.

Shatrughna, Veena. 1999. 'Foreword', in Bhargavi V. Davar (ed.), *Mental Health of Indian Women: A Feminist Agenda*, pp. 11–17. New Delhi: SAGE Publications.

Skultans, Vieda. 1991. 'Women and Affliction in Maharashtra. A Hydraulic Model of Health and Illness', *Culture, Medicine and Psychiatry*, 15 (3): 321–59.

Szasz, Thomas Stephen. 1971. *The Manufacture of Madness: A Comparative Study of the Inquisition and the Mental Health Movement*. London: Routledge and Kegan Paul.

———. 1974. *The Myth of Mental Illness: Foundations of a Theory of Personal Conduct*. New York: Harper and Row.

———. 2001. *Pharmacracy: Medicine and Politics in America*. Westport, CT: Praeger Publishers.

Thompson, Catherine. 1983. 'The Power to Pollute and the Power to Preserve: Perceptions of Female Power in a Hindu Village', *Social Science and Medicine*, 21 (6): 701–11.

Uberoi, Honey, Kishwar Shirali and Mira Sadgopal. 1995. *Dance of Madness*. Shimla: Kishwar.

Val, Resh. 2007. 'Speaking our Minds', *Aaina*, 7 (1): 12–13.

Vindhya, U. 2001. 'From the Personal to the Collective: Psychological/Feminist Issues of Women's Mental Health', in Bhargavi V. Davar (ed.), *Mental Health from a Gender Perspective*, pp. 82–98. New Delhi: SAGE Publications.

West, William. 2000. *Psychotherapy and Spirituality: Crossing the Line between Therapy and Religion*. London: SAGE Publications.

Winkelman, Michael. 2000. *Shamanism: The Neural Ecology of Consciousness and Healing*. Westport, CT: Bergin & Garvey.

Women's Studies Centre. 1994. 'Social Aspects Related to the Hysterectomies of Mentally Retarded Girls Placed in State Care', *Samajik: An Inquiry into Gender Construction*. (Special Issue on Hysterectomy of the Mentally Retarded), pp. 7–10. Pune: Department of Sociology, University of Pune.

Wurtzel, Elizabeth. 1999. *Prozac Nation: Young and Depressed in America — A Memoir*. London: Quartet Books.

15

Need for a Framework for Combined Disability and Gender Budgeting

ASHA HANS, AMRITA PATEL AND S. B. AGNIHOTRI[*1]

The immediate motivation for writing this paper comes from analysis of data on women with disabilities (WWDs) in the four states of Andhra Pradesh, Chhattisgarh, Orissa and West Bengal (Agnihotri, Hans and Patel 2007).[2] Among other things, the analysis reveals that the twin disadvantages faced by WWDs on account of gender and disability aggravate their 'entitlement failure'. The disadvantages do not just add up, they appear to multiply. Not surprisingly, WWDs with intellectual disability,[3] and widows among them, turn out to be the most vulnerable. Is there a way to mitigate the entitlement failure of these groups in order to guarantee their survival and promote their well-being?

Fortunately, the discourse in the disability sector has moved from the welfare-based charity approach to a rights-based perspective. There is no opposition to implementing measures for the welfare of persons with disabilities (PWDs) at policy levels either. What is needed is a specific mechanism to ensure that resources are allocated to translate policy statements into reality in the form of tangible outcomes. It is speculated that the availability of resources should not be a problem for the Indian state, given the current high growth rate of the economy. Further, the numerically small number of the 'most disadvantaged' groups mentioned earlier makes the task of providing them a minimal safety net feasible.

It is towards this end that we can draw upon the experience gained in the field of gender budgeting. In recent years, it has emerged as an effective tool for examining the gaps between the rhetoric of women's empowerment and the actuality of resource allocation for its realisation. The same paradigm can be applied to enhancing the welfare or empowerment of PWDs, making a logical case for disability budgeting. It needs, however, to be noted that the gender faultlines among the persons with disabilities are stronger than among persons without a disability. Among disadvantaged men and women with disability, the resource allocations made and the facilities created tend to be cornered by men with disabilities. Since WWDs are also not a homogeneous category, the more vulnerable women in the group tend to lag far behind.

There is, hence, a strong need to undertake a disability-cum-gender budgeting exercise to ensure that the more deprived segments are not left out or left behind in accessing the facilities and resources committed to them by the state under a rights-based framework. The most vulnerable persons within larger categories of vulnerable groups are often numerically manageable. Consequently, committing a full safety net for WWDs appears affordable for our fast growing economy. But being small in number also means being a less significant vote bank. Therefore, the need for a combined disability- and gender-based budget analysis becomes even more imperative. This is the aim of the present essay.

This chapter is organised into four sections. In the first section, the history of the gender budgeting exercise and its usefulness as a tool is traced. The second section presents a brief analysis of the disability data for the four states to highlight the vulnerable position of WWDs among the population with disabilities, particularly widows and persons with intellectual disability. Section three presents a disability budget analysis highlighting limitations of the existing data, as most data on allocation in the disability sector does not incorporate gender as an analytical category. The final section of the paper is the conclusion.

Gender Budgeting and Disability

Although gender budgeting has been defined in many ways, a common feature of all definitions is that it is a mechanism for gender mainstreaming of resource allocations and policies at all levels of government functioning (Banerjee, 2005; Dewan 2005; Goyal 2006; Sharp 2003; Sharp and Broomhill 2002). Gender budgeting attempts to find out whether a government's gender equality commitments translate into budgetary guarantees and allocations, the underlying rationale of the exercise being that 'without adequate resource allocation, gender equality commitments are unlikely to be realised, and government budgets will reflect political and economic priorities other than gender equality (Sharp and Broomhill 2002: 26).

Gender budgeting exercises check gender bias at the level of resource allocation in order to ensure transparency and accountability in the actual implementation of plans and programmes for women's development. It is, therefore, a useful tool for both economic assessment and advocacy. According to Sharp (2003: 10), the core goals of gender budgeting are:

a. raising awareness and understanding of gender issues and impact of budgets and policies that incorporate an explicit gender dimension;
b. making governments accountable for their gender budgetary and policy commitments; and
c. changing and refining government budgets and policies to promote gender equality.

Internationally, gender budgeting is a relatively new concept. Its history goes back to women's initiatives in Australia and South Africa. The Commonwealth Secretariat also promoted the concept in Fiji, St Kitts and Nevis, Barbados, Sri Lanka and Uganda among other countries (Lahiri, Chakraborty and Bhattacharyya 2001: 4). The 1995 Beijing Plan for Action paid special attention to gender mainstreaming in all budgetary exercises (Budlender and Hewitt 2002; Budlender, Elson, Hewitt and Mukhopadhyay 2002; Sharp 2003; Sharp and Broomhill 2002).

In South Asia, the United Nations Development Fund for Women (UNIFEM) has promoted gender budgeting at all levels of governance. UNIFEM's 'Follow the Money Series' of monographs was an outcome of the Beijing Plan for Action. The 23rd Special Session of the United Nations General Assembly (UNGA) in June 2000 also called upon all member states to implement the goal of gender equality in budgetary processes at regional, national and international levels. The outcome document of the UNGA 2000 urged all member states to integrate a gender perspective into key macroeconomic and social development policies through a framework of gender budgeting, which should include specific provisions for the most marginalised groups of women like WWDs. Some of the recent international commitments have the potential to reinforce gender-responsive budget initiatives. For example, the implementation and tracking of progress on the Millennium Development Goals (MDGs) involves a greater scrutiny of budgets from a gender-sensitive perspective (Sharp 2003: 7). The third MDG aims to 'promote gender equality and empower women', a goal shared by gender-responsive budgets. However, there are no specific references to disability, either in the eight MDGs, in the 18 targets set out to achieve them, or in the 48 indicators for monitoring their progress. Consequently, international organisations, UN bodies and states leave disability out of their policy agendas, indicator assessments and funding of MDGs.

Gender budget initiatives are a very recent phenomenon in India. Women's needs were reflected upon in passing in the Sixth Plan Document (1980–85), and somewhat more specifically in the Seventh Plan (1985–90). It was, however, only in the Ninth Plan (1997–2002), and in 2001 as part of the Women's Empowerment Policy, that the idea was mooted that 30 per cent funds be allocated for women in all development programmes. Yet its implementation at the national level could only take place after the intervention by the National Commission for Women (NCW) in 2005. Between 2005 and 2006, gender budgeting was started in many ministries at the national level. In fact, the 2005–6 budget speech of the finance minister made special mention of it. UNIFEM, the UNDP in India, universities, research centres, and many national and state-level non-governmental organisations (NGOs) have actively canvassed for gender budgeting in the 11th Plan (Eapen and Thomas 2005; Patel and Hans 2003; UNIFEM 2005).

Since the 1990s, globalisation and structural adjustment programmes have influenced implementation of policies that have adversely affected women. The NGO sector has used a gender budgeting approach to assess their macro- and micro-level impact. For instance, it has been used in trainings for groups on understanding *panchayati raj* finance (Bhat 2003; Sansristi 2006). Through an analysis of budget allocations and expenditures, it has been possible to know whether there has been gender equity in allocation and expenditure. Such exercises can, therefore, set the basis for a participatory budget preparation process by women in the future at all levels. So far, women's participation has only been possible in some areas of grassroots democracy where the *panchayat*s have been trained to prepare their budgets with a gender perspective (ibid.).

Budget analysis to assess allocation and utilisation for the benefit of oppressed groups like the Scheduled Castes and Tribes, and women, is an emerging field in India. For example, in 2003, the Tamil Nadu People's Forum for Social Development did a budget analysis for *dalits*. Disability and the persons with disabilities have so far remained outside the parameters of budget analysis because the latter is closely connected with political expediency. In such situations, budgets are consciously biased. WWDs are not a politically significant constituency, which pushes them to the background when it comes to issues of rights and entitlements vis-à-vis the state.

This essay attempts to analyse the disability budget in the four survey states from a gender perspective. Since allocation figures for disability are not available by gender, the analysis has been done for the sector as a whole. Even if the analysis is preliminary, it provides important insights not only into the gaps between budget estimates and actual expenditure, but also the per beneficiary allocation figures. If consistently done over a large cross-sectional and temporal database, budget analysis can emerge as an important advocacy and monitoring tool. If the results of this analysis are subsequently compared with the actual status of WWDs, it will be possible to make some assessment on whether government spending has made any impact on their lives.

Status of Women with Disabilities

The basic needs of WWDs from a life-cycle perspective have been identified through work in the field, particularly from the accounts of WWDs themselves. While healthcare and nutrition are critical concerns in early childhood, appropriate education and skill development are key issues during adolescence and in the prime reproductive years. WWDs are confronted with social stigma, domestic violence and mental harassment almost on a daily basis. Vulnerabilities in old age are high for women in general, and for WWDs in particular. Increasing employment opportunities for self-reliance, along with support from community-based organisations can make a major difference in their lives. Active participation in economic activities and exercising political and legal rights will not only improve the productivity of the WWDs but also promote their integration into society.

The 2001 Census highlights some important characteristics of persons with disabilities (PWDs). For every 1,000 males with disabilities, there are 738 females in India. Among the four states selected for the study, Chhattisgarh has the highest sex ratio (812) and West Bengal has the lowest (745). Orissa and Andhra Pradesh fall in the intermediate range.[4] Interestingly, while the general sex ratio is 933, the national disability sex ratio is lower than the lowest sex ratio in the population without disabilities, that is, 793 in the 0 to 6 age group in Punjab (Government of India 2001b). The masculine sex ratio of PWDs needs further investigation regarding whether it is attributable to under-reporting of the incidence of disability among women, or a higher incidence of disability among males. The two have different implications for policy and intervention.

Analysis of marital status by disability shows very small numbers of WWDs being married — one in every six in the study sample (Agnihotri, Hans and Patel 2007). The inter-state variation is significant, from 1:9 in Orissa to 1:4 in Andhra Pradesh. There is not much rural–urban difference in the marital status of WWDs, the exception being urban Chhattisgarh, where all respondents were reported to be unmarried. This is a non-representative situation. The analysis of marital status brings out some interesting findings. First, age-wise, married women appear clustered in the 26 to 36 age group (37 per cent), with only 8 per cent being married in the 18 to 25 age group (ibid.). Second, there is the harsh reality of the low likelihood of marriage, especially among those with intellectual disability (4 per cent).[5] Third, the existence of the practice of hypergamy also works against WWDs, since their bargaining capacity to get a spouse from a higher socioeconomic status than themselves is annulled by their disability. Fourth, widows emerge as one of the most vulnerable groups among married WWDs.

Marital status and unemployment may intersect to exacerbate the situation of WWDs. There was considerable unemployment among married and unmarried respondents, but the more disturbing finding was that 80 per cent of widowed WWDs were unemployed. They also emerge as the worst off in terms of economic status. This once again supports the hypothesis that disabilities multiply, and widowhood, female status and disability increase vulnerability non-linearly. The sizeable number of households being headed by women poses critical questions about safety net provisions and empowerment. Women-headed households are characterised by illiteracy or low literacy, high unemployment, little training and ownership of assets (mostly livestock, and not houses or land), and severe disability.

The 2001 Census paints a dismal picture of literacy rates among WWDs, pointing to entitlement failures. The literacy rate ranges from 32.41 per cent in Andhra Pradesh, 33.3 per cent in Chhattisgarh and 34.62 per cent in Orissa to 41.93 per cent in West Bengal. However, it goes down to 17.4 per cent in Raygada district in Orissa and 33.5 per cent in Bilaspur district in Chhattisgarh. There are, as expected, variations in literacy rate among disabilities. The highest number of the illiterate persons with disabilities has intellectual disability and mental illness, followed by the hearing impaired. A woman with either of these disabilities, without a disability certificate and no education, remains excluded from every facility the state may provide (except, perhaps, pension). Stipends and other benefits for the persons with disabilities notwithstanding, more than half the WWDs remain illiterate.[6]

Literacy does not automatically lead to work participation, which is abysmally low among WWDs. It varies from 1.2 per cent in Andhra Pradesh to 1.3 per cent in Chhattisgarh, 1.9 per cent in Orissa and 2.1 per cent in West Bengal. District-wise, it falls to 0.2 per cent in Hyderabad, 0.4 per cent in Kolkata and 0.8 per cent in Khurda (Government of India 2001a).

The story of entitlement failures continues as we move up the value chain: difficulties in acquiring disability certificates, lack of access to skills and wage/self-employment opportunities accruing thereof, lack of aids and appliances and necessary health check-ups, pervasive sense of insecurity and low levels of awareness (Agnihotri, Hans and Patel 2007). Even if these bottlenecks are overcome, it is still an uphill task for WWDs to get their entitlements, especially if budgets are minimalist and non-specific.

Gender Analysis of Disability Budget

The budget—broadly defined as an itemised summary of estimated/ intended expenditures for a given period of time, for example, a year — for the disability sector is part of the budget of the Ministry of Social Justice and Empowerment of the Central government. In the states, disability issues are addressed by different agencies, such as the Department of Women and Child Development (Orissa) and the Department of Social Welfare (Andhra Pradesh, West Bengal and Chhattisgarh). For purposes of this chapter, budget estimates (BE), revised estimates (RE), and actual expenditure (AE)[7] give an insight into the nature of allocation and utilisation of resources. A beneficiary incidence analysis shows the average expenditure accruing to each person with disability.

Central budget for the welfare of PWDs

Total allocation

The total allocation (budget estimate) towards programmes for PWDs under the Central government was ₹2364.1 million in 2002–3, which increased to ₹2577.1 million in 2005–6 (an increase of ₹2.13 million or 9 per cent). Although overall there has been an increase, during 2003–4, there was a decrease of ₹100 million (Figure 15.1).

Figure 15.1: Total Central Budget Estimate and Expenditure for Welfare of PWDs (in millions)

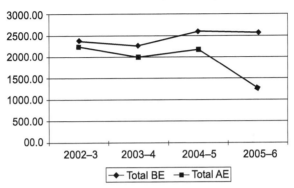

Source: Annual Reports of relevant years, Ministry of Social Justice and Empowerment, Government of India.
Note: 2005–6 figures are till 31 December 2005.

Expenditure from the Central allocation was always less than the budget estimates in all the years under study. The highest gap was in 2005–6 (₹1,303 million). Progressively, the gap between budget estimate and expenditure has increased. While in 2002–3, it was only ₹125.4 million, the gap increased to ₹1,303 million in 2005–6.

Allocation ratio for PWDs

Considering that the adult persons with disabilities population in the country is 2.2 per cent of the total population, of which 1.87 per cent is female (Government of India 2001a), the total Central government allocation on programmes for PWD is very small. And the fact that even that allocation is not being utilised totally is a cause for serious concern.

Non-Plan allocation[8]

Non-Plan allocation is the recurring committed expenditure of the state. The Non-Plan allocation of budget estimate of the Central government has been in the range of ₹300 million. The lowest was ₹303.5 million during 2003–4, while the highest was ₹341.1 million in 2005–6. The expenditure from the Non-Plan component has always been less than the budget estimates (Figure 15.2).

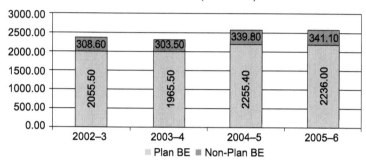

Figure 15.2: Central Plan and Non-Plan Budget Estimate for the Welfare of PWDs (in millions)

Source: Annual Reports of relevant years, Ministry of Social Justice and Empowerment, Government of India.
Note: 2005–6 figures are till 31 December 2005.

The Non-Plan component constitutes a small percentage of the total allocation towards programmes for PWDs. In the years under study, the Non-Plan budget (BE) was around 13 per cent of the total BE for PWDs. The Non-Plan expenditure was the lowest in 2005–6 at ₹237.9 million, while it was the highest in 2004–5 at ₹348.3 million (Figure 15.3).

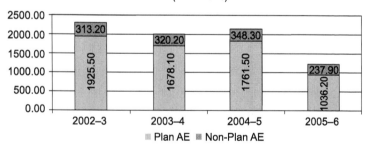

Figure 15.3: Central Plan and Non-Plan Expenditure for Welfare of PWDs (in millions)

Source: Annual Reports of relevant years, Ministry of Social Justice and Empowerment, Government of India.
Note: 2005–6 figures are till 31 December 2005.

State-wise analyses

Total allocation

The total allocation for the various programmes and schemes for persons with disabilities has a wide range in the states under study

(Governments of Andhra Pradesh, Chhattisgarh, Orissa and West Bengal for the years 2003–7). Demand for grants is made through proposals to the Legislative Assemblies of the states.

The BE of the disability budget in Orissa was ₹203.2 million in 2005–6, which declined marginally by ₹1.3 million in 2006–7. The lowest BE was ₹161.6 million in 2003–4 (Figure 15.4).

Figure 15.4: Disability Budget Analysis of Orissa: Total BE (in millions)

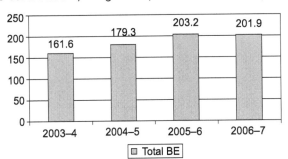

Source: Demand for grants for relevant years, Government of Orissa.

In West Bengal, the total allocation has been lower at ₹191.9 million in 2005–6, which is higher than the previous year for the state by ₹54.1 million (Figure 15.5).

Figure 15.5: Disability Budget Analysis of West Bengal: Total BE (in millions)

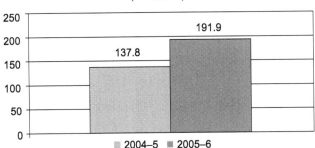

Source: Budget Publication nos. 24, 17 and 14, Government of West Bengal, relevant years.

The total BE allocation for the welfare of persons with disabilities in Andhra Pradesh was ₹210.7 million in 2003–4, which increased by ₹6 million the following year (Figure 15.6).

Figure 15.6: Disability Budget Analysis of Andhra Pradesh: Total BE (in millions)

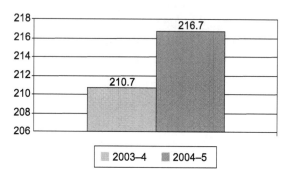

Source: Demand for grants of relevant years, Government of Andhra Pradesh.

The BE allocation of both Plan and Non-Plan expenditure in Chhattisgarh for 2005–6 was ₹173.4 million. The total BE for the disability sector during 2004–5 for the different states shows that it was highest in Andhra Pradesh and lowest in West Bengal (Figure 15.7).

Figure 15.7: Disability Budget Analysis of States: Total BE (in millions)

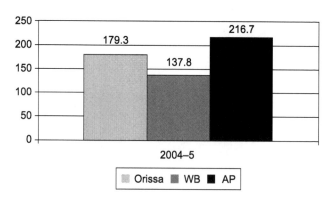

Source: Compiled from Figures 15.4, 15.5 and 15.6.

The total allocation for the disability sector serves only a small percentage of the actual population of PWDs. This is evident by calculating the allocation per person with disability. The per person ratio for the states under study is presented in Table 15.1.

Table 15.1: Allocation Ratio per Person with Disability in Andhra Pradesh, West Bengal, Orissa and Chhattisgarh

State	Reference Year	Total Population of PWDs	Total Disability BE (in million ₹)	Ratio per Person (in ₹)
Orissa	2003–4	1,021,335	161.6	158.24
WB	2004–5	1,847,174	137.8	74.60
AP	2003–4	1,364,981	210.6	154.33
Chhattisgarh	2005–6	419,887	173.4	412.93

Source: Census of India 2001.
Total disability BE: Calculated.
Ratio per person: Total disability BE/Total disability population.

The ratio of allocation per person with disability is the highest in Chhattisgarh (₹413) and the lowest in West Bengal (₹74). In both Orissa and Andhra Pradesh, it was comparable at ₹155. The high ratio per person in Chhattisgarh could be due to the lower number of PWDs reported in the state.

The disability sector allocation (BE) as a share of the total state expenditure is less than 1 per cent in the four states, as shown in Table 15.2.

Table 15.2: Disability Allocation as a Percentage of State Expenditure

State	Reference Year	Total Disability BE (in million ₹)	Total State expenditure (in million ₹)	%
Orissa	2003–4	16.16	230,262.9	0.07
WB	2004–5	13.78	1,296,369.2	0.01
AP	2004–5	21.67	457,471.1	0.05
Chhattisgarh	2005–6	17.34	102,179.4	0.17

Source: Census of India 2001.
Total disability BE: Calculated.
Total state expenditure: Budget of the concerned states of the relevant years.

Amongst the states under study, the allocation for the disability sector in Chhattisgarh is the highest share of its state's expenditure at 0.17 per cent. The lowest allocation for the disability sector is in West Bengal at 0.01 per cent, followed by Andhra Pradesh (0.05 per cent) and Orissa (0.07 per cent).

Committed allocation (Non-Plan) for PWDs

The Non-Plan component is an indication of the committed allocation and expenditure of the state towards persons with disabilities. The Non-Plan component is in the range of 85 to 91 per cent for the years under study in Orissa. The point to be noted is that the overall BE is low; consequently the high Non-Plan component actually covers very few PWDs, and even fewer WWDs. The Non-Plan BE was the highest at ₹183.6 million in Orissa in 2006–7 (Figure 15.8).

Figure 15.8: Disability Budget Analysis of Orissa: Non-Plan BE (in millions)

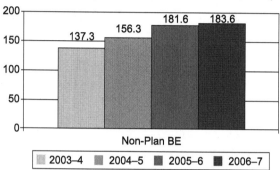

Source: Demand for grants of relevant years, Government of Orissa.

On the other hand, in Andhra Pradesh, the Non-Plan component is about 63 per cent of the total allocation, and in absolute values, it was ₹137.9 million in 2004–5 (Figure 15.9).

Figure 15.9: Disability Budget Analysis of Andhra Pradesh: Non-Plan BE (in millions)

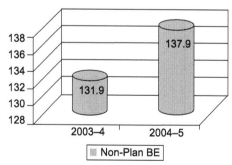

Source: Demand for grants of relevant years, Government of Andhra Pradesh (2004).

The Non-Plan component in West Bengal has a higher share in the total disability budget at 78 per cent in 2004–5 with an absolute value of ₹107.8 million (Figure 15.10).

Figure 15.10: Disability Budget Analysis of West Bengal for 2004–5: BE Components (in millions)

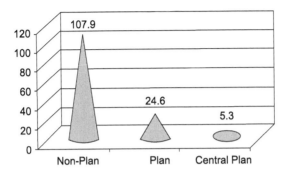

Source: Budget Publication nos. 24, 17 and 14, Government of West Bengal, relevant years.

Chhattisgarh has a Non-Plan component that is 56 per cent of the total disability allocation for the year 2005–6 (Figure 15.11).

Figure 15.11: Disability Budget Analysis of Chhattisgarh (Non-Plan and Plan) for 2005–6

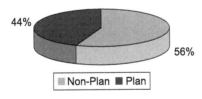

Source: Demand for grants of relevant years, Government of Chhattisgarh.

Among the four states, the Non-Plan component is the highest in Orissa, both in absolute values as well as percentage of total expenditure.

Central allocation

The Central government allocation towards various schemes and programmes in the disability sector forms an important component of the overall resource allocation in the states. Centrally-sponsored plans (CSP) cover all schemes fully or partially funded by the Centre and implemented by the states. The states may also contribute towards the funding of the schemes in a fixed ratio.

The Central Plan component has declined in Orissa. For example, the Central Plan BE, which was ₹14 million in 2003–4, was cut to only ₹5 million in 2006–7. This is, in any case, a very small component (9 per cent) of the total BE of Orissa. On the other hand, in West Bengal, the Central Plan is around 8 per cent of the overall BE in 2005–6 (Figure 15.12).

Figure 15.12: Disability Budget Analysis of West Bengal: Components

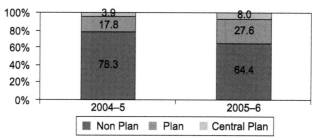

Source: Budget Publication nos. 24, 17 and 14, Government of West Bengal, relevant years.

Comparing the situation in West Bengal and Orissa, it can be seen that the maximum Central allocation has been not more than ₹20 million. While in Orissa it has declined, there has been an increase of ₹11.2 million in West Bengal between 2004–5 and 2005–6 (Figure 15.13).

Figure 15.13: Disability Budget Analysis: Central Plan Allocation (in millions)

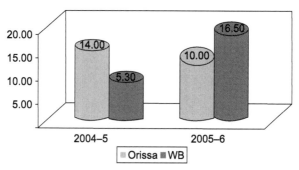

Source: Demand for grants of relevant years, Government of Orissa; Budget Publication nos. 24, 17 and 14, Government of West Bengal, relevant years.

In Andhra Pradesh, the Central allocation was only ₹97,000 for 2002–3.

Expenditure

In a situation where the allocation is meagre, expenditure becomes important to ensure that the minimal resources are put to good use. While data for 2005 onwards is not yet available for Orissa, it is seen that expenditure has declined from ₹175.6 million in 2003–4 to ₹160.3 million in 2004–5. Also, the expenditure was only 75 per cent of the RE in 2004–5 (Figure 15.14).

Figure 15.14: Disability Budget Analysis of Orissa: Total AE (in millions)

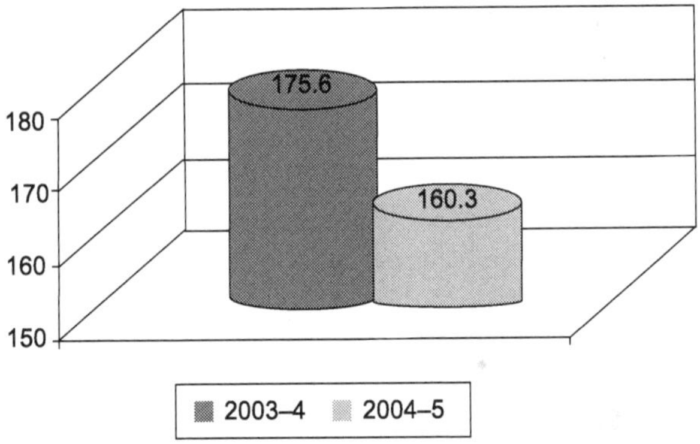

Source: Demand for grants of relevant years, Government of Orissa.

In West Bengal, the actual expenditure for 2003–4 was only ₹143.3 million. The highest AE (₹208.1 million) was in Andhra Pradesh during 2002–3.

The underutilisation of allocated funds is a cause of concern when the overall allocation is meagre in the first place, and the coverage per beneficiary is poor.

Budgetary allocation towards schemes (Central government)

There are many schemes for persons with disabilities under both the Plan and Non-Plan allocations.[9] Within the Plan schemes, the allocation for the Deendayal Disabled Rehabilitation Scheme (DDRS)[10] is the highest at 34 per cent, followed by the allocation for aids and appliances (26 per cent). The next highest share of the Plan allocation is for National Handicapped Finance and Development

Corporation (NHFDC) and the Persons with Disabilities Act (6.81 and 6.45 per cent, respectively).

Under the Non-Plan schemes, the National Institute for the Hearing Handicapped, Mumbai, has the highest share of 13.77 per cent, followed by establishment of rehabilitation centres at 12.96 per cent.

Budgetary allocation towards schemes (States)

There are many schemes and programmes under both Plan and Non-Plan heads undertaken by the state governments. In West Bengal, there are many schemes that are operational under the Plan, Non-Plan and Central allocations. Disability pension has the highest allocation of 30 per cent under the Non-Plan segment, while under the Plan segment, it has 20 per cent. The highest allocation under the Plan head is the development of institutions for the education of persons with disabilities (about 50 per cent). The only Central scheme operating in West Bengal is the Integrated Education for Children with Disabilities.

In Orissa, disability pension under the Non-Plan head has an 88 per cent share, while the next highest allocation is the grants-in-aid to voluntary organisations (8 per cent). Under Plan programmes, scholarships and stipends account for 30 per cent; and the highest allocation is also for grants-in-aid to voluntary organisations (57 per cent).

In Andhra Pradesh, the only Centrally-sponsored scheme operating for PWDs is the assistance to non-government schools. Under the Plan schemes for 2003–4, the Vikalanga Cooperative has the largest share of allocation (38 per cent), followed by allocation to government residential schools (19.4 per cent) and scholarships (18.5 per cent). On the other hand, in the Non-Plan part, the offices of the district headquarters have about 85 per cent share. There is an allocation of 13.6 per cent to government residential schools.

The Disabled Development Finance Corporation, social welfare schemes, and schools for the deaf and the blind[11] are the important schemes that are running in Chhattisgarh for the welfare of PWDs. Under the Plan programmes, District Disability Rehabilitation Centres (DDRCs) and the National Programme for Rehabilitation of Persons with Disabilities (NPRPD) are in operation.

Disability pension is perhaps the most important component of the Non-Plan allocation for the disability sector. State-wise comparison shows that it has been on the rise both in West Bengal and Orissa, but the quantum in Orissa is much higher than in West Bengal (difference of ₹111.6 million in 2005–6) (Figure 15.15).

Figure 15.15: Disability Pension in States (in millions)

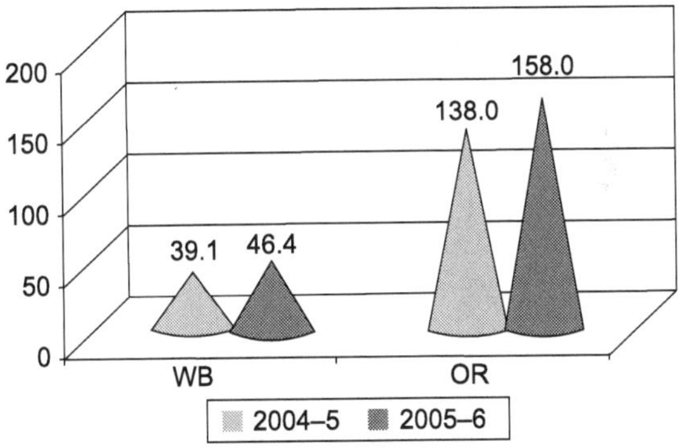

Source: Demand for grants of relevant years, Government of Orissa; Budget Publication nos. 24, 17 and 14, Government of West Bengal, relevant years.

The NHFDC scheme is available for PWDs in the 18 to 55 age group, but from the Census it is not possible to separate the population of PWDs in this age group. Hence, it is not possible to work out the percentage coverage of NHFDC loans out of the total population in the relevant age groups for a population cohort. At the same time, the gender differentiation is clearly visible, and the limited number of loans received by WWDs quite striking (Table 15.3).

Table 15.3: Beneficiaries of the NHFDC

Country/State	Total Population of PWDs (M)	Total Population of PWDs (F)	Loan Recipients (M)	Loan Recipients (F)
India	126,065,635	9301134	18,369	4,450
Andhra Pradesh	7,73,971	5,91,010	291	61
Chhattisgarh	2,31,768	1,88,119	188	39
Orissa	5,68,914	4,52,421	1,564	397
West Bengal	1,058,685	7,88,489	526	108

Source: Population is from Disability Census 2001 (Government of India 2001a); records of loan recipients are from NHFDC, Delhi.

Analysis of Disability Budget in a Gender Framework

Although women with disabilities represent a convergence of two divides in society — gender and disability — the two have infrequently been studied together (Ghai 2002; Hans and Patri 2003). This essay has tried to provide the missing link in research, with its special focus on the socioeconomic dimension. The data from the census and further empirical evidence from a survey reflect the adverse effects of improper budgeting on enhancing the status of women with disabilities.

According to the Census of India 2001, the population with disabilities constitutes 2.2 per cent of the total population, while WWDs are 1.87 per cent of the total female population of the country. Among the four states in the study, Orissa with 2.77 per cent and West Bengal with 2.23 per cent make higher contributions to the population with disabilities compared to the national average.

Considering that allocation and expenditure have a differential impact on men and women, it is important to assess whether expenditure reaches the WWDs at all, and if so, how and in what proportion. None of the schemes that are operating under the Central and state budgets are women-specific. Although there are female beneficiaries in many of the programmes in operation, targeted WWD programmes are missing. Gender budgeting guidelines decree that a minimum of 30 per cent of funds be allocated to women in each scheme. Detailed beneficiary incidence analyses of some of the schemes reveal that the women PWDs within the schemes meant for PWDs fall short of the stipulated level. The challenge lies in not only having women-specific schemes within the PWD community, but also reaching 30 per cent women beneficiaries within the general allocation and spending on programmes meant for PWDs.

In this context, it is important to assess whether the existing schemes and programmes address the issues of the WWDs partly, totally, or not at all. The broad findings in connection with government schemes for PWDs are:

    a. None of the schemes is totally women-specific.

b. Only the poverty alleviation programmes have a 3 per cent stipulation for persons with disabilities. Data on actual realisation by WWDs is sparse.
c. Issues of reproductive health and violence are not addressed at all.
d. Allocation for training in the disability sector is absent in West Bengal, highly inadequate in Andhra Pradesh (less than 1 per cent), and satisfactory in Orissa (10 per cent). However, there is no women-specific budgetary provision.
e. Resource allocation for improving educational standards and providing incentives to continue education for the PWDs is present in all the states under study. However, there is no women-specific allocation.
f. There is no specific budgetary provision for women with severe disabilities, including those suffering from intellectual disability.
g. Capacity building of carers is totally absent, considering that mothers play a very important role in the life of the WWDs.
h. Old age, health and social security are provided for in the disability pension, but there is no specific stipulation for the coverage of the WWDs.
i. There is no allocation specifically for improving awareness amongst the PWDs (particularly, the WWDs), parents and stakeholders regarding schemes and programmes.
j. In Andhra Pradesh, there is allocation for disability under the Tribal Sub-Plan (TSP) and Scheduled Caste component. This is absent in other states.
k. Gender budgeting for WWDs is absent.
l. Disability component is absent in women-specific programmes and schemes.
m. Expenditure is lower than allocation in most cases.

Conclusion

With low indicators of budgetary allocation and expenditure, the situation for WWDs is grim. This has been reflected in the study by Agnihotri, Hans and Patel (2007). The study also revealed the initial hurdles in carrying out the exercise itself, as there were no gendered data available in budget documents. Even in schemes like the Swarnajayanti Gram Swarozgar Yojana (SGSY),[12] where gender and disability data are provided for separately, there is no intersection, and so it is not possible to evaluate the status of WWDs in the scheme. It is only in the NHFDC loans that gendered data is available.

The total allocation made in the disability sector serves a small percentage of the population with disabilities. As no gender-disaggregated data on resource allocation is available, WWDs will have less resources flowing in for their welfare. In the absence of any women-specific schemes for the WWDs, or any reservation for WWDs in the general women-specific schemes, there is an urgent need to improve specific resource allocation and utilisation for WWDs.

A gendered budget framework for persons with disabilities will raise awareness on their needs. Gender-disaggregated data will enable optimal allocation and utilisation of resources in the disability sector for literacy, pension, aids and appliances, micro-credit, etc. A gendered budget will enable policymakers to take up a scheme like pensions to saturation level. This will bring out unrecorded, but eligible, cases and/or will actually provide full coverage to WWDs, both being desirable programme outcomes. Due to the lower number of WWDs in urban areas, it should be possible to implement the associated schemes for them in urban areas on a saturation basis, since training, transportation, marketing and monitoring infrastructure are stronger.

We suggest that there should be specific allocation for women in every programme/scheme for the PWDs. Gender budgeting of the disability sector should be carried out. Specific allocation should be made for skill and capacity-building of WWDs. Reproductive health and violence issues of WWDs should also have concrete allocations. There should be adequate budgetary provisions for training of carers, as well as specific programme for WWDs with intellectual disability and severe disabilities. Awareness programmes should have more allocation; and overall, there should be improved expenditure. Setting up of an independent and separate department for persons with disabilities, along the lines of the National Commission for Women, should be made a priority.

APPENDIX I

Plan and Non-Plan Central Government Schemes for Persons with Disabilities

Plan Schemes

National Institute for the Visually Handicapped, Dehradun
National Institute for the Orthopaedically Handicapped, Kolkata
National Institute for the Hearing Handicapped, Mumbai
National Institute for the Mentally Handicapped, Secunderabad
National Institute of Rehabilitation, Training and Research, Cuttack
Institute for the Physically Handicapped, New Delhi
National Institute for Empowerment of Persons with Multiple Disabilities, Chennai
Artificial Limbs Manufacturing Corporation of India (ALIMCO), Kanpur
Scheme to promote Voluntary Action for PWD: Deendayal Disabled Rehabilitation Scheme
Indian Spinal Injuries Centre (ISIC), New Delhi
Rehabilitation Council of India (RCI), New Delhi
National Handicapped Finance and Development Corporation, Faridabad
Science and Technology Mission
Institute of Rehabilitation Sciences, ISIC, New Delhi
Chief Commissioner for Persons with Disabilities, Government of India
Employment of handicapped

Non-Plan Schemes

National Institute for the Visually Handicapped, Dehradun
National Institute for the Orthopaedically Handicapped, Kolkata
National Institute for the Hearing Handicapped, Mumbai
National Institute for the Mentally Handicapped, Secunderabad
National Institute of Rehabilitation, Training and Research, Cuttack
Institute for the Physically Handicapped, New Delhi
ALIMCO, Kanpur

RCI, New Delhi
Chief Commissioner for Persons with Disabilities, Government of India
National Commission for Disabled Persons

Notes

* This essay first appeared in the *Indian Journal of Gender Studies*, 15 (2): pp. 233–60, 2008, New Delhi: SAGE Publications. Editorial changes have been made to the original published chapter with permission from the Centre for Women's Development Studies, New Delhi.
1. The views expressed by Dr Agnihotri are made in his personal capacity, and do not reflect the views of his institution.
2. The reference is to a multi-state socioeconomic study of women with disabilities in India, which examined their status in four states of the country: Andhra Pradesh, Chhattisgarh, Orissa and West Bengal. Using Census and National Sample Survey Organisation (NSSO) data, it looked at the position of women with disabilities (WWDs), governmental entitlements such as loans, education, vocational training, etc., for persons with disabilities in a gender-disaggregated manner. The empirical part was based on a sample size of 320 WWDs across the four study states. Some of the indicators used in the study to assess the status of WWDs were educational levels, marital status, and possession of disability certificates, aids and appliances, employment, credit availability, access to health services, violence and political participation.
3. 'Intellectual disability' has replaced 'mental retardation' (MR) in usage; however, the Government of India continues to use the latter terminology.
4. This data is in keeping with the general sex ratio among the four states: Chhattisgarh has the highest at 989 and West Bengal the lowest at 934. The two intermediate states are Andhra Pradesh at 978 and Orissa at 972.
5. According to NSSO data Report no. 485, p. 17 (Government of India 2002), out of every 1,000 WWDs, 309 are currently unmarried, 282 widowed, 24 divorced, and 385 never married. Of a sample of 1,000 WWDs with mental retardation, 911 have never been married, 28 are divorced, 19 widowed, and 41 currently married.
6. The target of eliminating gender inequality in all levels of education will not be achieved without considering disability. The gender gap in literacy among the persons with disabilities is greater than that in the overall Indian population.

7. Budget estimate (BE) is the estimated amount for a particular scheme or programme as projected in the annual budget of the state or Central government. Revised estimate (RE) is the amount as per the supplementary budget, which can be more or less or remain the same as the budget estimate. Actual expenditure (AE) is the expenditure made in a financial year against the revised estimate amount.
8. The Central and state governments draw up Five-Year Plans for carrying out a number of developmental programmes. Financial provisions are made in each financial year for execution of the programmes, and this expenditure is known as Plan expenditure. If felt that the scheme should continue even after completion within the Plan period, it is transferred under the Non-Plan expenditure. For instance, when a dam is constructed, it comes under Plan expenditure, but after the Plan period, the maintenance of the dam is covered under Non-Plan expenditure.
9. For a complete list of Plan and Non-Plan schemes, see Appendix I.
10. Formerly known as the Scheme to Promote Voluntary Action for Persons with Disabilities, DDRS provides financial assistance to voluntary organisations for running rehabilitation centres for leprosy-cured persons, for manpower development in the field of mental retardation (MR) and cerebral palsy (CP), and establishment and development of special schools for orthopaedic, speech, hearing, visual and mental disabilities.
11. The UNCRPD prefers the term 'sensory disability', but in this chapter, the use of 'blind and deaf' is as per the language used by the Government of India.
12. The Swarnajayanti Gram Swarozgar Yojana (SGSY) was launched as an integrated programme for self-employment of the rural poor on 1 April 1999 in India. The objective of the scheme is to bring the assisted poor families above the poverty line by organising them into self-help groups (SHGs) through social mobilisation, training, capacity building and provision of income-generating assets through a mix of bank credit and government subsidy. The SGSY has a special focus on the vulnerable groups among the rural poor. SC/STs account for at least 50 per cent, women 40 per cent, and persons with physical disabilities constitute 3 per cent of the recipients.

References

Agnihotri, Satish B., Asha Hans and Amrita M. Patel. 2007. 'A Multi State Socio Economic Study of Women with Disabilities in India (Report)'. Bhubaneswar: Shanta Memorial Rehabilitation Centre; and UNDP.

Banerjee, Nirmala. 2005. *What is Gender Budgeting?: Public Policies from Women's Perspective in the Indian Context*. New Delhi: UNIFEM.

Bhat, A. 2003. 'Building Budgets from Below: Lessons from a pilot project in two Gram Panchayats and two municipalities in Karnataka', in 'Proceedings of International Workshop on Gender Budget Initiatives in Orissa', pp. 41–65. Bhubaneswar: School of Women's Studies, Utkal University in coordination with Centre for Youth and Social Development (CYSD), Department of International Development (DFID), OXFAM, 22–24 September.

Budlender, Debbie and Guy Hewitt. 2002. *Gender Budgets Make More Cents: Country Studies and Good Practice*. London: Commonwealth Secretariat.

Budlender, Debbie, Diane Elson, Guy Hewitt and Tanni Mukhopadhyay (eds). 2002. *Gender Budgets Make Cents: Understanding Gender Responsive Budgets*. London: Commonwealth Secretariat.

Dewan, Ritu. 2005. *Gender Budget Perspectives on Macro and Meso Policies in Small Urban Manufactories in Greater Mumbai*. New Delhi: Human Development Resource Centre, UNDP.

Eapen, Mridul and Soya Thomas. 2005. *Gender Analysis of Select Gram (Village) Panchayat Plan Budgets in Trivandrum District, Kerala*. New Delhi: Human Development Resource Centre; and UNDP.

Ghai, Anita. 2002. 'Disabled Women: An Excluded Agenda of Indian Feminism', *Hypatia*, 17 (3): 49–66.

Government of India. 2001a. *Census of India: The First Report on Disability*. New Delhi: Director General of Census.

———. 2001b. *Gender Budget Analysis of Selected States: An Initiative*. New Delhi: Department of Women and Child Department and National Institute of Public Cooperation and Child Development.

———. 2002. *Disabled Persons in India*, National Sample Survey Organisation (NSSO), 58th Round.

Government of Andhra Pradesh. 2003, 2004, 2005. Demand for Grant. Hyderabad: Department of Social Welfare.

Government of Chhattisgarh. 2004, 2005. Demand for Grant. Raipur: Department of Social Welfare.

Government of Orissa. 2003, 2004, 2005, 2006. Demand for Grant. Bhubaneswar: Department of Women and Child Development.

Government of West Bengal. 2004, 2005. Demand for Grant. Kolkata: Department of Social Welfare.

Goyal, Anjali. 2006. 'Women's Empowerment through Gender Budgeting: A Review in the Indian Context'. Unpublished Concept Note, Department of Women and Child Development, Government of India.

Hans, Asha and Annie Patri (eds). 2003. *Women, Disability and Identity*. New Delhi: SAGE Publications.

Lahiri, Ashok, Lekha S. Chakraborty and P. N. Bhattacharyya. 2001. *Gender Budgeting in India: Post-Budget Assessment Report*. New Delhi: National Institute of Public Finance and Policy.

Patel, Amrita M. and Asha Hans. 2003. 'Proceedings of International Workshop on Gender Budget Initiatives in Orissa'. School of Women's Studies, Utkal University in coordination with Centre for Youth and Social Development (CYSD), Department of International Development (DFID), OXFAM, 22–24 September, Bhubaneswar.

Sansristi. 2006. *Handbook on Panchayat Finance and Gender Budgeting*. Bhubaneswar: The Organisation.

Sharp, Rhonda. 2003. *Budgeting for Equity: Gender Budget Initiatives within a Framework of Performance Oriented Budgeting*. New York: UNIFEM.

Sharp, Rhonda and Ray Broomhill. 2002. 'Budgeting for Equality: The Australian Experience', *Feminist Economics*, 8 (1): 25–47.

Tamil Nadu Peoples' Forum for Social Development. 2003. *Special Component Plan: Dalit Hopes Betrayed?*. Chennai: Social Watch.

United Nations General Assembly. 2000. 'Official Records: Twenty-third Special Session' (Supplement No. 3 [A/S-23/10/Rev.1]). New York: United Nations.

UNIFEM. 2005. *Gender Budgeting: Follow the Money Series*. New Delhi: UNIFEM.

16

Sameness and Difference: Twin Track Empowerment for Women with Disabilities

AMITA DHANDA*

Politics of Difference and Bivalent Collectivities

Human rights are often referred to as universal. This quality of universality contributes to the high moral value with which they are imbued, and reinforces their non-violable and inalienable character. These claims of universality have been challenged by excluded groups who have contended that the discourse of universal rights serves to suppress social differences, whilst reinforcing the power and authority of dominant groups and collectivities. The establishment of normative frameworks at odds with their world-view results in excluded populations facing two kinds of injustice: socioeconomic and cultural. The sequence in which or the simultaneity with which these injustices are confronted may vary for different excluded populations. To combat the first kind of injustice, redistribution strategies, which reallocate socioeconomic resources, may be required. The second kind may warrant the explicit recognition of the identity of the excluded group. It is important to note that redistribution efforts aim to reduce group differentiation, whilst recognition strategies enhance it. The question, then, is how to reconcile these competing demands of excluded populations.

Iris Marion Young (1990) in her theory of justice seeks to answer this dilemma by questioning the overarching emphasis on redistribution in theories of justice. She demonstrates through her five faces of oppression[1] how cultural forces and social processes play as great a role as economic factors in excluding populations; consequently, she asserts that the empowerment of these groups is not possible without a recognition and preservation of their non-oppressive group differences, that is, the uniqueness of their experiences and world-views. So, whilst she shows how redistribution without recognition makes for an incomplete theory of justice, she does not test this theory on individual excluded populations. That task has been undertaken by Nancy Fraser.

Fraser holds that the politics of difference or the right to recognition is not necessarily required by all excluded groups. The question that arises is: when is the right required and when is it unnecessary? Fraser (1997) makes an analytical distinction between socioeconomic and cultural injustice(s). In her view, projection of difference is emancipatory when used to combat cultural domination, non-recognition and disrespect. However, when the injustice is rooted in the economic structure, an assertion of difference, she contends, could prove to be counterproductive because it would preserve group identities that redistribution could undermine. Some groups — non-professionals, for instance — may only require economic empowerment, whilst others, such as homosexuals, may only need recognition to combat social injustice (Fraser 2001). In between these two opposing poles are excluded populations whom Fraser refers to as 'bivalent collectivities'.

Bivalent collectivities are described as those excluded communities that are marked out both by the politico-economic and the cultural structures of society. They are, thus, disadvantaged both by 'socioeconomic maldistribution and cultural misrecognition in forms where neither of these injustices is an indirect effect of the other, but where both are primary and co-original' (Fraser

1997: 19). Fraser posits gender as one such bivalent collectivity. This contention is made by pointing to the division between paid and domestic work, and how these divisions contribute to the exploitation and marginalisation of women. Economic remedies would be needed to address this occupational exclusion of women. Male preference and devaluation of all things coded as feminine are cultural disadvantages faced by women that cannot be counteracted by economic redistribution alone, but require cultural remedies such as the celebration of female identity and the exercise of freedom of choice.

Hugemark and Roman (2002) draw from Fraser's categorisation to suggest that persons with disabilities are also another bivalent collectivity, because 'the disadvantages facing disabled persons are rooted in the economic structure as well as in cultural beliefs, norms and attitudes'. The consequence of this bivalence is that 'collectivities of disabled persons need to simultaneously claim their specificity, and to deny it' (ibid.: 10).

Fraser's categorisation of bivalent collectivities, and Hugemark and Roman's application of the same to disability alert us to the disadvantages emanating from economic and cultural injustices to specified collectivities. These authors, however, do not explore the situation of those groups who find inclusion in both the collectivities of gender and disability. I seek to advance the analysis further by raising questions around the interrelationship among these bivalent collectivities. What is the relationship between women and 'women with disabilities'? And does disability have different impacts on men and women with disabilities? On which axis of the politics of difference should we place women with disabilities? Should it be gender or disability or both? How does feminism account for the disability experience?

Bivalence of Women with Disabilities

Women with disabilities have addressed these questions. Their writings acknowledge the relevance of feminist thought and method for politicising the disability experience, and they bemoan the silence of mainstream feminist thought on issues concerning women with disabilities (Begum 1992; Ghai 2003; Morris 1993).

If women found that philosophical accounts of man's nature were not about women, then women with disabilities discovered that women's accounts of woman's nature and woman's experience did not extend to all women. Illustratively, when feminist writings constructed the experience of caring, by only focusing on women as providers of care, without concerning themselves with women as recipients of care, they excluded women with disabilities from their discourse.[2]

Once it is recognised that gender is acted out on the human body, the next step is to examine how disability affects the gendering process (Gerschick 2000). While feminist theory has dwelt on the objectification and eroticisation of the female body, women with disabilities report how they have been unsexed due to their bodies. If mainstream women's writings condemn the social control functions of the beauty myth (Wolf 1991), women with disabilities find that the possession of atypical bodies renders their very womanhood problematic. As women question their womb-driven roles,[3] women with disabilities seek the freedom to assume these very roles (Dhanda 1994; French 2005; Goldhar 1991; Hans 2003). Significantly, both experiences show the absence of freedom to decide.

Both women and women with disabilities experience sexism; only the latter experience 'sexism without the pedestal' (Fine and Asch 1988: 1). It is my contention that the stark and unmediated experiences of women with disabilities throw the disempowering nature of gender into sharp relief. These experiences allow for a more complex challenge to social constructions of womanhood. For these parallels to be drawn between the experiences of women and those of women with disabilities, it is necessary that both the sameness and the difference between women in general and women with disabilities be appreciated.

CEDAW and CRPD

The Convention on the Elimination of All Forms of Discrimination against Women (CEDAW) did not encourage the making of these connections since it dealt with discrimination in monolithic terms. All women, irrespective of region, religion, ethnicity, colour, sexual orientation or disability, were inducted within the same normative framework. This was done because it was believed that any normative deference to diversity would dilute the challenge to patriarchal norms (Jain 2005). Such diversity could be addressed in the implementation of the Convention.[4] However, as the CEDAW approach did not obtain unanimous approval,[5] the question of double discrimination or intra-group disadvantage has continued to be raised.[6] It again came to the fore for women with disabilities during the deliberations on the Convention on the Rights of Persons with Disabilities (CRPD).

The Ad Hoc Committee negotiating the CRPD[7] was required to consider whether it should adopt the universalist approach and propose a single normative framework for all persons with disabilities; or whether, in view of the cross-cutting relevance of gender, it should acknowledge the intersections between disability and gender, and specifically address the concerns of women with disabilities. These questions were answered in different ways by governments and by civil society. The reason for seeking mainstreaming is to underscore the overarching relevance of gender and the ubiquitous presence of discrimination. Special measures are suggested because, without them, it would be difficult to scale off the deep layers of gender discrimination. However, both approaches have yielded specific difficulties. Whilst mainstreaming has marginalised gender, special measures have ghettoised it.

Finally, the Committee adopted what is termed the 'twin track' approach. In accordance with this approach, the CRPD, along with inducting the gender dimension in relevant articles, incorporated a dedicated article on women with disabilities. This article examines the various single and twin track proposals to assess how double discrimination has been addressed in the CRPD, the first human rights Convention of this century. Subsequently, the potential and limitations of the strategies adopted by the Convention will be evaluated. The article concludes by considering the possible effects of the twin track approach on the empowerment of women with disabilities.

Single and Twin Track Proposals to Address Gender Discrimination

Confronting the question

The CEDAW dilemma surfaced with a different face in the negotiations on the CRPD. In CEDAW, the question was whether specific differences, such as ethnicity, colour, sexual orientation or disability, should find mention; in CRPD, the concern was whether gender should be explicitly included.[8] After all, the economic and cultural injustices experienced by women with disabilities also affect men with disabilities. Wouldn't an explicit reference to gender discrimination fragment the challenge to ableism[9] which was being mounted by the Convention?

The Committee was confronted with this question by the Republic of Korea, which proposed an amendment to the Convention text seeking to incorporate an article expressly addressing the concerns of women with disabilities. The text of the proposed article, presented at the third session of the Ad Hoc Committee in June 2003, is as follows:

1. States Parties undertake to ensure the enjoyment of full and equal rights and freedoms by women with disabilities and their equal participation in political, economic, social and cultural activities without any discrimination on the basis of their gender and/or disabilities.
2. States Parties shall take the following steps from a gender perspective so as to ensure that women with disabilities are able to live with dignity in freedom, safety and autonomy: (*a*) Include a separate reference to the protection of the rights of women with disabilities in laws pertaining to women and persons with disabilities; (*b*) Incorporate women with disabilities in social surveys and statistics collection efforts and collect gender disaggregated data on persons with disabilities; (*c*) Protect the motherhood of women with disabilities by developing and disseminating policies and programs for assistance based on the recognition of the special needs of women with disabilities in pregnancy, childbirth and post-partum health care and child care;

(*d*) Ensure that women with disabilities are not deprived of their right to work due to their pregnancy or childbirth, and provide the necessary assistances in this regard; (*e*) Ensure that women with disabilities are protected from sexual exploitation, abuse and violence at home, institution and communities.[10]

The Korean proposal stemmed from the understanding that:

> The plight of women with disabilities is not the simple sum of the barriers faced by people with disabilities and the barriers faced by women. The combination of their disabilities and inferior status as women goes beyond the mechanical doubling of discrimination to a situation of utter social alienation and policy neglect. Women with disabilities have remained invisible in legislative and policy efforts at both national and international levels, without an anchor in disability discourse or women's rights discourse.[11]

The Koreans maintained that the inclusion of an article on women would not start a race for listing other vulnerable groups among persons with disabilities because 'women with disabilities comprise half the subject population of this convention and gender is a cross cutting dimension of a different order than other defining characteristics of vulnerability'. Even as the Koreans endorsed references to gender in the general provisions, they were not content with these provisions. Without a special article, they contended, 'women with disabilities could slip through the fingers of the government ministries in charge of implementation of the convention'.[12]

The Korean proposal received the support of a number of countries, but it also had its share of detractors. The opposing countries did not dispute the marginalisation of women with disabilities; but they did not agree that a stand-alone article was the way to address this discrimination. It was feared that recognition of the disadvantages of one group could trigger similar demands from other groups who face particular disadvantages, such as indigenous women or aged women with disabilities. A number of articles focusing on specific groups, the European Union opined, 'would do this convention a disservice . . . as it would then lack a strong statement on the rights of all persons with disabilities'. It, therefore, suggested that:

The convention would be stronger, more authoritative and more beneficial to people with disabilities if its provisions apply equally to all disabled people, and there was no "picking and choosing" of rights and standards. Such a convention would then also be stronger and more authoritative for women with disabilities.[13]

The objections of the European Union, which were supported by several countries,[14] bore allegiance to a certain perspective towards the institution of law. This perspective requires legal instruments to be unambiguous and certain. The introduction of a separate article on women with disabilities was not acceptable because it undermined this certainty. If the special articles on women and children were included, then 'there could be confusion between the interpretations of CEDAW or CRC and this convention. There could be the suggestion that CEDAW and CRC are inadequate for the protection of the rights of women and children with disabilities'. Further, this twin track approach could create

> an uneven comparison between disabled men and disabled women.... An example of such legal uncertainty lies in the inclusion of violence against women. While this may serve to provide further protection for women with disabilities it detracts from a general article on abuse, leaving men with disabilities in weaker position, when men are also very vulnerable to such abuse.[15]

Whilst the narration above captures the polarised opinions on the issue, the Chair's report at the sixth session of the Ad Hoc Committee provided a more balanced description of the deliberations. The report said that:

> All delegations agreed that the Convention needed to adequately address the situation of women with disabilities. There were different views expressed, however, on how best to achieve this aim in the Convention. Some delegations supported the proposal for a stand-alone article. Others suggested that a reference in the preamble combined with language in the general principles, the general obligations, or the monitoring section best met the aim. Others proposed to mainstream gender issues throughout thematic Articles of specific relevance to women. Others supported both a separate article in addition to mainstreamed references.[16]

In order to arrive at a consensus, the question on how the CRPD should address the concerns of women with disabilities was referred to a Facilitator.[17]

Before I analyse the specific proposals addressed to the Facilitator, it is important to remember that the fact of gender discrimination and the necessity to redress it were not being questioned in the Committee negotiating the CRPD. The dispute was not on the necessity of providing redress, but on how best to provide it. While States Parties proffered different opinions in the matter,[18] human rights institutions[19] stressed mainstreaming but were neutral about a special article;[20] disabled people's organisations, on the other hand, were nearly unanimous in asking for the adoption of a twin track approach.[21] This unanimity explains why it became increasingly more difficult for opposing states to persist with their more legalistic stand; whilst the move of the Ad Hoc Committee towards the less radical text can only be understood if the concerns of the opposing states are kept in view.

Proposals before the Ad Hoc committee

The proposals before the Ad Hoc Committee on issues concerning women with disabilities can be broadly categorised as minimal, middle-of-the-road and optimal.

Preamble plus proposal

The preamble to a convention contains its guiding philosophy. This philosophy is evocative in import, as the text of a preamble is not binding by law. Whilst it may be desirable for a State party to obtain guidance from the preamble, its failure to seek such guidance would not invite any sanctions. The European Union acknowledged that gender discrimination was rife and it also accepted the need to act in the matter; but it feared that an excessive concern for women with disabilities could weaken the Disability Convention. Therefore, in order to demonstrate its support in principle, it proposed that a clear commitment to address the issue of gender discrimination should be included in the preamble.[22]

The article containing the general obligations is a generic provision that specifies how states should fulfil their obligations under the Convention. As the European Union conceded that distinct implementation efforts may be required for improving the life situation of women with disabilities, it proposed that a specific clause dealing with gender discrimination should be included in the article listing the general obligations[23] or in the monitoring provisions. These proposals addressed the question of gender discrimination, with minimal modification to the main Convention, and thus can be said to adopt a minimalist approach.

Mainstreaming

Mainstreaming, like the minimalist approach, is an anti-discrimination strategy that has been devised to deal with the problem of unequal implementation. Whilst the minimalist approach attempts to tackle discrimination by a single mention in any one article dealing with implementation, mainstreaming is an exercise in repeatedly alerting the state to its gender equalisation responsibilities. Even as a number of states expressed a preference for this approach to address the problem of gender discrimination, Canada presented the most elaborate proposal for mainstreaming.[24]

The Canadian proposal required: first, a clear principle guaranteeing equal protection of the rights of women, along the lines of Article 3 of the International Covenant on Civil and Political Rights (ICCPR);[25] second, a general obligation to mainstream a gender perspective in all policies and programmes relating to persons with disabilities; and third, the inclusion of specific references in key articles of particular concern to women. Canada asked for such references to be specifically inserted in the articles dealing with equality and non-discrimination, violence and abuse, family, education, health and work. It is important to note that this approach does not posit any change in the normative structure to address the concerns of women with disabilities; it only serves to guard against the inequitable implementation of the norms. In the UNCRPD, mainstreaming aims to ensure equality of treatment to both women and men with disabilities. It is a middle-of-the-road approach that does not construct any special norms for women with disabilities, but uses the technique of reiteration to stress the need for overcoming gender discrimination.

Twin track

The twin track strategy sought to, simultaneously, incorporate both sameness and difference. On one track this strategy asks for mainstreaming; and on the other it demands special measures to address the injustices faced by women with disabilities. Even as the Republic of Korea was the flag-bearer of the twin track formula, there were other proposals from states[26] and civil society[27] also advocating, in the main, the same. All such proposals accorded greater importance to the special article, while the suggestions for mainstreaming were generally more open-ended.[28] This could be because the advocates of the twin track approach used the special article to outline their concerns for women with disabilities, even when a general article on the issue had been included in the Convention. For example, the case for reproductive rights, which was common to several proposals, was included in the special article and not in the general article on the right to health. Of similar purport were inclusions relating to violence and abuse, gender segregated social surveys, or non-discriminatory work environments. And since these values were easily compromised in relation to women with disabilities, explicit guarantees to uphold their respect, autonomy, dignity and safety were demanded in a number of proposals.[29]

The focus areas were not common to all proposals. Some proposals departed from the beaten track in the kind of interventions that they desired. For example, the Kenyan proposal asked for awareness programmes on 'single parenthood, negative cultural practices, and negative religious beliefs and practices'. This proposal also asked States Parties 'to address the special needs and provide necessary support, security, safety, and counselling for women with disabilities in situations of civil or natural calamities'.[30]

The most comprehensive list, however, came from the IDC.[31] The dedicated article was being proposed to obtain equality for girls and women with disabilities with boys and men with disabilities, as well as with non-disabled women and men. Whilst some states and civil society groups were content with mentioning these equalising aspirations in their lobbying documents, others wanted this objective to be appropriately reflected in the text of the special article.[32]

Even though the Facilitator's report showed a narrowing of differences between the various perspectives, the core issue of a special article on women with disabilities remained unsettled. The

Facilitator was not able to obtain a consensus on the issue of a special article, but succeeded in arriving at a text that could either be included in the article on general obligations or in the special article.[33] She also identified a number of other articles in the Convention in which a special mention of the concerns of women with disabilities could be made.[34]

Treaties that contain one of the most authoritative manifestations of international law like the CRPD are negotiated legal instruments. The law is arrived at through a process of agreement; and agreement requires consensus. The necessity for consensus often requires international law to be settled at the lowest common denominator. The final text on women with disabilities was produced, consequent to the interplay of the aforementioned competing perspectives, as also further refined by the Facilitator's report. This interplay was informed by the need to arrive at an agreement. It is, thus, not what each party wanted, but what it could not give up, that is reflected in the final text.

The adopted text

In due course the specific and detailed proposals of the early rounds gave way to all-encompassing but brief articles[35] — and the final text of the standalone article in the CRPD is both broad and brief. When the Republic of Korea initiated discussions, the proposed text required States Parties to undertake 'to ensure the enjoyment of full and equal rights and freedoms by women with disabilities and their equal participation in political, economic, social and cultural activities without any discrimination on the basis of their gender and/or disabilities'.[36]

The final text of the CRPD lists neither the rights nor the different kinds of discrimination. Instead, Article 6 (1) states that: 'States Parties recognize that women and girls with disabilities are subject to multiple discrimination, and in this regard shall take measures to ensure the full and equal enjoyment by them of all human rights and fundamental freedoms'.[37]

The text of the special article (Article 6 of CRPD) is a refined version of the Facilitator's text. The Facilitator, in her report, had not said that the text suggested by her should constitute the entire special article. The explanation for the adoption of the brief article probably lies in the give-and-take that informs international law. The foregoing narrative of the varied perspectives shows that while the minimalists were willing to recognise gender in the implementation provisions, they were not agreeable to any normative concessions. Their opposition to a dedicated article stemmed from this disagreement. The adopted Convention contains a dedicated article, but the article is not about the rights of the marked constituency, but about the obligations of States. Here, again (Article 6 [2]), the overarching motif is implementation. And to that end, States Parties are required to: 'take all appropriate measures to ensure the full development, advancement and empowerment of women, for the purpose of guaranteeing them the exercise and enjoyment of the human rights and fundamental freedoms set out in the present Convention'.[38]

Other than the special Article, gender concerns find mention in the Preamble[39] and in the Articles relating to: general principles;[40] awareness raising;[41] freedom from exploitation, violence and abuse;[42] health;[43] and adequate standard of living and social protection.[44] It can be seen that with the induction of the special article on women with disabilities, there has been a clear shrinkage in the number of articles meriting explicit mention of gender from the initial proposals, through the Facilitator's report, to the final text. Most significantly, there is no mention of gender discrimination in the article dealing with equality and non-discrimination. And despite a persistent demand, there is no explicit obligation to collect gender-specific statistics.[45]

Twin Track Approach: A Substantive Evaluation

The twin track approach for eradicating gender discrimination was put forward to provide for both sameness and difference to women with disabilities. In the previous section, I have recounted the process by which it was finally incorporated in the CRPD. In this section, I discuss the gains and losses of this strategy, and also speculate on its potential and limitations.

The twin track approach is driven by a weak engine due to the diluted text of Article 6. Such a description captures the weaknesses, but misses out on its strengths. The main strength resides in its demonstrative effect. The twin track approach is an acknowledgement of multiple discriminations, and an admission that women with disabilities need both sameness and difference. This admission, in an authoritative international legal instrument, could augur the initiation of complex strategies to eradicate gender discrimination. It may not be the strongest of beginnings, but that it is a beginning is undeniable. Moreover, it is a beginning with immense possibilities.

Although the Canadian proposal of mainstreaming may seem textually stronger, it did not win too much support. Consequently, the real contest was between the minimalist and twin track approaches. The final text seems to bear the form of the twin track and the content of the minimalist approaches. Consequently, States Parties will now have to specifically report on what measures they are taking for women with disabilities to advance the realisation of general human rights and rights under this Convention.[46] If the same duty had been included in the list of general obligations, it would have been one of several obligations of the State, and reporting on it could have been more easily fudged and diluted.[47]

A major limitation of Article 6 is the general wording of the text. At the same time, it is only because of this that consensus on inclusion of the Article could be arrived at in the first place. The fact is that general terms, such as 'multiple discrimination' and 'all rights', were easily agreed upon because they could encompass detailed lists of rights. According to the rules of treaty interpretation,[48] the preparatory papers can be used to obtain guidance on the objectives and meaning of a treaty's provisions. This rule can be used to tease out the abandoned elaborate proposals from the general terms used in the special articles. Disabled people's organisations, along with national and international monitoring authorities, could perform the task of culling specific proposals from the all-inclusive general provisions.[49] The all-encompassing right to participation, recognised in the Convention, would greatly assist these organisations in the performance of this duty.[50]

The mainstreaming track of the strategy can also be criticised for only taking on board the victim and marginalised visage of women with disabilities. This is borne out by the fact that freedom from exploitation (Article 16) and adequate standard of living and social protection (Article 28) of the CRPD expressly mention women. The proposals for introducing a gender dimension in the rights to education and work were evidently rejected.

Once the law and politics connection in international law is acknowledged, this track can also be seen in a different light. So, once a special article was agreed upon, it became difficult to contest the hard evidence of the violent and deprived lived reality of women with disabilities. It is the same life experiences that have caused gender to be explicitly mentioned in the article on health in the Convention (Article 25). These lived realities can be drawn upon to show why special measures are necessary. For the twin track to work, it is important that the provisions of both sets of articles are read in tandem. Thus, without an explicit acknowledgement of the deprivations, the raison d'être of the special measure would not be understood; and without the commitment to proactive initiatives, the victimhood trap would close in on women with disabilities.

This argument may not negate the desire for a stronger text, but wishes have to be ridden on available horses. International law is primarily the law of the possible; or rather the law of teasing out the desirable from the possible. Furthermore, there is a continual need to appreciate the symbiotic relationship between life and legal texts. It is this relationship that prevents legislators from racing ahead of their times, whilst encouraging adjudicators and administrators to dynamically interpret the law when it lags too far behind. The twin track is a soft induction of a complex new strategy to eradicate gender discrimination. This may seem limited in its textual form. Ironically, it is the same open-ended text that holds the promise of setting in place a complex process of eradicating discrimination against women with disabilities.

Conclusion

This essay began with the conundrum of universalism for excluded populations who draw upon the moral force of universal norms to challenge the unequal and discriminatory treatment meted out to them. Yet, this very process of seeking the same can result in a second round of exclusion for some excluded groups. This is so because the sameness of the universal has not been constructed keeping excluded populations in mind. This situation is difficult for bivalent collectivities, and especially for individuals and groups who are members of two bivalent collectivities, because they have to battle two kinds of cultural stereotypes. Identity politics and assertion of difference have been used to challenge cultural imperialism. However, women with disabilities are hard put to employ this strategy as they are confronted with a situation where society uses their disability to deny them access to the stereotypical roles of womanhood — that is, getting married, becoming mothers, and setting up a home and family.

The negotiations around the CRPD show that women with disabilities[51] have employed the human rights discourse to assert those very stereotypical roles that women are chafing under. In having to make this assertion, they are demonstrating the socially constructed nature of these roles. What they should or should not do with their bodies is socially dictated, both for women in general and for women with disabilities. The stereotype is a source of oppression for both categories of women; the former is oppressed by imposition of the stereotype and the latter by the exclusion from the stereotype. Even as these connections have been made in the writings of disabled women, they have not informed mainstream feminist theory and practice. Article 6 (1) of the CRPD, which requires States to take measures to ensure the full and equal enjoyment of all human rights and fundamental freedoms by women with disabilities, forges a vital link between CEDAW and the CRPD, along with other human rights instruments. This connection with CEDAW is not just an opportunity to root out numerous discriminatory practices perpetrated against women with disabilities; it is also to foundationally challenge the social construction of womanhood. It is an opportunity to create a feminist discourse that allows all women to escape the forced dichotomies surrounding family, work, beauty, femininity or motherhood, and to construct an enabling relationship between self and society. The feminisation of human rights through a celebration of human diversity and an acceptance of human interdependence could lead to the empowerment of all human beings.

Notes

* This essay first appeared in the *Indian Journal of Gender Studies*, 15 (2): 209–32, 2008, New Delhi: SAGE Publications. Editorial changes have been made to the original published chapter with permission from the Centre for Women's Development Studies, New Delhi.
1. The five faces of oppression that Iris Marion Young (1990) identifies are: exploitation, marginalisation, powerlessness, cultural imperialism and violence.
2. See Morris (1993: 60–61) for a critique of Dalley (1988), Finch and Groves (1983), Keith (1990), and Meekosha and Dowse (1997).
3. For the discrimination faced by women in employment due to pregnancy, see Huckle (1981) and Davis, Neathey, Regan and Willison (2005), and for the structural embedding of this discrimination, see Faber (2007).
4. This was done by General Comment 18 of CEDAW, which asked States Parties to devote special attention to women with disabilities.
5. This may be because the exhortative General Comment 18 of CEDAW has not yielded the expected results. It is also pertinent to point out that the choice made in CEDAW was of a piece with the manner in which the issue of gender discrimination was dealt with during the deliberations on the Universal Declaration of Human Rights (UDHR) and the Human Rights Conventions. The issue of normative distinctiveness was not raised. It was felt that a special committee could watch over the implementation of women's rights. The comfort with the logic of universalism can be seen from the fact that even the case for more inclusive terminology had to be vociferously argued. Eleanor Roosevelt, who was chairing the UDHR Committee, saw no need to substitute 'man' with 'person', whereas Hansa Mehta, the delegate from India, insisted on the change as she feared that 'man' could be used to exclude women. However, progressively, the surveillance on implementation of the strategy was found to be insufficient; and the need for explicit human rights instruments, which protected women's rights, came to be voiced. It is this advocacy that first resulted in the Declaration on the Elimination of Discrimination against Women (DEDAW), which in turn graduated to CEDAW. For an analytical narration of these developments, see Jain (2005).
6. In contrast to CEDAW, the Convention on the Rights of the Child (CRC) dealt with this issue by incorporating a dedicated article on children with disability (Article 23).
7. By resolution 56/168 of 19 December 2001, the General Assembly of the UN established an Ad Hoc Committee to consider proposals for a

comprehensive and integral international Convention to promote and protect the rights and dignity of persons with disabilities.
8. Along with women, children were the other population whose concerns were sought to be explicitly mentioned in the CRPD. The twin track approach was also adopted for children; and the working out of that approach makes a fascinating comparative story that needs to be told.
9. Ableism may be defined as discrimination in favour of the able-bodied and against disability.
10. 'Proposed Article 15 bis: Women with Disabilities', Report of the third session of the Ad Hoc Committee on a Comprehensive and Integral International Convention on the Protection and Promotion of the Rights and Dignity of Persons with Disabilities, UN Enable, 2003, www.un.org/esa/socdev/enable/rights/ahc3reporte.htm (accessed 6 May 2007).
11. 'Ad Hoc Committee — Daily Summaries', UN Convention on the Human Rights of People with Disabilities, UN Enable, 2 August 2005, http://www.un.org/esa/socdev/enable/rights/ahc6sum2aug.htm (accessed 6 May 2007).
12. Ibid.
13. Ibid.
14. Amongst the countries lending support were Australia, the former Serbia and Montenegro, New Zealand, Costa Rica and Mexico.
15. See http://www.un.org/esa/socdev/enable/rights/ahc6sum2aug.htm (accessed 6 May 2007).
16. Ibid.
17. The Chair's report at the sixth session on the matter stated that the facilitator, Theresia Degener of Germany, was asked 'to explore further the best approach and examine . . . gaps in the convention that needed to be addressed from a gender perspective', http://www.un.org/esa/socdev/enable/rights/ahc6reporte.htm (accessed 6 May 2007).
18. For example, the European Union, New Zealand, Australia, Mexico, Japan and Costa Rica supported a mention of the issue in the implementation provisions; Canada, India and Jordan favoured a mainstreaming approach; and Korea, El Salvador, Morocco, Thailand, Israel, Kenya, Sudan, Yemen, Uganda and Iran spoke in favour of a special article with or without the twin track. These opinions were voiced by the different States at the sixth session. For a report of the discussion of the day, see http://www.un.org/esa/socdev/enable/rights/ahc6sum2aug.htm (accessed 6 May 2007).
19. The Human Rights Commissions of various countries were accorded independent representational status in the negotiations, and were referred to as the 'human rights institutions'.
20. However, the human rights institutions did suggest that should there be a special article, then it should only be a statement of principles without

getting into specifics; see http://www.un.org/esa/socdev/enable/rights/ahc6sum2aug.htm (accessed 6 May 2007).
21. While the twin track approach was endorsed by the Korean Women's NGO, Disabled Peoples' International (DPI), Council of Canadians with Disabilities and the World Blind Union, the European Disability Forum Women's Committee asked for the adoption of the Canadian government's mainstreaming approach; see www.un.org/esa/socdev/enable/rights/ahc6sum2aug.htm (accessed 6 May 2007).
22. The European Union proposed the inclusion of two paragraphs in the preamble. The first paragraph addressed the issue of multiple discrimination by 'recognising that women and girls with disabilities are often subject to multiple discrimination and therefore face particular disadvantages, and bearing in mind the obligations of States Parties to ensure the full enjoyment of all human rights and fundamental freedoms by women and girls with disabilities on an equal basis with others'. The second paragraph dealt with the issue of violence by 'recognising that persons with disabilities, in particular women and girls, are often at greater risk, both within and outside the home, of violence, injury or abuse, neglect or negligent treatment, maltreatment or exploitation, including their gender based manifestations'; see www.un.org/esa/socdev/enable/rights/ahcstata6sscomments.htm#eu (accessed 6 May 2007).
23 The proposed obligation required States Parties 'to take all necessary measures to ensure the full and equal enjoyment of all human rights by women with disabilities on an equal basis with others, bearing in mind the general obligation to ensure equality between women and men'.
24. Other than Canada, preference for this approach came from India, Jordan and the human rights institutions.
25. Article 3 of the ICCPR lays down that 'States Parties to the present Covenant undertake to ensure the equal rights of men and women to the enjoyment of all civil and political rights set forth in the present Covenant'.
26. Thus, whilst Kenya put forth a separate proposal in the sixth session (www.un.org/esa/socdev/enable/rights/ahcstata6sscomments.htm#kenya, accessed 6 May 2007), Australia (www.un.org/esa/socdev/enable/rights/ahcstata6sevscomments.htm#australia, accessed 6 May 2007), China (www.un.org/esa/socdev/enable/rights/ahcstata6sevscomments.htm#china, accessed 6 May 2007) and South Africa (www.un.org/esa/socdev/enable/rights/ahcstata6sevscomments.htm#sa, accessed 6 May 2007) made proposals amending the Facilitator's text in the seventh session. And Korea also submitted a modified version of its original proposal in this session (www.un.org/esa/socdev/enable/rights/ahcstata6sevscomments.htm#korea, accessed 6 May 2007).

27. Such proposals came from the International Disability Caucus (IDC) and the Women's IDC (www.un.org/esa/socdev/enable/rights/ ahcstata6sevscomments.htm#idc, accessed 6 May, 2007), International Disability Convention Solidarity in Korea (IDCSK) http://www.un.org/ esa/socdev/enable/rights/ahcstata6sevscomments.htm#idcsk, accessed 6 May 2007) and People with Disability, Australia (www.un.org/esa/ socdev/enable/rights/ahcstata6sevscomments.htm#pwda, accessed 6 May 2007).
28. The proposal of the IDC was, to that extent, an aberration, as it named the Convention articles where it sought gender mainstreaming, that is, in the general principles (Article 3) and the general obligations (Article 4) and in Article 5 on equality and non-discrimination.
29. See, for example, the proposals from the Republic of Korea, International Disability Caucus (IDC) and the International Disability Convention Solidarity in South Korea (IDCSK).
30. See www.un.org/esa/socdev/enable/rights/ahcstata6sscomments. htm#kenya (accessed 6 May 2007).
31. The Proposal of the IDC asked States parties to develop 'pro-active measures and policies to ensure that women and girls with disabilities of all ages enjoy the same opportunities and rights as others. To this effect States Parties shall ensure that women and girls with disabilities shall ensure: (*a*) full access to programs and measures related to areas such as, but not limited to information, finances, family relations, education, training, health care, habilitation and rehabilitation and employment; (*b*) the right to sexuality, motherhood, adoptions, support during pregnancy and childbirth, postpartum health care and child-care and necessary assistance in this regard; (*c*) freedom from abuse, violence, sexual exploitation, marginalization and forced medical and pharmaceutical experimentation; (*d*) full access to development programs such as microfinance and independent economic viability programs in order to overcome poverty and financial dependence; (e) access to all programmes and measures for the general population, whether gender mainstreamed or gender specific; (*f*) participation in public decision-making, policymaking and self-representation through organizations, on a basis of equality between women and men; (*g*) participation in policymaking related to gender on a basis of equality with other women, and participation in policymaking related to disability on a basis of equality between women and men; (*h*) participation, on a basis of equality between women and men, at all stages of implementation and monitoring of this Convention'. See http://www.un.org/esa/socdev/ enable/rights/ahcstata6sscomments.htm#idc (accessed 6 May 2007).
32. See, for example, the suggestion for change made by South Africa, where it sought that women and girls with disabilities enjoy all human rights and fundamental freedoms on the basis of equality not just with men and

boys with disabilities, but also with women and girls with no disabilities (www.un.org/esa/socdev/enable/rights/ahcstata6sevscomments. htm#sa, accessed 6 May 2007). And the IDC supported the twin track approach so that women with disabilities enjoy equality with men with disabilities and non-disabled men and women (www.un.org/esa/socdev/ enable/rights/ahcstata6sevscomments.htm#idc, accessed 6 May 2007).

33. States Parties recognise that women and girls with disabilities are subject to multiple discrimination, and that focused empowerment and gender-sensitive measures are necessary to ensure the full and equal enjoyment by women and girls with disabilities of all human rights and fundamental freedoms. States Parties shall take all appropriate measures to ensure the equal rights of women with disabilities to the enjoyment of all rights set out in this Convention; see www.un.org/esa/socdev/enable/rights/ ahcstata6sevsfacilitator.htm (accessed 6 May 2007).

34. These concerns were: awareness raising; freedom from exploitation, violence and abuse; respect for home and family; health; statistics and data collection; national implementation and monitoring; and international monitoring; see www.un.org/esa/socdev/enable/rights/ ahcstata6sevsfacilitator.htm (accessed 6 May 2007).

35. See, for example, the four different proposals on Article 6 that were floated as consensus texts in the eighth session by Canada; Egypt, Morocco, Sudan, Syria, Qatar and Saudi Arabia; the European Union; and El Salvador, Venezuela, Guatemala, Mexico, Chile, Colombia, Argentina, Costa Rica, the Dominican Republic, Panama, Cuba, Trinidad and Tobago, and Jamaica (www.un.org/esa/socdev/enable/ rights/ahc8gpcart6.htm, accessed 6 May 2007).

36. See www.un.org/esa/socdev/enable/rights/ahcstata6tscompilation. htm (accessed 6 May 2007).

37. See www.un.org/esa/socdev/enable/rights/convtexte.htm (accessed 6 May 2007).

38. Ibid.

39. Paragraph (q) of the Preamble of CRPD recognises 'that women and girls with disabilities are often at greater risk, both within and outside the home, of violence, injury or abuse, neglect or negligent treatment, maltreatment or exploitation'; and paragraph (s) emphasises 'the need to incorporate a gender perspective in all efforts to promote the full enjoyment of human rights and fundamental freedoms by persons with disabilities'. Paragraph (p) flags the whole gamut of multiple discrimination by expressing concern 'about the difficult conditions faced by persons with disabilities who are subject to multiple or aggravated forms of discrimination on the basis of race, colour, sex, language, religion, political or other opinion, national, ethnic, indigenous or social origin, property, birth, age or other status' (ibid.).

40. Paragraph (g) of Article 3 of the CRPD includes 'equality between men and women' along with respect for dignity, individual autonomy and independence of persons; nondiscrimination; full and effective participation and inclusion in society; respect for difference and human diversity; equality of opportunity; accessibility; and evolving capacities of children with disabilities as the general principles of the CRPD.
41. Article 8 (b) of the CRPD requires States Parties to adopt immediate, effective and appropriate measures 'to combat stereotypes, prejudices and harmful practices relating to persons with disabilities, including those based on sex and age, in all areas of life'.
42. In Article 16 of the CRPD, the States Parties are required to undertake their protective, preventive, investigative and rehabilitative activities in a gender-sensitive manner. Gender and age, either cumulatively or separately, find mention in all the five paragraphs of the Article.
43. The grant of appropriate health services and protection of reproductive health found mention in virtually every proposal advocating the rights of women with disabilities. The heading of Article 25 acknowledges this concern by asking States Parties to 'take all appropriate measures to ensure access for persons with disabilities to health services that are gender-sensitive, including health related rehabilitation'. In paragraph (a) of Article 25, an obligation to provide persons with disabilities with programmes in the area of sexual and reproductive health has been expressly mentioned.
44. While setting out the social protection obligations of the state, Article 28: 2 (b) of the CRPD requires States Parties 'to ensure access by persons with disabilities, in particular women and girls with disabilities and older persons with disabilities, to social protection programmes and poverty reduction programmes'.
45. See http://www.un.org/esa/socdev/enable/rights/ahc8gpcart6.htm (accessed 6 May 2007). This recommendation, incidentally, even made it to the Facilitator's report. See note 47.
46. States Parties are required to file implementation reports before the Treaty Monitoring Body. The States Parties are mandated by the reporting process to file specific reports for each article.
47. Here, it may also be noted that the text of the special Article 6 is more explicit than the one proposed by the European Union for inclusion in the general obligations.
48. Article 32 of the Vienna Convention provides for consultation of the preparatory papers to confirm or clarify an ambiguous meaning.
49. Article 33 of the CRPD provides for national monitoring, and Article 34 establishes the treaty body that will oversee international monitoring.
50. Article 4 (3) of the CRPD requires States Parties to closely consult and actively involve persons with disabilities in the development and implementation of legislation and policies to implement the Convention.

51. It may be pertinent to point out that the Women's IDC was primarily composed of women with disabilities. The NGO leadership was assumed by the Women's IDC, which forged alliances with various women with disabilities who were members of State delegations.

References

Begum, Nasa. 1992. 'Disabled Women and the Feminist Agenda', *Feminist Review*, 40 (1): 70–84.

Dalley, Gillian. 1988. *Ideologies of Caring: Rethinking Community and Collectivism*. London: Macmillan Education.

Davis, Sara, Fiona Neathy, Jo Regan and Rebecca Willison. 2005. 'Pregnancy Discrimination at Work: A Qualitative Study', Working Paper Series No. 23, Equal Opportunities Commission, Sydney.

Dhanda, Amita. 1994. 'Womb Removal of Women with Mental Retardation: Constitutional Constraints on State Power', *Samadhan News*, 11 (1): 3–15.

Faber, Emily Miyamoto. 2007. 'Pregnancy Discrimination in Latin America: The Exclusion of "Employment Discrimination" from the Definition of "Labour Laws" in the Central American Free Trade Agreement', *Columbia Journal of Gender and Law*, 16 (1): 297–336.

Finch, Janet and Dulcie Groves (eds). 1983. *A Labour of Love: Women, Work and Caring*. London: Routledge and Kegan Paul.

Fine, Michelle and Adrienne Asch. 1988. 'Introduction: Beyond Pedestals', in Michelle Fine and Adrienne Asch (eds), *Women with Disabilities: Essays in Psychology, Culture and Politics*, pp. 1–37. Philadelphia: Temple University Press.

Fraser, Nancy. 1997. *Justice Interruptus: Critical Reflections on the 'Postsocialist' Condition*. New York and London: Routledge and Kegan Paul.

———. 2001. 'Recognition without Ethics', *Theory, Culture and Society*, 18 (1): 21–42.

French, Catherine M. 2005. 'Protecting the "Right" to Choose of Women Who are Incompetent: Ethical, Doctrinal and Practical Arguments against Fetal Representation', *Case Western Research Law Review*, 56 (3): 511.

Gerschick, Thomas J. 2000. 'Toward a Theory of Disability and Gender', *Signs*, 25 (4): 1263–68.

Ghai, Anita. 2003. *(Dis)Embodied Form: Issues of Disabled Women*. New Delhi: Shakti Books, Har-Anand Publications.

Goldhar, Jeff. 1991. 'The Sterilization of Women with an Intellectual Disability', *University of Tasmania Law Review*, 10 (1): 157–96.

Hans, Asha. 2003. 'Introduction', in Asha Hans and Annie Patri (eds), *Women, Disability and Identity*, pp. 11–39. New Delhi: SAGE Publications.
Huckle, Patricia. 1981. 'The Womb Factor: Pregnancy Policies and Employment of Women', *Western Political Quarterly*, 34 (1): 114–26.
Hugemark, Agneta and Christine Roman. 2002. 'Disability, Gender and Social Justice Claims for Redistribution and Recognition in the Disability Movement'. Working Paper Series, Uppsala University, Sweden, http://www.soc.uu.se/Download.aspx?id=38wjQVqspBY%3D (accessed 22 August 2012).
Jain, Devaki. 2005. *Women, Development, and the UN: A Sixty-Year Quest for Equality and Justice*. Hyderabad: Orient Longman.
Keith, Lois. 1990. 'Caring Partnership', *Community Care*, pp. 5–6, 22 February.
Meekosha, Helen and Leanne Dowse. 1997. 'Enabling Citizenship: Gender, Disability and Citizenship in Australia', *Feminist Review*, 57: 49–72.
Morris, Jenny. 1993. 'Feminism and Disability', *Feminist Review*, 43: 57–70.
Wolf, Naomi. 1991. *The Beauty Myth: How Images of Beauty Are Used Against Women*. New York: William Morrow.
Young, Iris Marion. 1990. *Justice and the Politics of Difference*. Princeton, NJ: Princeton University Press.

17

Participation, Inclusion and the Law: Moving beyond Rhetoric

JEEJA GHOSH

This essay begins with the rhetorical query whether law is adequate in itself to ameliorate the plight of disabled persons, particularly disabled women, in society. Subsequently, the author, a disability rights activist herself, highlights the need for actualising social participation which she identifies as the most important vehicle for social inclusion. The author concludes that without social and economic inputs, law cannot on its own bring about substantial change.

In recent times, there has been a paradigm shift in the way disability and disabled people are viewed and understood. We have moved from a medical and individual-based approach to a human rights-based approach. This shift has resulted in the signing of the landmark United Nations Convention on the Rights of Persons with Disabilities (UNCRPD). The main slogan here is 'nothing about us without us' (Charlton 1998). The UNCRPD is an unconventional legislation, which, for the first time, acknowledges that disabled people have the same rights as non-disabled persons to participate in family life: marry, give birth, or adopt children.

The Convention identifies disabled women as a doubly marginalised group, whose specific interests need to be protected. The interests of disabled women are not particularly prevalent within the Indian disability legislation. Except for the National

Policy for Persons with Disabilities, the major disability legislation is silent on the issue of disabled women. Even the National Policy limits itself to issues of education and employment. The concerns of sexual and reproductive health are completely overlooked in this document.

The most common word in the vocabulary of the contemporary social milieu is inclusion. Inclusion simply means that all people of diverse backgrounds (irrespective of their caste, class, religion, ethnicity, gender, or sexual preference) have equal rights in all spheres of life. Inclusion is a holistic concept with six prerequisites: namely, attitude, acceptance, access, accommodation, assimilation and acknowledgement. Total inclusion cannot be actualised without social participation. For the purpose of this discussion, social participation includes access to leisure activities, participation in social functions, interaction with family, friends and outsiders, and opportunities to socialise with the peer group to develop intimate relationships. Our conservative social norms lay down stringent rules on disabled people's expression of their sexuality. Social inclusion becomes a reality when a synthesis takes place among the above mentioned criteria. In other words, inclusion is possible with the removal of both structural and attitudinal barriers.

The extent of social participation and expression of sexuality is also regulated by gender. Disabled people, especially disabled women, are relegated to the backwaters as far as sexual expression is concerned. Disabled women themselves internalise this subtle oppression, and are socialised to negate their sexuality.

This can be understood under the purview of internalised oppression. The concept of internalised oppression finds place in the writings of Reeve (2002). According to Reeve, the psycho-emotional dimensions of disability point to what disabled people can be, ignoring their abilities. This kind of reaction, rooted in the negative attitudes and prejudice of the society towards disabled people, leaves them being hurt, made to feel worthless and unattractive. One important aspect includes the way people respond emotionally to social exclusion and physical barriers, such as feelings of anger and frustration, when they encounter inaccessible buildings. Another aspect of this form of oppression can include the emotional responses to the social reactions of other people. This can be manifested in instances such as feeling ashamed when stared at in the streets. This kind of emotional disablism can be called internalised oppression.

The concept of internalised oppression has been aptly captured in an example cited by Ghai (2003). The author cites that in the north Indian culture, girls are not allowed to sleep in the same room as male members of their family, particularly cousins. This custom, however, does not hold true for disabled girls and women, thus giving them the signal that their sexuality is the least important aspect of their existence, and proclaiming them as asexual.

This is further reinforced by the priority and importance given to beauty and body perfection to promote the consumerist market. Advertisements of products reiterate the social approval of conventional beauty and perfection, and rejection of the imperfect. Thus, for the physically disabled woman, her impaired body becomes a symbol of imperfection and rejection.

Social inclusion is directly linked with economic inclusion. In a consumerist society, leisure is not free. Ironically, given the status of employment of disabled people, it is apparent the free access to leisure becomes a barrier both in terms of economic amenities as well as physical infrastructure. Thus, this is also a contributing factor to social isolation.

While being a critical tool of empowerment, legislation alone is not adequate to attain social inclusion of disabled people. A whole range of social, economic, political and cultural factors have to be simultaneously confronted to create the necessary conditions for disabled persons to participate in the social mainstream as equal citizens; only then can the goals of total inclusion be achieved.

Paradigm Shift

There has been, over the course of the last few decades, a change in the perspective of how disabled people are viewed by society. This change is the outcome of a paradigm shift. The focus has shifted from the medical or welfare approach towards a social and rights-based model. The underlying philosophy is that disabled people are no longer objects of welfare and pity, but instead are subjects having equal rights to all amenities enjoyed by their non-disabled counterparts. The Disabled Peoples' International (DPI) came up with the slogan 'Nothing about us without us' — disabled people claimed to be equal partners in all decisions regarding their lives and not just passive recipients of charity.

The rights-based approach shifts the cause of disablement of a person from individual impairment to the barriers in the physical environment and to social attitudes. There has been an overall transition in the perspective in the way disability and disabled people are viewed and understood. Research and advocacy have shifted from treatment, cure and rehabilitation to inclusion and empowerment. Indeed, there is a shift in focus from the disabling society to emancipation and empowerment of disabled people. The solution to the problem of disablement has been located in the creation of barrier-free environments, a distinct shift from medical treatment and expert advice.

Looking at the national laws and policies on disabled people in India, we find that the most prominent legislation, namely, The Persons with Disabilities (Equal Opportunities, Protection of Rights and Full Participation) Act, 1995, completely overlooks the particular concerns of disabled women. Sexuality and reproductive child health issues are absent in its provisions. The Act is silent on the disabled people's right to marry and set up a family. The National Policy for Persons with Disabilities, which was announced in February 2006, lays emphasis on employment and training of disabled women; but again, sexual and reproductive health concerns of disabled women are missing in this policy document.

Strategies for Inclusion

The belief in the rights-based approach has given rise to the historic UNCRPD, which was declared an international law in May 2008. India is a signatory to this Convention. The Convention promotes and protects the civil, social, economic, political, cultural, health and reproductive rights of disabled people, unequivocally guaranteeing their entitlement to full and equal enjoyment of all human rights and fundamental freedoms. If effectively used,

UNCRPD has the potential to bring about an inclusive society through social participation. For the first time, there is a legal recognition that disabled people are people first, with all human needs. Their rights are not just restricted to education and employment, but extend further to include rights to a family life, recreation and leisure.

UNCRPD talks of 'universal design', which holds that all products, environments and services are to be designed in a manner so that they can be used by all persons to the fullest possible extent. This implies that disabled people are to be considered an integral part of society, and there is a mandate to guarantee their inclusion in all policies and programmes. Article 9 has broadened the concept of accessibility, which is not just restricted to the physical or built environment. It incorporates accessibility to transport, information and communication technologies. Hence, accessibility is an all-encompassing concept covering all areas of life. The UNCRPD also recognises the right of disabled people to participate in cultural life, leisure and sports. Article 30 acknowledges sign language and Deaf culture as a separate cultural entity.

Article 6 of UNCRPD states that the signatory countries should recognise that disabled women are subject to multiple discriminations and, therefore, specific measures are required to ensure full enjoyment of their human rights and fundamental freedoms. The Convention further ensures the expression of sexuality of disabled people is not overlooked. Article 23 stipulates that the signatory countries will take action to stop discrimination against people with disabilities, when it comes to issues of marriage and family relations. People with disabilities have the same rights as other people to lead a sexually active life, to marry and have children, to decide how many children to have and when to have them. They should get information and be educated on reproduction health and family planning; and they should receive assistance, wherever and whenever necessary, to understand this information. Guardianship and adoption also have to be addressed, with the most important issue being the children's interest. Support to people with disabilities in accomplishing responsibilities related to raising their children also have to be guaranteed by the signatories to the Convention.

Legislation, including international laws like the UNCRPD, is a significant tool to ensure the rights of disabled people. However, legislation alone is not enough to bring about marked changed in their lives. There are other social factors which need to be considered for enhancing the social participation of disabled people. The major barriers to social participation of disabled people are discussed in the following sections.

Barriers to social participation: The gender factor

Incident 1:

In a special school for disabled people, the teachers had taken a decision to introduce sex education classes for adolescent girls. This was vehemently opposed by the parents who felt such classes have the potential to ignite false aspirations in their daughters, which, in turn, are likely to hamper their wellbeing. In another sense, they implied that the presence of visible impairments was a justification for denial of their existence as sexual beings.

Gender is a determining factor as far as social participation is concerned. This holds true for both disabled and non-disabled people. The suppression of women stems from the patriarchal nature of Indian society. Social and religious order in Indian society lays stringent regulations on expression of sexuality, especially of women. Sex and sexuality in the Indian social context are legitimately accepted only within the parameters of marriage.

Sexuality is given least importance in the case of disabled people, especially disabled women. Disabled people are usually labelled asexual — thus totally negating their identity as sexual beings. Disabilities, as well as gender, are products of society's conceptualisations on, and attitudes to, both disability and gender. The notion that disabled people are asexual is even reflected in the disabled women's own conception of themselves.

While conducting her study on disabled women, Indian feminist and disability activist, Anita Ghai (2003), found that the most difficult discussions were around sexuality. Most disabled women she talked to did not have the words to express their sexuality. According to Ghai, in our Indian culture any departure from socially accepted standard norms is marked as a deviation.

Hence, an impaired body becomes a symbol of imperfection. The myth of the beautiful body defines the impaired female body as unfeminine and unacceptable. Since sexuality is defined within the parameters of marriage and disabled women are generally held to be asexual, therefore, they are not considered eligible to enter matrimony. Ghai cites an example from north Indian culture where disabled girls are allowed to sleep in the same room as their male cousins. However, this norm is not applicable to non-disabled girls, the underlying assumption being that a disabled girl, being intrinsically asexual, is not likely to invite any sexual advances, even in such an intimate setting.

Incident 2:

> Riya is a married working woman. Her mobility has been severely impaired by polio in childhood. Her parents were furious with her when she conceived — they blamed her husband for taking advantage of her.

Jo Campling (1981) also cites a similar example where a visually impaired woman was advised by medical professionals to undergo an abortion, because they considered her incapable of shouldering the responsibilities associated with motherhood.

There is almost a universal attachment with the non-disabled body. As Priestley (2003) writes, the body is a powerful symbol of identity in a consumer culture, and the mass marketing of the youthful body image has created a near universal attachment to the goal of 'eternal youth'. Thus, the consumerist idealisation of the youthful body is associated with both normative construction — as fit and functional — and its aesthetic beauty and sexual potential. The normalisation of youthful bodily ideals, in terms of functional and sexual desirability, contributes directly to the negative construction of disability as the obvious and natural obverse. Disabled people are disadvantaged by the enforced normalcy of bodily appearance arising from regulating physical characteristic. Thus, 'the myth of body perfection' becomes an important and long-standing factor in portraying people with visible physical impairments as inferior and damaged. This, in turn, becomes a source of social exclusion.

Barriers to social participation: The economics of leisure

Sexuality, social participation and social and economic inclusion are intertwined. It is difficult to achieve one without the other. Access to amenities entails access to economic resources. In a consumerist society, leisure activities are not really 'free' — they relate to people's position in the family and labour market (ibid.). This has particular relevance to disabled people's absence in leisure activities.

Researches on leisure activities show that participation in leisure and sporting activities is generally low in the case of young people with physical impairments. Access barriers and lack of money play a significant role here. This is of particular importance in a country like India. According to the Census of 2001, only 34.49 per cent of the disabled population is employed. In such a situation, 'buying' leisure activities become difficult and, indeed, luxurious for this group.

Barriers to social participation: Architectural and social factors

However, even those who have the resources to purchase leisure are faced with structural barriers. Hardly any places of entertainment are equipped to accommodate disabled people. Ramps, lifts and wheelchair-accessible toilets still remain a distant reality. The few cinema halls and shopping malls that boast of providing access for all are too highly priced, and are thus out of bounds for most disabled people. In such circumstances, disabled people are left with very little option but to remain confined to their homes.

Here again, the attitudinal barrier comes into play. Disabled people often find themselves socially isolated, as neighbours are sometimes reluctant or hesitant to interact with them. Hence, the family remains the only outlet for many disabled people. This is also liable to undergo change as siblings set up their own families and move on in life, while old parents are mostly left to provide company to the disabled individual.

Conclusion

Social inclusion of disabled people cannot simply be achieved through legislation, even though it is likely to play an important role in ensuring the human rights of all citizens, including disabled people. As discussed earlier, the UNCRPD envisages a society where disabled people become an integral part of the social milieu, and inclusion is achieved in its true sense. However, social participation of disabled people requires something more than mere legislation. It involves a change in perspective to view disabled people as 'people first' beyond their visible impairments. It calls for a change in attitude and the flexibility to unconditionally accept and accommodate them.

References

Campling, Jo (ed.). 1981. *Images of Ourselves: Women with Disabilities Talking*. London/Boston: Routledge and Kegan Paul.

Charlton, James I. 1998. *Nothing About Us Without Us: Disability Oppression and Empowerment*. Berkeley and London: University of California Press.

Ghai, Anita. 2003. *(Dis)Embodied Form: Issues of Disabled Women*. New Delhi: Har-Anand Publications Pvt. Ltd.

Priestley, Mark. 2003. *Disability: A Life Course Approach*. Cambridge: Polity Press.

Reeve, Donna. 2002. 'Negotiating Psycho-emotional Dimensions of Disability and their Influence on Identity Constructions', *Disability and Society*, 17 (5): 493–508.

ABOUT THE EDITOR

Renu Addlakha is Associate Professor at the Centre for Women's Development Studies, New Delhi. Her areas of interest include the sociology of medicine, mental illness and the psychiatric profession, public health, anthropology of infectious diseases, bioethics, gender and the family, disability and society. She is the author of *Deconstructing Mental Illness: An Ethnography of Psychiatry, Women, and the Family* (2008) and *Contemporary Perspectives on Disability in India: Exploring the Linkages between Law, Gender and Experience* (2011), and the co-editor of *Disability and Society: A Reader* (2009).

NOTES ON CONTRIBUTORS

S. B. Agnihotri is currently Consultant to UNICEF Kolkata on policy analysis and child nutrition. He joined the Indian Administrative Service in 1980 and has held executive positions in Orissa. He holds a Ph.D. and an M.A. in Rural Development from the School of Development Studies, University of East Anglia, Norwich. He also has M.Sc. degrees in Physics and Environmental Science and Engineering from the Indian Institute of Technology (IIT), Bombay. His research interests include gender inequality, policy research on infant and child mortality, child nutrition programmes, and use of mapping techniques in social policy research.

Shilpaa Anand is Assistant Professor at the Department of English Literature, The English and Foreign Languages University, Hyderabad. She received a Ph.D. in the Disability Studies Programme at the University of Illinois, Chicago. She also has an M.A. in English from the University of Hyderabad, and a diploma in Cultural Studies from the Centre for the Study of Culture and Society, Bangalore. Besides working as a special educator, Anand works with a women's grassroots organisation in the old city area of Hyderabad. Her research interests include the history of disability, disablement as a concept, theories of cultural difference, and epistemology.

Partho Bhowmick is a business consultant and freelance photographer based in Mumbai, initiator of the 'Blind With Camera' project, and the founder of Beyond Sight Foundation, Mumbai. He is an independent researcher on 'Art by the Blind' and is involved in promoting disability art and culture in India.

Upali Chakravarti is pursuing a Ph.D. in the area of disability and health from the Centre of Social Medicine and Community Health, Jawaharlal Nehru University, New Delhi. She also teaches

Psychology at the Department of Elementary Education, Miranda House, University of Delhi.

Jagdish Chander is Associate Professor at the Department of Political Science, Hindu College, University of Delhi. He completed his post graduation and M.Phil. in Political Science from University of Delhi and joined the teaching faculty at Hindu College in 1992. He is a Ph.D. candidate in Disability Studies at Syracuse University, New York. He was among the founding members of the Disability Rights Group, the first cross-disability rights organisation in Delhi. Chander was also a member of the special committee set up by the Chief Commissioner on Disability in July 2001 to recommend amendments in the Constitution of India for ensuring equal rights of disabled persons. He has presented papers at several international conferences and has published on the role of residential schools in advocacy movement of the blind and on inclusive education in India.

Bhargavi V. Davar is Director at the Centre for Advocacy in Mental Health in Pune. A pioneering researcher and mental health activist, Davar has written extensively on mental health from a range of perspectives. Her major publications include *Mental Health of Indian Women: A Feminist Agenda* (1999) and *Mental Health from a Gender Perspective* (2001).

Amita Dhanda is Professor at the National Academy of Legal Studies and Research (NALSAR), Hyderabad. She is also Visiting Fellow at the Faculty of Law, University of New South Wales, where she has been exploring the intersections between CEDAW and the newly adopted Disability Rights Convention. Her services have been utilised by the Supreme Court of India to investigate and advise on the problem of persons with mental illness being housed in prisons. She also headed a high-powered committee formed by the Government of India to suggest amendments to the Persons with Disabilities (Equal Opportunities, Protection of Rights and Full Participation) Act, 1995. More recently, she has been actively involved in the deliberations of the United Nations Ad Hoc Committee which negotiated the Disability Rights Convention. She is the author of *Legal Order and Mental Disorder* (2000).

Michele Friedner has a Ph.D. in Medical Anthropology from the University of California, Berkeley. She has researched on Deafness in India and published a number of pioneering articles on identity construction, vocation training, neo-liberal economics and disability.

Anita Ghai is Associate Professor at the Department of Psychology, Jesus and Mary College, University of Delhi. She researches in the area of disability focusing especially on education, health and gender. She is the author of *(Dis)Embodied Form: Issues of Disabled Women* (2003) and *The Mentally Handicapped: Prediction of Work Performance* (with Anima Sen, 1996). She is on the editorial board of *Disability and Society, Disability Studies Quarterly, Disability, Culture and Education,* and *Scandinavian Journal of Disability Research*. She has served on the executive boards of many NGOs as well as Planning Commissions. She was appointed by the National Trust for Welfare of Persons with Autism, Cerebral Palsy, Mental Retardation and Multiple Disability, Government of India, to be a member of the local guardianship committee for southwest Delhi.

Jeeja Ghosh is a disabled rights activist. She completed her M.A. in Social Work from University of Delhi, and an additional M.A. in Disability Studies from Leeds University, UK. She has been involved in the advocacy movement for people with disabilities for the last 14 years with a special interest in women with disabilities. She now works with the Spastics Society of Eastern India.

Nandini Ghosh is Assistant Professor at the Institute of Development Studies, Kolkata. She received her Ph.D. from the Tata Institute of Social Sciences, Mumbai, in the area of gender and disability. She has a B.A. in Sociology from Presidency College, Kolkata, and an M.A. in Sociology from the University of Kolkata. She has worked for nearly eight years in the field of disability as a development worker and activist with grassroots-level organisations in West Bengal and Jharkhand.

Asha Hans is former Director of the School of Women's Studies, and Professor and Head of the Department of Political Science, Utkal University, Bhubaneswar. A Fulbright Scholar and recipient of the Kathleen Ptolemy Award from York University, Canada, her work has mainly focused on issues of gender, international relations and, more recently, gender and disability. She has co-edited (with Annie Patri) *Women, Disability and Identity* (2003).

Rachana Johri teaches Psychology at Lady Shri Ram College for Women, University of Delhi. Her work explores gender and motherhood in cultural contexts. Her Ph.D. dissertation examines the experience of mothering daughters in the context of son-preference. Her other areas of interest include disability.

Sandhya Limaye is Associate Professor at the Centre for Disability Studies and Action, School of Social Work, Tata Institute of Social Sciences, Mumbai. She has an M.Phil. and Ph.D. in Social Work. Her dissertation examines parental efforts in the developmental tasks of adolescent children with hearing impairment. She has published on deafness in national and international journals as also books.

José Abad Lorente is an artist, curator and Director of Abadi Art Space in New Delhi. He has an M.A. in Photography and Urban Cultures from Goldsmiths College, University of London, and a degree in Advanced Studies in Chinese Art and Calligraphy from the Central Academy of Fine Arts, Beijing. Some of his recent art projects and exhibitions in India include 'Engendered Space: Can you see Me?' (2012), 'Decadence — a Present History' (2012), 'The Solo Show Project' (2011–12), and 'The Colours Exhibition' (2011–12). Lorente has also curated exhibitions in China, Spain and the United Kingdom. He conducts workshops that explore social themes, and addresses his works to marginal communities where self-expression, interaction and communication play the main role.

Nilika Mehrotra is a social anthropologist and Associate Professor at the Centre for the Study of Social Systems, Jawaharlal Nehru University, New Delhi. Earlier, she taught at the departments of Anthropology and Sociology, University of Delhi. She has been researching on gender issues for nearly two decades. Her previous work was on women's organisations and activism in India. She has also worked on gender, property and development issues. Of late, she has been working on gender and disability with special reference to north India.

Amrita Patel is Lecturer at the School of Women's Studies, Utkal University, Bhubaneswar. She has been engaged in research, training and advocacy on women's issues for more than a decade. She was involved in the first gender budget analysis undertaken for the state of Orissa. Patel has worked with the government, NGOs, the United Nations (UNDP, UNIFEM, UNICEF-DFID), and a number of other donor agencies such as the Commonwealth Foundation, Dan Church Aid, and Catholic Relief Services.

N. Sundaresan is an independent researcher and advocate on disability issues. He received his Ph.D. from Pondicherry University, which he completed after leaving his service with the government. His dissertation is entitled 'Law and the Disabled: Implementation and Strategies in the Indian Context'. He has participated in a number of conferences, workshops and seminars on disability in India and overseas.

Amit Upadhyay is pursuing his doctoral research on conceptual history of rights in India at the Department of Sociology, University of Hyderabad. He has an M.Phil. in Evidence-Based Social Work from the University of Oxford, and and M.A. in Sociology from the University of Hyderabad. He is a member of the Oxford Human Rights Hub, and has worked as a Research Officer at the Institute for Social and Economic Change, Bangalore. His recent publications include study material for the M.A. programme in Gender and Women's Studies at the Indira Gandhi National Open University.

Shubhangi Vaidya is Assistant Professor at the School of Inter-Disciplinary and Trans-Disciplinary Studies, Indira Gandhi National Open University, New Delhi. She completed her Ph.D. from the Centre for the Study of Social Systems, Jawaharlal Nehru University, New Delhi. Her dissertation is on the sociological study of families of autistic children in Delhi. A parent of a child with autism, she is interested in research pertaining to disability, family and culture which is informed by a rights-based approach. Her other research interests include gender and development, and qualitative methods.

INDEX

Aadhaar 158–59, 161
ableism 74, 226, 395; definition of 407n9
abnormality, notion of 2, 40, 220, 222, 291, 339
abortion: circumstances to opt for 101; grounds for 107; legitimisation of 102; right to 99
Action for Ability Development and Inclusion (AADI) 14, 123, 125–31, 135–37, 143n4
Action for Autism (AFA) 157–62; future goals of 160
adolescents, with hearing impairment: autonomy 274–75; awareness of changing body 269–71; developmental challenges 264, 269–80; economic independence 277–78; gender roles 271–72; marriage and family life 275–77; peer relationships 272–74; personal identity 278–80
adopted text strategy, to address gender discrimination 401–2
adult-onset Huntington's 107
advocacy movement of the blind 70, 72
All India Federation of the Deaf (AIFD) 249, 253
All India Institute of Speech and Hearing 290
All India Sports Council of the Deaf 250
altruism, womanhood in context of 140–41
American Deaf community 248
American Psychiatric Association 353
American Sign Language (ASL) 290, 291
Americans with Disabilities Act (ADA, 1990) 24, 65, 72
ancient discourses, disabled people in 48
anencephaly 102, 118n6
antenatal screening 98
antidepressants 352, 353, 357n4
anti-psychiatry 334, 345, 357n3
antipsychotics 352, 357n4
Appadurai, Arjun 242–43
Arpan Institute For Mentally Handicapped Children, Rohtak 154–57, 162–63
Asch, Adrienne 113, 224
Asia-Pacific Decade of Disabled Persons (1993–2002) 80
assisted reproductive technologies 112
Augustine of Hippo (354–430 CE) 41–42
autism 28n10; action for 157–62; awareness through mass media 161; case from Delhi 157–62; symptoms and diagnostic criteria 158
awareness of changing body 269–71

Balagangadhara, S. N. 49–50,

56n13, 57n15
Bandewar, Sunita 98
Banerjee, H. C. 289–90
Bangalore–Chennai–Hydera-bad Sign Language 290
Bangalore–Madras Sign Language 290
Baquer, Ali 73, 218
Barua, Merry 158
Beijing Platform for Action (1995) 86, 223, 365–66
bhalo meye, notion of 17, 205–15, 216
Bhatt, Usha 43–44, 54, 70–71
biological/intellectual condition, medicalisation of 42
biological markers 353
biomedicine 11, 152
biosociality, concept of 252–53
birth abnormality 13
bivalent collectivities: Fraser's categorisation of 391–92; politics of difference and 390–92; of women with disabilities 392–94
black civil rights 5, 11, 61
Bleak House (Dickens) 323
Blind With Camera Project 303; approach to photography 308–11; objectives of 307; origins of 306–7; ways of visualising the world 304–6; workshop format 308
Body Calligraphy 286, 296, 302n2
Bombay Institution for Deaf and Mutes 289
Bombay Sign Language 290
brain abnormality 358n12
Breivik, Jan-Kåre 247, 257–58
Brill, Richard G. 264
British Sign Language 290, 291
budgetary allocation towards schemes: central government 379–80; state government 380–81

Cairo Programme of Action 86
Calcutta Sign Language 290
Campling, Jo 420
Caraka Samhita 44, 56n12
care: definition of 122; form and consequences of 122
'career of caregiver' 123
caregiver, for a child with a disability: career of 123; caring and caregiving 134–38; community, family and gender, influence of 138–41; gendered nature of 138; narratives of 124–34; stressful life situation, consequences of 123; support from the extended family 134
caring for self 343
caring functions, in relation to child rearing 137, 139
Carter, Betty 264
Center for Independent Living 64
central budget, for the welfare of PWDs: allocation ratio 371; non-plan allocation 371–72; total allocation 370–71
centrally-sponsored plans (CSP) 377
Centre for Women's Development Studies (CWDS) 1
cerebral palsy (CP) 14, 28n8, 122–25, 133, 162, 172, 208, 387n10
charity, concept of 41
Chesler, Phyllis 335
children with special needs 137
child's training programmes 155
child with disabilities 14; medical and social assistance 137
Chinese calligraphy 286
Chowdhry, Prem 153
Chronicle of Higher Education, The 66
church doctrine, development of 41
civil rights movement of the blacks 61
colonial consciousness 50

colonial medicine 48
Commission for Social Development's Special Rapporteur on Disability 89
common mental disorders (CMDs) 349, 351
community-based rehabilitation (CBR) 84, 149, 165n5
competence, notion of 150
compulsory altruism 140
Confederation of Indian Industry (CII) 186
connected body-selves, notion of 150
Convention on the Elimination of All Forms of Discrimination against Women (CEDAW) 393–94, 395
Convention on the Rights of Persons with Disabilities (CRPD) 78–79, 248, 355–56, 393–94, 395, 401
Copenhagen Declaration (1995) 86
cost of disability 105–7
creativity–disability dyad 21
Crippled Children's Bill of Rights (1931) 80
cultural representation of disability 66
cystic fibrosis 107, 113
Dalley, Gillian 139
Darnovsky, Marcy 116
Darwinian notion of monstrousness 51
Das, Veena 112, 150, 252
Deaf Cultural Festival of India 244
Deaf culture 19–20, 243, 246–49, 257, 418
deaf education in India 21, 289
Deaf empowerment movement 247
deaf–hearing miscommunication 291
Deaf identity 19, 247–48; development of 291; domestic sphere (family and home) and 252–57

deafness, notion of 246-49, 253
Deaf Olympics 257
deaf people: marriage programme 250; societal discrimination against 249; vocational programmes for 250
Deaf President Now (DPN) 247
Deaf pride 19, 246–48, 256, 291
deaf-run institutions 247
Deaf schools, residential 246, 289
Deaf Studies 19, 29n12, 243, 246
deaf traditional literary forms 291
Deaf Way 290, 292, 301n1
Deaf women's empowerment 251
Declaration of the Rights of Mentally Retarded Persons (1971) 79
Declaration on the Elimination of Discrimination against Women (DEDAW) 406n5
Declaration on the Rights of Disabled Persons (DRDP, 1975) 79, 82
Declaration on the Rights of Mentally Retarded Persons (1971) 81
Deendayal Disabled Rehabilitation Scheme (DDRS) 379
Delhi Foundation of Deaf Women (DFDW) 19, 242, 244, 249; cultural and social events 250; vocational programmes 250
Delhi Sign Language 290
depression 104, 127, 335, 344–45, 349, 352
Derrida, Jacques 5, 304
designer shadow (Mahesh Umrrania) 320
Devanâgarî script 290
dharma, theory of 71
Diagnostic and Statistical Manual of Mental Disorders (DSM) 353
Dickens, Charles 323
Diploma in Special Education (Autism) 158

disability: aesthetics and creative diversity 20–22; categories of 145; concept of 1; cost of 105–7; cultural representation of 66; destigmatisation, recognition and empowerment, issue of 22–25; femininity and 16–20; gender budgeting and 365–70; in general UN programmes 86–87; Hindu perspective on 151; at home, work, and community 13–16; individual model of 68; Marxist idea of 39; medicalisation of 102–4; medical model of 4–5, 7, 25, 39–40, 63, 65, 67–68, 70, 73, 82, 102, 170–71, 222–23, 242; and mental illness 353–56; millennium development goals (MDGs) and 90–91; minority model of 65, 68; models of 69; social model of 4–5, 11, 66, 69, 78, 109, 170, 222; specialised UN agencies and 87–91; status of women with 368–70

disability activism, development of 5, 9, 25, 98

disability budget, gender analysis of: Andhra Pradesh 374, 376, 380; central budget, for welfare of PWDs 370–72; central government expenditures 379–80; central plan allocation 378; Chhattisgarh 377; in gender framework 382–83; Orissa 373, 376, 379; state government expenditures 380–81; state-wise analyses 372–78; West Bengal 373, 377–78

Disability Discrimination Act (1995), UK 24

disability history in India: comparative analysis of 43–48; monstrosity and feeble-mindedness 50–54; proposal 48–50; sample survey of histories of 45–46; subjects and themes, overview of 36–43

disability legislation 12, 24, 71, 150, 414–15

Disability Rag, The 65

disability rights movement 11–12, 61, 169; and origin of disability studies in United States 64–66

disability-specific activism 12, 64

disability studies: application of 4; definition of 2–3, 66–70; features of 3; historicising disability and 11–12; in India 8–11, 70–74; social model of 4–5, 11; *vs* study of disability 2–8; in United States 64–66

disabled children, birth of 107, 111

Disabled Development Finance Corporation 380

disabled girls, in Bengali culture: adolescence of 207–9; adulthood of 209–11; childhood of 206–7; gender-based socialisation 207; household chores of 210; sexuality of 211–15; special status of 206

Disabled In Action 64

disabled people: in ancient discourses 48; barriers to social participation, architectural and social factor 421; barriers to social participation, economics of leisure 421; barriers to social participation, gender factor 419–20; disadvantages facing 392; discrimination towards 45; historical attitude towards 43; institutional support for long-term care 138; paradigm shift in approach towards 416–17; population in United States 65; practices of killing 43–44;

principal aspirations of 151; reservations in government jobs 71–72; sexual education for 419–20; strategies for inclusion 417–19; support systems for care of 138; transport and transfer experiences of. *See* transport and transfer experiences, of disabled persons; vocational rehabilitation of 44; workplace-related barriers for. *See* workplace-related barriers, for disabled people
Disabled Peoples' International (DPI) 408n21, 417
Disabled Persons' Organisations (DPOs) 28n4
disablism 74, 226, 416
'discreditable' identity, of intellectually disabled people 157
disease, concept of 42
District Disability Rehabilitation Centres (DDRCs) 380
Down's syndrome 42, 102, 107–8, 110–13

Economic and Social Commission for Asia and the Pacific (ESCAP) 80
economic inclusion of disabled people, concept of 416
economic independence, of adolescents with hearing impairment 277–78
Edgerton, Robert 147
electroshock, as form of mental treatment process 342, 351
emotional disablism 416
emotional distress 143n10, 336, 341, 348
employer's attitude, towards disability 183–85; equal opportunity imperative 185–87; government offices and disabled-friendly imperative 187–89; middle class respondents and 189–90; social class, role of 189–91; socioeconomic class and management of fatigue 191–92; working class respondents and 190–91
'equal pay for equal work' principle 84
Erikson, Erik 29n13
Erikson–Goldthorpe Class Schema 174, 194n5
Erwadi 137–38
Ethnologue 290
eugenics movement 149, 164n2

family-based care 140
fatigue, experience and management of 181–82
feeble-mindedness 11, 50–54, 153
femininity and disability 16–20; anomalous and normative embodiment of 228–36; characteristic of 231; features of 237; parenting issues 233; relationship between 222–28
feminist disability studies 202; adolescence impairment 207–9; adulthood impairment 209–11; childhood impairment 206–7; contradictions and constraints in 205–15; methodology for 203–5; sexual impairment 211–15
feminist movement. *See* women's movement
First Founding Congress of Disabled Peoples International 83
fluoxetine (Prozac) 352
foetal abnormality, 97, 103
Food and Drug Administration (FDA) 352
Foucault, Michel 5, 39–40, 42, 49, 57n17, 148, 221
Fragile X syndrome (FXS) 149, 164n4
Fraser, Nancy 391–92

Gallaudet University 244, 247, 260n5
Galton, Francis 164n2
'Gay Pride' movement 357n2
gay rights movements 61, 65, 67
gender budgeting and disability 365–70
gender discrimination, single and twin track proposals to address: adopted text strategy 401–2; CEDAW 395–98; mainstreaming 399; preamble plus proposal 398–99; proposals before the Ad Hoc committee 398–402; twin track strategy 399–401
gendered care for the disabled 123, 143n10
gender roles, of adolescents with hearing impairment 271–72
gender-sensitive health programmes 87, 347–51
gender socialisation, among disabled girls 206
genealogy, Foucault's notion of 49
Gilmore, David 147
girls with hearing impairment: developmental tasks in 264; Hasina, story of 268–69; language usage and communication 266–67; Radha, story of 267–68
global Deafness 243, 246, 249
Goffman, Erving 4, 66–67, 146, 149, 157, 163
Gottlieb, Roger S. 116
government health centre 126
Green, Josephine 103
guardianship and adoption 418

handicapism 74
Hasina, story of (case study) 268–69
Havighurst, Robert James 263
hearing impairment: adolescents with. *See* adolescents, with hearing impairment; girls with. *See* girls with hearing impairment; parent-child relationship and 265
Heathen in his Blindness, The (Balagangadhara) 56n13
heteronormativity, notion of 214
heterosexism 114
Heumann, Judy 64
Hindu perspective on disability 151
History of Disability, A (Stiker) 40
Holocaust 38, 55n5, 56n10
homophobia 114
homosexuals 67, 391
hospital schools 63
human consciousness 342, 354
human rights: institutions 79, 86, 88, 398, 405, 407n19; protection of 338

immunisation programme 126
impairments: meaning of 62–63; medical rehabilitation approach for curing of 63; sociology of 170–71
inclusion, strategies for 417–19
Indian Deaf community 244, 250
Indian disability legislation 414
Indian feminism, politics of 340
Indian Journal of Psychiatry 349
Indian Lunacy Act (1912) 338
Indian Red Cross Society 155
Indian Sign Language (ISL) 21, 259n4, 286, 290, 292, 301
individual model of disability 68
industrial capitalism 5
infant physiological system 352
Ingstad, Benedicte 241–42, 248
insanity 337; philosophical validity of 338–39
institutional care, for disability 135, 137

institutional criminalisation of madness 38
intellectual disability 15, 41, 42; autism, action for 157–62; case from Delhi 157–62; conceptions in non-western societies 150–62; institutionalisation of 149; management of 149; normalization principle 149; perspectives on 148–50; special needs of 155; state and NGO intervention 154–57; in the state of Haryana 152–54; stigma of 148, 151
internalised oppression, concept of 415–16
International Classification of Functioning, Disability and Health (ICF) 80
International Classification of Impairments, Disabilities and Handicaps (ICIDH) 80, 82
International Convention on the Elimination of All Forms of Discrimination Against Women (CEDAW, 1979) 81, 85, 393–94, 395, 397, 405
International Convention on the Elimination of All Forms of Racial Discrimination (ICRD, 1969) 81
International Convention on the Rights of the Child (ICRC, 1989) 81
International Covenant on Civil and Political Rights (ICCPR, 1966) 81, 399, 408n25
International Covenant on Economic, Social and Cultural Rights (ICESCR) 79, 81
international development organisations 247–48
international disability rights movement 1, 3
International Labour Organisation (ILO): activities of 87; Vocational Rehabilitation and Employment (Disabled Persons) 79; Vocational Rehabilitation of the Disabled 79
International Year of Disabled Persons (1981) 80, 82–83, 88, 248
IQ protocol 164n3
Ishara Foundation 290
ITI Secunderabad 290

Jagori 358n10
Johnson, Mary 65
juvenile sex ratio 97

karma, theory of 44, 62, 71, 151
Kennedy, John 306
Kent, Deborah 110
*khap panchayat*s 165n8
Kleinman, Arthur 141
Klotz, Jani 147, 152

Lang, Raymond Paul 151
League of Nations 80
learning disorders 152
legal writings, on women and mental health 336–38
lesbian women 344
Life Bricolage project 20, 286; body, sign communication and art 291–300
limb deformity 152
liminality, anthropological concept of 146
Linton, Simi 2–4, 63, 66, 220
literacy rates, among women with disabilities (WWDs) 369–70
locomotor disorders 153; definition of 194n3; employer's attitude towards 183–92; fatigue, experience and management of 181–82; getting to a bus stop and boarding the bus 176–77;

information, transport and employment issues 175–76; public transport *vs* self-driven transfer 177–78; sampling for research on 173–75; transport and transfer experiences 175–78; workplace-related barriers 178–81; work-related experiences 172–81
long-term institutional care 137

McGoldrick, Monica 264
Madness and Civilization (Foucault) 40
madness and psychoanalysis: activism and healing perspectives and strategies 342–44; legal writings on women and mental health 336–38; personal or political apprehension 338–41; privacy, issue of 341–42; women's movement in India 335–36
'mad' women 344
Mahabharata 44, 45, 47–48
mainstreaming approach, for redressal of gender discrimination 399
Manu's laws 44, 47–48, 62
marginalisation of women, with disabilities 22, 74, 392, 396
marital status by disability, analysis of 368–69
marriage and family life, of adolescents with hearing impairment 275–77
marriage programme, for deaf people 250
maternal physiological system 352
medicalisation of disability 102–4
medical model, of disability 4–5, 7, 25, 39–40, 63, 65, 67–68, 70, 73, 82, 102, 170–71, 222–23, 242

Medical Termination of Pregnancy Act (1971) 13
Meekosha, Helen 225
Memoirs of the Blind (Derrida) 304
mental disability, notion of 8, 85, 101, 110, 156, 234, 333, 335
mental distress and illness 23, 334; political discourses of 348
mental health 336–38, 347; violence and 348
Mental Health Act (1987) 12, 336, 337
mental health services 343, 356; gender-sensitive 347–51; profit markets for 351–53; quality of 347; relief measures 347
mental hospitals 337–38, 346, 351
mental illness 8; and disability 353–56; as experience 344–46; inhuman and degrading treatments for 349; phenomenology of 346; reasons for recognition of 346–47
mental retardation 8, 28n9, 82, 85, 124, 386n3
micro-credit loans 244
Miles, M. 45, 48, 53
Millennium Development Goals (MDGs) 366; and disability 90–91
minority model of disability 65, 68
MI Principles 85
models of disability 69
monstrosity: concept of 49–50, 51; Darwinian notion of 51; and feeble-mindedness 50–54
Morris, Jenny 220, 224
mudras 289
Mumbai–Delhi Sign Language 290
Murphy, Robert 146
My Name Is Red (Pamuk) 304

National Association of the Deaf (NAD) 252, 256, 259

National Blind Youth Association 70
National Centre for Education 301
National Commission for Women (NCW) 366, 384
National Conference of Deaf Women 244
National Curriculum Framework (NCF) 290
national disability sex ratio 368
National Federation of the Blind (NFB) 70, 72
National Federation of the Blind Graduates. *See* National Federation of the Blind (NFB)
National Handicapped Finance and Development Corporation (NHFDC) 379–81, 384; beneficiaries of 381
National Mental Health Programme (NMHP) 338, 351
National Policy for Persons with Disabilities (2006) 417
National Programme for Rehabilitation of Persons with Disabilities (NPRPD) 380
National Sample Survey Organisation (NSSO) 172–73, 194n3
National Trust Act for the Welfare of Persons with Autism, Cerebral Palsy, Mental Retardation and Multiple Disabilities 162
natural sign language 292, 297
Nirje, Bengt 149
non-directive counselling 103, 118n7
non-governmental organisations (NGOs) 169, 242, 248, 366
normalization, principle of 149–50
normate bodies 67

Oliver, Michael 7, 66, 68–69, 74, 78, 114, 150, 201, 291

Open Door (model school for autistic children) 158
orthopaedic disabilities 45, 202, 204

Padmanabhan, Manjula 100
Pamuk, Orhan 304
panchayati raj finance 367
parental autonomy, in support of prenatal diagnosis 107–12
Parenting India (magazine) 102
parents' support group, formation of 143n4
Parmenter, Trevor 148–49
Parsons, Talcott 39, 56n8
peer relationships, in adolescents with hearing impairment 272–74
personal identity, of adolescents with hearing impairment 278–80
personhood, notion of 147, 150
persons with disabilities (PWDs) 363, 364; central budget for the welfare of 370–72; characteristics of 368; masculine sex ratio of 368; plan and non-plan central government schemes for 385–86
Persons with Disabilities (Equal Opportunities, Protection of Rights and Full Participation) Act (1995) 1, 12, 24–25, 72–73, 154, 165n6, 174, 417
Philosophical Transactions of the Royal Society 51
photography, by the visually impaired 304; 'ear has eyes' concept 315–19; 'eye has new eyes' concept 324–28; 'hand has eyes' concept 312–14; 'memory has eyes' concept 319–23; reading of pictures 311–28; *see also* visually impaired persons,

approach to photography
political activism and healing 342–44
Postpartum Depression (PPD) 352
Pranay Milan Sammelan 250
preamble plus proposal, for addressing discrimination against WWDs 398–99
prenatal diagnosis: in context of sex selection 100–102; and cost of disability 105–7; of foetal characteristics 112; individual choice 112–16; and legitimacy of motherhood 99; and medicalisation of disability 102–4; parental autonomy in support of 107–12; for sex-selective abortions 97; technology of 112
Pre-Natal Diagnostic Techniques (Regulation and Prevention of Misuse) Act (PNDT Act, 1994) 13, 97, 100
prenatal screening 107–8, 112, 116
Principles for the Protection of Persons with Mental Illness and the Improvement of Mental Health Care (1991) 79, 85, 355
privacy, issue of 341–42
prozac nations 334
psychiatric disorders 349
psychiatric treatments 346
psychiatry, interrogation of 338, 346–47
psychological empowerment 340
psychological ill health 348
psychological suffering 334, 348, 350
psychosocial disabilities 333–35, 340, 343, 346, 355–56; concept of 23; women suffering from 344
psychotropic medicines 351
public health 347
public interest litigation (PIL) 97, 338

qi, concept of 286
queer women 344

Rabinow, Paul, concept of biosociality 252
Radha, story of (case study) 267–68
radical communist movements 71
Ramayana 45
Rapp, Rayna 105, 254
recuperation and self-recovery, process of 346
Rehabilitation Council of India 290, 385
rehabilitation programmes, for deaf people 248
reservations in government jobs, for disabled persons 71–72
Rich, Adrienne 225
rights of women 108, 237, 395, 397, 399, 410n33, 411n42
right to care 22, 334, 344–53
Roberts, Ed 64

Sacks, Oliver 305
Salamanca Statement and Framework for Action on Special Needs Education 80
SAMA Resource Group for Women and Health 112–13
Saxton, Marsha 99, 114
self-advocacy, philosophy of 2, 12, 64, 80, 222, 236
self-care activities 122
self-help groups (SHGs) 387n12
sexism, notion of 393
sex-selective abortions 97, 101, 118n3
sexual abuse 212, 215, 234–35, 351, 358n11
sexual and reproductive health 411n42, 415, 417
sexual education, for disabled people 419–20

sexual exploitation 17, 218, 234, 396, 409n31
sexual harassment, of persons with disabilities 130, 227, 235
sexuality and disability discourses, in women's movement 343
sexuality, gendered notions of 211–15
Shah Daula's *chuha*s 50, 52–53, 57n18
Shirur Home for Mentally Handicapped Women, Pune 336
shock treatment, of mental illness 349
sickle-cell anaemia 107
sick role, concept of 39
sign language 21, 247, 288–91; distinctiveness of 289; growth of 289–90; as natural language of deaf 292; regional dialects 290; use of 289
Sihaya Samooh, Pune 348
Singer, Peter 107–8
smallpox 43, 56n11
social acceptability, notion of 214–15
social attitude, towards persons with disability 43, 51–52, 70–71, 138, 417
social constructions of womanhood 393
social inclusion of disabled people, concept of 165n5, 307, 414–16, 422
social inequality of women 141
social justice and empowerment discourses 339, 370
social model of disability 4–5, 11, 66, 69, 78, 109, 170, 222
social network, of kinship and community 156
social participation by people with disability, barriers to: architectural and social factor 421; economics of leisure 421; gender factor 419–20
social reform 41
social security insurance schemes 173
social stigma 40, 368
social therapy 350
societal discrimination, against deaf people 249
socio-political minority group 65, 69
solitary confinement 349
sound-based languages 288
Spastics Society of Northern India 123
spirituality, in human consciousness 354
Sraban School, Rohtak 155
Stainton, Tim 41–42
Standard Rules on the Equalization of Opportunities for Persons with Disabilities (1993) 79, 85, 89, 248
state-wise analyses, for allocation of disability budget: central allocation 377–78; committed allocation (non-plan) for PWDs 375–77; total allocation 372–75
sterilisation, for prevention of birth of feeble-minded children 42, 85
stigma: of intellectual impairment 148; sociological analysis of 146; theory of 66
Stigma: Notes on the Management of Spoiled Identity (Goffman) 66
Stiker, Henri-Jacques 40–41, 146
suicide prevention 347
Sundberg Declaration on Actions and Strategies for Education, Prevention and Integration 79–80
Swarnajayanti Gram Swarozgar Yojana (SGSY) 384, 387n12

Tallinn Guidelines for Action on Human Resources Development in the Field of Disability (1989) 79, 84–85
Tamil Nadu People's Forum for Social Development 367
Titchkosky, Tanya 4, 6
Todas (Indian tribe) 43
transport and transfer experiences, of disabled persons: getting to a bus stop and boarding the bus 176–77; information, transport and employment issues 175–76; public transport vs self-driven transfer 177–78
Tribal Sub-Plan (TSP) 383
Trust Fund for the International Year 83
Turner, Bryan 170–71
'twin track' approach, for eradicating gender discrimination 394, 399–401; substantive evaluation of 402–4

UN agencies and disability 87–91
Unani system of medicine 143n6
UN Convention against Torture (CAT) 81
unemployment, issue of 154; and social security insurance schemes 173
UN International Conference on Population and Development 86
Union of the Physically Impaired Against Segregation (UPIAS) 4, 69, 238n4
United Nations Children's Emergency Fund (UNICEF) 80, 87–88
United Nations Convention on the Rights of Persons with Disabilities (UNCRPD) 1, 9, 12, 88–90, 165n6, 414

United Nations Decade of Disabled Persons (1983–1992) 80, 84
United Nations Declaration of Human Rights 248
United Nations Development Fund for Women (UNIFEM) 365–66
United Nations Educational, Scientific and Cultural Organisation (UNESCO) 80, 87
United Nations General Assembly (UNGA) 79, 366
United Nations programme, for welfare of persons with disabilities 86–87; beginning of 81–82; intensification of efforts 82–86
Urban Indian Sign Language (UISL) 291
'users and survivors' of psychiatry 348, 355–56, 357n1

Vienna Declaration and Programme of Action (VDPA) 86, 92n18
Vikalanga Cooperative 380
visually impaired persons, approach to photography: dominance of senses 310; learning session 309–10; seeing what they click 310–11; visual connection, assessment of 308–9
visual reality 305, 308–9, 311–12
vocational programmes for deaf people 250
vocational rehabilitation, of disabled people 44, 80, 87
Voluntary Fund for the United Nations Decade of Disabled Persons 84

Wendell, Susan 171, 220, 225
Western societies, approach towards disability 67–68
Whyte, Susan Reynolds 150,

241–42, 248
womanhood, in the context of altruism 140
women and mental health, legal writings on 336–38
women in emotional distress, personal risk of 341–42
women's movement: for empowerment 22, 350, 369, 394; as mental health movement 335–36; sexuality and disability discourses in 343; social justice 350
women's reproductive health 352
Women's Studies and Development Centre (WSDC) 1
women with disabilities (WWDs): bivalence of 392–94; budgeting guidelines for 382–83; disadvantages faced by 363; gender budgeting and 365–70; literacy rates among 369–70; marital status of 368–69; politics of difference and bivalent collectivities 390–92; social stigma 368; status of 368–70; twin track approach on the empowerment of 394; unemployment among 369; women-specific schemes for 384
workplace-related barriers, for disabled people: restroom access 179–81; staircase and railings 178–79
World Deaf Congress 257
World Federation of the Deaf (WFD) 244, 247, 249, 253
World Health Organisation (WHO) 8, 80, 145
World Programme of Action Concerning Disabled Persons (WPA) 79, 83–85, 88–89, 248

Yong, Amos 42
Young, Iris Marion 391